THE
BEST
MAN

OTHER TITLES BY NATASHA ANDERS

THE
BEST
MAN

Natasha Anders

Montlake Romance

Published by Montlake Romance, Seattle

www.apub.com

Amazon, the Amazon logo, and Montlake Romance are trademarks of Amazon.com, Inc., or its affiliates.

ISBN-13: 9781503901520
ISBN-10: 1503901521

Cover design by Eileen Carey

Printed in the United States of America

Dedicated to Nathan, who will never read this book because eww (his word, not mine). Sorry I threw soap in your eye, made you believe you were adopted, hit you when you were a kid, and beat you at every game ever invented. Thanks for always being ready to bird sit or dog sit at the drop of a hat and for always grudgingly doing all the handyman stuff in my house.
You're the best brother ever!

CHAPTER ONE

"Thirty-two is *not* old," Daffodil McGregor muttered under her breath while pasting a simpering smile on her face for the benefit of her elderly, "well-meaning" hag of an aunt. The one who had just told her that being cute and spunky lost its charm once you left your twenties behind. Horrible crone. If Daffodil were younger, she would slip some laxatives into the old girl's tea and gleefully watch her desperately dodder her way to the toilet. Being a responsible adult could be so boring at times.

"Daff, I need your advice, please." Her youngest sister, Daisy, wrapped an arm around her waist and turned her away from Aunt Ivy, who was still lecturing Daff about her waning charms. "Sorry, Auntie, I just need to borrow her for a few seconds."

Daisy hurriedly dragged her away from Ivy, and Daff frowned at her shorter sister.

"What advice?"

"None." Daisy grinned. "Auntie Ivy looked like she needed rescuing from the impending Daffsplosion."

"She was pissing me off, harping on and on about how old I was getting. *Why* are they even here? Who invited them?"

"Daff, I can't not have the aunties at my engagement party," Daisy admonished, and Daff rolled her eyes.

"It's just an engagement party, not a wedding or anything." Daff scowled, and Daisy dimpled at her adorably.

"It's still a big deal," she said. Daff sighed and tucked one of Daisy's errant curls behind her ear.

"I can't believe my baby sister is getting married," she said, and Daisy grinned.

"I know, right? And to such a *stud*." Daff's eyes drifted over to where Daisy's frankly gorgeous fiancé, Mason, was earnestly conversing with his older brother, Spencer. She had to admit, Mason Carlisle did fantastic things for a three-piece suit. Her attention shifted to the man standing beside him. Spencer didn't look as comfortable in a suit. In fact, he looked too big, too rough, and too damned barbaric to do the Alexander McQueen suit any justice. He kept tugging at the tie, which—added to his overly long hair and dark stubble—gave him a generally disheveled appearance.

Mason—always aware of where Daisy was in a room—glanced over and graced her with a very hot, very intimate smile. Daff rolled her eyes when her sister sighed and practically melted in pleasure. Seriously, these two were perpetually horny. It was downright embarrassing to be in their company at times.

Spencer also looked over, and his stormy dark-green eyes clashed with Daff's for a second before she deliberately looked away. She couldn't stand the man. She had once harbored a smidgen of affection for him, but that was before he hurt Daisy in a misguided attempt to get closer to Daff. She peered over at her flushed sister, who was still eye-fucking Mason, and sighed. Okay, so everything had worked out in the end and Daisy had forgiven and forgotten because the whole debacle had won her Mason. But Daff was made of sterner stuff and Spencer had pissed her off. She didn't forgive as easily.

Still, Daff was the maid of honor and Spencer was the best man, so for the sake of harmony it was probably better to declare a truce. The last McGregor wedding hadn't ended well—her middle sister, Lia, had thankfully called the whole thing off—so Daff wanted to be sure this one was without any drama. Establishing some kind of peace with Spencer would probably go a long way toward making things easier for Daisy.

Mason was coming over, looking like a lovestruck fool floating on a sea of pheromones. The guy was practically drooling, for God's sake.

"Hey, angel. Miss me?" His voice was pitched low and clearly intended for the only person currently in his field of vision. Daff might as well not have existed.

"Always." Daisy smiled. Jesus, they lived together, spent every spare moment in each other's company, and had been dancing together less than five minutes ago. Daff couldn't fathom this kind of yearning for anybody. Once, long ago when she had been little more than a naïve, foolish girl, it might have been something she aspired to. Now, hard-earned experience had taught her that those innocent dreams of romance and love were not for her, and she hoped never to actually feel anything remotely similar. How terrifying that would be. And yet . . . sometimes it physically hurt Daff to see them together. She was pleased for Daisy—her sister deserved all the happiness in the world and Mason made her ecstatic—but looking at them made Daff feel . . . lonely. The thought made her uncomfortable, and she just wanted to get away from them.

"Anyway, thanks for the rescue, Deedee," she said. No response. "I'll just be heading . . . over there somewhere." No response. "To, you know, dance on the tables. Naked, probably. Haven't decided yet." No response. All righty, then.

She turned away, grabbing a glass of bubbly from one of the tables on the way. She looked around the crowded room. Her parents were hosting this party in their own home. It was early days yet, but Daisy had opted to do her entire wedding at home. The ceremony would be in the huge backyard, beneath the weeping willows out by the large duck pond. The farm was really an ideal setting for this wedding, and for veterinarian Daisy, who had always been happy to run around with the geese and ducks and cows, it was a perfect fit.

Daff circled the room restlessly, feeling out of sorts and a little bit moody, like a shark circling the shallows looking for a potential victim. She spotted her prey just a couple of meters away and made her way to his side. He was a big bastard, topping her five foot seven by at least seven inches. He was massively built with shoulders that could block out the sun; he was easily twice her size, but all muscle. She knew he kept fit, always out playing sports, swimming, cycling, and surfing. While Mason had a lean elegance to his gorgeous body, Spencer was all brute force.

"Stop fiddling with that tie," she said when he tugged at the length of fabric again. "You've done enough damage."

"What do you care?" he sneered, glaring at her from beneath that fall of black hair. He looked like a beast, hulking, menacing . . . His hair fell over his eyes, a wild, sleek mane. It was kind of thrilling how savage he seemed at times. Barely civilized. No wonder he always messed up flirting with her—he had all the finesse of a stampeding bull.

"Fine, if you want to continue looking like an absolute primitive, then by all means, fiddle away." She continued to stand beside him, sipping her bubbly, while he wavered for a few seconds before his hand discreetly went up to touch the knot of his tie, obviously checking if it was as bad as she'd said. She glanced at the dance floor, where Daisy and Mason were now dancing together, still completely wrapped up in each other.

"So your brother finally popped the question," she said.

"I think he started asking her about six months ago. She finally said yes," Spencer corrected, and Daff grinned. The younger couple's relationship had been anything but ordinary, so the news didn't surprise her in the slightest.

"And you're the best man?" She framed it as a question, despite already knowing the answer, and he nodded. "Well, since I'm the maid of honor, we'll be partnered and expected to *do* stuff together. I just wanted to be sure you were okay with that."

"Why wouldn't I be?"

"We haven't really been on good terms."

"I hadn't noticed. You don't exactly feature prominently in my life."

Ouch. That hurt.

"Right. Anyway. Bygones?"

"If you say so." He shrugged, clearly not caring less. Feeling foolish, Daff walked away and wished she'd never approached him in the first place. She was annoyed with herself for allowing him to get the better of her. He wasn't exactly the sharpest tool in the shed. Years of repeatedly getting thumped on the head couldn't be good for the brain, and Spencer typified the term *dumb jock*. She chose not to acknowledge the fact that he was a successful businessman with a highly lucrative sporting goods business. He had capitalized on the minor fame his short-lived rugby career had generated, and it had resulted in the right doors opening at the right time. He was still that big, sulky brute who had been two years ahead of her in high school. The bad boy with the seemingly delinquent tendencies. A causeless rebel who—she initially believed—had seen her as yet another trophy to be won.

She tossed back her drink and looked around for another tray of the stuff. Finding nothing close by, she put the glass on the closest surface and indulged in one—or several—of the delicious canapés instead.

"Why are you hiding back here?" her middle sister's light voice asked from behind her, and Daff guiltily turned to face Lia—cheeks stuffed with tiny canapés.

"Hey."

"Jeez, Daff, hungry?" Lia asked playfully, handing her a napkin. "You have cream cheese on your face."

Daff took the napkin with a nod and swallowed down the delicious little treats before wiping her mouth. Lia's finger indicated left, and Daff swiped the napkin across her cheek.

"Got it?" she asked and Lia nodded with a sweet smile. Her middle sister was always sweet and too damned *nice* for her own good. Just over a year ago, she'd nearly allowed herself to be railroaded into marriage with a guy who was entirely wrong for her, but she had thankfully come to her senses at the eleventh hour.

"So *are* you hiding?" Lia asked, and Daff shrugged.

"Auntie Ivy had a go at me. I'm old, blah blah blah. Better catch a man before the last of my looks fade, and so on and so forth." Lia snorted and daintily picked out one of the canapés for herself.

"Aunt Mattie was helpfully informing me that I shouldn't sulk over Clayton forever. Got to get myself back on the market ASAP. Before my ovaries wither and I die a bitter, childless old maid. Or something to that effect." She smiled, inviting Daff to share the joke, but her eyes were shadowed as ghosts—barely dead and buried—surfaced to haunt her.

"They're harmless, silly old ladies who are stuck in the dark ages. Independent women are foreign concepts to them."

"And yet none of *them* ever married," Lia said and glumly contemplated the canapé in her hand before taking a delicate nibble.

"Maybe they want to save us from the same terrible fate?" Daff suggested with a grin before sobering. "Don't let them get to you, Lia."

"Maybe it's not entirely progressive of me," Lia confessed, keeping her eyes glued to the canapé, "but I *want* a husband and a family. I want everything I thought I would get with Clayton."

"Years of verbal put-downs, a man who flirted with—and possibly fucked—everything in a skirt, who made our baby sister feel both sexually harassed *and* physically lacking?" Daff asked skeptically, the latter referring to Daisy's condemning revelations about Clayton on the eve of Lia and Clayton's doomed wedding. "Because that's all you would have gotten from that ass."

"I know." Lia's voice was a mix of exasperation and pain. "I know that, okay. And I meant I wanted the fantasy of the perfect marriage, with the perfect children and the perfect life."

"Sounds perfectly boring." Daff shrugged.

"To *you*, maybe. But it sounds like bliss to me." Daff made a non-committal sound, not sure how to respond to that. While Lia's dream life was not one that particularly appealed to her, Daff envied Lia her certainty. Her sister knew what she wanted, and Daff still had no clue.

She managed an exclusive clothing boutique in the center of their small tourist town. Business was sluggish in winter and crazy busy over summer. Pretty much like all the other businesses in town. It was dead boring at the moment, with a few loyal patrons who popped in more for a chat than anything else. Daff was the only employee during winter, and the sheer boredom nearly drove her insane. The owner had a few other boutiques set up around the country and rarely visited Riversend, content to let Daff run the place as she saw fit as long as they were turning a profit, no matter how small.

It was a dead-end job with very few prospects and not the least bit challenging, but it was all Daff was currently qualified to do. She had fallen into the management thing, getting the promotion simply because she'd worked there longer than any other employee. A high school temp job had turned into her only work experience, and she was too damned scared to try anything else. She'd started there when she was sixteen, and before she knew it another sixteen years had passed and here she was. Same job, same life, same mistakes over and over again. It was literally all she knew, and she was terrified that it was all she would ever know.

Spencer tugged at his tie again—he swore to God the thing was getting tighter with every passing second. He knew a frown was settling on his face and that his heavy, dark brows, overly long hair, and day-old stubble probably made him look terrifying, but he was well past caring. He hated events like these, but his brother was getting hitched and he was determined to be a good sport and do the whole big brother thing. He was the only family Mason had, and while he knew he wasn't ideal, he would damned well do his brother proud, even if it killed him.

His eyes searched for the younger man; Mason was laughing—a deep belly laugh—and hauling Daisy into his arms for a kiss.

Little Daisy McGregor. She made Mason ridiculously happy. It was the damnedest thing; his brother was hot for the most overlooked, underappreciated woman in town. Not only hot for her but head over heels in love with her. And Spencer had to admit, since getting to know her, he could understand why Mason felt the way he did.

Daisy was a sweetheart. Funny, smart, and cuter than anybody had ever given her credit for. Just showed how superficial people could be. Nobody had ever considered her remotely pretty, with her weight issues, frizzy hair, and huge glasses, until Mason had come along. Now every eye was drawn to her. There was something about her, and Mason had seen it and snatched her up before anyone else could even appreciate it.

Spencer scanned the rest of the room, his eyes unconsciously seeking the one person who intrigued and frustrated him in equal measures. Daffodil McGregor was chatting with her other sister, Lia. The two women were strikingly similar, nearly equal in height, the same dark-brown hair, clear gray eyes—a trait that they shared with Daisy—and willowy bodies. But while Lia looked soft and delicate, Daff had a harder edge to her. A nervous energy that made her seem impatient and restless. It hadn't been there when she was younger. She had been a carefree, independent, irreverent girl, and Spencer had been drawn to her like a moth to a flame. He always felt hopelessly out of her league, of course, but that hadn't stopped him from not-so-secretly pining for her in high school.

A fledgling flirt, she had managed to keep him hopeful with the occasional smile, greeting, or slow, seductive sweep of those long, dark lashes of hers. And she had always given him *just* enough attention to make him think he had a chance. Which often resulted in him making a complete fool of himself.

What a pathetic, lovesick idiot he had been, sending her all those heartfelt notes and flowers and truly awful poems. He winced at the recollection now. She had had him wrapped around her pretty, spiteful little finger.

He had grown out of it, of course, or so he'd thought, until last year when—fresh out of a failed relationship—he had tried and been shot down again. Only this time both Mason and Daisy had been casualties of his stupidity. Luckily his mistake had eventually yielded positive results for the other couple, but Daff had irrationally accused him of hurting her sister, when—as far as Spencer was concerned—she had been just as much to blame for the entire debacle.

Spencer dragged his eyes away from her and surveyed the rest of the room. A shitload of beautiful people wearing beautiful clothes and dripping in expensive jewelry. Spencer didn't belong here—he should be at home eating pizza, drinking beers, and watching TV. Mason fit into this world; he knew how to talk to these people, but Spencer felt completely exposed, like an impostor pretending to be more than he was. He didn't know what to say or do. Literally the only person he felt comfortable with in this room was his brother, and Mason was wholly preoccupied with Daisy. Spencer tried not to feel a sting of betrayal and hurt by that. Mason was getting married; this was how it was going to be from now on, how it was *supposed* to be. But rationalizing didn't make him feel any less excluded from his brother's changing life. It was just that after Mason had returned home following twelve years abroad, Spencer had believed they'd have more time together. Instead, Mason had spent a year traveling around the country and had been back in Riversend for just a short while before meeting Daisy, falling in love, and setting up house with her.

Spencer sighed and chugged down his drink.

"We've been watching you, young man." The creaky old voice coming from right beside him startled him, and his head jerked down to stare at two of the four old ladies who had been glaring at everybody from the comfort of their sofa all evening. The one who had spoken looked likely to keel over any second; she was hunched over, holding onto a cane with a gnarled, shaking hand, and glaring up at him through Coke-bottle lenses. Spencer had heard about Daisy's aunts from his brother and knew that nothing good could come from this confrontation. He peered over at the sofa, where the other two old women were avidly watching the exchange.

"Hello," he ventured tentatively, but she merely sniffed—a disturbingly wet sound—before carrying on with what she'd been saying before.

"We've been watching you lurk in the shadows like a thug. Am I going to have to tell Millicent to count the good silver after you leave?" Insulted, Spencer glared at the horrid old woman and said nothing. "Strong, silent type, are you? That won't get you anywhere in this family. You've got to speak up for yourself."

"Maybe he's a little . . ." The other woman spoke up for the first time. She did little loops at her temple with her index finger and crossed her eyes. This woman was even shorter and older than the one with the cane and sported a few impressive dark whiskers on her jaw. Even her wrinkles had wrinkles. She cackled, showing off her ill-fitting, startlingly white dentures. "Hit your head a few too many times, didn't you, boy? Bless."

Spencer frantically scanned the room, searching for an escape route, but the other two women had left the sofa to join their cohorts and Spencer was surrounded by gray-haired little old ladies. How the fuck had they managed to ambush him like this?

"Why aren't you married and making babies yet?" one of them—he didn't know which—demanded in an obnoxiously loud voice. "You're not getting any younger, you know. And the older you get, the more your sperm loses its motility and desire to swim. I read that on the Google."

"I, uh . . . I think my brother's calling me," Spencer prevaricated desperately.

"Nonsense, he's too busy making cow eyes at our Daisy. So why aren't you talking to anyone? You've been standing in this corner all evening, barely sparing a word for anyone."

"That's not true." The most fairy-godmother-ish of the quartet spoke up in a sickeningly sweet voice that perfectly matched her snow-white hair and rosy apple cheeks. "He spoke with Daffodil." She graced Spencer with a beneficent smile before adding, "She's single, you know."

Oh hell no!

"I really have to go," he lied, trying very hard to keep the desperation from his voice.

"Where to?" Glasses asked.

"I wanted to tell Lia something."

"She's single, too," Fairy Godmother offered.

"But she's fragile." This from Dentures. He looked at the other one with the hairy white eyebrows. She hadn't said a word so far, and it made him hope for some kind of merciful intervention, but she merely gave him a measuring look in return, telling him not to hope for much in the way of help from her.

"She is fragile, so if all you want from her is sex, then stay away from her, mister," Dentures warned him, and Spencer swallowed back a groan.

"Spencer, I see you've met my great aunts." Daisy's very welcome voice sounded from behind him, and he turned to face her with a relieved smile.

"We haven't been formally introduced," he said. They'd been too busy haranguing him to bother with social niceties like introductions.

"Oh, well then, allow me," Daisy said, her eyes alight with mischief and laughter. "These are my aunts Ivy"—Glasses—

"Helen"—Dentures—"Mattie"—Eyebrows—"and Gertrude." Fairy Godmother.

"Nice to meet you all," he gritted, forcing a smile when all he wanted to do was run for the hills.

"Aunties, I hope you don't mind, but Spencer has promised me a dance." She didn't wait for a response but took his hand and dragged him away from the four old women and onto the dance floor.

"Oh my God, I think I'm in love with you," he muttered fervently, and she laughed.

"That bad, was it?" she asked sympathetically, and he groaned.

"You have no idea."

"Oh, trust me, I have an inkling." The song playing was romantic and dreamy, and she stepped into his hold, fully prepared to slow dance with him. He put his hands on her shoulders and pushed her slightly away from him in order to achieve what he felt was maximum safe distance between their bodies. She laughed at him and wriggled under his arms to snuggle close against his chest.

"Daisy, I may be older and taller than my brother, but he *was* an elite soldier and is fully capable of kicking my ass if he thinks I'm getting too touchy-feely with you."

"We're just dancing." She laughed. "Keep your hands off my butt—he's possessive over it—and you should be okay."

Spencer sighed and acquiesced. She was a nice armful, and once again he applauded his brother for spotting this gem when the rest of the town's male population had been stupidly blind to her charms.

"So what did my aunts say to you?"

"Warned me not to steal the silver, asked me why I wasn't married and producing babies, and then advised me that these are my best sperm-producing years. Kind of reminded me that both your sisters are single, but also cautioned me against hurting Lia. She's very fragile right now, you see?"

"Jeez, they couldn't have been talking to you for more than five minutes and they managed to offend you in how many different ways? That may well be a new record for them."

"Awesome," he deadpanned, and she chuckled.

"Don't take it too personally, Spencer. We've all fallen victim to their so-called pearls of wisdom. They think because they're older than time it gives them special license to say whatever they like."

He was about to respond when he felt a heavy hand on his shoulder. He sighed and removed his arms from around Daisy's waist and turned to face his steely-eyed brother.

"Hands off my woman, Spence. Go find one of your own."

"You're being silly." Daisy laughed. "I'm enjoying my dance with him."

"Were you going to do the chicken dance with him?" Mason barked, narrowing his eyes at her as she grinned unrepentantly.

"I was considering it." Spencer rolled his eyes when Mason growled and grabbed her against him. This weird thing the two of them had about that ridiculous dance was completely unfathomable.

"Thanks for sending her to my rescue, bro," he said as he stepped away and allowed Mason to take over the dance.

"No idea what you're talking about," Mason said, his face like granite while his eyes shone with repressed laughter.

"Sure you don't," Spencer retorted as he swiveled on his foot and strode away, making sure he was heading in the opposite direction of the old ladies. He wondered how long he'd have to stick around before he could leave. They'd already finished dinner—surely that meant he could make his escape without looking too obvious. He was tired after a long day at work, and while he was happy for his brother and Daisy, he'd had about all the family togetherness he could take with the McGregors.

He cast a discreet look around the room. Everybody was laughing and drinking and chatting. Daisy and Mason were so completely wrapped up in each other he doubted anybody would notice if he left now.

He edged his way toward the doorway of the large room and stepped out into the relative quiet of the big old house's foyer. Nobody was out here, and he wondered where his coat had disappeared to. He didn't have a clue and decided to get it from Mason in the morning. He made a beeline for the front door before anybody could come out of the other room and spot him. He gratefully stepped outside into darkness, relishing the cold, fresh air on his overheated skin.

There were way too many cars parked all over the lawn and front yard, but thankfully Spencer had had the foresight to park his 4x4 outside the farm's front gate. It was a short walk to the gate, but at least he wasn't blocked in. He didn't even mind the sluggish drizzle, just happy to be away from all those people.

The farm was situated about three and a half miles outside Riversend, and the short dirt road that connected the farm to the main road was unlit. Because it was so dark, Spencer jumped and then cursed out loud when his headlights picked up a single slender figure walking briskly in the dark ahead of him. The cursing became more potent when he realized who it was.

"Fuck, fuck, *fuck*!" She was literally the last person on earth he wanted to see right now, but he couldn't in good conscience let her continue to walk into town alone. He slowed his car down when it was abreast of her, but she kept her gaze straight ahead and continued to walk, ignoring him as he kept pace with her. He let down his passenger window.

"Daff?" At the sound of his voice, she finally stopped, her pale face lit only by his dashboard display.

"Spencer."

"Why the fuck are you walking out here alone in the dark?"

"My car was blocked."

"Where are you going?"

"Home."

"Don't you live at the farm?"

"No, I've been renting Daisy's house since she moved in with Mason."

"Get in, I'll drive you," he commanded reluctantly.

"That's fine, it's not far."

"It's a fifty-minute walk. Probably longer in this weather and in the dark. Get in."

"Spencer . . ."

"Get in the goddamn car, Daff!"

"Hey, watch it! You don't get to talk to me like that."

"I do when you're being an idiot." Her perfectly arched brows puckered into a frown as she glared at him. She wrapped her coat more tightly around her slender frame and continued walking. His car crept along beside her.

"Leave me alone, Spencer," she huffed a few moments later.

"No. If you won't get in, I'll damned well keep driving beside you to be sure you get home safely. Of course that'll take about fifty minutes when I could get you there in, what? Five? Less?"

She stopped again and, with a muttered curse, yanked the passenger door open and clambered into the seat.

"I'm only doing this because I'd rather not deal with you for longer than I have to," she seethed, and he shook his head.

"No argument from me," he agreed. "Fasten your seat belt." He watched her do that before gunning the engine and heading toward town.

God, she smelled really, really good. He couldn't quite place the fragrance; he wasn't very good with stuff like that. Honeysuckle, maybe? Or was it vanilla? Did those two things even smell the same? He had no clue, but he couldn't get enough of it. It made him want to lean toward her and bury his nose in the elegant, silken curve of her neck and just inhale her.

"For the record, walking down an isolated dark road in the middle of the night is a dumb thing to do."

"It's safe enough. I've done it heaps of times."

"Have you forgotten what happened to your sister last year?" he growled, infuriated by her blasé response. Daisy had been ambushed and attacked on a similarly dark road.

"It's safer here," she pointed out, and he scoffed at that.

"You never know who could be out there lurking in the dark, Daff. Don't do it again."

"You have no right to tell me what to do, Spencer."

"Somebody has to. Might as well be me."

"Why did you leave the party?" she asked. She was staring out the window while her hands fidgeted in her lap. Her restlessness was contagious, and he found himself tapping nervously on his steering wheel.

"Not my scene. Why did you leave?"

"I'm tired. I have work in the morning, and I didn't feel much like socializing." It was a more detailed answer than he'd been expecting, and he mulled over it for a moment.

"I didn't really know anybody there," he admitted. "And I wanted to avoid being ambushed by your aunts again."

Her head swiveled, and a grin lit her face. Spencer cursed the lack of decent light in the car because he couldn't see every nuance of that smile.

"They can be a little overwhelming." Understatement of the century.

"No shit. The mean one with the thick glasses—"

"Ivy."

"Yeah. She accused me of making off with the silver. And I swear to God, the one with the toothache-inducing voice—"

"Gert?" There was no disguising the blatant amusement in her voice by now.

"She was trying to set me up with you or Lia. Possibly both of you."

"Oh *hell* no!"

"My sentiments exactly. But I *should* probably consider settling down, because apparently my sperm are losing their will—and ability—to procreate by the second."

She laughed. The sound was so unexpected and completely charming that Spencer's hand jerked on the wheel and the car swerved for a microsecond before he righted it. She didn't notice but continued to chuckle quietly to herself.

"Welcome to our world. Daisy, Lia, and I have been hearing about our various shortcomings all our lives." The words, while light, were laced with an undercurrent of bitterness. "I love my aunties to death, but they can be a bit . . . trying sometimes." The turnoff to the main road into town came moments later, and Spencer focused on negotiating it before glancing at her again. The streetlights allowed more illumination into the car, and he was struck by the absolute sadness on her face. It intrigued and disturbed him. He'd always considered Daffodil McGregor a pretty, pampered princess. What did she have to be sad about?

He drove through their quiet, tiny town. The only places that were still open at this time of night were the local pub, Ralphie's, and the more family-friendly eatery, MJ's. Everything else was dark and closed, and there were no other cars on the road. It didn't take long to reach Daisy McGregor's tiny house, which was situated just on the edge of Riversend. It was a quaint little place and resembled something out of the book of fairy tales he'd secretly hoarded when he was a boy. A sweet little gingerbread house, with a picture-perfect lawn.

"Why did you move here?" he asked after drawing the car to a stop outside the gate, and she shrugged. For a moment he thought that was the only answer he would get until she unexpectedly elaborated.

"I'm thirty-two, and still living with my parents was just sad."

"The farmhouse is huge—it's not like you guys are all up in one another's space."

"It was starting to get claustrophobic. I felt smothered." Another startlingly candid revelation.

"I see." He didn't. Not really. For as long as he remembered, it had always been just him and Mason, with their parents coming and going whenever the hell they pleased. He didn't know what it was like to feel smothered by family. To him it sounded like paradise to be surrounded by people who cared about you.

"Anyway, thanks for the ride. Sorry I gave you grief about it." She hopped out of the cab without waiting for a response from him, and he watched as she rounded the front of the car and kept watching until she made her way to the front door and then into the house. It was only after the interior lights switched on that he drove off.

CHAPTER TWO

"I've never been so grateful for a half day." Daff sighed while she was locking up the shop. Saturday was Daff's favorite day of the week—she closed the shop at one, with an entire day and a half of rest stretching seemingly endlessly ahead of her—and Lia had popped around for the last half hour to gossip about the previous night's festivities.

She'd had a grand total of two customers that day and had been bored out of her mind for the most part. Lia showing up had been a godsend and had kept her from ruminating over her ride home with Spencer Carlisle. The dark interior of the car had created a disturbingly intimate setting, and she'd found herself revealing way too much about herself to Spencer—literally the last person to whom she wanted to expose her vulnerabilities.

"Grab some lunch?" Lia asked as Daff tugged down the security shutters, and Daff nodded.

"Yeah, I'm starving." MJ's was a minute down the road and they both picked up the pace, knowing that the place would be packed at lunchtime on a Saturday.

"Ugh, looks like the whole town came out today," Lia observed as they stepped into the noisy interior of the restaurant. At first glimpse it seemed filled to capacity, and Daff knew they'd probably have to wait for a table to free up.

"It's the weather," Daff said. It was a rare sunny late-winter day. The whole town would start blooming over the next couple of weeks with the advent of spring, and before too long the tourists would start flocking back, turning their sleepy town into a tourism mecca. Business would pick up and Daff would hopefully get over her debilitating bout of boredom. She couldn't remember it ever being this bad before.

"Hey, guys, join us?" Daisy called from halfway across the room. She, Mason, and Spencer were seated at one of the larger tables in the middle of the floor. Daff stifled a groan at the thought of having to keep company with Spencer again, but Lia was already making her way toward them, so Daff sighed before following reluctantly.

Spencer was sitting opposite Mason and Daisy, an empty chair on either side of him. He looked like he was about to slide over to the chair on the end, but of course, Lia—ever accommodating—sat down on his left before he could move. Daff fought back a glower and sat down gracelessly on his right. Immediately aware of the big, hulking presence beside her, she bit the bullet and offered him a perfectly insipid smile of greeting.

"Hey."

"Hey," he returned with an equally bland smile.

"So I guess you closed up shop before I did?" Spencer's sporting goods store—by far the biggest and most popular business in town—was across the road and just a few doors away from the boutique. It was always busy, even in the middle of winter, since people drove from miles around to shop there. She could see the store whenever she looked out the window. Something she had fought against doing today, especially since part of her knew she would only be looking outside in the hopes of catching a glimpse of Spencer.

"I delegate," he informed her succinctly. "No need to be there for the close of business."

"Nice to be the boss, I guess."

"I trust my people to get the job done." He shrugged. He was wearing his usual uniform, a gray sweat suit with the logo of his store—SC Sporting Solutions—discreetly embroidered in red on the breast of the jacket. He wore the clothes with the ease of an athlete. He looked magnificent as he leaned back, one arm hooked around the back of his chair, massive thighs spread and broad chest pushed out like the dominant male he was.

"How did you get home last night, Daff? Your car was still at the farm when we left," Daisy asked suddenly, and Daff cast Spencer a circumspect look before replying.

"I was blocked in. Spencer was on his way home and offered me a ride." His eyebrows, those straight, dark masculine slashes above deep-set emerald eyes, rose almost to his hairline, but he didn't negate her story.

"Why'd you leave without saying goodbye, Spence?" Mason asked, and this time she watched him carefully for his response. He looked uncomfortable; his mouth—beautiful and bow shaped with just enough fullness in the lower lip to make it highly kissable—tightened for a second, emphasizing the deep, craggy grooves in his lean, tan cheeks.

"You were busy," he muttered. Spencer always muttered or growled or grunted. It fostered the perception that he was a big, dumb jock, but Daff was beginning to doubt her long-held belief about him. A few of their more recent interactions were making her really question everything she thought she knew about him. "I didn't want to interrupt."

"Don't be silly," Daisy dismissed. "We're never too busy for you."

"Hold up," Mason said, tugging at one of Daisy's curls. "There will be many, *many* occasions when we'll be far too busy for him."

Daisy blushed before elbowing Mason in the ribs.

"You know what I mean, Spencer," she said, ignoring Mason's chuckle.

"Thanks, honey," he said with a grin, and the grooves in his cheeks turned into full-on dimples. The smile had a weird effect on Daff, and she touched a quick hand to her chest, not sure what to make of the suddenly off-kilter beat of her heart.

Their beleaguered waitress eventually made her way to the table and everybody paused for a moment to place their orders, nobody bothering to check the menu they all knew by heart.

"Thanks, Thandiwe." Daisy smiled at the young waitress, who also happened to be an intern at the veterinary practice where Daisy partnered with their father.

"So while you're all here, Daisy and I have some news," Mason said, toying with Daisy's fingers. Daff's eyes flew to her youngest sister's face, and she was alarmed to note that Daisy looked . . . subdued. "After the wedding, we'll be moving to Grahamstown while I complete my studies."

Mason would be studying architecture, they all knew that, but until he just spoke the words aloud, Daff hadn't thought any of them had considered that the only way he could do so would be for him to leave Riversend.

"We picked it because it's closer than Cape Town, so we can still make the drive back to Riversend on some weekends and for the holidays."

"What about the practice?" Lia asked Daisy, her voice shaking slightly.

"We considered me staying here and Mason commuting back every weekend, but in the end decided that we didn't want to be apart for such long stretches at a time. I've spoken to Daddy about it, and he says he'll hire someone to help out and when Mason and I return I'll take over the practice."

"That sucks," Daff said, more devastated by the news than she allowed them to see. She leveled an accusatory glare on Mason. "You just had to take her away from us, didn't you, asshole?"

"I'll bring her back," he said with a somber smile. "This is our home. We want to raise our kids here."

"The five years will fly by, and we'll visit so often it'll be like we've never left," Daisy added.

"Five years?" The dismay was evident in Lia's voice, and her eyes shone with tears. She lowered her head quickly to hide them, but everybody had already seen them. Not that Daff blamed her—she felt like howling, too. She sneaked a peek at Spencer, but his face was downcast and unreadable. Only the slight tightening of his lips betrayed how he might be feeling, but other than that he was a closed book.

"When will you move?" Daff asked.

"Probably late January, so we'll have time enough to get settled and find a place before the semester starts."

"That's less than five months away," Lia stated unnecessarily. "And you haven't even set a date for the wedding yet."

"We thought the first Saturday in November," Mason said, and Lia gasped.

"Does our mom know? I can't imagine she's too thrilled about that!"

"She's not. But because it's a backyard wedding, I'm not anticipating too much work," Mason said, and all three women shot him identical incredulous looks, which he returned with a blank, confused stare.

"What? What did I say?" Mason asked, and Spencer chuckled softly. The unfamiliar sound startled Daff into looking at him. His handsome, rugged face was alight with laughter as he grinned at his brother.

"I'm thinking they don't agree with you."

"But it won't be a huge production like Lia's wedding was," he retorted. "No fancy hotels and gift bags and froufrou crap like that. I imagine it'll be more like a *braai* or something . . . won't it?" The last two words sounded uncertain when Daisy shot him a lethal glare.

"Mason, our wedding isn't going to be some common *braai*, where people show up in shorts and drink beers with their barbecued steaks!"

"I mean, I know we'll put a fancier spin on it, but . . ."

"No! We're hiring caterers for the three- to four-course dinner. There will be proper tableware and silverware, no paper plates, no paper napkins, and *no* plastic forks." Daisy's face was going an unbecoming shade of red and Daff, her earlier sadness shelved for the moment, sat back and enjoyed her youngest sister's rare display of temper.

"I'm sorry, angel. Of course it will be beautiful and romantic and everything you want it to be," Mason asserted hastily, and Daff snorted. The guy was thoroughly whipped and it was glorious to see. Daisy's bottom lip quivered ever so slightly and Mason swore beneath his breath before dropping an arm around her shoulders and dragging her close to whisper in her ear. He followed up whatever he said with a kiss to her neck, and a reluctant smile softened her lips.

The show of intimacy made Daff uncomfortable and she shifted her eyes, only to meet Spencer's hooded green gaze. He looked grim, and again she wondered how he felt about the news that Daisy and Mason would be leaving soon.

She wasn't sure how to break eye contact and was grateful when their food arrived to distract everyone. The rest of the conversation centered around wedding plans, and Mason wisely kept his mouth shut this time and offered input only when asked.

"I'll take you to the farm to pick up your car, Daff," Lia offered between bites of her lasagna, and Daff smiled gratefully. She hadn't exactly been relishing the thought of walking back to the farm in the cold. Spencer barely said a word as the meal continued, which was kind of unnerving when one considered how he had once seized every opportunity to talk to her in the past. His bumbling conversational attempts hadn't been very sophisticated or remotely successful, but Daff was honest enough to admit to herself that she hadn't made it very easy on him. Depending on her mood, she would half-heartedly encourage him or completely ignore him. It had taken him long enough to get fed up with her mixed signals, and part of her mourned the loss of his earnest attempts at conversation. Another—much smaller—part of her was happy he no longer seemed interested in her.

She considered his strong, masculine profile again while he spoke with his brother, and she sighed. Yes, only the very smallest part of her was happy about the loss of his attention.

He turned his head unexpectedly and nailed her again with his penetrating stare. Her throat went horribly dry at the latent heat she saw in that burning regard. Why had she never noticed that before? Never seen all that intensity beneath the formidable brow and the flop of shaggy hair? It made her knees feel so shaky she was happy to be sitting down.

She broke eye contact and focused on her salad. She tensed when she felt him lean toward her. He smelled absolutely wonderful, and she bit back a moan as her awareness of him seemed to heighten even further.

"You should eat real food. Meat, potatoes, corn. I don't know what that is, but it wouldn't even satisfy a rabbit." Startled by his observation, Daff's envious eyes fell to his sirloin steak and baked potato. A man-size meal for a formidably sized man.

"Spoken like a guy who's never had to worry about the size of his ass."

"Hmm," he rumbled. "I do, however, worry about the size of yours. You continue to eat like this and the nice handful you have there will fade to nothing."

Her jaw dropped—that was so much more brazen than she was used to from him, and judging by the way his eyes shuttered, he immediately regretted his words.

His body moved subtly so that he was practically leaning away from her, physically putting as much distance between them as he could without alerting anyone else around the table.

"That was uncalled for," he said, his voice pitched low. "I'm sorry."

"Uh . . ." Daff wasn't sure how exactly to respond to his initial observation and subsequent apology and knew she should simply let it go. Accept the apology and pretend it had never happened.

"I'm on a diet," she confessed and then wondered at the admission as well as the complete lack of artifice in her voice. The prospect of dieting made her miserable, and her voice conveyed that very sentiment.

"That's bullshit," he growled, his own voice surprisingly angry. "You're perfect the way you are. What is it with women and this quest for imagined perfection when there's nothing wrong with you in the first place?"

His voice rose, and the rest of the table fell silent.

"What's going on?" Daisy asked warily, and Spencer gestured toward Daff.

"Your sister's on a diet." Daff cringed when every eye turned to her, all expressions conveying various degrees of disbelief.

"You are? Why?" Daisy asked, her eyes wide in surprise. "You've never dieted before." Daff knew Daisy often lamented the fact that neither Lia nor Daff ever found it necessary to diet, while she constantly battled with her weight.

"I just . . ." Daff shrugged uncomfortably. "I think it's best to maintain a healthy lifestyle. It's a lot harder to keep the weight off after thirty—best not to let it creep up on me."

"Let what creep up on you?" Lia asked blankly. "You still fit into your high school uniform. Your weight has remained constant since your late teens."

"Does this have anything to do with the stuff the aunties were saying last night?" Daisy asked, and Daff laughed.

"They've had a lot to say over the years and I haven't let it bother me yet," she dismissed and refused to meet their skeptical eyes, digging into her horrible Caesar salad without dressing—*eww*—with pretend relish.

"But you were eating those canapés last night," Lia reminded her, her sweet face screwed up in confusion.

"I started the diet this morning," Daff informed her around a mouthful of lettuce. "Look, can we stop talking about this? I'm not the first woman in the world to eat a salad, for God's sake."

"But . . ." Daisy began, but her voice trailed off when Mason's hand dropped over hers and gave it a quelling squeeze, obvious to everyone at the table. Daisy bit her lip and focused her frown on her glass of wine instead.

Happy that the subject had been dropped, Daff crunched another mouthful of crisp, bland, water-flavored lettuce and tried her best to look like she was enjoying it.

"So last night's party was—"

"Wait, that's it? No well-meaning intervention for your clearly delusional sister?" Spencer's incredulous voice spoke over Lia's, and Daff bit her lip before leveling a glare at him.

"Back off, Carlisle, this is none of your business," she gritted, and he met her glare unflinchingly.

"You're hating every bite of that salad," he stated, so much arrogant masculine certainty in his voice.

"Still none of your business," she reminded him, and he shook his head, looking genuinely pissed off. She had no idea why he was so offended by her salad. His reaction seemed unnecessarily extreme. She speared a slice of cucumber with her fork, bloodthirstily wishing it was his thickly muscled thigh. Like she needed his stupid opinion. Like she didn't have enough people telling her what she should be, how she should look, talk, act, and feel. She didn't need another voice to add into the crazy mix.

Daisy eyed Spencer and Daff apprehensively.

"This isn't going to be a problem, is it?" she asked bluntly, and both Daff and Spencer blinked at her in confusion until she elaborated. "The best man/maid of honor thing? I won't have to be refereeing you guys at every turn, will I? Because that would be exhausting."

"They're both adults, Daisy," Mason said with an affable smile, while his cold eyes promised instant retribution to the next person who upset his fiancée. *Whoa.* It was the first glimpse Daff had had of lethal Special Ops Mason, and she gulped a bit. "I'm sure they'll be able to work through their differences." The silent *or else* tacked on to the end of that sentence was clear as a bell.

"No problem here," Spencer said with an easy shrug, his unfathomable scrutiny raking over Daff with frigid indifference. And she struggled to achieve a similar expression on her face.

"Yeah, none whatsoever." Daff hoped her smile looked sincere, even though it felt unnatural. She ducked her head and went back to her salad, signaling an end to the discussion. The rest went back to discussing the previous night's party, while both Spencer and Daff remained silent.

Daff continued to poke at her salad, not even pretending to eat it now, and when she caught Spencer's critical gaze on her again, she exhaled sharply and, heartily fed up with his judgmental crap, excused herself before escaping to the bathroom.

It was a unisex bathroom, nothing fancy, just a single room with four stalls. And it was blessedly empty now that the lunchtime crowd was thinning. She rinsed her face with cool water and swore softly when she reached for the paper towel dispenser, only to find it empty.

"Typical," she muttered beneath her breath before slamming into one of the cubicles and dragging some toilet paper off the roll. It was the horribly cheap, soft paper that broke when you so much as folded it. She crumpled a handful and dabbed her face with it, cringing when she felt bits sticking to her damp skin.

The door opened, letting in the noise from the restaurant, and light footsteps came all the way to her cubicle. Daff looked up, a resigned sigh escaping when she saw Lia leaning against the cubicle door, arms folded over her chest.

"So, seriously, what's up with you and Spencer?" Lia asked without preamble, and Daff sucked in an irritated breath.

"Absolutely nothing. You know Spencer and I have been amicable enemies for years now."

"I know no such thing." Daff was so focused on her sister that she only dimly registered the noise level increasing when the restroom door opened again. "You never seemed to actively dislike the guy, and he definitely didn't dislike you. Whatever is going on now seems different."

"It's not. I'm just not used to seeing so much of him. He's better in small doses, right?"

"Spencer's a nice guy."

"He's okay. Just not very interesting. I mean, the guy is good-looking, if you go for the big, hulking types, but that's about it. He has the personality of a mushroom. Bland, boring, insipid. And yes, I know those words all mean the same thing, but, I mean, can you say *boring*? How can so much hotness house so much blahness?" Daff felt nasty saying the words, but it was better than letting on how she really felt. Or how uncomfortable she felt around him lately and how much she wished she had cultivated a different relationship with him. One that didn't make her always seem like a rampant bitch. She hadn't been kind or fair to Spencer Carlisle, she knew that, and the childish interactions of her youth had somehow bled into her adult relationship with him. Well, if it could be called a relationship.

She was so wrapped up in her own thoughts that she barely noticed Lia's gasp and horrified step back. It was only when Lia swore—something the younger woman never, *ever* did—that she tuned back in to the present and to the unpleasant reality that Spencer Carlisle was standing behind Lia. He was glaring down at Daff with an expression on his face that was shocked, pissed off, and hurt all at the same time. It was the latter—quickly disguised—that hit her right in the gut, and she lifted a shaking hand to her mouth as she tried to formulate the apology that he deserved.

She didn't get so much as a squeak out before his lips compressed and he swiveled on his heel to leave the restroom.

"Shit," Daff whispered, and Lia was staring at her with eyes so huge they practically swallowed her face.

"How could you say all those terrible things about him?" she asked, her voice shaking.

"Look there's no need for *you* to get all uptight about it, okay? I'll apologize to him and fix it. He's a guy, he's probably shrugged it off already. Water off a duck's back and all that."

Lia didn't look very convinced, and, truthfully, Daff felt like a complete jerk, but for God's sake, why the hell did he feel the need to eavesdrop on them in the first place? Didn't he know that eavesdroppers never heard good things about themselves? Okay, so maybe he'd been coming to use the bathroom, but couldn't he have waited until they had returned to the table? He knew it was a unisex bathroom; it was super awkward—and a little creepy—to come in while she and Lia were using it.

She scrubbed her hands over her face and winced when she felt damp bits of toilet paper rolling beneath her palms. She wiped her cheeks on her shoulders, hoping she got most of the paper off, and gestured for Lia to follow her.

When they rejoined the table, everything seemed normal. Spencer and Mason both got to their feet and held out Lia's and Daff's chairs. It was something she had found corny about them in high school. They had always done cringey stuff like that. Held doors, helped girls into their coats . . . smarmy, nerdy stuff that seemed to come straight out of old movies. Like they had learned their manners and mannerisms from old-school, long-dead actors in musicals. Recently, watching Mason's interactions with Daisy, Daff had started to find it charming and sweet. And with the insight that she had lacked as a teenager, she wondered if indeed the brothers hadn't learned their old-world chivalry from movies. They'd certainly had no other role models around to teach them.

Once they were all seated again, she lifted her eyes to Spencer's face, but his expression was carefully neutral and he kept his eyes averted. He didn't seem particularly disturbed by anything she had said earlier, and she wondered if maybe she had imagined the hurt she'd seen in his eyes.

Lia was completely unsettled and upset and kept trying to do things for Spencer. When he reached for a napkin, she grabbed it before he could and handed it to him; if he wanted salt, she passed it to him before he could fully formulate the question. She still looked on the verge of tears, and when she took the saltshaker from him before he could place it on the table, he smiled and took her shaking hand and brought it to his lips for a kiss.

He leaned over and whispered something into her ear, and whatever he said seemed to release Lia's tension. She practically melted and favored him with a lovely smile, which he returned warmly.

He released her hand before glancing around the table and then levering his bulk out of the chair with more grace than such a big man should ever possess.

"I'm off. Got plans." Concise. The man didn't believe in wasting words.

"Yeah? Do I know her?" Mason grinned and Spencer slanted him an unfathomable look.

"I'll talk with you tomorrow. This should cover my bill," he said without inflection, dropping some money on the table before nodding at the rest of the group in general. He left without any further comment.

"Okay, what's up with him?" Daisy asked Mason as soon as Spencer was out of earshot. Mason was staring at his brother's retreating back with a slight frown on his face.

"Not sure. He's been a bit distant recently."

"How do you think he took the news about us moving?" Daisy asked, and Mason shook his head.

"Not good."

"How can you tell? The man's expression barely changed," Daff said, and Mason looked at her with speculatively raised brows.

"Watching closely, were you?"

"I'm just observant," Daff muttered defensively, and Mason snorted.

"Not observant enough. His body language immediately changed. He shut himself in. He does that when he's trying to shield his emotions—he battens down the hatches, so to speak. I think he feels . . . left out. Lonely, maybe."

He looked disturbed by the notion, and Daisy leaned in to him and lifted a hand to his cheek.

"We'll talk to him. Make sure he knows he's important and welcome and included." Mason lifted his hand to cover hers and turned his head to plant a kiss in her palm. Daff peered over at Lia and found her sister staring at Daisy and Mason with a kind of wistful envy on her face. Daff sighed; Lia really needed to get over this whole marriage and happily ever after thing. It helped to lower one's expectations. Daisy was lucky and the exception. That kind of lightning-bolt, romantic shit didn't happen every day.

"Lia, you ready to go?" Her question startled Lia out of her dreamy funk, and she stared at Daff blankly.

"What?"

"I need to get home," Daff said. "Got some housecleaning to do."

"Ah, your semiannual cleaning spree?" Daisy teased her. Daff was the slob of the three sisters and the victim of many hours of ribbing because of it.

"You're going to need a shovel and a wheelbarrow," Lia said. "Should I ask Daddy to drop them off for you?"

Mason was laughing his ass off by now, and Daff glared at the three of them.

"Why don't you just hire someone to do your cleaning?" Mason asked between chuckles.

"I can do my own cleaning," Daff grated, a little fed up with this by now.

"No, you can't," Daisy said, shaking her head. "Mason is right; you should get some help. It's really nice to see the floor and be able to find your shoes—"

"Or your feet, for that matter," Lia interrupted her.

"Jesus, it's not that bad," Daff growled, embarrassed. "You make me sound like one of those hoarders."

"If the shoe fits," Daisy said.

"She wouldn't know if it fits, she can't find it beneath the rubble," Lia retorted, and the other three screamed with laughter.

"Oh, for God's sake. Lia, are you taking me to my car or should I walk?"

Lia wiped her eyes, her shoulders still heaving with her silent chuckles.

"Yes, okay. Get your panties out of that twist."

"This is what happens when she doesn't eat. She gets mean and feral," Daisy observed, and Daff glared at her.

"Watch it, Deedee," she warned. "I know where you keep your girl porn."

Mason sat up, immediately on high alert.

"Her what?" he asked eagerly.

"Nothing. Ignore her, hunger has made her delusional," Daisy said, and Daff smirked, knowing that her sister's fiancé would keep hounding Daisy until he found out exactly what Daff had meant by that comment. It wasn't exactly porn, just a small stash of erotica that Daisy had been meaning to give away for years. She was too embarrassed to donate the books to the local library or clinic, because everybody would know it was from her. Daff had once suggested Daisy make anonymous donations, and her sister had confessed that she still had the childish habit of writing "this book belongs to Daisy McGregor" on the inside cover of every book she bought. Now Daisy's eyes promised painful retribution as Mason immediately leaned toward her and started badgering her.

"What girl porn, Daisy? C'mon, I know you're keeping something from me."

"I don't know what she's talking about," Daisy maintained, not meeting his eyes.

"Aw, angel, why you gotta be like this? If you have girlie porn, maybe we could have a read through together, see if there's anything interesting to try." Daisy's chest hitched and her breathing increased as she lifted her eyes to meet his. The expression in them was shockingly sultry.

"You're not exactly lacking in imagination," Daisy said, a husky note entering her voice.

"*Okay.*" Daff surged to her feet and added a couple of bills to the money Spencer had left in the middle of the table. "I'm out of here. Coming, Lia?"

"Oh my God, yes, please." Lia was on her feet in seconds, tossing her own money onto the growing pile, while Daff threw a disgusted look at the couple who barely seemed aware of their surroundings anymore.

"Ugh, sometimes you guys are a bit much," Daff complained, and Lia made a strangled sound of agreement. They left the overly affectionate couple who acknowledged their departure with half-hearted waves before going back to their intimate whispering.

"Thanks, Lia," Daff said after Lia parked beside her tiny hatchback VW at the farmhouse.

"You coming in to say hi?" her sister asked, unbuckling her seat belt.

"Nah, I just want to get home," Daff responded, reaching for the door handle. Truth be told, she needed to figure out what she was going to do about the Spencer thing. Until she apologized to him, she wouldn't feel right. She had said some truly awful and unfair things and now felt like the bitch everybody already thought she was.

"What did he say to you?" Daff asked, pausing with her fingers wrapped around the handle, and Lia frowned in confusion.

"What?"

"Spencer," Daff clarified. "You were all eaten up with guilt about our conversation earlier until he whispered something in your ear. So what did he say?"

"Oh." Lia hesitated, as if contemplating whether to divulge the information. "He said words don't hurt, only actions do, and then he said that my actions have only ever shown me to be a kind and caring person."

"He really said that?"

"Yes? Why? Surprised that a bland, insipid, boring guy like Spencer Carlisle would have insightful gems like that to offer?" *Ouch!* Turned out words *did* hurt, especially when they were thorny zingers laid on you by the sweetest person on earth.

"He's full of shit," Daff dismissed, and Lia surprised her by nodding.

"He is. Because words *do* hurt. You said terrible things and they hurt him, but he was sweet enough, *kind* enough to let me know that he didn't hold me accountable for your words. So I will do him the courtesy of pretending that he meant what he said. In order to preserve his dignity and pride."

Daff chewed on her lower lip, feeling justifiably put in her place.

"He wasn't meant to hear what I said."

"And yet he did."

"Yes."

Lia sighed. "Let me know if you need help with the cleanup."

Somehow Daff didn't think she meant the cleanup of the house, and that made her feel small and petty. Despite clearly being pissed off with her, Lia was still offering her moral support. Something Daff definitely didn't deserve.

"I feel like crap, okay?" she admitted, and Lia leaned over to give her a one-armed hug.

"I know."

Daff sighed heavily. "I'll sort it out."

"I know."

Damn it. Her sister's unwavering faith killed Daff. That was a hell of a lot to live up to.

CHAPTER THREE

Bland!

Thwack.

Insipid!

Thwack.

Boring!

Thwack! Thwack! Thwa—

"Fuck! Balls! Shit!" Spencer swore when his ax lodged in the fallen tree he'd been attempting to split for firewood. It wasn't his favorite chore and he'd been delaying the job for days, but he needed to get the anger out of his system and could think of no better outlet than violent physical activity. It was this or beat the shit out of the punching bag in the makeshift gym that doubled as his home office. He had chosen this option because at least it yielded positive results from released negative energy.

Well, that was the idea, anyway. He glared at his stuck ax and swore again, wiping his forearm across his forehead to prevent the sweat beading there from dripping into his eyes. He tugged at the ax before releasing his breath on yet another curse word. He wasn't getting the damned thing unstuck anytime soon. He'd need a chain saw or something to dislodge it.

God. Sometimes she pissed him off.

She made him feel capable of conquering mountains one day and smaller than a bug the next. It was very fucking unhealthy, and he knew it. But today . . . to hear those words from her. The wake-up call had been a long time coming, but it was welcome nonetheless. Just what he needed to get her out of his head once and for all. He didn't know how someone with such a rancid personality could have come from such a perfectly lovely family. It was baffling, really. And she was one to comment on his character, when hers was as grating as nails on a chalkboard.

Frustrated, he lifted his arms and linked his fingers behind his head as he glowered blindly at the wind-felled tree. Why did he always let her get to him? Daffodil McGregor had been treating him like a second-class citizen since . . . well, since forever, really, and he was done with her. She was unreasonable and a little unhinged and it would be better if—after this wedding—he stayed as far away from her as humanly possible.

On the upside, at least her obnoxiousness had taken his mind off the fact that his brother was leaving again. The news, while unsurprising, had shaken him more than he cared to admit. After Mason and Daisy left, he'd be alone once more. He had some friends, sure, cultivated relationships with the occasional woman, but he never felt like he was truly a part of something. For a while, when he was dating Tanya, he'd felt like he finally belonged somewhere and with someone. Only to find her sandwiched between two guys in his bed one day. She'd had the nerve to smile when she spotted him in the doorway. Smile and invite him to join them.

He'd tossed them all out on their naked asses and then he'd burned the bed.

He'd loved that fucking bed.

Awesome. Now he was remembering Tanya spit-roasted between two guys. Not pretty, and yet the memory didn't sting half as much as the recollection of Daffodil McGregor saying he had the personality of a mushroom. A mushroom, for fuck's sake!

He growled. He actually growled like a wild animal, shocking himself in the process. He threw a longing stare at his ax before wearily making his way to his home gym.

It looked like the punching bag was going to get that workout after all.

The following night, Daff glared at her phone screen in frustration. There they were, in stark black and white. Two words. Sincere and yet completely inadequate.

I'm sorry.

She couldn't send it to him. She wanted to. She so desperately wanted to send it and then be able to tell Lia in all honesty that she had apologized, but she knew that it was a cop-out and she also knew that Spencer deserved more. It had already taken her more than twenty-four hours to get to this point. She had spent the rest of Saturday and all of Sunday cleaning and telling herself to get busy apologizing to the man. Yet she still hadn't plucked up the courage to do anything more than stare at the two simple words on a phone screen.

She hit "Delete" and watched the words disappear from her screen. One tiny letter at a time. She scrolled through her contacts until she found his name, and her thumb hovered over the "Call" button for a very long time. She should go to his store tomorrow, apologize in person. But if she called first, paved the way, so to speak, it might be easier than just going in cold. She could start laying the groundwork now. It would be better if she didn't have to look at him when she did it.

But it was just as much of a cop-out as a text message. No . . . it was better than a text message. He would be able to hear the sincerity in her voice and know that she meant it.

She hit "Call" before she could talk herself out of it and put the phone on speaker. Somehow, lifting it to her ear and hearing his voice so intimately close felt too personal. Especially when she was in bed, wearing nothing but panties and a tank top.

The phone rang, twice . . . three times . . .

This was a terrible idea. She was about to cancel the call when his voice rang out in the dark silence of her room. He sounded groggy, angry, unutterably sexy . . . and like he was right there in bed with her. The rogue thought made her uncomfortable, and she immediately regretted making this call from her bedroom.

"Daff? It's twelve thirty. Why are you calling so late? Are you okay? Mason? Daisy?" Okay, she couldn't lie to herself—she found it sweet as hell that he was immediately concerned for her well-being.

"Daff?" he prompted, irritation and fear mounting in his voice when she didn't respond straightaway.

"I didn't know it was so late," she admitted. It was the truth—she'd been stressing about this matter all evening, and the time got away from her. The silence stretched between them, taut, uncomfortable, and incredibly awkward. Daff wasn't sure how to break it. She heard the faint rustling of crisp, clean bedsheets as he shifted.

"It couldn't wait till morning?" he finally asked, and she was relieved that he had spoken and not merely hung up on her.

"I—I had to apologize." Even though it was something she wanted and needed to do, the words still had the consistency of sawdust in her mouth.

"Had to, huh?" He sounded speculative, and she heard the bedsheets rustling again. Was he sitting up? What was he wearing? Was he bare chested? Had the covers just slid down his chest to pool in his lap? Was he more than bare chested? Did he sleep naked?

The distracting thoughts made her groan, and she pinched the bridge of her nose to get herself back on track.

"I said some pretty nasty things," she admitted, and he grunted. It sounded like agreement. "I should apologize for them."

"You should," he agreed amicably and then felled her with a zinger. "But do you *want* to?"

Her answer didn't take much thought. "Yes. I want to." She was surprised to find that she meant it.

"You mean you don't think I'm . . . what was it? Bland, boring, and insipid?"

"I mean, I barely know you," she prevaricated, and that prompted another grunt from him. She couldn't quite interpret this one. "So I can't be the best judge of what you actually are."

"As apologies go, this one is pretty shitty," he said, stifling a yawn.

"I'm trying, okay?" she snapped. Then immediately regretted the slight lapse in temper.

"If I have the personality of a mushroom, you have the disposition of a wasp—skinny, sometimes good to look at, with a propensity to go on the attack with little to no provocation."

She gasped, his words immediately getting her back up, but she forced herself to take a deep breath and fought to get her temper under control.

"Okay, you earned that shot. We're even now."

"Still waiting for my apology," he reminded her, and she scowled at her phone screen.

"You could be a bit more gracious about this," she hissed, and he sighed.

"Daff, it's nearly one in the morning. Why not get this over with so that we can both get a decent night's sleep? I don't know about you, but Monday is my busiest day and if I don't get enough sleep I won't be able to function very well at all."

"Fine," she snapped through clenched teeth, before swallowing and screwing her eyes shut. "I'm really sorry I said those things about you. It was wrong and I do regret it."

"Okay." Her eyes flew open and she stared at her phone—the only source of light in the room—in disbelief.

"'Okay'? That's it?" Didn't he know how much the stupid apology had taken out of her? And that was all he had to say in response to it?

"Yeah. And thank you."

"But—"

"I'll see you soon, Daff. Sleep tight." He hung up before she could say another word, and Daff gritted her teeth before lifting a pillow to her face and screaming in frustration. She immediately picked up her phone, did a quick Google image search, and loaded a new profile picture and name to replace the white-on-gray *SC* that had formerly been on the screen next to his name. There. *Much better.*

She flung her phone aside and threw herself down on the bed and spent the rest of the night tossing and turning and fuming. Getting little to no sleep at all.

Daff sat with her chin in her hand—one fingertip absently tracing the rim of her warm coffee mug—and watched even more customers enter SC Sporting Solutions. They'd had a steady stream of customers all morning, and most exited the store with huge shopping bags. Daff sighed and scanned the boutique grimly. The place was neat as a pin, had beautiful couture clothing on display, and had attracted just one customer that morning—a window-shopper who, after one discreet glance at a price tag, had hastened back out.

God, she was so bored.

She looked out again. She had opened slightly after nine this morning, feeling groggy and a little hungover from lack of sleep, and had missed Spencer's habitually brisk walk past the huge boutique window on his way to work. Daff usually arrived at eight thirty in the morning, a full fifteen minutes before Spencer. She liked to ease into her day—put on the coffee in the tiny back kitchen, start up the soothing ambient music, which she hated with an absolute passion, and then check her e-mails and inventory. As if there were any danger at all of running out of stock. She snorted at the thought. She should be so lucky.

Now she wondered if Spencer was at work already. More than likely. She had never seen him arrive late. Always eight forty-five on the dot. It was Monday, so he would probably be wearing the black sweat suit instead of the gray one. He looked good in both, of course, but she preferred the black one. It made him look sleek and less overwhelmingly brutish. He tended to alternate the colors every day. Monday was black day.

Daff would cut off her own left thumb rather than divulge how familiar she was with Spencer's wardrobe changes. Her job was boring, she tended to notice things, and since she saw Spencer every day, of course she would start to pick up on silly details like that.

Such as the fact that he always carried a refill mug—presumably of coffee—and a doughnut box from MJ's on Monday mornings. Every other day of the week he had only the mug, but Monday was doughnut day. The box was large enough to feed his entire staff of ten, so she figured it was a beginning-of-the-week staff treat. That was really nice of him.

Daff lifted her mug to her lips and took a cautious sip, wrinkling her nose when the bitter brew hit her tongue. Well, that was what happened when you rushed through the coffee-making process. The stuff was undrinkable. She sighed and put the mug aside. She'd have to brew another pot.

She considered going over to SCSS and apologizing in person, but she lacked the courage to face Spencer so soon. Maybe this afternoon. Possibly tomorrow morning.

She glowered across the road again. Oh look, more customers wanting sporting goods. She muttered something vile beneath her breath and dragged out a tattered secondhand historical romance novel. Might as well catch up on her reading. Would Duke Sexy rescue Lady Gorgeous from the Pornstache Villain's clutches?

Chapter fifteen revealed all and yeah . . . no big surprise, he rescued her and she gratefully swooned into bed with him.

Daff was so absorbed in her reading that she didn't see the figure approaching the store until the bell above the door tinkled. She dropped her book guiltily and plastered a smile on her face. A smile that faded seconds later.

"Spencer?" What was he doing here?

"Hey. What are you reading?"

"Why are you here?"

"Rude," he admonished before dragging over an expensive, ornate, and purely decorative chair to the opposite side of the checkout counter. He sat down with a satisfied sigh. "Thought we could have lunch together."

Seriously. What the hell?

"Why?"

"Give you the opportunity to apologize in person. I know you must be desperate to."

"This is really weird. And it's way too early for lunch."

"How good is that book if you've lost complete track of time?" She checked the clock, and sure enough, it was after twelve. Retail people rarely took lunch at midday, but since Spencer was the boss and Daff hardly ever had customers, there was nothing stopping them from eating right now.

"I have plans for lunch."

"Hmm?" He sounded way too skeptical for her liking. "Too bad, I have more than enough to share with you." He lifted a brown paper bag to the counter and removed a cellophane-wrapped sandwich from its depths. "Smoked hickory ham, cheese, tomato, lettuce, and mustard on rye."

God, that sounded delicious, and considering that she just had a small salad and an apple for lunch, it was also highly tempting.

"That barely looks like enough to feed you," she pointed out. No way half a sandwich would sustain a man Spencer's size.

He rumbled in agreement and lifted a second sandwich from the bag.

"Which is why I have two," he said.

"Is that from MJ's?" she asked faintly, unable to resist asking.

"Made them myself."

She didn't know why, but somehow that made it seem even more irresistible.

"Are your lunch plans really that urgent?" he asked, unwrapping the tasty-looking sandwich and holding a perfectly cut triangle up in front of her nose. Gosh, it looked good. Her stomach rumbled eagerly, and she blushed when he chuckled at the sound.

"I suppose I could postpone them till tomorrow or something," she conceded, reaching for the sandwich with both hands. He handed it over and rummaged around in a separate bag that she hadn't previously noticed before placing two clear bottles of orange juice and a large bag of salted potato chips on the counter between them. He nudged one of the bottles toward her.

"To wash it down," he said before taking a hearty bite from his sandwich.

They didn't exchange another word until they had both polished off their sandwiches and started on the salty deliciousness of the potato chips.

"So," she began, reaching for a chip and crunching down on half of it before continuing, "I really am sorry about the things I said."

"Pissed me off a little," he confessed placidly, and she leveled a surprised look at him. For all that he looked brutish, Spencer always seemed personable and mild mannered. She couldn't imagine him angry at all. What did that even look like? Her breath hitched in her chest as she imagined a furious Spencer. Would he go all quiet and deadly or would he be loud and blustery? Somehow she couldn't picture the latter at all and decided that he would be cold and aloof, like Duke Sexy in her romance novel.

Ugh, and what was she doing, romanticizing Spencer Carlisle?

Get a grip, Daff! she warned herself sternly, but she still couldn't help feeling a bit hot and flustered at the thought of Spencer Carlisle getting his mad on.

"It did?" she asked stupidly, and he frowned at her.

"Well, of course it did. Nobody wants to be compared to a fucking mushroom."

She twirled the other half of her chip for a few seconds before popping it into her mouth.

"The mushroom thing really bothered you, didn't it?" she said in dawning realization, but he didn't reply—just glowered at her. "I said I was sorry."

"You did."

"So can we drop it now?"

His jaw clenched for a moment before he shrugged. "I don't bear grudges," he said between gritted teeth, the words so strained that she had a hard time believing them.

"Well, that's good, since we're going to be forced to do a lot of stuff together over the next few months."

"Will it really be that bad? Just a couple of dances at the wedding and that's that, right?"

"I'm pretty sure they don't want to do separate hen and stag nights. So we're going to have to collaborate on that."

He looked so horrified by the notion that Daff was bordering on seriously offended until he spoke.

"A mixed stag and hen? What the hell is that about? It goes against the laws of nature," he exclaimed, and, a little relieved that the look of horror hadn't been at the thought of them working together, Daff laughed.

"I know, right? I don't even know how to go about planning something like that."

"I suppose we could start off with separate events and have them mix halfway through the evening?" he ventured and Daff nodded, thoughtfully crunching away on another chip. She washed it down with some juice.

"That would be . . . not entirely horrible. We could get the strippers out of the way before the parties mingle," she acknowledged and then grinned when he snorted in amusement. She was starting to differentiate between his grunts and sniffs and snorts. Go her. "Look at *us* collaborating like pros."

"It might not be too bad," he agreed.

"We should probably double-check if they want a mixed event, but Daisy did say something to that effect."

"Mason never mentioned it."

"He's a guy, of course he never mentioned it."

"Watch it. Guys are people, too."

"Ooh, witty."

"Yeah, I'm not quite the Neanderthal you think I am," he said, crumpling up the empty chip bag and shoving it—along with their sandwich wrappers and empty juice bottles—into one of the empty paper bags.

"I don't think you're a Neanderthal," she hedged, and he slanted her a blatantly disbelieving look from beneath his heavy brows. He leaned over the counter, his face uncomfortably close to hers before responding.

"Liar." The word was barely a whisper, a breath of warm air fanning across her cheek, and she flinched slightly in reaction to both his closeness and the shivery blaze of awareness that skirted down her spine. He withdrew and got up, gracefully easing his large frame out of the tiny chair, which had surpassed all expectations by bearing his weight admirably.

"I'll see you tomorrow," he said abruptly. She was still trying to process his words when he left. He'd see her tomorrow? Did he mean like in passing? On his way to work? She was still trying to work it out when the bell tinkled again and his head popped back in.

"Don't bring lunch."

"Whoa . . . hold on a sec—" The door closed on her protestation and he was walking down the road to his store before she could even begin to formulate a proper response.

It was colder than a witch's tit this evening, and Spencer hadn't really expected much of a turnout. The kids were barely interested in any of the activities he organized at the best of times, and Spencer figured freezing temperatures combined with an outdoor activity would definitely serve as the ultimate turnoff for most of them.

He was stomping his feet to keep the circulation going, steam from his own breath clouding his vision, as he hopefully watched the local sports field's entrance. The field generally served as a rugby, soccer, and cricket arena, and a lot of people used the track for jogging. In summer it hosted the community fete and various other social functions. Old ladies did their tai chi here when the heat in the gym got too claustrophobic. But in winter—aside from the high school soccer or rugby matches—it remained relatively unused. Spencer had had the—probably misguided—idea to rope Mason in to teach a few self-defense classes for his youth outreach program. He figured the kids would love to learn from a pro like Mason, but on a night like this even someone with as much badass cred as Mason might not be enough of a drawcard for already unmotivated kids.

"Why couldn't we have done this at the gym or the community center?" Mason groused, blowing hot air into his cupped hands and swearing under his breath.

"You're getting soft, Mase. I thought the weather didn't bother you."

"Easy living will do that to you," his brother said with a cocky grin. "I can tolerate the weather when necessary. This doesn't seem necessary. Not when we have perfectly good interior alternatives."

"Yeah, well, Harry 'the Ass' Walters doesn't want a bunch of 'young hooligans'—his words—fucking up his expensive gym equipment. And I told you, man, the community center has a water leak. The place is flooded. We're working on fixing the problem, but until then this is the only place we can come to for the youth program."

"I don't think anyone is going to show up, Spence," Mason said, his voice almost apologetic. He knew how much the program meant to Spencer.

"Let's give them a few more minutes. Some of them have to travel a distance to get here. I'm thinking of chartering a bus or something to pick them up every week. But it's tough finding a driver who's willing to go to some of the places these kids live."

Mason nodded, and they stood in silence for a moment before the younger man spoke again.

"I didn't mean to spring the news on you like that. About moving to Grahamstown, I mean."

"Well, I was kind of expecting it. You can't exactly go to university in Riversend, can you?"

"Yeah, but five years is quite a stretch."

"Better than twelve years," Spencer responded, referring to the last time Mason had left. "And at least this time you won't be on the other side of the world."

Spencer wasn't happy to be losing his only family again, but he wasn't about to reveal to Mason how he felt. His brother had enough on his plate without having to worry about Spencer's feelings.

"Daff says you and Daisy want a mixed stag and hen?" Spencer said, changing the subject. Mason grimaced.

"It's weird, right?" he said with a slight shake of his head.

"Off-the-charts weird," Spencer agreed. "What the fuck, bro?"

"Daisy mentioned it, and she looked so damned cute and hopeful I found myself agreeing to it before I knew what I was doing."

"Come on, Mase. At least put up a semblance of a fight. If you're already crumbling over shit like this, you'll never have a say in anything in your marriage."

Mason laughed.

"It's not like that. The stag thing isn't important, and if it makes Daisy happy then that's all that matters. I just think it's bizarre as fuck to have a mixed thing, is all."

"Daff and I were thinking we could start off separately and the two parties could merge later in the evening."

"Daff, huh?" Mason crossed his arms and tucked his hands beneath his armpits.

"We're just getting a jump on the whole maid of honor/best man thing."

"You guys aren't going to kill each other and break my fiancée's heart, right?"

"Depends on how much more of a bitch Daff is."

"Come on, she's not that bad." Spencer said nothing in response to that, merely watched Mason with raised brows, and the latter laughed.

"You're the one with the hard-on for her," Mason pointed out, and Spencer ran an irate hand through his hair.

"I'm over that." And he *was*, despite giving in to his really odd whim to take her lunch that afternoon. Even odder was the fact that it couldn't be dismissed as an impulse. He had prepared the extra sandwich before work, fully intending to give it to Daff. He couldn't explain what had motivated the act any more than he could explain the knowledge that he was going to do the same thing tomorrow. Maybe it was because he knew that she'd probably packed a salad in her misguided attempt to diet. He was pissed off with her, sure, but he didn't really want her to starve herself.

"Spence, no one's coming," Mason said after another beat of silence, and Spencer sighed and nodded.

"It's the shitty weather. Who can blame them? Maybe we can reschedule for next week."

"Suits me." Mason moved to quickly and efficiently stack the half dozen exercise mats they had brought into a neat pile. "Want to grab a beer after this?"

"Shouldn't you be getting home to do wedding stuff?"

"Nah, I already committed to spending the next few hours with you, so we might as well hang out. Besides, Daisy's still pissed off with me for even mentioning the word *braai* in relation to the wedding, so I'm kind of in the doghouse as far as wedding plans go at the moment."

"That was a dumb move." Spencer chuckled as he lifted one side of the stacked mats and Mason grabbed the other. They carried the mats to the back of Spencer's huge pickup truck with Spencer ribbing Mason all the way.

"You Carlisle?" The young, gruff voice came from behind them, and both men looked over to see a slight boy, probably no more than fourteen or fifteen, watching them warily. Spencer assessed the boy. He had never seen the kid before. Small, skinny, hands thrust in jeans pockets, and shoulders hunched defensively. His black hair was cropped short and spiky, he had warm, golden-brown skin, and—as with a few of the other mixed-race kids Spencer worked with—had striking light-green eyes.

"Hmm. I'm sorry, we're packing up. We didn't think anybody was going to come. You must be new. I'm Spencer Carlisle. This is my brother, Mason." He held out a hand in greeting, but the boy kept his own hands firmly tucked into his pockets.

"I know who you are," he snapped.

"And you are?" Spencer prompted, ignoring the rudeness. The kid said nothing at first, merely stared at them with those unnerving eyes.

"Charlie," he finally replied.

"Well, Charlie, if you don't mind skipping the self-defense class, we can maybe grab something to eat before I take you home? Or will one of your parents be picking you up?"

"I don't need your charity," the kid snapped. His jeans looked at least two sizes too big, and the belt had a few extra holes punched into it to accommodate his small waist and to keep the baggy trousers up.

"It wasn't meant to be charity. I usually order a pizza for the kids anyway, and I figure you came out in this weather, the least I can do is offer you something to eat since we're not doing the class. Kind of as an apology for wasting your time."

Charlie narrowed his eyes on Spencer's face, as if he were trying to gauge the older man's sincerity.

"I'm all right. Thanks. I'll just go home."

"You need a ride?"

"It's close by." Now it was Spencer's turn to try to figure out if the boy was being truthful, but he couldn't see anything beyond defiance and challenge in his eyes.

"Check the community center announcement board tomorrow to see when our next self-defense class will be."

The boy shrugged.

"I hope to see you there."

"Whatever." The kid turned away and kicked at the muddy ground as he trudged away, leaving the two tall men to watch his retreating figure.

"You ever seen that kid before?" Mason asked, and Spencer shrugged.

"Never."

"She seems familiar."

"*She?*"

"Yeah, man. Don't tell me you fell for that gruff act." Spencer scrutinized the kid's back speculatively and had to admit that there was a definite feminine gait to Charlie's stride.

"Why the hell would she pretend to be a boy?" Spencer speculated.

"I can think of any number of reasons, none of them pleasant."

"Do you think she needs help?"

"Beyond the obvious, you mean?"

"I'm just wondering if she's in immediate jeopardy."

"I think she probably does have a safe place to stay tonight—she didn't seem that desperate."

Casting another look at the boy—*girl*—and contemplating whether he should push the issue of food and possibly shelter, Spencer decided that it would probably succeed only in alienating her. Best to tread carefully with a prickly personality like hers. He wanted her to come back so that he could better ascertain what kind of help she needed. He just hoped she really had a decent place to stay and that she wasn't in a dangerous situation.

"I'll ask *Oom* Herbert and Principal Kane if they know her," he decided out loud, and Mason nodded.

"Good call." Oom—or Uncle—Herbert was the popular local minister who ran the homeless shelter. And old man Kane had been the principal at the high school since Mason and Spencer were kids. They would know if the girl was local and what her situation was. Then again, Spencer knew pretty much all the at-risk kids in and around town, and he had never seen her before. Somehow he doubted that young Charlie was local.

He sighed and climbed into the cab of his truck. He was going to worry about her all night; it was really bucketing down by now and she was skinny as hell—she could get sick easily. He hoped she really had decent shelter close by. He would never forgive himself if anything happened to her.

Daff was in the middle of reorganizing her overstuffed closet when her phone rang. Her eyes skimmed the room, and she wondered which pile of clothes hid the clamoring device.

"Shitsticks," she muttered as she dug through the nearby charity heap. Not there. She dived through a few more heaps: skirts, blouses, and jumpsuits—how in the hell had she managed to accumulate so many jumpsuits?—before she finally found it beneath a smaller pile of scarves. Naturally, the second she laid her hands on the damned thing, it stopped ringing, and she swore colorfully while she checked the screen to see who had messed with her cleaning mojo. Her language got even more creatively foul when she saw who the call had been from.

She had a brief moment of hesitation before jabbing at the screen to return the call.

"Hey." He answered on the first ring, and she glared at the mess she had made of her packing system while searching for the phone.

"Why were you calling me?"

"Must you always be so rude?" he chastised, and that made her even more irritable. She hated being called out on her bad behavior. And she discovered that she hated it that much more when it was Spencer doing the calling out.

"It's ten o'clock . . . at night." She tacked on the last two words for emphasis, and he chuckled; the rich sound startled her and sent a wave of warmth through her.

"Yeah. I got that."

"There is no reason to be calling me at ten p.m., Spencer."

"I beg to differ."

She said nothing in response to that, merely waited silently for him to elaborate. But the silence stretched for what seemed like an endless moment and she sighed.

"Well?"

"Well, what?"

"Why the call?"

"Oh." She could practically hear the smile in his voice, and she wondered what possible joy he got out of annoying her like this. But at the same time, she sat down on the soft sofa and folded her feet under her butt, wriggling slightly to get comfortable. "I was wondering if you're allergic to eggs."

"What?" *The fuck?* The last two words were unspoken but had to be pretty apparent in her tone of voice.

"I was thinking of making something eggy for lunch tomorrow."

"Don't bring me lunch tomorrow, Spencer."

"Why not?"

"Because it's weird. I told you, I don't understand why you'd do something like that."

"I'm a giving kind of guy. And we can start strategizing our BM/MOH stuff."

"What?"

"Best man, maid of honor. Apparently it's the *thing* to use acronyms—MIL, FIL, BM, and so on."

She fought back a smile; he sounded so pleased to actually *know* that bit of information. She toyed with the frayed edge of a silk cushion for a few moments before talking again.

"No," she said, and he was quiet for a couple of seconds.

"No, what?"

"I don't have an egg allergy."

"Cool."

"But I don't like eggs," she continued smugly.

"Who doesn't like eggs?"

"I don't." Nobody else really knew that. Back in the sixth grade, a cute boy had offered her half of his egg-mayo sandwich, and she had accepted the hateful thing with a gracious smile before swallowing it down without even flinching. A week later, Daff and young Byron Blake had been going steady. Ugh, she winced at the memory . . . and at the thought of his name. His parents had named his sister Barrett and his younger brother Browning. Apparently back in the day, it had been all the rage to give your kids dumb alliterative names that would make them cringe when they were adults. Her own parents had also fallen prey to the unfortunate trend. Her innocent relationship with Byron had set the tone for every relationship that followed. She liked whatever her guy of the moment liked, wanted what he wanted, ate what he ate, and after years of the same, it was hard for Daff to know what her real likes and dislikes were.

Except eggs. She knew that she hated eggs, and she had relished telling Spencer that. Almost as if admitting it confirmed that she didn't find him attractive. She had no wish to put up her usual perfect potential partner façade. It was liberating.

"Okay, no eggs," he said easily. "Do you like mayonnaise?"

Did she? She thought about it for a moment before shrugging.

"It's okay, I guess."

"So what are you doing?" he asked, his voice intimate and gentle in her ear. He sounded too far removed from his usual awkward self, and it was making her very uncomfortable.

"Irrelevant," she replied.

"But interesting."

"Not really . . . I'm rearranging my closet."

"I was doing some accounts." Again, she could hear a smile in his voice, and once more she wondered what he found so amusing. This was probably the most infuriating conversation she'd ever had, nothing amusing here at all.

"And you probably want to get back to that."

"Not really. It's frustrating the hell out of me."

"Why?" she asked before she could stop herself. She heard the muffled sound of fabric against fabric and pictured him making himself more comfortable in his chair. She imagined him lounging, legs stretched in front of him and thighs spread. Again she found herself wondering what he was wearing. It was pretty late; he must have had a shower by now. Once more the image of him bare chested and in boxers floated to mind, and she swallowed down the saliva that suddenly flooded her mouth. Why was she salivating at the thought of Spencer Carlisle's bare chest and thighs? She needed serious help.

"Well, I was trying to find the funds to fix the plumbing at the community center."

"Why is that *your* problem?" she asked curiously.

"The youth outreach program," he replied succinctly. "Our last couple of meetings were washed out by the rain and the community doesn't appear to have enough money to fix it, so I figured maybe I could work something out."

Of course. It had been stupid of her to ask; everybody knew how strongly he felt about that program. In fact, he was the one who had taken it to where it was today. Over the last four years, since he had started helping Oom Herbert with the program, three at-risk kids had gone on to college or technical school, thanks directly to Spencer's influence and help. He was doing admirable work, but until now, Daff had only been peripherally aware of it.

"It doesn't seem right, using your own money to fix the community center. It belongs to the town—surely there are funds allocated toward maintenance?"

"This isn't your run-of-the-mill maintenance job. Looks like all the pipes will have to be replaced. They're over a hundred years old and should have been sorted out long before now. There just isn't enough money in the budget for it."

"How do you know that?"

"I'm on the town committee."

"I thought only old people were allowed on that committee," she mused.

The high school principal, the Catholic priest, the township minister, the librarian, the alderman, and also Daff's dad, the vet, were all middle-aged or older. Daff couldn't picture a strapping thirty-four-year-old like Spencer sitting on that committee.

"I have an old soul," he quipped, and she frowned. Who the hell was this witty guy? She didn't like feeling so completely wrong-footed by him, it was too unsettling.

"Well, good luck with that. I have to get back to what I was doing."

"Cleaning out your closet, you mean?" Why did he have to make it sound like a metaphor?

"Yes. Good night." She severed the connection before he could respond and stared blindly at the lit screen of her phone for a few long moments.

CHAPTER FOUR

The following afternoon, Spencer showed up at the boutique just after twelve. This time Daff was ready for him; she didn't have her novel out, instead she was industriously changing Maggie—one of her trendy silver mannequins—into a ridiculously expensive designer dress. She enjoyed this aspect of her job. Window dressing, marketing, trying to attract clients. In summer she consistently had the best-dressed windows on Main Road, and the boutique had won the best Christmas store display three years in a row.

"Hey," he greeted casually as he dragged the same spindly chair as yesterday over to the checkout counter.

"I'm really busy today, Spencer," she grunted, dragging the mannequin's arm up in an attempt to shove it through the dress's armhole. It was an exercise in frustration, since the dress was stupidly strappy and Maggie's splayed fingers were getting caught on the straps.

"Hmm." The low, rumbling sound could have been interpreted as agreement. She kept her attention on the task at hand but was fully aware of his every move. He ignored her while he unpacked plastic containers and plates and cutlery from the big brown paper bag. Once he had everything laid out to his liking, he refocused his attention on her.

"Need help?" He drifted over to where she was building up a fine sheen of sweat, struggling to get Maggie's stupid fingers untangled from the millions of spaghetti straps.

"I'm fine. Just super busy."

"Uh-huh," he muttered, hanging back to watch her. He shoved his hands into his jacket pockets and rocked slightly back and forth on his heels. His silent perusal unnerved her and made her clumsy.

"*Shit,*" Daff hissed when she seemed to be making absolutely no progress. The dress, dripping with sparkly beads and sequins, weighed a mother-loving ton, and Maggie was starting to wobble precariously. It would look amazing in the window display, but Daff was starting to regret her decision to start this task just before she knew Spencer would arrive. She had wanted to look busy, not completely clumsy and *incompetent.*

"It has nipples," Spencer suddenly said, his deep voice layered with incredulity. "Why the fuck does it have nipples?"

"What?" She stopped what she was doing and met his wide green eyes over one of Maggie's narrow shoulders.

"The mannequin. Why does it have nipples?"

"Oh." Daff gaped at where one of her hands was resting on Maggie's perky breast, the lifelike little nipple peeking out between her fingers. She reddened and snatched her hand away, but Maggie started to topple and Spencer made a grab for the heavy mannequin. This time *his* huge mitt of a hand covered the small breast completely, and Daff's throat went dry. Maggie's breasts were almost exactly the same size as hers . . . and seeing Spencer's hand so completely engulfing it made her stomach flutter alarmingly. She couldn't help but wonder how that same hand would feel on her breast, and it was messing with her head.

Spencer, unaware of Daff's wayward thoughts, held on to Maggie while yanking the strap over her hand and then her arm, his longer reach making the task look easy. Determinedly shoving her unexpected and inappropriate thoughts aside, Daff felt her face settle into a glower.

"I don't need your help," she protested, and he silenced her with a long, speaking look that really made her feel like a petulant child. When he was certain that he had silenced her protests, he refocused on the task at hand.

"Why the hell does this thing have so many straps?" he growled beneath his breath as he wrestled with Maggie's other arm. Daff eased the straps over the mannequin's fingers and up over the smooth, plastic arm. The task was much easier with his help. She tried to ignore his closeness, the heat coming off his huge body, and the warm, delicious musk of his aftershave. He made her feel small and delicate, and Daff didn't like feeling small and delicate—it made her uncomfortable.

Once they had Maggie dressed, they both stepped back and took in the effect. The dress had a plunging cowl neck, dipping very low between the mannequin's breasts and resting just above the perky nipples that had so disturbed Spencer. The confounding off-the-shoulder straps settled beautifully on her upper arms.

"Seriously, why the nipples?"

"I don't know," Daff said, resting her hands on her hips as she tilted her head, trying to figure out how to accessorize with the dress. Because it was so damned sparkly, it didn't need much embellishment, so she decided to leave it as it was. It was going to look fantastic backlit in the window at night.

"They seem pointless as fuck," he said, still on about the damned nipples. Daff was trying very hard to forget the image of his big hand over that small boob, because the memory deeply, *deeply* unsettled her. She crossed her arms over her chest in an attempt to hide her own perky nipples, which were starting to stand up and beg for attention. They were probably well hidden by the padding of her bra, but she wasn't going to chance him figuring out that she'd had a rogue moment of attraction toward him.

"Ready for lunch?" he asked, giving the nipples a rest, and Daff huffed impatiently.

"I told you I'm busy."

"Not leaving till you eat," he said in that terse way of his, and she shoved a stray strand of hair out of her face before sighing.

"What did you bring?" she asked, recognizing that the fastest way to get rid of him was to just get this over with.

"Couscous, grilled chicken, and some fruit."

"That sounds"—*delicious*—"nice."

He shrugged and started opening up the containers he'd laid out on the counter. He'd placed everything on a tea towel, which he'd brought with him, and she found the gesture unexpected and really thoughtful.

"Hmm. You can eat healthy without starving yourself," he pointed out as he began to heap a large pile of cold couscous onto one of the plates. He stabbed a piece of grilled chicken with his fork, dumped it onto the plate, and pointedly put it down in front of her. Daff's eyes widened as she took in the huge portion.

"Eat," he commanded, stabbing his fork in her direction. Daff cleared her throat and sat down before delicately dipping her fork into the fluffy pile of couscous and lifting it to her mouth.

God, it was good.

"This is delicious," she said around a mouthful of the stuff, and he merely grinned in response. He'd garnished the grain with cucumber, olives, tomato, avocado, feta cheese, coriander, and some lemon juice, and it tasted light and fresh and very satisfying.

He grunted suddenly and reached into the bag to produce a couple of bottles of water, which he plonked down between them. Daff didn't say anything, merely nodded her thanks. She was starting to understand that Spencer didn't need much in the way of conversation, and Daff—the consummate talker—was strangely okay with that.

They both devoured their lunch before speaking again.

"I was wondering if we should have the parties out of town. Plett, maybe?" Spencer said after taking a sip from his water.

"Like an overnight thing?"

"Hmm." He picked up an apple and held it out to her, and she accepted with a soft "thanks" before crunching into the ripe, red fruit appreciatively.

"That's a really good idea," she said around a mouthful of sweet apple, and when he didn't respond, she looked up and caught him staring. Wiping self-consciously at her chin, where some of the apple juice had dripped, she lowered her eyes.

"So . . . uh . . . what exactly did you have in mind?" she asked, taking another, smaller bite of the apple.

"I don't know; it was just an idea. Figured we could brainstorm together," he said almost shyly, and she raised her eyes to meet his. His expression was hard to read. He really was the most frustratingly enigmatic man. It was weird how she could see that now, where before she'd simply dismissed that closed-off personality as a man without much intelligence, having nothing of note to say. An unfair assumption based on nothing more than the fact that he was good at sport, rarely spoke, and couldn't flirt worth a damn.

"Well, it's a start," she said, and he nodded.

"That's what I thought."

"How do you feel about Mason and Daisy moving?" she asked, the words tumbling from her lips without warning. Maybe she wanted to see if Spencer was as affected by the news as his brother had said he was.

"I knew it was coming," he said, his voice and face without expression, and Daff was about to dismiss Mason's words of the other day as sheer bollocks when she saw it—the brief tightening around his eyes and mouth, the tense set of his huge shoulders. He looked like he was bracing for a hit.

"You knew it was coming but you were upset by it," she elaborated, and he shifted uncomfortably, saying nothing in response. Not even a grunt this time.

"Not my place to be upset by it." He shrugged, gathering up the empty containers.

"Bullshit, you're his brother. I'm bummed Daisy's leaving. I'll miss the hell out of her. We were just starting to reconnect, and I think it sucks that she's leaving just when we're starting to act like sisters again."

"You seemed sisterly enough before," he said.

"Not really. We got along and loved each other, but we never seemed to have very much in common. It's been a lot better since your asshole move last year." He grimaced at the reminder.

"So maybe you can thank me instead of constantly bitching about it?" he suggested, and she laughed incredulously.

"You're joking, right? Dude, you treated my sister like she didn't matter."

"Yeah, and I've apologized. More than once," he reminded her through clenched teeth. Spencer Carlisle looked seriously pissed off and Daff—perversely—found herself mildly turned on by that. She was beginning to discover that she liked pushing his buttons. It kept her in control. She preferred being in control these days. She had allowed others to control her too often in the past. She was done with that.

"Anyway, I was saying that you have a right to be upset about your brother leaving."

"It's none of your business how I feel," he muttered, carelessly dumping all the cartons into the large brown paper bag. He shoved to his feet, looming threateningly above her, and Daff was secretly thrilled by the deliberately intimidating display. Big, bumbling Spencer Carlisle seemed almost scary, and it was pretty damned awesome.

God, I'm so messed up, she thought, shaking her head slightly. One second wanting to be in control and the next thrilled because of his show of dominance.

"I've got to get back to work," he snapped.

"Okay. Thanks for lunch," she said in a sickly-sweet voice with a matching smile. He said nothing in response to that, just glared at her before slamming his way out of the store.

"Touchy," she said softly, exhaling on a whistle.

How the hell did she always manage to get the upper hand like that? Spencer seethed as he walked the short distance back to SCSS. One minute he was staring at her luscious mouth while she devoured that fucking apple, and the next she had him on the back foot about some ancient history that nobody else even cared about anymore. And worse, why the fuck would she nose around about his feelings concerning Mason's imminent departure? What did she care?

She was the most frustrating woman. He didn't know how to converse with her, and it didn't help that he was semihard every time he was in her general vicinity. He didn't know why the hell he was so turned on by her. Sure, she was pretty, but she'd never been anywhere near civil to him. Maybe he liked being treated like dirt. It was familiar—it was how most people had treated him for the entirety of his life. And it was disturbing to think that he was still such a victim that he would willingly seek out this treatment from someone like Daff, someone he desired, someone he couldn't seem to stay away from.

What the fuck was wrong with him?

"Hey, boss," Claude Meintjies, his manager, greeted him when Spencer stepped back into the store, and Spencer lifted a hand in greeting. The salesmen and women all looked up with smiles and waves, too. They were a friendly lot, hardworking, efficient, and he valued every single one of them. He kept them incentivized and well paid, and he made sure there was room for growth within the company. SCSS was so much more than just this store. He intended to expand and branch out. And he made sure his staff knew that they would be right there along with him.

"I'll be up in my office, Claude," he informed, striding past the smaller man as Claude gave him a thumbs-up. Spencer made his way to the back of the store, through the storeroom, and up a short, winding staircase to the small glass office upstairs. The second floor of the building was a huge empty space, housing only the staff break room, Claude's cubicle, and Spencer's office. But Spencer had big plans for this space.

He shut himself into the office, closing the door and the blinds. His staff would know not to disturb him. He lowered himself into his desk chair and threw his head back on the rest. He examined the stained ceiling board above his desk, the remnant of a damp problem that had long since been taken care of. He should have replaced the board, but he liked the familiarity of the elephant-shaped stain.

His phone beeped and he dragged it out of his pocket and raised it to his line of sight, blocking out the elephant in the room. A text message . . . from Daff.

Seriously. Thanks for lunch.

He sighed and chewed the inside of his cheek for a second before sending a thumbs-up emoji.

He waited for a moment, but no response was forthcoming . . . she wasn't even typing. He was about to lower the phone when it pinged and her response—a grinning emoji accompanied by a thumbs-up—popped onto the screen.

He stared at the two cheery little pics for a moment before screwing his eyes shut and then opening them to type two words. Words he knew he'd live to regret.

Dinner? Tonight?

"For fuck's sake," he gritted, furious with himself. He was a sucker for punishment. Clearly he was a masochist. Who knew?

She was typing . . . and typing . . . and typing. Jesus, how many words did she need to spell out a rejection? In the end, after endless amounts of typing, he found himself staring at just one word: Okay.

No shit?

He nearly dropped the phone in his haste to respond. He fumbled and caught it before it fell and sent his response before he could change his mind.

Pick you up at 6:30

Another thumbs-up in response, and that was it.

Someone knocked on her door at six that evening. Daff was in the middle of getting dressed for her dinner—*date?*—with Spencer, and she cursed the timing of this unexpected visitor. A quick peek through the peephole had her groaning and she unlocked the door with palpable reluctance. Daisy stood on her doorstep, a huge canvas bag tucked beneath her arm and clutched protectively to her side. Her entire demeanor was furtive, and Daff's curiosity was immediately piqued.

The younger woman pushed her way into the small house and Daff stepped aside, allowing the intrusion. It was Daisy's place, after all, even though her youngest sister would never really intrude unless she absolutely had to.

Daff closed the door, shutting out the cold, and followed her sister into the living room.

"Thank God you're home," Daisy was saying, gingerly placing her bag on the coffee table. "You have to hide these."

"Hide what?" Daff asked blankly and then watched as Daisy carefully unloaded the contents of her ugly canvas bag.

"*Ugh!* No, I don't want to hide your creepy caterpillars," Daff protested as Daisy gently placed her entire caterpillar collection onto the coffee table. A little revolted, Daff gawked at one complacently smiling little caterpillar, a ceramic thing wearing a jaunty sailor uniform.

"Come on, please, Daff," Daisy begged. "You even have the perfect display case for them, right there." She pointed at the empty cabinet that had previously housed the unsettling caterpillars that Daisy had always found so inexplicably fascinating.

"Why?"

"Mason keeps swapping them out for these weird butterfly trinkets."

The information startled a laugh out of Daff, which she quickly stifled when Daisy scowled at her.

"Why would he do that?" she asked, trying very hard to keep a straight face.

"Some nonsense about me letting go of my negative self-esteem issues and embracing my inner butterfly."

Aw, hell! That Mason was constantly surprising Daff. She honestly couldn't have asked for a better man for her baby sister.

"I'm not keeping them."

"But I like them," Daisy insisted.

"You do *not*. You collected only a quarter of these before everybody else started showering you with the hideous things and you found yourself drowning in them."

"I've grown attached to them. I'm not holding on to them because I have negative self-esteem. Not anymore. They've become . . . I don't know . . . a collection. Mine. I don't want to part with them."

"So explain that to Mason," Daff said reasonably. "He loves you, he'll understand."

"I know. But he can be stubborn, and I just want to give my caterpillars a temporary safe haven until I can convince him of that fact. He's already disappeared three of them and he won't tell me where they've gone."

This was absurd. But kind of cute, too.

"I suppose I can keep them for a while."

"Oh thank you . . ."

"*Not* for long," Daff warned her sharply. "You don't sort this out soon and I'll start disappearing them myself. So you and Mason find a way for caterpillars and butterflies to safely coexist."

Daisy grinned cheekily at that and nodded.

"Definitely," she said and hugged Daff before taking a step back to peruse her appearance. "You look nice. Are you going out?"

"Yes."

"On a Tuesday night?"

"Yes, *Mom*. I have a social life even during the week," Daff said with a roll of her eyes.

"Jeez, no need for sarcasm, I was just asking."

"It's just a . . . a meeting, kind of. With Spencer," Daff confessed, trying not to look or sound self-conscious.

"*Spencer?* Really?" Daisy looked inordinately pleased by that news, and Daff smiled. "That's great, Daff."

"We've been planning your crazy mixed 'last glorious days of single-dom' party," Daff elaborated, and Daisy smiled widely in response to that.

"Thank you," she said and then surprised Daff by enfolding her into another warm hug. "I know you guys don't always get along and I've been worried, even though Mason has been telling me that I'm stressing for nothing. I'm so glad to know he was right."

"We love you guys," Daff said into Daisy's neck. "And we want your wedding to be perfect and stress-free. That's more than enough reason for us to set aside our differences." She tried not to wince as she showered her sister with comforting half truths, but who knew, maybe tonight would be the night they actually, for real, set aside their differences.

Daff still had no idea why he had asked her to dinner, or—more pertinently—why she had accepted. In fact, she shouldn't have texted him in the first place, but once her smugness in provoking a reaction from him had worn off, she'd immediately felt bad for pushing him like that. She'd felt the need to end their lunch on a more positive note. She certainly *hadn't* expected a dinner invitation after the way they had left things.

"What time are you meeting him?" Daisy asked, stepping out of the hug.

"He's picking me up in about ten minutes."

"Oh gosh, and you were getting ready? I'm sorry I disturbed you."

"It's nothing." Daff shrugged, feeling a bit awkward. "It's not like it's a date or anything."

Except she'd been fussing over her clothes and makeup almost exactly like it was a date. She now found herself grateful for Daisy's interruption, because it put everything back into context.

"Maybe not, but I'm sure you still want to look nice."

Daff lifted her shoulders casually. "Makes no difference to me. I mean, we're probably just going to Ralphie's or MJ's. Not exactly fancy."

"Well, you still look very pretty," Daisy said warmly, and Daff looked down at the black jersey knit dress that she'd fully intended to change before her sister's untimely interruption. It was too low in the neck, too high in the hem, and definitely clung to her slender curves a little too lovingly. It was entirely inappropriate for a casual dinner with Spencer Carlisle. An authoritative rap sounded at the door and Daff stifled a sigh. It was too late to change now. She squared her shoulders, smoothed her hair, and moved toward the door. She swung it inward just as he lifted his hand to knock again, and he lowered his arm and his eyes ran over her body solemnly.

"You look nice," he observed, his voice so neutral he might as well have been commenting on the weather. His regard shifted from Daff to a point beyond her left shoulder, and his mouth quirked while his eyes wrinkled at the corners.

He smiled with his eyes. Daff had never noticed that before. It was as distinct as an actual smile—his expression warmed and his eyes shone. It was devastatingly attractive and she was quite taken with it. Sadly, the warmth wasn't directed at her but at the person standing behind her.

"Daisy, I didn't expect to see you here."

"Hi, Spencer." Her sister moved toward him and stood on her toes while he hunkered down, allowing her access to kiss his craggy cheek. "I was just dropping something off. I'm on my way again. I just wanted to thank you for going the extra mile with Daff. Mason and I really appreciate it."

His eyebrows lifted to his hairline and his scrutiny moved to Daff, who lifted her shoulders behind Daisy's back.

Go with it, she mouthed, and his head dipped for a very brief instant, acknowledging her words.

"We just want your big day to be cool," he mumbled, and Daisy wrapped her arms around his waist and hugged him for good measure. The embrace was over before he could figure out what to do with his comically outstretched arms and Daff bit back a grin, loving how flustered he looked.

"Anyway, happy planning, guys. I'm sure whatever you come up with will be awesome. Daff, I'll call you tomorrow, okay?"

"Sure," Daff responded and waved her happily smiling sister off. The silence after Daisy left felt weighted with both expectation and uncertainty, and Daff wasn't sure what to make of it.

"I should probably drive myself," she said, voicing the thought that had occurred to her just seconds after their text conversation the previous evening. "More convenient that way."

"Convenient for whom?"

Whom?

"You? Me? Both of us?" she supplied, her voice breathless.

"Since I just drove here with the intention of picking you up, it wouldn't be convenient for me," he pointed out.

Daff couldn't fault that logic.

"Ralphie's or MJ's?" she asked, reaching for the coatrack alongside the front door. He beat her to it and grabbed her double-breasted cashmere coat—not the one she would have chosen considering the rain—and held it open. Damn it. She would *not* be charmed by his unconsciously courteous little gestures.

Deciding not to say anything about his choice in coats, she slid her arms into the armholes and buttoned and belted it efficiently. She tensed when he unexpectedly dropped a hand onto one of her shoulders and slid the other beneath the hair at her nape, his fingers brushing against the sensitive skin there as he lifted the shoulder-length fall from the neck of the coat. He smoothed a gentle hand over her hair, patting it in place before stepping back without a word and reaching past her to open the door.

Still staggered by the alarming intimacy of his previous action, it took Daff a moment to readjust and even out her jagged breathing and erratic heartbeat. This was crazy. It was Spencer, he was harmless . . . he wasn't the kind of guy who normally attracted her.

Then again, considering how spectacularly all her previous relationships had crashed and burned, maybe that wasn't such a bad thing.

She shook herself. Allowing herself to think like that was dangerous. Spencer Carlisle wasn't someone with whom she could have any kind of romantic interaction. When it failed—and it *would* fail—she wouldn't be able to simply erase him from her life. He'd always be around, at family gatherings, in town, at work . . . reminding her of yet another failure in her life.

"Daff?" The gruff sound of her name in his voice didn't help. Why was *everything* about him suddenly so damned sexy?

"Yes. Sorry. I was trying to remember if I had my wallet or not." The words sounded lame and unconvincing to her, but it was all she had.

"Doesn't matter. You won't need it."

Rolling her eyes at that bit of macho nonsense, she chose not to respond. She'd fight that battle when she had to. She waved him ahead, and when he gave her that truculent look she was becoming so familiar with, she fought against rolling her eyes again.

"I know you're a gentleman and ladies first and all that, but I have to lock up, so move your ass." He stood there for another second before, with obvious reluctance, moving ahead and exiting the house. He stopped on the tiny front porch, opening the umbrella and waiting for her to lock up.

When she turned to join him, he hooked his—much too familiar—arm around her waist and dragged her to his side to shelter her beneath the umbrella before leading her out into the rain. She was in his car before she even had time to protest, watching him run around the front, not bothering with the umbrella this time.

She had been expecting the pickup truck, but this sleek, masculine automobile was a lot more elegant and beautiful than the truck he normally drove. She'd seen him drive by in it a couple of times, of course, but not often enough for her to begin associating this sexy ride with the Spencer Carlisle she'd known all her life.

Because of his humility, the fact that he drove around in an old pickup truck, and dressed in sweats most of the time, it was easy to forget how successful he was. This car was tangible evidence of that success and wealth. A gorgeous, metallic-blue panther of a machine.

"Nice car," she said drily when he climbed into the driver's seat, and he glanced at her for a second before starting the engine.

"I like it," he said without inflection after he had himself belted in.

"What is it? Maybe I'll add this one to my Christmas wish list or something."

"Audi R8, and you should stick to your VW. You'd be a menace on the road in one of these." He eased the car onto the road, and she gasped at the slur.

"What's that supposed to mean?" she asked indignantly.

"I've seen you drive. I've had the bad luck to be stuck behind you on occasion. You never use your turn signals and *God*, woman, you're a road hog. You tailgate, speed, weave in and out of lanes like you're doing some kind of crazy dance. And that's just in an ancient, shitty little hatchback. Can't imagine you in one of these."

It was the most she'd ever heard him speak at one time, and every word was an insult. What an asshole.

She'd be a lot more pissed off by his words if they weren't also true—she had a few (dozen) traffic violations to her name to corroborate what he was saying. Both of her sisters would rather walk than get into a car with her behind the wheel.

"I'm an awesome dri—" she started to say, but a rude sound from him, this one unmistakably scathing, shut her up.

"*You* don't even believe that," he said, and she glared at him before crossing her arms over her chest and diverting her attention out of the window. She sat up a moment later, her mien alert as she watched the scenery slide by.

"Where are you taking me?"

"Dinner."

"We're heading in the wrong direction," she stated. "Town's the other way."

"We're not having dinner in town."

"But . . ." Panic flared in her chest. This wasn't the plan. She wasn't comfortable with the thought of seeing him outside the usual familiar settings.

"I'm bored with MJ's and Ralphie's." He shrugged and she chewed on her bottom lip, wondering if she should insist they head back to town. It seemed like an unreasonable response to a casual dinner, and she bit back the words.

"So Knysna?" It wasn't a long drive, twenty minutes to half an hour at most. Maybe faster when the roads were this empty.

"Yeah, I read about this great place."

"I see." She nervously folded and unfolded her hands in her lap, a habit she had developed in an attempt to stop chewing her nails but that had just devolved into a different nervous tic. Still, it was preferable to ruining a perfectly good manicure.

She continued to fidget until he reached over and engulfed both of her hands with his free one. He gave them a brief squeeze before lifting his hand back to the steering wheel. The gesture made her breath catch, as did the lingering warmth of his touch, and she found herself striving to appear casual after the fleeting contact.

"Relax," he growled. "I'm not driving you to some remote location to murder you or anything."

"Wow. That thought hadn't occurred to me . . . till now." Her voice was tart and—despite the dimly lit interior of the car—she could see his lips tilt just enough to reveal one of those masculine dimples to her. It took everything in her not to reach up and trace her thumb over the indentation in his stubbled cheek.

"So what kind of place is this? Am I overdressed?" Considering the rough and ready guy he was, it wasn't beyond the realm of possibility that he'd simply take her to a pub much like Ralphie's.

"You look perfect." His gravelly voice sounded intense, and Daff felt her face heat at his words.

"Thank you. You look quite nice, too." And he did. He was dressed in a pair of faded jeans that fit him perfectly; her eyes drifted over thickly muscled thighs and the snug pull of fabric over his crotch before she hastily diverted her attention upward. The view was no less unsettling—a pale-blue dress shirt, slightly damp in spots from where it had caught the rain, lovingly draping and dipping over his broad chest. The top two buttons were undone, leaving her with a tantalizing glimpse of smooth, tanned skin. She couldn't see much because of the dim car interior, but it put her imagination into overdrive and made her breath quicken.

God, Spencer Carlisle was seriously good-looking. Not conventionally handsome, but so damned sexy it made her skin feel tight and uncomfortable. Like she had an itch that was just out of reach.

He had slipped into one of those contemplative silences he seemed to enjoy so much, and not feeling the need to break the silence, Daff fumbled for her phone and pretended to check her messages and Facebook. He left her to it and only when she saw the lights of Knysna rapidly approaching about ten minutes later did she put her phone away again.

"I'm starving," she said, and he grunted in agreement.

"Nearly there," he informed her, and she stretched luxuriously, curling her toes in her shoes.

"Awesome." She sighed, paying closer attention to their surroundings. "We're headed toward Leisure Isle." She didn't know why that surprised her. Leisure Isle was a residential suburb surrounded on all sides by the tidal estuary and only accessible by a narrow causeway. Daff had never visited the tiny lagoon island before and was both flustered and impressed with his choice of destination. It was touristy and upmarket. Maybe he wasn't taking her to a pub after all.

"I've been meaning to try this restaurant for a while—this is as good an excuse as any to give it a go."

"This isn't a special occasion," she hastened to remind, and she could hear his sigh even over the engine noise.

"Never said it was."

"Just saying."

"Hmm."

Frustrating man.

"This is a hotel," she pointed out suspiciously when he finally drew the car to a standstill, and he slanted her an exasperated look.

"It's a lodge," he corrected before continuing, "with a great restaurant. Don't worry, Daff . . . I didn't bring you here to seduce you. I know better."

What was that supposed to mean? She nearly asked before thinking better of it and keeping her mouth shut. Instead she perused the exterior of the whitewashed building. It looked sublimely luxurious and was situated right on the lagoon's edge, promising fantastic views. A shame they wouldn't be able to enjoy it on a dark, rainy night like this.

"Fancy," she observed when he held the passenger door open for her. She was suddenly grateful for the little black dress she was wearing and then instantly peeved with Spencer for not warning her that he'd be bringing her to a place like this. What if she'd dressed for Ralphie's or MJ's? She'd have looked distinctly out of place in jeans and a T-shirt.

He led her to the restaurant's separate entrance, where they were greeted by a smiling maître d'.

"Carlisle," Spencer said succinctly, and the officious little man's smile broadened.

"Yes, of course, Mr. Carlisle." He picked up a couple of leather-bound menus and tucked them into the crook of his arm. "Right this way, please."

He led them through a maze of white-clothed round tables—some empty, some filled with smiling, relaxed people—toward the back of the restaurant.

"Here you go. Your server will be right with you," he said. The table was in a great location, right beside one of the huge picture windows, with a fantastic view of the night-black lagoon. There were a few blinking lights from boats and reflected lights from homes and buildings, but it was eerily dark out there. Especially with the cloud cover. Still, the view was amazing, and Daff would have loved to see it on a sunny day, when it would probably be brilliantly blue and ethereally beautiful. She turned her avid scrutiny back to her immediate surroundings and was impressed by the gorgeous decor of the place. Everything was white and cream and airy. The austere color palette worked in this setting.

"This is a little much, don't you think? We could just as easily have discussed the party plans over a beer and some pretzels," she said, her eyes meeting Spencer's.

"No skin off my nose," he said with a shrug before lifting his hand to summon a waiter. "Ralphie's it is."

The waiter was there in seconds.

"Ready to order your drinks, sir?" he inquired.

"We've changed our—"

"Not yet," Daff interrupted hastily, sending a glare Spencer's way. He merely lifted a brow and folded his arms over his chest before leaning back in his chair and watching her with something like a smirk on his brutally handsome face. "Give us a few more minutes, please."

"Certainly, ma'am," the young man said with a polite little bow before retreating.

"Thought you wanted to leave."

"I'm starving," she complained. "And I can't stand the thought of another long drive on an empty stomach. We're here, we might as well eat something."

"Hmm." He turned his attention to the wine list, his overly long hair sliding forward as he bent his head.

"Use your words, for God's sake," she groused beneath her breath, and he tilted his jaw just enough to look at her from beneath the long flop of hair. Daff grinned before reaching for her purse and digging around a bit until she found what she was looking for.

"Need a hairclip?" she offered, holding the tiny sparkly butterfly clip out to him. He ran a sheepish hand through his hair, pushing it back from his face in the process.

"No time to get to the barber. Been meaning to hack it off myself." He sounded charmingly embarrassed, and Daff's grin widened even while she was appalled at the thought of Spencer doing a hack job on that gorgeous mane. She acted without thought, reaching across the table to slide her fingers through the silky hair that kept falling over his eyes and used the ridiculously feminine clip to pin it back. She snatched her hands back almost immediately and hid them in her lap beneath the table. Spencer reached up and touched the clip with the tip of his long index finger. He surprised her by leaving it in place and thanking her gruffly before bending his head to contemplate the wine list again.

Daff, in the meantime, kept rubbing her palms against the material of her skirt, trying—and failing—to rid herself of the feel of his luxurious hair on her skin.

CHAPTER FIVE

Spencer very slowly and very carefully released the breath that had caught in his chest when Daff had so unexpectedly reached out to touch him. His grip on the wine list tightened in an effort not to betray his trembling hands to her, and he immediately lowered his unseeing gaze back to the stark black-on-white letters in front of him, even though none of the words currently made an iota of sense.

Shit.

Was that really all it took to turn him on these days? One whisper of a touch? The answer to those burning questions had to be a resounding yes, if the straining bulge of his crotch was any indication. He sneaked a peek at her. A tiny little furrow between her perfectly arched brows marred the smoothness of her skin. She looked pensive, her attention directed out at the dark lagoon instead of her menu.

"Ready to order?" he asked, happy to hear that his voice sounded relatively normal. Her startled eyes flew back to his and she blinked slowly, looking like she was coming out of a deep sleep.

"Uh. You order. Whatever you choose will be fi—" She stopped, the frown deepening, before she reached for the wine list determinedly. "On second thought, give me a minute. I haven't really looked at the menu."

"I'll be happy to choose." He shrugged.

"Yeah? Well, you don't know what I like. And I doubt we like the same things. So . . . I'll pick my own wine. And food. And dessert."

"Of course." He wouldn't have chosen her whole meal, damn it. He'd just meant the wine. Although he'd definitely feel more comfortable if she chose that.

Bringing her here had to be one of the worst decisions he'd ever made. He'd taken one look at the place and known that it was way too romantic for a casual dinner, and he'd been more than willing to call it quits earlier when she kept on nagging about it. But then she'd changed her mind again.

Confusing woman. It was hard to keep track of her lightning-fast mood changes. He contemplated her shiny down-bent head, marveling slightly at how soft and silky her dark-brown hair was. He recalled the texture of it beneath his roughened palm. He shouldn't have touched her, but it had been an instinctive move—he'd seen the hair trapped in the collar of her coat and had tugged it free without much thought.

Stupid.

The move had been too intimate and had made the situation awkward. Then again, Spencer was a pro at being awkward. The eternal loner, his best friend had always been his brother, and after going to college, he'd bonded with his rugby teammates but hadn't really forged deep and lasting friendships with any of them. He could barely function in civil society and preferred to keep his mouth shut in social situations. The second he opened it, he always seemed to shove his foot right down his throat.

Still, he couldn't sit here tongue-tied all evening. The woman already thought he had the personality of a mushroom.

"It's rainy," he observed inanely. *Yeah, way to state the fuckin' obvious, Spence!*

"The forecast says it'll be this way for the rest of the week," she said, barely looking up from the menu.

"We need it, but it's getting a bit problematic." Christ, still with the weather.

"How so?" she asked, looking up, her eyes frank and assessing. All the McGregor girls had the prettiest gray eyes, but Daff's was the only gaze Spencer ever found himself lost in. And the shittiest part of it was that he knew she didn't find herself in the same predicament with him. Ever.

"Uh. With the kids and the center."

"Oh yes, of course." She looked away—without any fucking hesitation—and went back to perusing the wine list. "I think I'll have a glass of this 2013 cabernet sauvignon."

"Why don't we just get a bottle of that?" Spencer shrugged and tossed aside his menu.

"You'll have the same thing?" Daff looked surprised by that, and Spencer lifted his shoulders again.

"Sure. I trust your taste." He did. A hell of a lot more than he did his own. When it came to choosing wine, he always felt like a complete philistine. He lacked the knowledge to make an informed choice and usually only went with the house red or white. He never knew if he should sniff or swirl the stuff before sipping it and took his cues from those around him. He always felt exceptionally awkward when he was around people he perceived as more learned on the subject. He supposed it was one of the hazards of being nouveau riche, so to speak.

Daff looked a little taken aback by his words and fiddled with the ends of her hair for a moment. Thankfully the waiter returned before another awkward silence could descend.

Daff watched Spencer expectantly after the young man asked if they were ready to order and, belatedly recognizing what they were waiting for, he self-consciously asked the guy for the wine she'd mentioned. From the way the waiter jumped and Daff rolled her eyes, Spencer knew he'd probably barked the words. It was something he did when he was nervous and he was aware that it came across as rude or bossy, but he'd take that over people knowing what he was really feeling.

After the waiter scurried away like a frightened mouse, Spencer heaved a sigh and shook his head. He put aside the wine list and focused his attention on the menu. He was aware of Daff's scrutiny and ignored it for a moment while he gathered his thoughts.

But Daffodil McGregor wasn't a woman to be ignored.

"You didn't have to snarl at the poor guy," she chastised, and Spencer stared levelly back at her. It was a look meant to intimidate, one that had gotten him out of a few uncomfortable situations before. But she didn't react the way other people did. No lowered eyes or hastily mumbled apology—she just returned his look unflinchingly.

"Didn't mean to," he finally admitted. "Sometimes it just comes out like that."

She pursed her lips as she considered his words.

"I see," she said thoughtfully, and the words drove Spencer a little crazy. What did she see? He was on the verge of asking when the waiter rushed back with their wine. Gracing them with a nervous smile, his eyes darted to Spencer for a second before he focused all his attention on Daff. Clearly he was too intimidated by Spencer to hold his stare for long.

Fuck, how badly had he snapped at the poor guy earlier?

He made an effort to loosen up when the waiter—Liam, as his name tag helpfully informed—popped open the bottle and poured a sample into Spencer's glass. Daff and Liam both gawked at him expectantly, and Spencer sucked in an irritated breath before lifting the glass and— without bothering to do any of the swirling, sniffing crap—downed the entire portion in a gulp. Sometimes, brazening it out crassly was the only way to go. Putting up a front of impatience and arrogance was an excellent—if obnoxious—way of hiding any feelings of uncertainty.

"Awesome," he said dismissively before pointing at Daff's glass. "Fill up."

"Yes, sir." Liam leapt to it and practically genuflected before leaving with a promise to be back soon for their food orders.

Daff lifted her glass by the delicate stem, swirling it between her thumb and forefinger before taking a small mouthful. He watched her eyes close as she savored the taste of the wine—a taste he'd barely registered when he'd swigged it down—before swallowing it with a delicate movement of her slim throat.

"Good?" he asked, fascinated by that beautiful throat, and her eyes opened before she lifted her shoulders and placed the glass back on the table.

"Full-bodied. With subtle hints of black pepper, a mere suggestion of berries, that slight tang of woodsmoke—oak, if I'm not mistaken—and just the tiniest suggestion of vanilla."

Spencer contemplated his glass dubiously before lifting his eyes back up to her somber face. That full lower lip was trembling ever so slightly, and Spencer felt his own lips curve.

"Bullshit."

"Well, yeah!" she said, the "duh" unspoken but very present. "It tastes like red wine. I like red wine. It's yum . . . but I never taste the hints of this and the overtones of that. Pretentious crap, if you ask me."

"Right?" he agreed, feeling a chuckle rise up in his throat and escape before he could choke it back.

"Oh, he can laugh," she observed, and he felt his cheeks heat. Did he give the impression that he couldn't?

"Only when I find shit funny," he said self-consciously.

"Well, then, do tell: What kind of 'shit'"—she made air quotes—"do you find funny?"

"I don't know. Random shit."

"Like what? Adam Sandler movies?"

"Fuck no."

"Ricky Gervais movies?"

"Who?"

"Work with me here, Carlisle. Tina Fey movies?"

"She's pretty good."

"What? I totally didn't see that coming. You like chick coms?"

"When they're funny. Y'know?"

"No I don't, 'cause you won't elaborate," she complained, and he felt his smile widening.

"I don't watch too many comedies; I find the humor forced."

"Action man?"

"I wouldn't say no to something with guns, fast cars, hot babes, and lots of explosions."

"Improbable stunts? *Fast and Furious* style?"

"I've watched a few of those," he confessed. "An okay way to spend a couple of hours."

"We're veering dangerously off topic, Carlisle. Come on, spit it out, what do you find funny?"

"Okay, so the other day," he started, and Daff wriggled forward in her chair, eager and attentive. It was a little unnerving to be her sole focus, and he took a fortifying sip of the wine. "Customer comes in, asking if we sell branded condoms, you know, like Nike or Adidas condoms, and Claude, my manager, tells him"—he chuckled to himself at the recollection—"he says—"

He snorted when he recalled the expression on Claude's face and his tone of voice. "He says, 'I'm sorry, sir, the only Adidas latex we sell are those running shorts over there. Comfortable fit and ribbed for your pleasure and, yes, we do stock them in extra large.'"

By the time he finished his anecdote, he was practically clutching his sides. Usually he wouldn't have condoned such attitude toward a customer, but this particular guy was a bored asshole who came in regularly with impossible requests. And Claude had such a genuine warmth to him that it was really hard to take offense to anything he said.

He wiped his streaming eyes and comprehended that Daff was sitting there with a polite smile on her face. He winced a bit.

"You—uh—you probably had to be there," he said lamely, and the polite smile widened sweetly. It was a novelty seeing such a warm expression on her face, and he gaped.

"If the mere memory of it still has the ability to make you laugh like that, then I really wish I had been there."

"Claude's a funny guy," he said, taking another drink. "He always says exactly the right thing at the right moment. Dry, quick wit."

He knew he sounded wistful, but he did envy his store manager the ability to joke and put others at ease. He was a real people person, and Spencer had lucked out employing him. Claude was much better at interacting with the employees at SCSS. Spencer liked his staff, enjoyed being around them, and would move heaven and earth to ensure they were all treated fairly and enjoyed the best benefits. But while they were friendly and polite toward him, they maintained a certain reserve whenever they spoke with him. He knew that it was their way of showing him deference, and Spencer had to respect that reserve. He made an appearance at staff parties but never stayed long, knowing they would enjoy themselves more without him there.

Claude—with the easy smile and great sense of humor—was the guy they went to when they needed something. None of them would ever dream of approaching Spencer directly. And Spencer had long since made peace with that fact.

"So you find Claude funny?" Daff's voice jerked him back into the present, and he smiled vaguely.

"Yeah."

"Claude and Tina Fey movies. That's a short list," she said, chewing the inside of her cheek thoughtfully.

"And other stuff, of course," he added, lifting his menu in the hopes of changing the subject. "I read that the food here is quite good."

They both went back to studying the menu, and when Spencer caught sight of poor Liam hovering close by, he warded him off with a look and a curt shake of his head.

"Wait, you sell latex shorts?" she suddenly asked, and he grinned.

"Of course not. Claude was just bullshitting, but it was enough to send the guy packing."

"I don't think I've ever met Claude," she said.

"You must have seen him; he cycles to work every day. He's passionate about his cycling; he's entering the Argus next year." The Cape Town Cycle Tour—commonly referred to as the Argus—was the largest individually timed cycle race in the world and attracted participants from every corner of the globe. It was a pretty grueling endurance test, and Daff was suitably impressed.

"Yes, I've definitely seen him. Great thighs," she said admiringly, and Spencer instantly felt less than charitable toward his likable manager.

"Can't say I've noticed," he said, ice in his voice.

"Hard not to when he wears those spandex cycle shorts. Maybe I should pop into your store sometime." That made him frown.

"It's not like he wears them at work. He showers and changes before we open."

"How tragic. Imagine how many female customers he'd draw to the store."

"He's married with four kids."

"Four?"

"Happily married," he stressed, and she sighed wistfully.

"The hot ones are always taken."

Well, what the fuck was Spencer, then? Chopped liver? He couldn't hide his frown and kept his attention on the menu to prevent her from seeing how her words had affected him.

"This all looks amazing," Daff moaned. "How on earth are we supposed to choose?"

"I was thinking of trying the chef's tasting menu—no need to choose then."

She looked torn, obviously not wanting to agree with him.

"I suppose that's a good idea," she admitted reluctantly, and he hid his smile from her. He'd refrained from telling her earlier that she was on the very short list of things and people he sometimes found amusing. She was so damned prickly and combative and contrary as fuck. Which, while annoying, could also be kind of funny.

"I've been known to have those on occasion," he said drily. He summoned Liam, who had been watching from much farther away, and placed the order. The man enthused about their excellent choice, asked them if they wanted to pair each course with specially selected wine—they did not—and hastened away purposefully.

"So this party." Spencer figured he'd better get the ball rolling.

"What about it?"

"Any ideas?"

"Not a clue. You?"

"Not really. I'm not into planning parties. You may have noticed that I'm not the most social guy around."

"No," she gasped, and he narrowed his eyes at her sarcasm.

"So you agree we should do an out-of-town thing? Plett or farther afield?"

"I think Plett is good," she said. "People can carpool and get there quickly. And we can rent a few hotel rooms and confiscate keys at the beginning of the evening to prevent the more stubborn drunken assholes from trying to drive back."

"Yeah."

"I suppose the first order of business is to figure out the guest list."

"Mason doesn't have a lot of local buddies. And most of the guys will be flying in a few days before the wedding."

"So we'll have to figure out when exactly they're all arriving so that nobody gets left out of the plans."

"Yeah, I suppose." He watched her reach down for her purse and drag out a tiny notebook and pen.

"Can you guesstimate how many guys, approximately?"

"I've barely spoken with Mason about this. I mean, we have like three months left to plan. I didn't think it was that urgent."

She made a tsking sound and set the notebook aside.

"No, it's two months, three weeks, and it's nowhere near enough time to plan an event like this, Spencer," she admonished. "Your first order of business after tonight is to sit your brother down and ask him how many guys will be coming to his stag. Does he even have groomsmen picked out?"

"I'm his best man," he reminded her, feeling a little defensive and not entirely sure why.

"Yes, I know. But Daisy will have at least two bridesmaids—that's not including any random cousins she may want to include. Mason will need a matching number of groomsmen."

"I thought this was going to be a no-fuss wedding."

"There's no such thing as a no-fuss wedding."

"God, if I ever get married, I think I'll elope to fuckin' Bali or something," he muttered beneath his breath.

"Screw that, I'm never getting married," she snorted, and that snagged his attention. He was about to question her about it when Liam returned with something tiny and decorative on a plate.

What the fuck? It didn't even look like food.

"An amuse-bouche. With Chef's compliments," he announced with a smile and flourish as he placed the tiny black plates with cubes of perfectly pink meat and splotches of unidentifiable sauce and purple bits of something sprinkled artfully about. "Duck and honey jus, served with lightly toasted lavender sprigs."

Right.

Daff looked genuinely delighted.

"How pretty," she gasped, and the gorgeous smile that followed made the trip out here entirely worthwhile.

"Enjoy," Liam urged them before beating a hasty retreat.

Daff lifted one of the smaller forks and Spencer quickly took her cue, finding the same fork before looking at his plate again. He cautiously stabbed a tiny cube of pink along with a miniscule sprig of purple and swiped it through a dab of golden sauce. Feeling braver than a man ought to when having dinner, he put it into his mouth.

His eyes widened as the flavors burst over his tongue. He didn't do much fine dining—the fanciest he ever went was a good steak at a brasserie. This was . . . something else entirely. He polished off the small plate before Daff had even finished her first bite.

He was immediately happy he'd finished first, because he discovered that he really liked watching her enjoy every aspect of those couple of mouthfuls. The way her gorgeous lips closed over the fork, the tiniest bit of suction as she drew it back out. The suckling motion of her lips just before she chewed and then again that beautiful throat working as she swallowed it down.

Fuck, it was hot, and he was transfixed. He shifted slightly, his breathing jagged, his cock hard, his heart thudding heavily in his chest as he pictured those lips closing over his length and suckling in the same delicate motion. His eyelids grew heavy and he could practically feel those full lips engulfing the head of his dick, hot, moist . . .

Pull yourself together, asshole!

He jerked his eyes away, fighting for control over his crazy hormones. What the fuck was wrong with him? He was worse than a randy teenager. He was used to wanting Daff. Used to yearning for her. But this visceral reaction was new. Maybe because it was the first time he'd actually spent real time in her company. Having a civil conversation instead of just stuttering his way through yet another attempted flirtation. Turned out that spending time with the real, live Daffodil McGregor was a much bigger turn-on than worshipping Fantasy Daff from afar.

Who knew?

"Yum." Her voice startled him, and he raised his eyes to meet hers. She was grinning from ear to ear, and it struck him that she was smiling a lot easier around him tonight.

"Good?"

"Yep. I love an amuse-bouche, it's like getting a fun little predinner gift. I can get really comfortable in a world that gives you predinner presents."

"So why do you think you'll never get married?" he asked, remembering her statement before Liam's arrival and grateful for a topic that could take his mind off his rampant hard-on.

"I don't think, I know." She seemed vehement about that.

"Why?"

"I'm not suited to it."

"Why not? Your parents are happily married, Daisy and Mason are clearly in it for the long haul . . . you're surrounded by nothing but happy couples. Why wouldn't you be suited to it when it's in your DNA?"

"Lia's wedding fell through," she reminded him.

"Lia deserved better than that asshole. As far as I'm concerned, that was a happy ending for her. And you know as well as I do that it's only a matter of time before she falls for some other lucky guy and winds up happily married. I always figured you were headed the same way."

"Not with the assholes I've dated in the past."

"There must have been a good guy or two in the lot," he probed, not really wanting to hear about her previous douchebag boyfriends, but curious nonetheless.

"Nah, rotten apples, the lot of them. I seem to attract losers and freaks."

"Freaks? How so?" Her eyes slid from his and she started to look a little cagey, sending his curiosity into overdrive. What was she hiding?

"What about you?" she hedged. "You still holding out for that happily ever after, even after what Tanya did to you?"

Ouch. Living in a small town blew big-time. It hadn't taken long for everybody from the priest to the local grocery packer to hear all about Tanya's threesome. In fact, he estimated it had been less than a day before the whole town heard that he had caught her cheating. The humiliation had been unbearable, but he'd kept his head down and refused to discuss it with anybody. The only reason it got out was because one of Tanya's asshole lovers—the local mechanic—was a blabbermouth who couldn't wait to brag that he'd stolen the local rugby hero's girl. As if he could steal Tanya—she didn't belong to anybody, she belonged to everybody. She'd apparently flirted and fucked her way through half of the male population in town, seniors and high school kids included. A lot of them while she'd been with Spencer.

"I'm the eternal optimist," he said grimly, and she giggled—as he had intended—at those words delivered in that tone of voice.

"Were you in love with her?"

"No." He hoped the curt tone in his voice would discourage further questions, but she scooched forward in her chair and rested her chin in the palms of her hands, her eyes intent.

"You were with her for three years."

"Habit." Even more curtly. It didn't deter her at all.

"Yes, but . . . three years. I was expecting a wedding announcement soon."

"It never felt completely right with her."

"Maybe that's why she cheated? She knew you weren't entirely into her."

"Way to blame the victim, Daff," he chastised. "But maybe it never felt completely right because she was fucking everybody she could almost from the moment we started seeing one another."

"Yikes." She winced theatrically.

"Come on, everybody knew."

"I didn't . . . not while it was happening. I found out afterward, of course, but I never knew it went that far back."

"As far as I could tell, she was never faithful to me. She said that—" The memory of her exact words made him press his lips together in an attempt to stifle the laughter rising to the surface. He wasn't wholly successful and pinched the bridge of his nose and lowered his face as the chuckles escaped in fits and starts.

Alarmed, Daff watched Spencer lower his eyes and cover his mouth. His shoulders started to shake and she gaped, horrified to discover how very raw the whole Tanya situation still was for him. Was he sobbing?

Oh God.

She cast an embarrassed look around the room, but nobody else seemed to notice his reaction, and she scooted over to the chair on his left.

"Hey, come on now, buddy. She's not worth this," she soothed, running a hand over one shaking shoulder. He looked up, and tears were gleaming in his eyes. His face was red and he seemed to be attempting to curb his sobs.

Wait. Were they sobs? His eyes widened at her sympathetic words, and his shoulders shook even more. She tugged at the hand he had clutched over his mouth, and when she managed to draw it down she saw that Spencer was laughing. Huge guffaws shook his body, and her concern seemed to set him off even more.

Exasperated, she flounced back to her chair and sat with her arms crossed over her chest, waiting for the chuckles to subside.

Part of her was enjoying the display, though. He looked boyishly handsome when he laughed, young and ever so slightly innocent. She'd noticed it earlier when he was telling that god-awful anecdote about his manager. He had an amazing laugh, warm and carefree, and she felt privileged to hear it when she knew that few others did.

Still, it would be nice to be let in on the joke. He reached for a napkin and wiped the corners of his eyes, finally seeming get himself under some semblance of control.

"I'm sorry," he said, still trying to keep the chuckles at bay. "It's just . . . the look on your face made it even worse."

"What set you off?" she asked.

"Tanya—what she said in defense of her cheating—she said trying to keep her in a committed relationship was like caging a mermaid. When she was meant to swim free and frolic with dolphins."

Daff blinked and then pressed her lips together.

"As mermaids do," she said with a somber nod.

"Wild and free. With the dolphins."

"A mermaid?"

"Yep. A freaking mermaid."

"I mean . . . she knows mermaids aren't real, right?" He grinned at the question, stifling another chuckle.

"Who knows? Although, since mermaids don't have sexual organs and she was fucking everything with a dick, I don't know why she'd go there."

"Why were you with her so long? I've had a few conversations with her in the past and . . . she's not exactly the sharpest tool in the shed."

"Like I said before, habit. She was a warm body to come home to. She was sweet and affectionate. And I liked that she made no demands. She seemed happy enough in the relationship."

"Were you hurt? By her infidelity?"

"I think you mean infidelities," he corrected, a shadow crossing his expression. "I felt betrayed, obviously. And humiliated."

The last was conceded almost reluctantly, and he looked like he immediately wished the words back. Before he could say anything more, the waiter returned with their first course and Daff was suitably distracted by the beautifully arranged sliver of yellowtail, accompanied by a swirl of lemon jus and fennel foam.

She looked up to share her delighted smile with Spencer and caught him glaring at the plate in front of him.

"Should have eaten before this," she heard him mutter beneath his breath, and her smile widened. He was entertaining as hell. Something she hadn't expected at all. His sense of humor was odd, but it was gratifying to know that he had one. No matter how offbeat it was. She was already borderline addicted to the sound of his laughter, and she could watch him smile all night.

He was ridiculously attractive, and she was trying her level best not to succumb to that attraction. She did stupid things when she liked a guy, and for the first time in years she found herself without a significant other. It was revelatory. She liked herself more when she wasn't trying to impress some man. It was like unearthing a whole new Daffodil McGregor, and she found that she liked the person she was discovering beneath the layers of pretense that she hadn't even known were there.

An attraction to Spencer Carlisle might halt that discovery process entirely.

Put it out of your head, Daff, she admonished herself severely. *It's not going to happen.*

She lifted her fork and noticed that Spencer mirrored her movement. He'd done that earlier as well, with the amuse-bouche, and she clued in to the fact that he wasn't as familiar with the place settings as she was. She found it curious that he'd chosen to come here, despite the fact that it appeared to be outside his comfort zone.

"Why did you choose this place?" she asked, and his fork halted halfway to his mouth.

"Don't you like it?"

"It's beautiful, and the food's fantastic. I was just curious. You said you've been meaning to try it for a while. It just isn't the type of place I pictured you liking."

"Why not? Because I'm a Carlisle? Because I once did whatever it took to survive and grew up in a dilapidated old house with broken windows and no heating?"

Jesus, Daff hadn't known that his childhood was that dire. She'd heard snippets from Daisy, but to hear it from Spencer himself was . . . sad.

"No." She finally found her voice and responded to his defensive questions. "Because you seem like a down-to-earth, meat and potatoes guy like—"

"Like who? My deadbeat alcoholic father?" He bristled, and she rolled her eyes.

"Hate to break it to you, buddy, but I barely remember your father. I was going to say, like my dad. But you're acting like a hormonal chick, so I take back that particular compliment. My dad is awesome, and you're being less than awesome right now."

He paused, his face clearing as he lowered his fork back down to his plate.

"I'm sorry," he said softly, the words brimming with sincerity. "It's a touchy subject. My dad, I mean."

"You brought him up."

"Hmm. I also feel a little uncouth in a place like this." The confession was hushed, and his eyes were directed out over the dark lagoon in an effort to avoid meeting her stare. Daff could barely hear him over the piano music in the background and the chatter of the other restaurant patrons. "With its weird wine rituals and place settings and unrecognizable food."

"Then why come here?" she asked again, her voice gentling.

"I thought you'd like it."

Oh.

For God's sake. Why was he so damned sweet?

"I do," she said after a beat. "Thank you for bringing me here."

His eyes swung back in her direction, and she met his scrutiny head-on. Her expression was serious, but she hoped that he could see that she was being sincere. His eyes darted back and forth between hers for an excruciatingly long moment before he smiled. The parting of his lips was slow and hesitant, like a foal taking its very first steps. It was like watching the sun come out from behind a cloud, and the subsequent brightness was almost blinding after so much gloom.

"You're welcome."

"Now try the fish. It's freaking awesome."

"There's barely enough here to feed a fuckin' gnat," he complained, and she laughed.

"This is the first of seven courses. You'll be stuffed after this, trust me."

He looked dubious but lifted his fork nonetheless.

"I hope so, or we're stopping at a McDonald's on our way home."

"Trust me," she repeated, keeping her gaze level, and he nodded.

"Hmm."

"What a fucking revelation *that* was," Spencer groaned in the car a few hours later. The evening had gone surprisingly well after his stupid, embarrassing first-course rant. They had kept the subjects neutral and limited to mutual acquaintances and party planning. Daff was an easy-going, witty companion, and his fascination with her was stronger than ever by the time the long and shockingly good meal was finally done.

"I mean, most of that stuff looked like art—how the hell did they manage to make it so delicious and so filling at the same time? I don't get it. It's like some weird sorcery."

"You ate *seven* courses, Spencer," she reminded him. "That's a lot of food."

"It didn't *look* like a lot of food." He shook his head, still astonished.

"But it was."

"I didn't hate it." He could hear the shock in his own voice, and she laughed.

"I didn't hate it, either. In fact, I found everything about it quite enjoyable. The company included."

He nearly swerved from the road in his rush to look at her.

"Hey, watch the road, buddy," she criticized.

"Sorry. I just . . . I enjoyed your company, too." And now he sounded like a teenage boy after his first date, and he cringed a little.

"Good to know we can spend a few hours together without killing one another, huh? Bodes well for this partnership."

"I never find your company a hardship," he said, focusing his attention back on the road. Disturbed by her words. "If anything, you're the one with some inexplicable grudge against me." He heard the questioning lilt in his statement, inviting her to elaborate on exactly why she always seemed to have it out for him. But she didn't respond, just kept her attention on the darkness outside.

Fuck it. He was going to ask and let the words fall where they may.

"Why *don't* you like me?"

And didn't that just sound needy as fuck?

"I don't *not* like you," she said, her voice completely emotionless, which frustrated the hell out of him.

"You always seemed to." Why was he pursuing this? It was humiliating, but for some reason he couldn't seem to help himself.

"I just don't think we have much in common, that's all," she elaborated. "You were a *rugby* player." She said the words in the same tone of voice one might use to say *serial killer.*

"Not sure what that's supposed to mean," he muttered.

"Nothing, I just tend to get along with more *cerebral* people." The dashboard lights highlighted her immediate wince, telling him she regretted the words as soon as she said them. "I didn't mean that the way it sounded."

"You think I'm dumb." He was hurt and completely offended by her words and her attitude. And was sorry to witness the resurgence of her snobbery, which had been refreshingly absent all evening. "Guess that explains the mushroom thing."

"No, I don't think you're dumb. I didn't mean it like that."

"Correct me if I'm wrong, Daffodil," he said, quite fucking fed up with this bullshit, "but you barely finished high school and didn't go to college, right?"

Silence.

"Because while I may have been *just* a rugby player and it may have been what got me into college, it *wasn't* what helped me graduate summa cum laude. It wasn't what made me start a sports shop from scratch and turn it into one of the most thriving businesses in the area. That all came from *here*"—he stabbed his forefinger against his forehead and then lowered his hand to jerk a thumb at his chest—"and *here*."

"Spencer—"

He'd had more than enough and leaned forward to turn on the radio, flooding the car with loud rock music. She was still trying to talk and he cranked the volume, ignoring her and whatever trite apology she felt the need to throw at him this time.

When would he learn his lesson where Daffodil McGregor was concerned? He was like a dog that kept going back to someone who beat it constantly. It was humiliating. It was past time to grow some balls where this woman was concerned.

The rest of the ride was punctuated by loud, angry music, and when he slid to a stop outside her house, he was still so pissed off he didn't bother to get out and open the passenger door for her. He could tell from the way she sat and watched him for a few moments that she was expecting him to, and when he didn't she sighed and opened the door.

Before exiting the car, she reached forward and pushed the mute button on the radio. The immediate silence thundered between them, but he still refused to acknowledge her, maintaining a death grip on his steering wheel as he glowered grimly ahead.

"I'm really sorry, Spencer. I had a pretty great time tonight."

He wasn't going to soften, no matter how sweet her damned voice. He'd fallen for that bullshit before—it was the way she operated. Pretend to let him in before shutting him down so hard his head reeled. He'd experienced a few concussions during his rugby days, but none of them had ever left him as dazed and confused as Daff did.

"I'll see you at lunchtime tomorrow?" His hands tightened on the wheel, and he ground his teeth so hard his jaw ached.

"No."

"I'm sorry to hear that. Good night." She left without a further word, and much as he wanted to just speed the hell out of there, he still felt compelled to make sure she got into the house safely. Once the door was shut and the lights were on, he took off like a bat out of hell. Promising himself that he would never allow her to fool him again.

CHAPTER SIX

Daff tossed and turned all night. The way things had ended between her and Spencer weighed heavily on her mind, and she felt awful about it. No matter how much he blustered to the contrary, she knew she had hurt him, and it bothered her. He was a decent man and she was smearing all her *crazy* and her *wrong* off onto him. But she couldn't leave it the way it was. She just couldn't.

She picked up her phone and checked the screen for the umpteenth time since she'd sent her message just after arriving home from dinner. Her apology remained unread, and that stung a bit. Not that she deserved anything better, it was just . . . she didn't want to ruin whatever it was that seemed to be building between them. She was beginning to discover that liking Spencer was a good habit to have and a hard one to break.

She tossed and turned some more, checked her phone again, and at around 2:00 a.m. knew that she wasn't going to get any sleep. She sat up and pushed her hair out of her face. She could go around to his store in the morning, take him and his staff some doughnuts, even if it wasn't their usual doughnut day. Or maybe she could take *him* lunch for a change.

She drew her knees to her chest and wrapped her arms around her legs, resting her chin on top of them. She stared off into the darkness pensively, wondering how to fix this.

He hadn't even bothered to open the car door for her this evening, and that had bugged her so much. Not the fact that he hadn't done it, more the idea that she'd taken a decent guy and angered and corrupted him to such an extent that he'd willingly forgone his hard-earned impeccable manners. And knowing Spencer, she figured he must have fought his chivalrous instincts very hard to make that point. She hadn't missed that death grip on the steering wheel.

She groaned and got out of bed, dragging on a pair of jeans, a T-shirt, and a thick cable-knit sweater. She put her hair up in a sloppy ponytail, shoved her feet into comfy fur-lined boots, and grabbed her keys on the way to the front door. She had to make this right tonight. Somehow.

The house was dark and quiet. A modest two-floor white building with gingerbread trim and a peaked roof. It looked almost too feminine for a man like Spencer, but rumor had it Mason had designed it to Spencer's exact specifications. This beautiful family home with the white picket fence and the huge front and back yards was the home of a man who longed for a settled life with a wife and kids. The home of a man who didn't have room in his life for a woman like Daff. But here she was anyway, knocking, at nearly two thirty in the morning. And when that didn't get a response, she leaned on the doorbell.

A few short minutes later, an upstairs light switched on, then another, and she could hear, even above the thundering rain, the sound of him cursing roundly at the interruption of his sleep. The door unbolted, and her breath hitched in her throat as she grasped that he probably hadn't even had a chance to drag on a robe to cover his nudity. Again she pictured his naked chest and thighs, and that anticipation zipped along her nerves in addition to the anxiety already bubbling there as a result of this insane move. This wasn't the behavior of a rational person, she knew that . . . but she didn't know what else to do. She had to make him understand that she was sorry . . . that she . . .

The door was yanked open, and she gaped at the hulking figure silhouetted there in absolute shock.

"P-pajamas," she heard herself stuttering like an idiot. Yes, there he stood, this big, sexy beast of a man, resplendent in his flannel pajamas. Plaid, red-and-black *pajamas*. They were buttoned all the way up to his throat. Only his hands, face, and large feet were naked.

It was . . . unexpected, to say the least. And Daff's throat went dry as she discovered that reality—this buttoned-down image that was nothing close to what she'd been picturing for days—was *so* much better than her imagination. He looked absolutely, unexpectedly gorgeous. He'd cut his hair since dinner, she noted regretfully, before immediately wanting to run her fingers through the newly shorn, inch-long locks.

"*Daff*, what the fuck?" She came back to reality with a bump as she jerked out of her lustful haze to remember that she was dripping in the man's doorway.

"I—I wanted to t-tell you . . ." Her teeth were chattering, and she couldn't tell if it was because she was nervous or cold. "It's not that I don't like you, Spencer. It's that I like you *too* much. I think I've always liked you too much. And that t-terrifies me. I don't want to like you. Not when I'm just starting to like myself."

He looked confused and a little alarmed.

"Jesus, have you been drinking? Come in, for Christ's sake, it's freezing and you're turning blue." He dragged her over the threshold and grabbed a huge coat from the coatrack to drape around her shivering body. He then ran his hands vigorously up and down her arms, returning some of the sensation she hadn't even known she had lost, before enfolding her in his arms and enveloping her in his delicious warmth. She sighed and cuddled closer, only vaguely aware that she was getting his sexy pajamas wet.

"I'm sorry," she sobbed.

"Oh darling, you're a complete mess," he murmured into her hair, and her eyes filled with tears at both the words and the old-timey endearment. Of course Spencer would use an endearment like *darling*—it was exactly like him and it made her feel treasured.

"I *am*." She nodded with a wet sniff, and he sighed.

"You are what?"

Your darling.

"A mess. And I didn't mean to drag you into my mess. I just wanted to tell you something."

"That you like me?" he said on a questioning lilt.

"And something else." He lifted his head at that and looked down at her, his striking, savage face much too close to hers.

"What?" he asked curiously.

"This." She went onto her toes and lifted her lips to his, wanting so very desperately to taste the full lower curve of that beautiful mouth. He jerked, her move obviously surprising him, but then he sighed and deepened the kiss. His lips firming beneath hers and taking charge. He lifted a hand to cup her cheek, his thumb lovingly tracing the curve of her jawline as he changed the angle of her head to allow him better access to her mouth.

The kiss was . . . *everything*. More than everything. All those other mediocre kisses—those immature fumblings by inadequate men who could never be the measure of this one perfect man—they had all led to this moment here. Now. With him. His mouth was fire . . . ice . . . *elemental*, and his tongue, when it finally teased its way inside, was like sunshine casting light over all the dark stains on her soul.

Her arms came up, wrapped around his neck, her hands burrowing through the hair she had fantasized about stroking just moments ago.

She felt *his* hands moving up to her arms, encircling, tightening, and then . . . pushing her away.

She sobbed and tried to burrow back into his warmth, but he kept her firmly at arm's length, his delicious, stern mouth much too far away.

"Please . . ." she moaned, and he shook his head. His chest heaving with each breath, clearly as affected by their embrace as she had been.

"No." The word was harsh and completely without emotion.

"Why not?" She heard the whimper in her voice and despised herself for that weakness.

"Because I don't know what this is. I don't know where it's coming from, and I sure as hell don't know where it's going."

"I was hoping . . . to bed?" She tried to get close again, and his throat worked as he swallowed.

"Damn it. No."

"Oh." How humiliating. She'd thought . . . she'd figured he wanted her, too. He'd been trying to hook up with her for years. "I'm sorry. I should . . . I should probably leave."

He swore, and his hands tightened on her arms. His fingers were going to leave bruises. But unlike the others, she knew that Spencer would regret leaving marks on her skin.

"You're hurting me," she said quietly, testing that theory, and he immediately loosened his hold, his hands instinctively stroking over the bruised area.

"You're not leaving," he said. "You're going to dry off, have a hot drink, and we're going to fucking talk about this."

"Okay," she said meekly, and his eyes narrowed.

"I mean it, Daff."

"I know."

Spencer was confused, horny, and mad as hell. What in the ever-loving fuck was this about? If he hadn't tasted her clean—*hot*—mouth himself, he'd have sworn she was drunk. That left drugs, but her pupils and responses seemed pretty normal, she didn't seem doped up. She was just . . . odd. And it scared the hell out of him. She seemed much too vulnerable, like one wrong word or action would shatter her completely. He didn't want to be the one to break her. Not when all he'd ever really wanted was a chance to cherish her.

He marched her into the guest bathroom and handed her a bathrobe and a towel.

"Get out of those wet things and dry off. I'll be waiting in the kitchen." It was an open-plan home, so she wouldn't have trouble finding him. "Bring your clothes out with you and I'll stick them in the dryer." His voice was sharp, but he needed it to be, to snap her out of whatever the hell was wrong with her. She nodded slowly, as if she had a hard time understanding his words, but thankfully she turned toward the basin, allowing Spencer to shut the door.

He heaved a huge sigh after closing the door and rested his forehead against the wood for a brief moment before shaking himself and heading to the kitchen. He braced his hands on one of the granite countertops and regarded the glossy, marbled dark surface for a moment. He wasn't sure what to say to her after all this. She clearly needed help, but he wasn't sure what kind, and he wasn't sure if he was the man for the job. He didn't want to fuck her up any more than she already was.

She stayed hidden in the bathroom for nearly ten minutes, but he didn't rush her, just kept the kettle going until the door creaked open and a small, bare foot tentatively stepped out from behind the door. He followed the foot up, over the much too large bathrobe that seemed to swallow her whole. The only reason it wasn't puddling over her feet was because she had the front gripped in both hands, to prevent it from tripping her when she walked. Her wet hair was a mess, and her eyes and nose were red from an obvious bout of crying.

He smiled at her and hoped his face didn't reflect the grimness he felt.

"Would you like a cup of tea?" He was happy that his voice sounded gentle, and she hesitated before nodding. He had never seen her this uncertain before, and it made his chest ache.

She stepped up to the island and sat on one of the tall bar stools. Completely stripped of makeup, with her skin red and blotchy, she looked a bit like a child playing dress-up in his huge robe. Spence rubbed at his chest as the ache intensified.

"Milk? Sugar?"

"Two sugars, no milk." Her voice sounded hoarse. He finished her tea and a comforting cup of cocoa for himself and handed it to her. He positioned himself on the other side of the island, directly opposite her. He reached across and thumbed away the remnants of a tear from her cheek, ignoring the way she flinched at the movement.

He took a long, restorative gulp of his hot chocolate, watching her over the rim the entire time. She was doing her best not to look at him.

"You're going to have to meet my eyes sometime, Daff," he told her with a slight smile.

"Yes, but not right now," she whispered.

"Hmm." He allowed the silence to continue for several minutes, not pressuring her, hoping she would be the first to speak. After a few long moments, she finally rewarded his patience.

"I'm so sorry."

"You spend way too much time apologizing to me."

"Because I keep saying and doing stupid things." She sniffed before shaking her head and holding up a finger. "No, don't argue."

Spencer hid a grin at that, since he'd had absolutely no intention of arguing. He said nothing, wanting her to do the talking for now.

"Anyway," she continued, "I felt bad about what happened in the car tonight. I don't think you're dumb. If anything, I'm a little jealous because you did the whole college thing and made something of yourself. I'm such a loser. Same dead-end job for sixteen years, moving from one crappy failed relationship to the next. I mean, I lived with my parents up until a year ago, for God's sake."

"You moved from store clerk to manager. I wouldn't call that a dead-end job," he reminded her, and she laughed bitterly.

"Please, if I took my *credentials* elsewhere, they'd laugh at me. The only reason I got that promotion was because nobody else stuck around as long as I did. I know how the business works. And instead of taking the time to find, and possibly train, a new manager, Alison"—her boss—"just slapped the label onto me and barely increased my salary to reflect the title. And the worst of it is . . . I *hate* my job. I hate the sight of that store every morning, hate the smell of it, the very *thought* of it. But I have no idea how to do anything else."

"Why did you kiss me?"

"I thought it was what you wanted," she whispered, the words timid.

"Was it what *you* wanted?"

Her eyes widened a little, as if his words shocked her. "I don't . . . I think . . . if you wanted it, then I wanted it." That answer was so fucked-up on so very many levels, and it pissed him off beyond reason. He fought hard to hide his flare of temper from her and took a deep, fortifying breath before he trusted himself to speak again.

"Yes, but was it what *you* wanted?"

"I think so."

"Daff, it's a straightforward question, requiring a yes or no answer."

"Didn't *you* want to kiss me?" Again in that tiny, timid voice that was so unlike the brash, outspoken Daff he knew.

"Why is this so hard for you?" he asked, confused, and her eyes welled with tears.

"I don't know if I wanted to kiss you, I just felt that I *should*. It's what you do when you like someone. Right?"

"No, it's not," he corrected. "You talk with them, get to know them, you decide if you *really* like them, and then, when you're absolutely convinced that you can't take another breath without feeling their mouth on yours, that's when you kiss them."

"What about chemistry? What if you just know?"

"And did you? Just know? Is that why you kissed me? Because you just *knew* you had to?"

Her brow furrowed, and she looked completely confused.

"You're complicating this. It was just a kiss, for God's sake," she said with some of her old spark. "Why do you have to overthink things like this? Why can't we just be in the moment and share a kiss?"

"Because we weren't *just* in a moment. You showed up at my house at two thirty in the morning, soaking wet, rambling on about liking me, and then you planted your mouth on mine in the most desperate excuse of a kiss I've ever had the misfortune to experience."

"You liked it, I *know* you did. You were hard!"

"Physically, yes, but emotionally it left me stone cold, because it felt . . . frantic and forced."

"What kind of man is ruled by his emotions when his *cock* is hard?"

"Clearly not any kind of man you've ever been with."

"What's that supposed to mean?" she asked, her voice strained and the tears now flowing freely. He knew that acknowledging them, or hugging her close the way he was desperate to, would be met with rejection. So even though it was one of the hardest things he'd ever had to do, he ignored them.

"It means that I'm not like the assholes you've been with before, Daff. You want to kiss me, you'd better fucking mean it. You'd better want it with everything in you, because I'll want every part of you. Body and soul."

"What is it with guys?" The words practically exploded from her, rife with frustration and . . . *fear*? "Why do you all feel the need to *own* me?"

Whoa.

"That's not what I meant," he corrected calmly. "I'm talking about you opening up and willingly sharing those parts of yourself. Not demanding ownership of your body and mind."

"I fail to see the difference."

"There is one, a big one."

"Oh, do elaborate," she invited him sarcastically. She was definitely getting her spark back, and it relieved him.

"You'd have every part of me, too. Body and soul."

Shit. His words didn't have quite the effect he was hoping for—panic immediately rose to the surface. He could see it in the way her shoulders tensed as she retreated emotionally.

"I don't think that's something I'd want," she denied shakily.

"Why not?"

"T-too much responsibility. I mean, I prefer to keep things casual. I like you and I think maybe we'd be good together, but why does it have to be more than that?"

"So what are you after? No-strings sex, that's it?"

"Yes, and you're turning it into this big, serious *thing*. I think you've completely missed the point."

Had he? Maybe he was completely misreading the situation. It would be just like him to be Mr. Commitment in what was essentially a sex-only situation. It was exactly what had happened with Tanya. She'd never been into the whole relationship thing, and hindsight told him that he'd been willfully blind to that fact, forcing a relationship when she'd only ever been after a good time.

Was he doing the same thing with Daff? Had he turned her big seduction into an embarrassing and uncalled-for "let's discuss our feelings" session? He went over the entire encounter from the moment he'd opened the door to now and shook his head.

No, there was definitely something else going on here, and she was covering it up with this . . . *bluster* now.

"So we fuck each other and when it's out of our systems, we move on? That's what you're saying?"

"Yes." Her voice sounded breathless and a little uncertain.

Spencer placed his cup carefully down on the granite counter and sighed softly before rounding the island and coming to stand behind her, moving fast in order to catch her off guard. He turned the bar stool until she was facing him and reached down, placing one hand on each knee and gently moving them apart. He immediately shifted his hips between her thighs, until nothing but a deep breath separated them. He moved his hands to the counter on either side of her, effectively caging her with his body.

"Okay," he muttered. "Have it your way." Her face was downcast, her regard determinedly fixed on his chest, but that wouldn't do at all. "Look at me, Daff."

She tilted her head back obligingly, and he smiled, just a grim parting of his lips.

"That's better." He lowered his head and captured her mouth with his; her soft, full lips immediately softened beneath his, and he groaned his satisfaction.

His mouth was gentle, so much gentler than anything she was used to. He finessed instead of claimed, his lips coaxed and requested instead of demanded. The tenderness was new to her, and it made her respond in ways she never knew she had in her. It made her want more, and she opened her mouth willingly when his tongue traced along the seam of her lips, bidding entry.

His hands never left the counter, but hers took on a life of their own and she reached up to explore that beautiful face, her palms tracing the strong contours of his stubbled jaw before moving up over his lean cheeks and then sweeping by his temples until she finally had two fistfuls of his thick hair clenched between her fingers.

She waited for him to deepen the kiss, but he kept it gentle and that lack of insistence made her—for the first time ever—crave more. Her nipples were hard and aching, and between her legs, where she could feel his heat of his erection not even an inch away from her nakedness, she was completely drenched. She slid forward and wrapped her legs around his tight, muscular butt, dragging herself closer until *finally* she could feel his steel length up against her cleft.

He groaned, lifting his mouth from hers and burying it against her neck, where he landed a soft, suctioning kiss in the cove beneath her ear. The next suckling kiss was lower, then lower, until he got to the neckline of the robe, which he nosed aside to land another one of those gentle, wicked kisses on the curve of her breast.

Daff watched him move lower and lower, her hands cupped around the back of his head.

"Please," she begged when he dragged his tongue lightly over the rippled seam of her areola. "Oh please, Spencer . . ." When his mouth finally closed over her nipple, she writhed beneath him, bucking wildly against his erection. His mouth remained so incredibly gentle, using just the lightest of suckling motions, before he raised his head to blow on the wet tip.

She sobbed, trying to pull his head back down, but he was working his way to the other breast, and he was soon driving her crazy with another one of those sweet, tender kisses. Done with that breast, he moved down, still using only his lips and tongue, his soft kisses leaving a scorching trail over her torso, then her stomach—where he spent a moment, tracing the shape of her belly button with his tongue—and then down over her abdomen. The loosely knotted belt proved no obstacle for him, as with just one tug of his teeth, he had it undone with nothing between her nudity and his scrutiny at all. He took a moment to appreciate the display before smiling and going back to work.

Daff's legs went slack when his objective became clear, and she watched in disbelief as he knelt in front of her. His hands still on the countertop, he looked up to meet her eyes. His gaze scorching hot while his panting breath fanned out over her delicate flesh, and she shuddered at the delicious sensation.

"Put your feet on my shoulders, please," he murmured. She had a moment's doubt—this was so far beyond anything she'd ever experienced before. Were they moving too fast? Probably. Was that going to stop her? Probably not.

Embarrassed to be on such lewd display when he was essentially fully dressed, she swallowed nervously. If not for his half-mast eyes, his uneven breathing, and the rampant hard-on tenting the fabric of those pajama bottoms, she would have wondered if he was turned on at all. He seemed completely in control, and it was . . . *unnerving.*

But still . . . she was so hot and so close to orgasm that a strong breeze would probably set her off right now. She lifted her legs and slotted the arches of her feet neatly over the curves of his shoulders. He grunted his approval and gave a long appreciative look at what she had just revealed to him before leaning forward and closing his mouth over her hard, aching clit.

She gasped, then sucked in and held another breath when her back arched and her palms slammed down onto the counter beside his hands. "Uhhhh!"

The suction of his mouth was relentless but not strong enough to make her come—it was driving her insane. His tongue soon joined the party, and Daff cried out again while he kept her on edge with his soft little butterfly licks and tender suckling. Because he never ramped up the intensity, she just remained hovering on the brink. Her feet pushed down against his shoulders, her back flat on the countertop by now, her head tilted over the other end, while her arms spread out on either side of her and gripped the edge.

"Oh God, oh please," she begged, opening her eyes to stare fixedly at the upside-down cabinets on the other side of the room. His hands finally came into play, one splayed flat over her abdomen to hold her still when she tried to push herself closer to his mouth and the other curved over her right thigh, spreading her a little wider.

The pressure of each suctioning kiss was starting to intensify; the licking got a little more purposeful. He was finally giving her more, and it was wrecking her. She wasn't sure she'd be able to stand it for much longer, but he continued to take his time, savoring her taste in the same way he had enjoyed every morsel of the haute cuisine they'd been served at dinner, with little sighs and appreciative groans.

He kept her balanced on a knife edge while he toyed with her relentlessly . . . until eventually he drew her hypersensitive, extremely swollen clitoris into his mouth and sucked . . . *hard*. Daff's entire body convulsed, her back and shoulders leaving the counter as her body bowed beneath the intense, wrenching pleasure of her climax. She cried out, the sound loud and piercing and unexpected, and covered her face with both hands as her bones and muscles turned to warm liquid as she melted back onto the counter in a messy puddle.

She felt undone, like Spencer Carlisle had systematically taken her apart and left off important pieces when he put her back together.

Spencer got to his feet and watched the small, vulnerable woman crying on his kitchen counter. He shouldn't have done it. He should have sent her off to bed in one of the spare rooms and they could have discussed the matter again in the morning. He truly hadn't meant for it to go this far.

It was supposed to have been a kiss only. But she'd been so receptive and then so damned shocked by every gentle caress that he found himself both unwilling and unable to stop. Now she looked fucking ruined, and he felt like an asshole.

He moved quickly, scooping her up into his arms, where she drew up her legs and curled her arms around his neck, burying her wet, weeping face in his chest. Not sure what to do, he carried her to his bedroom and laid her down under the covers of his unmade bed before crawling in behind her and tugging her into his arms. She turned so that she was facing him and again buried her face in his chest, still crying.

He stroked her back soothingly, not asking questions, not saying anything, just holding her until her trembling abated and her tears stopped. He leaned back and reached for a tissue from the box he kept on the nightstand, and she took it gratefully.

"You're probably the only man I know who keeps tissues next to his bed."

"I'm sure there are quite a few guys who keep tissues at their bedside, for a myriad of reasons," he said inanely, relieved to hear the teasing note in her voice.

"I'm sorry for turning into a gooey mess on you."

"There you go, apologizing again."

"Then allow me to thank you."

"For?" he asked, baffled.

"*Seriously?* You don't know? You couldn't tell?"

"No, what?"

"That was the first time . . ." She paused and he frowned. "That was the first time anybody has ever done that for me."

"You're shitting me."

"I shit you not."

"What kind of fucking morons have you been dating?"

"Selfish ones," she said, her voice slurring a bit. Her hand reached down between them, dipped beneath the waistband of his pajama bottoms and found his throbbing cock with unerring accuracy. He sucked in a startled breath, releasing it again with a soft groan. "You didn't finish."

"Because I never started," he said, not sure if the words made sense at all—nothing currently made sense to him except that firm grip on his hot, painful erection. She slid her hand up to the sensitive tip and then all the way back down to his aching balls. He allowed her a few more strokes—he was only human, after all—before his hand closed over hers, tightening for a brief moment, and he relished the feel of the tighter grip on his shaft. He pulled her hand away gently, lifting it out from beneath the covers and dropping a kiss into her palm. "We're both exhausted, darling. Go to sleep."

"But I want to make you feel good, too," she whispered, sounding exhausted but a little vexed at the same time.

"I appreciate that, but what would make me feel good right now is sleep. Just sleep. With you in my arms. Okay?"

"This is just sex, Spencer," she felt obligated to remind him, and he rolled his eyes before turning to switch off the bedside lamp. He quickly gathered her back into his arms and she settled into them with a happy sigh.

"Just sex. Got it." Over his dead body.

"I like it when you call me that." She sounded all but gone by now.

"What?"

"*Darling.* I like that. It's old-fashioned and sweet."

"Good. Because I like calling you that, and I'm not about to stop." She yawned.

"Good night, Spencer."

"Daff?"

"Hmm?"

"No regrets, okay?"

"No regrets." He kissed the top of her head and, ignoring his angry, demanding penis, settled down to sleep.

Of course, she had regrets, big-time regrets. They hit the second she opened her eyes just three hours later. She was alone in the king-size bed, but Spencer's side of it still retained some of his body heat, and she sighed softly before stretching languorously.

Her mind was screaming, *oh fuck what have I done!* while her body was purring, *hmm more, yes please!* It was confusing, and she wasn't exactly certain how she felt this morning. All she knew was that it was seven in the morning, she'd allowed Spencer certain intimate liberties just a few hours ago, and she had to get out of here and get ready for work. Preferably before the whole town woke up and saw her do the drive of shame from Spencer's place back to her home.

She looked around for the robe she'd been wearing but couldn't find it anywhere and then blushed hotly when she recalled that it had come off while she lay sprawled on Spencer's kitchen counter. She had been naked when he carried her to his bedroom. She saw his discarded pajamas at the foot of the bed and dragged the top on. It fell to just above her knees and the sleeves ended well below her fingertips. But it smelled of his spicy, masculine scent, and she tugged the collar to her nose to inhale deeply. Okay, so maybe the regrets were waning a bit— there were definite positives to this situation.

The hardwood floor was cold beneath her bare feet as she padded her way out of the bedroom and downstairs to the living area. She found Spencer in the kitchen behind the island, sweeping up shards of ceramic that she recognized as the cups they had used last night. She must have unknowingly swept them off the counter. She went bright red at the thought and could barely look at the counter without blushing even more.

Spencer caught sight of her, and his eyebrows went all the way up into his hairline at the sight of her in his pajama top.

"Morning," she murmured self-consciously, pushing her hair out of her eyes.

"Morning," he replied, dropping the shards of glass into the recycle bin and rounding the island to stand in front of her. He was dressed for work already, and he dug into one of his jacket pockets for something. "I wanted to hang on to this in case I had some kind of hair-related emergency in the future. But you look like you need it."

He scissored her messy bangs between his middle and forefingers and used the tiny butterfly clip she'd put in his hair just the night before to pin her hair back and out of her eyes. He trailed his fingers down over her cheek and leaned down to drop a sweet kiss on her mouth.

"Breakfast?" he asked after ending the all-too-brief caress.

"I should get home." He nodded before turning away to reach for something.

"Not without coffee," he instructed, dropping a mug on the counter in front of her. Daff hummed happily as her senses perked up at just the smell of the freshly brewed coffee and gratefully wrapped her hands around the warm mug.

"Sit down, I wouldn't want you to slice your feet. I'm not sure I got all the shards."

"Where are my things?" she asked, moving far away from the island and taking a seat in one of the huge easy chairs in his living room instead.

"You didn't bring them out of the bathroom last night, so I put them in the dryer about ten minutes ago. They may still be a bit damp, I'm afraid."

"It's okay, I won't have to be in them for too long."

"Finish your coffee, we'll take them out of the dryer after you're done." He grabbed a mug for himself and joined her in the living room, taking the chair opposite hers.

"Dinner tonight?" he asked nonchalantly, sprawling in the chair with his long legs stretched out in front of him. He looked *much* too relaxed for her liking.

"Can't," she said. "I'm meeting my sisters tonight; Daisy wants to discuss bridesmaid dresses."

"Afterward?"

"I'm not sure how long it'll be. I can't give you a definite time."

"I'll be here," he said with a shrug, taking a sip of his coffee.

"Will I see you at lunchtime?" she asked, hating the hopeful note in her voice.

"No." She was ridiculously disappointed by his curt, unyielding response and strove to maintain a casual demeanor.

"Okay. Cool."

They sat drinking their coffee in silence, and Daff couldn't tell if it was an awkward silence or a comfortable one. He seemed comfortable enough, but she felt awkward as hell.

"I should get going," she said after a few minutes, and he nodded, placing his mug on the coffee table and pushing to his feet when she jumped to hers. He was beside her in half a stride and cupped her cheeks in his large palms.

"Hey," he said calmly, forcing her to meet his tranquil green gaze. "Relax. No regrets, remember?"

She reached up and closed her hands over his.

"No regrets," she repeated determinedly, hoping to make it her mantra.

"So," he said, keeping his hands on her face and his eyes steady on hers, "how do you want to play this no-strings sex thing? Nobody knows? Everybody knows? Only a select few know?"

"I'm not sure."

"Siblings?"

"Daisy's going to flip her shit if she thinks this may affect the wedding."

"Hmm."

"I don't know what that one means," she confessed, and his brow furrowed.

"What do you mean?"

"That particular grunt. I've been learning to decipher them, but that one always leaves me stumped."

"They don't mean anything," he denied, and she scoffed.

"Please, you say more with your noises than most people do in a full conversation."

"They're just fillers."

"They're so not fillers, and nothing you say will convince me otherwise."

"Hmm." She giggled in response to that, and he frowned again.

"Wiseass," she dismissed.

"It was just a grunt," he maintained, looking a little freaked out.

"Nope, that one was facetious and meant 'Believe what you want, Daffodil McGregor, you're a nutcase.'" She deepened her voice to imitate his, and his resulting smile was a charming mixture of bemusement and amusement.

"First, I do not sound like that. Second, you *are* a nutcase. And third, it's *just* a grunt."

"Ri-iight." He huffed in amusement and planted a kiss on her mouth without any warning. He took advantage of her openmouthed shock by immediately plundering with his tongue and leaving her completely shell-shocked and shaky after the stealth attack.

"Get dressed, darling," he said hoarsely after ending the kiss. "Or I'll be tempted to call in sick and keep you here in nothing but that pajama top—or less—all day. You look sexy as hell in it."

She carried that kiss with her throughout the morning. She got to work after him and so missed his walk past her shop window for the second time that week. She sighed regretfully as she sipped her third cup of coffee—including the one she'd had at his house.

She couldn't believe how fast things had happened between them over the space of just days, after so many years of buildup. If anybody had told her last week she'd be contemplating a sex-only arrangement with Spencer Carlisle this week, she'd have laughed them out of the room, and yet here she was, thinking about nothing but his tongue on her most intimate body parts. Reliving their moments together over and over again.

She was recalling it again, flushed and hot and breathless, when the bell above the front door tinkled and jerked her out of her little fantasy world. For the brief moment between looking down at her book and up at the door, she hoped with everything in her that it was Spencer with lunch, but she was doomed to disappointment. It wasn't Spencer, instead it was a familiar-looking woman whom Daff was sure she'd seen before but never really spoken to. The woman was wearing an SCSS uniform, which explained why she seemed familiar. She probably walked past Daff's store every day.

"Good afternoon," Daff greeted uncertainly. "May I help you?"

The woman—girl, really—smiled broadly, revealing two gold-capped front teeth and a pair of sweet dimples.

"Hi, miss, I'm Chantal. Mr. Carlisle asked me to bring you this." She held out a brown paper bag with a white notepaper clipped to the folded top. Daff took it automatically.

"Thank you, Chantal."

"No problem, miss. Have a nice day." Chantal waved and left the store immediately, leaving Daff to stare at the package in her hand like it was a ticking time bomb. She placed it carefully on the counter and unclipped the note.

Daff,

Sorry I couldn't come around for lunch today, I have a business meeting at twelve. I don't trust you to eat a decent lunch, so I prepared this for you.

Eat up, darling.

See you later.

S

CHAPTER SEVEN

"No! Mom, tell them I look terrible in yellow," Daff complained after dinner with her sisters and mother. They were at Mason and Daisy's place, and Daisy had prepared dinner. Well, actually, she had *ordered* dinner from MJ's.

Daff had been completely distracted all evening, and they appeared to have finalized bridesmaid dress colors while she was off in Happy Horny Dreamland.

"Well, you agreed to it," Lia pointed out a little smugly, and Daff sent her a death glare. Everybody liked to think that Lia was the nice one. Maybe because she dressed like a librarian, taught children, and spent all her free time helping others.

"I did *not*."

"We literally placed the swatches on the table, Daisy asked what we thought about this one, I said I loved it, and you said, 'Yes, very nice.'"

"Come to think of it, you've been saying 'yes, very nice' to *everything* tonight," Daisy chimed. "Cravats for the men? Yes, very nice. Four-inch snakeskin stilettos for the bridesmaids? Yes, very nice. Daffodils for the bouquets—"

"I did *not*. I would *never!*" Daff shook her head, horrified. She absolutely hated her namesake flower. Every time a guy brought her flowers it was daffodils. Ugh. They always just *assumed* she must love daffodils.

"Yes, very nice!" her sisters and mother all chimed at the same time and then giggled hysterically. Cooper, Mason's gorgeous mixed Labrador retriever, peered up briefly when the high-pitched laughter woke him from his nap.

"We're not really going with any of those things, by the way," Daisy said.

"Except the yellow for the dresses," Lia chimed in.

"No! I hate that yellow."

"But it's my accent color," Daisy pouted, and that's when Daff knew they had to be pulling her leg. Daisy never pouted. Well, she had started recently with Mason, and the guy was a complete sucker when the lower lip came out. Did her every bidding. It was sad and embarrassing, really.

"Come on, girls," their mother chastised as she absently stroked Daisy's toy Pomeranian, Peaches. The little fluff ball always managed to wind up on their mother's lap. "You know she looks sickly in yellow."

"Mom," Daff whined, hating to have her shortcomings pointed out.

"You do, you know it, and that's why you refuse to wear it."

"Well, okay, but you don't have to rub it in."

"We just wanted to see what would snap you out of your semi-fugue state." Daisy smiled.

"And we want to know what's up with you."

"Just distracted," she said dismissively.

"You had dinner with Spencer last night," Daisy recalled gleefully. "Does this have anything to do with that?"

"Oh my goodness, she's blushing," Lia said, sounding completely shocked. Daff raised her hands to her hot cheeks.

"I'm not."

"Oh, but you *are*," their mother confirmed. "You always were my best blusher. Couldn't tell a lie without going the color of a ripe tomato."

"What's going on between you and Spencer, Daff?" Lia asked.

"Nothing. He's just a lot nicer than I ever gave him credit for."

"That he is," Millicent McGregor agreed. "A lovely young man. Very shy, though."

"Shy?" Was he?

"Of course he is. He never has a word to say in company, always kind of tries to hide in a corner and blend in with the furniture. But so sweet. Even when he was a boy and everybody else thought he and Mason were troublemakers, he always had a friendly greeting, helped carry my groceries—and never accepted a tip, mind you, no matter how dire their situation was at home. He was a little gentleman in the making. But never had much to say for himself. Then or now."

"Why didn't the town help them when their mother died?" Daisy asked, her voice sharp and a little resentful. "Did you know the police picked them up after they'd spent all night in the hospital with their dying mother and detained them for a day, thinking they were the ones who wrecked Mr. Richards's store?"

Daff's heart seized in her chest at the thought of what an ordeal that must have been for both boys. How cruel.

"I had no idea the boys had been suspected of that." Their mother sounded appalled. "I heard about the vandalism a couple of days after the fact. At that point they had no suspects. It must have been after they questioned and cleared the Carlisle boys."

"So are you and Spencer finally hooking up, Daffy?" Lia asked.

"Don't call me that," Daff said irritably. "And what do you mean, *finally*?"

"Just that the guy's been trying for years."

"And years," Daisy added with a nod.

"He has?" Their mother looked startled by the information.

"Yep, he's had a crush on her since high school."

"He used to send her poems," Daisy added, and Lia giggled.

"Oh my gosh, I forgot about that," Lia said. "'Daffodil. Tell me you will . . .'"

"'Be mine. Your smile is like gold and like diamonds your eyes do shine,'" Daisy continued. She grabbed Lia's hand and they went in for the big finish together.

"'I'll love you forever and forget you never.'"

They collapsed against each other and screamed with laughter while Daff glared at them and their mother smiled in delight.

"Oh my, how sweet," Millicent said once the cackles had died down. Daff was less than impressed with her sisters for bringing up the poetry. They'd teased her relentlessly about it at the time, and she couldn't believe that they'd actually gotten their hands on one long enough to memorize it.

"Do you remember that, Daff? All those poems?" Lia asked.

"Of course I remember it," she grumbled. "It wasn't *that* long ago. And there's nothing going on between Spencer and me, so can we please focus on the task at hand? We have under three months to plan this thing and the clock is ticking, ladies."

That got them all refocused immediately, and Daff heaved a silent sigh of relief when they all started looking at color and fabric samples again.

"That's the fourth easy shot you've missed tonight. What's going on with you?" Mason asked as he lined up his own shot and sank yet *another* ball. At this point, Spencer might as well stand back and enjoy the show, because Mason wasn't going to let him in with another chance. Spencer rarely lost at pool and he'd known—with his atrocious lack of form—that it would be only a matter of time before Mason figured out something was up.

He watched as his brother lined up yet another perfect shot and allowed his thoughts to drift back to Daff. He had a raging case of blue balls and had barely been able to focus at work today. Even an intense wank session in the shower just before coming out tonight hadn't done much to take the edge off his horniness.

He thought back to the prim thank-you text she'd sent him earlier, accompanied by a selfie of her licking the hot sauce from the home-made burrito off her fingers. Like she didn't know *exactly* the effect that picture would have on him.

He barely swallowed back a groan now.

"I've been instructed to ask you how many groomsmen you think you'll have."

"*Instructed*, is it? Daff running the show?"

"Only as much as I'll let her." He thought back to how he had kept her hovering on the brink of orgasm for nearly half an hour, then flushed—grateful for the low light in Ralphie's pub that disguised both flush and instant hard-on—at the entirely inappropriate memory.

"And it's a valid question. I need to know how many people to plan for." He willed his dick to go down and was happy when he managed to wrangle some control over the unruly boner.

"What's the rush? It's three months away."

"Apparently that's nowhere near enough time to plan a wedding and all the flash and fuckery that goes along with it."

"Hah? I'm beginning to get that."

"So? Any idea?"

"Yeah. You're my best man, with Chris and Sam as groomsmen." Christién was one of Mason's modeling friends—now a trained chef with a restaurant in the area—and Sam Brand was one of his army buddies, as well as his former business partner. Spencer hadn't met either man yet, but he'd heard that Sam had saved his brother's life—and vice versa—more than a few times.

"You can't have just three guys at your stag party, Mase."

"I have three more ex-army buddies flying in, and there's also my future father-in-law."

"You're inviting Dr. McGregor? Man, what if I wanted to hire a stripper?"

"Fuck, Spence. No strippers . . . Daisy would kill me."

"She would?"

"Okay, maybe not," he confessed sheepishly. "She's curious. She'd want to know what the strippers' go-to moves were and then she'd—" He stopped talking abruptly and cleared his throat. "Anyway, no strippers."

Fascinated by the way his brother refused to meet his eyes, Spencer grinned. Well, then, wasn't Daisy McGregor the little dark horse? He was tempted to hire a stripper just to give his brother a fun night of role-playing, but he didn't think Mason and Daisy needed any help in that department.

"Okay, so the good doctor will be joining us. Anyone else?"

"Daff and Lia aren't seeing anybody right now, are they?"

"You're about to become their brother-in-law, wouldn't you be more qualified to answer that question? And why do you want to know, anyway?" He sounded cagey, even to himself.

"Well, they may want their boyfriends included, and it'll pad the numbers."

"You need more friends."

"I have a shit ton of friends, just not in this country. If *you* had more friends, we could invite them."

"Not my wedding."

"What about old school friends? We may have a few of those in common."

"We didn't have school friends," Spencer reminded.

"Who needs friends when I have you?" Mason quipped, but there was a note of sincerity in his voice and Spencer smiled.

"Ditto, bro. Okay, so seven guys? We can make that work."

"It'll be awesome, man."

"I just hope Daisy's lady friends don't outnumber us when it comes time to merge the parties."

"She doesn't have too many friends, either. Her sisters, her mom, that chick Tilda, and a few others. It doesn't matter if the numbers are uneven—it's not a hookup party."

"Yeah."

Mason focused on his game and sank two more balls. He sized up the table while dusting the tip of his cue with some chalk.

"So Daisy tells me you and Daff had dinner last night." Spencer, who'd been in the process of taking a sip of beer, nearly choked and quickly lowered the bottle, clearing his throat vigorously in the process.

"Hmm." He grunted for lack of anything better to say.

"That go okay?"

"Uh-huh."

"Where did you go? Daisy and I were at MJ's last night and didn't see you there."

"Why'd you go to MJ's? Spying on us?" Spencer asked suspiciously and then instantly regretted the question when Mason gaped at him.

"Why the fuck would we do that, man? Daisy burned dinner last night, and instead of starting from scratch, we decided to eat out. We thought we'd run into you guys."

"Sorry." Spencer scrubbed a hand across the nape of his neck. "I don't even know why I said that. I took her to Leisure Isle."

"In *Knysna*?"

"Figured it'd be a nice change and right up her alley."

"Like a date?"

Spencer winced at the incredulous note in Mason's voice. "What's wrong with that?"

"Spence, c'mon, you know she treats you like dirt most of the time. Why put yourself in the position to get rejected yet again?"

"Don't worry, it wasn't like a date. She made sure to point that out a few dozen times." Mason grimaced. "Sorry, buddy."

"Nothing I wasn't expecting." Spencer shrugged. "We managed to have a pretty pleasant evening for the most part." Followed by unpleasantness . . . followed by the most confusing and intense sexual encounter of his life.

Speaking of which, it was time he wrapped this up and got home, just in case Daff decided to grace him with her presence tonight.

"Daisy still with her sisters?" he asked casually, and Mason checked his phone.

"Looks that way. She said she'd text me after they left."

"Can't believe they kicked you out of your own home."

"Apparently a lot of this wedding stuff is super-secret, in addition to being a crap ton of work."

"I always figured it was a party, and how hard can planning a party be?"

"Right?"

"This stag party, I thought you, me, a bunch of guys, some alcohol, and music. Sorted, right? But now it's become an 'event' with 'activities' and 'speeches.'"

"You're using air quotes," Mason scoffed, and Spencer snorted.

"That's because I'm quoting Daff." These were some of the things they'd discussed over dinner last night.

"Wait, why would there have to be speeches at a stag party?"

"I don't know." Spencer threw up his hands in frustration. "Man, I don't fucking know. It makes no sense to me. But Daff . . . she seems to know what she's talking about."

"She *did* help plan Lia's wedding," Mason said dubiously. "So she has some experience."

"That wedding was a failure."

"But it was flawlessly planned."

"I'll take your word for it." Spencer grinned, reaching into his front jeans pocket and dragging out a bill. "This should cover my beers. I'm headed home."

"Hey, hold on a second, I was winning," Mason protested. "You can't just leave in the middle of the game."

"Sure, I'll give you this win," Spencer said magnanimously. Mason had never beaten him at pool, and he knew this was going to seriously piss his brother off. Which was exactly why he was doing it.

"That sucks, man."

"Hey, I said you can have the win," he emphasized, knowing it would drive his brother nuts.

"You can't *give* it to me! I've earned it."

"Of course you have. No arguments from me. That's why I said you could have it."

"Stop giving me the win, asshole! It's already mine." Mason was going slightly red in frustration.

"Sure it is," Spencer said agreeably.

"Just hang on a second, I'm about to sink the eight ball," Mason said desperately.

"Ooh, sorry. No can do. I'm running late." He deliberately turned away and grinned when Mason swore behind him.

"Running late for fucking what? Bedtime?"

"I like to stay on schedule, you know that. See ya."

"Spencer, wait. Look . . ."

He left before Mason could finish the sentence and chuckled to himself as he walked to his 4x4. His brother would never forgive him, and even though he'd eventually get over it, he'd still be bitching about it years from now.

It was nearly midnight when his doorbell rang. Spencer heaved a sigh of relief and pushed himself to his feet to get the door.

"Hello, darling," he greeted the apprehensive-looking woman at his door warmly. "How'd the wedding planning go?"

"Ugh. Can we please talk about something *other* than freaking wedding plans? I feel like this wedding is starting to take over my life."

"How was work?"

"Boring," she complained, peeling her coat off. He took it and hung it on the coatrack beside the front door. "You're in your pj's already. Nice."

He grinned, not sure what her fascination with his pajamas was about, but he'd take the admiring looks she was giving him over her usual animosity anytime.

"Oh my *God*, and what's this?" Her eyes widened as she looked him over and he almost made a self-conscious move to cover his erection with both hands. But she wasn't focused on his groin—instead she was staring up at his face, and he wondered if he had food on his cheek or . . .

"You wear glasses?" He lifted a hand to touch one of the arms of his heavy, square, black-framed glasses.

"Yeah, to watch TV."

"It's so sexy," she breathed. "Nerdy hot, like Clark Kent."

"Uh . . . thanks?"

"I want to change out of these clothes. I went straight to Daisy's after work and came directly here after that. I didn't bring anything to wear. Can I borrow your pajama top?" She didn't wait for his answer; she was too busy unbuttoning his top. The thought of her in it was unbearably sexy, and he helped her by slipping the thing over his head before she even had it half-undone and handing it over without any fuss or complaint.

"I'm going to grab a quick shower, 'kay?"

"You eat?" he asked, bemused by how very at home she seemed.

"Yep." She hooked a finger into the collar of the top and tossed it over her shoulder before sauntering to the downstairs bathroom, her hips swaying gently as she walked. His mouth went dry and he couldn't take his eyes off her sweet, round ass in the formfitting pants she was wearing.

She threw him a sexy little grin over her shoulder, telling him with just a cheekily raised eyebrow that she knew exactly how she was affecting him.

"Be right back."

"Hmm." The sound came out more feral than he'd intended, and she laughed huskily as she closed the bathroom door behind her.

He watched the closed door for a second, tempted to join her, but joining her in that shower—even if it was what she expected him to do—was not an option. He had the feeling that Daff was playing by a very specific set of rules known only to her, and he refused to play her game. No matter how fucking titillating it was. This was more than just a game to him.

He groaned and forced himself to return to the living room. He stoked the fire he had going, sat down on the sofa, and tried to shift his focus back to his movie. Even though his concentration was shot to hell and all he could think about was the very naked and very beautiful woman in his shower.

He didn't join her. Daff didn't quite know what to make of that. She'd made all the right moves, the *expected* moves, and he hadn't responded in the predictable way. Her brain was working overtime by the time she'd soaped and rinsed herself. Delaying any longer was pointless. He wouldn't be joining her, and it confused her. She wasn't sure what to do next.

She dried herself and dragged on his top, inhaling deeply and relishing the scent of him. This was a green-and-black version of the one he'd worn last night. Same old-timey design, with lapels and a breast pocket, so perfectly suited to Spencer. She towel dried her hair and held a hand to her chest for a moment to still the frantic fluttering of her heart before throwing back her shoulders and leaving the bathroom.

The kitchen and living area were lit only by the cozy, flickering fire and the television set. Spencer seemed to be watching something loud and full of shouting and explosions. He looked up when she stepped out of the bathroom, his glasses gleaming from the light of the television screen.

"Hey, the movie's just started, you haven't missed much." He held out a hand, motioning her to join him, and she hesitated. He wanted to watch a *movie*? Seriously? That was . . . that was truly flippin' weird. Did she have to wear a sign saying "easy lay" for him to understand that he didn't have to go through the usual tedious motions to get lucky with her?

Not sure what to do, she took a couple of tentative steps toward the man-size, comfy-looking sofa. When she got close enough, he grabbed her hand and tugged her down next to him. He lifted the little lap blanket—seriously, a lap blanket, this guy was adorable—and dragged her legs over his lap, cupping the soles of her feet in one large hand and hooking his free arm around her shoulders to tuck her snugly beneath his armpit.

This wasn't half bad. She snuggled close to his seriously ripped bare chest—*ah*, the perks of stealing his pajama top—one cheek resting on a firm, smooth pec, his tight nipple just an inch away from her mouth. She tucked one hand into the dip of his taut waist and rested the other in the small of his lower back, just where the curve of his butt began.

Beneath her calves, she could feel the swell of his penis, and it was hard, which gave her hope that she wasn't a complete failure at the seduction thing. Still, he did nothing about it, just gently kneaded the balls of her feet with one hand and toyed with her hair with the other.

"What are we watching?" she asked. Feeling so safe and warm and comfortable that she could barely form the words.

"*Captain America.*"

"First one?"

"Second."

"Oh, I've seen that one."

"Me too, but it's a fun one to rewatch." His voice rumbled beneath her ear. She traced little patterns on his chest, and his breath hitched. She smiled at the reaction, but he lifted his hand from her feet and plastered it over her wandering fingers. Pressing her hand flat against his chest.

"Behave. We're watching a movie."

"But I've seen it." She could hear the pout in her voice and was appalled by how girlish she sounded. What on earth was this man doing to her?

"Nevertheless, we're watching it."

"Spoilsport," she grumbled, but she decided to go with this for the moment and see where it led . . .

Where it led was to the end of the movie. He did *nothing* for nearly two hours, just watched the movie while stroking her hair, then her back, her feet and occasionally her calves. His erection waxed and waned . . . mostly waxed. The thing had been an almost constant companion throughout the movie. And occasionally she'd rub her legs against it to get some kind of reaction from him, but he'd just still her movements with his quelling hand. He had some serious Jedi mind tricks when it came to controlling his hard-on, because any other man would have had her pinned and staked hours ago. Spencer had phenomenal willpower.

The credits started rolling, and he made a satisfied sound.

"Great movie," he said, letting go of her toes to stretch luxuriously. He turned his attention on her, his eyes heavy lidded and intent.

"Nobody's ever thrown me over for Steve Rogers before," she complained, and his lips quirked.

"You haven't been thrown over, just put on hold for a moment."

"Still, I'm a little irked."

"Yeah?"

"Yes." It was hard to get a mad going when you were snuggled up to the hardest, hottest, and sexiest chest in town, but Daff was for damned sure going to give it the old college try.

"I didn't mean to irk you," he said and quickly shifted his hands to her waist and dragged her into his lap. "C'm'ere, darling."

Before she knew it, she was straddling his lap, her naked mound coming into immediate contact with the hard, thick ridge beneath the crotch of his flannel pants.

"Hmm," he purred, the long, drawn-out sound brimming with satisfaction. "You're so fuckin' wet."

She was, embarrassingly so, and had been for most of the movie. A result of all his petting and cuddling and the feel of that constantly hard penis beneath her legs. Her moisture immediately dampened the crotch of his pants, leaving absolutely nothing of what lay beneath to the imagination.

"And you're *so* hard," she replied, her voice sultry. He lifted his hands to her hair and tugged her down for a kiss. She crossed her forearms around the back of his head, her elbows digging into his shoulders as she clung to him while his mouth ravaged hers. His tongue was hot and demanding, and she was very willing to acquiesce to his every demand right now. He dragged his mouth away and, with shaky hands, fumbled with the buttons on the pajama top before losing patience and ripping it open. The plastic buttons went flying, landing on the wooden floor with little pings.

He peered at her breasts for a long moment before going to work. Oh, but the man knew how to play. Daff had never even known how sensitive her nipples were before Spencer. He sucked, he licked, he grazed with his teeth and with his stubble and drove her crazy. She still had her arms crossed behind his head, and she arched her back, writhing wildly in his lap as she bordered on orgasm just from having her nipples sucked. It wasn't anything that had ever happened to her before, and she was almost mindless with passion.

Without moving his mouth from her breast, his hands slid from her waist to her hips. He stilled her frenzied movements and then led her, showing her the rhythm he wanted from her.

"*Oh,*" she whispered when she slid up against his massive hard-on and the rigid shaft aligned perfectly with her naked furrow. As her clitoris rode up and then down the heavy erection, she realized that her movements had dragged his pants down enough to uncover the plump glans. Her clit bumped against the underside of the broad head with every upward slide, and that, combined with his continued lavish attention at her breasts, felt absolutely *incredible*. His hands steered her to move faster and she happily obliged, sensing that they were both nearly there.

"*Spencer,*" she gasped. "Don't stop. Please. I'm nearly . . . *Oh! Oh! My! GOD!*"

Spencer grunted and his arms wrapped around her back in an almost bone-crunching hug; his mouth went slack at her breast as he gasped and then jerked. Daff was too focused on her own orgasm in that moment to recognize Spencer's. She could not stop coming, her body remaining clenched and spasming for what seemed like hours, before she finally came down from her intense climax.

Spencer was panting against her chest, and she could feel his penis throbbing beneath her still gently thrusting pussy. Judging from the sticky wetness on her abdomen, he had climaxed, too. *Hard,* if the still-frantic jerking was any indication.

Her blurry eyes focused on the television, and she laughed, her voice sounding hoarse.

"What?" He sounded completely spent, as if just formulating the single-syllable word had taken all the energy he currently possessed.

"The credits are still running," she said with a chuckle, and he opened his eyes with effort to focus on the television. Where the end credits of the movie they had just watched were rolling to a close. The after-credits bonus scene popped up, and he chuckled.

"Just a little something," he managed to huff. "A little something to . . . take the edge off."

She laughed weakly and collapsed onto his chest, content to just stay there for now. A very happy, very sticky, and *very* replete mess.

They sat there for a while, Daff still straddling his lap. Her knees were drawn up on either side of his chest, and his arms were wrapped around her narrow back. They were both in dire need of another shower, but Spencer didn't want to move right now. He was so content to just hold her.

Her perfect little breasts were flattened against his chest, and he relished the memory of how responsive they'd been to his every touch.

She was getting heavier as her body went slack with sleep, and he grinned. She had to be exhausted. They'd both had only three hours of sleep the night before. He checked the clock above the mantelpiece. It was late. Time for bed.

He hated to disturb her, but there was no way he could pick her up without waking her, not from this position.

"Daff? Daff, darling," he whispered into her ear, and she groaned. "Come on, let's get you to bed."

"Just a little longer," she pleaded.

"We'll both be more comfortable in bed." He shifted her until she was lying sideways on his lap and picked her up in the same way as the night before. Her eyes opened, and she looked at him with a dreamy smile.

"You can't keep carrying me everywhere, I'll get spoiled."

"You deserve to be spoiled," he replied, and her smile widened.

"Silly man." She rested her head on his shoulder while he carried her upstairs. Once there he deposited her on his bed—he could get used to seeing her there—and unfastened the one remaining button on the pajama top. He went to the en suite, returned with a warm, damp cloth, and gently wiped the stickiness off her belly. She smiled gratefully, her eyelids heavy with sleep.

"Thank you," she said in a slurred voice.

"We could both do with a shower, but I'm too fucking tired to bother right now."

"Me too."

"Sorry about the mess."

"It's *your* mess," she said hazily. "I didn't mind it."

And wasn't that just fucking mind-blowing as hell? Not sure what to make of her words, he cleared his throat and climbed into bed next to her.

"We're not doing the sex bit of the no-strings sex thing properly, Spencer," she said, her voice thick with sleep when he tugged her into his arms, spooning her in front of him.

"Says who?" he asked, planting a kiss on her temple.

"We haven't even had sex yet."

"You in some kind of rush?" he asked, turning off the light. "You got a sex deadline or something? An intercourse record you need to break?"

She giggled and then yawned.

"It's just this is the second night without sex."

"You came, I came, everybody came. That's a win for Team . . . Spaff? Dense? Both of those are terrible, let's never do *that* again." His improvised couple names just made her laugh even harder, while he kept a perfectly straight face. "Now get some sleep, darling. Maybe we'll get the sex thing right tomorrow."

For the second day in a row, Daff found herself waking up—alone—in Spencer's bed. She crawled out of the warm bed and winced when she heard the thundering downpour outside. Fabulous. More late-winter rain.

For the first time—yesterday morning she'd been too freaked out and last night and the night before she'd been way too exhausted—she looked around Spencer's bedroom. It was lovely. That was the only word that came to mind. It was light and airy and just incredibly welcoming. Decorated in creams and browns, it suited Spencer's old-fashioned sensibilities to a T. The king-size sleigh bed appeared to be handcrafted, with intricate carvings in the head and footboards. The rest of the furniture had been made to match the bed, all carved from multigrained walnut. She ran her hand over the curved footboard of the bed, marveling at how warm and silky the wood felt beneath her hand. She looked out the window, to Mason's house just a few yards away. Spencer's house was very new, having just gone up in the last year, after Mason had designed it. The Carlisles now shared the town's overlook hill. The houses were far enough away to allow the brothers their privacy, but also easily within walking distance of each other. The lights were on, and she imagined Daisy was getting ready for work. Her sister's fantastically wealthy fiancé lazed about the house all day, but Mason would soon realize his dream of becoming an architect, of course. Taking her sister away for five years in the process.

Daff sighed at the thought, wishing Daisy could stay, even while knowing it wasn't that far and the couple would visit often. Still, it would be a huge adjustment, and Daff hated change.

The smell of freshly brewed coffee was starting to seep into the room, and Daff groaned as it coiled around her then sinuously wound its way up to her nose. Feeling like a character in a cartoon, she followed her nose and was halfway down the stairs by the time she comprehended that the pajama top was held together by just the one button between her breasts. The rest of her very naked body was on display. She dragged the two ends of the shirt together and used one hand to secure it.

Spencer, already fully dressed, was fussing around in the kitchen.

"You're having breakfast this morning," he said by way of greeting, not bothering to look around. His tone brooked no arguments.

"Fine. I'm starving."

"No eggs, right?" She shuddered at the thought.

"If you're making it, I suppose I'll have some, too." The words left her mouth before she could stop them, and she froze.

Shit.

This was exactly what she had feared, getting involved with Spencer, that she would start compromising again. Start pretending and putting up an act. Being who *he* wanted her to be and not who she really was. Even if she didn't truly know who she was.

His shoulders tensed, and he turned around to pin her with a stare.

"You don't *like* eggs, right?"

She opened her mouth to answer in the affirmative, but what came out was, "I mean, I don't *mind* them."

His dark, heavy brows slammed together, making him look formidable.

"Yeah, but do you like them?"

"What are you having?"

"What does that matter? What I'm having has no bearing on what you're having."

"I don't want to be any trouble." His eyes widened, and he folded his arms over his huge chest while he continued to look at her like she was some kind of lab experiment.

"I feel like we've had this conversation before. You seem to have difficulty answering yes or no questions, Daff," he pointed out gently. "Tell me, very quickly, without thinking about it, do you like eggs?"

"No." She paused, then shut her eyes miserably. "I don't know."

"Oh darling." He sighed. "Come over here and give me a good-morning kiss."

She padded over to him, her head downcast, feeling miserable and stupid and spineless. He fisted the lapels of the top and dragged her to him for a very thorough, *very* enjoyable kiss. He lifted his head and smiled sweetly at her.

"You like that?" he asked, his voice a sexy rumble, and she sighed contentedly, wanting to rub herself all over him like a cat.

"Yes." Another, longer kiss. But this time when he lifted his head, she went up on her toes and followed his mouth hungrily. He kept his lips *just* out of reach.

"And that?"

"Oh yes." Her eyes were fixed on that gorgeous mouth of his. She needed more.

"Now tell me," he began, bending his head to nuzzle her neck. "Do you like eggs?"

"No," she admitted.

"What about as an ingredient? Like in pancakes or waffles?" His lips were so close they brushed against hers when he spoke, and Daff was so desperate for his kiss that she was grateful for even that small touch and finding it hard to concentrate on his words.

"I like pancakes," she said softly. "Eggs are okay if I can't really *taste* them."

He lifted his head and smiled at her. Daff smiled back, feeling more lighthearted than she had in years.

"Grab a shower and get dressed while I fix your breakfast," he instructed, and, still dazed from the kisses, she nodded and walked to the bathroom where she had left her clothes last night.

She thought about the exchange while she luxuriated beneath the gloriously hot shower. A silly, seemingly inane conversation about eggs that meant *everything* to her. She was so used to pretending with men and lying to herself, and that trite little chat had been the most honest talk she'd ever had with a man. The recognition was both frightening and wonderful. She was terrified that he was rapidly becoming . . . essential to her. And while part of her wanted to keep him at arm's length in case he hurt her, another—braver—part of her was certain he could and would keep her heart safe.

CHAPTER EIGHT

Once again, Spencer didn't join her for lunch, and an earnest young man named Alton delivered the food. This time the note was sealed in an envelope and stapled to the bag like the day before. Daff couldn't wait for Alton to leave so that she could read it.

Daff,

I have another meeting today. Don't know how I'll get through it. I've been hard all day, thinking about how hot and wet and messy and very fucking sexy our encounter was last night. I suggest we keep trying this sex thing till we get it right. Because getting it wrong feels pretty damned amazing.

Enjoy your lunch. Eat every bite—you're going to need your strength.

XX

S

Daff sighed and held the note to her chest for a moment, a dreamy smile on her face as she considered his words.

Damn it, why did he have to be so irresistible? The man was very swiftly becoming the most all-consuming force in her life. She couldn't stop thinking about him—her hair smelled like his shampoo, her body like his soap. Her mouth and breasts were still tender from his kisses, and everything south of her waist tingled and buzzed and clenched at the memory of his solid heat grinding against her softness.

Daff had never really liked sex, but with Spencer, maybe the humiliation and wrongness she'd always felt wouldn't be so bad. She'd certainly felt no regret after their last two encounters. But that could very well be because they hadn't truly had sex. She dreaded the inevitability of that particular intimacy, but for once had hope that it would turn out okay. Spencer was different. He wasn't as arrogant or as brash and condescending as any of the guys she had formerly dated.

"What are you mooning about?" The voice was unexpected, and Daff swore and nearly dropped the note in fright. Daisy had managed to walk right up to the counter without Daff hearing the bell at the door or her sensing her presence.

"Shit, you scared me, Deedee!" Her youngest sister grimaced at the nickname—she had never liked it—before homing in on the brown paper bag on the counter in front of Daff.

"You were so busy mooning over your love letter that you didn't even hear me come in," Daisy said while opening up the bag to peek at the contents. "*Yum!* New boyfriend? Is he a chef? Because this looks awesome."

Daisy stuck her hand into the bag and withdrew several of the now-familiar plastic containers. Where did Spencer find the time to pack these lunches? Daff hadn't noticed him preparing anything that morning. Or the day before.

"Oh my, is this lamb tagine?" Daisy asked, practically drooling, after opening the biggest box. "It smells divine. I'm starving and there's enough here for two. Want to share with your poor, hungry baby sister?"

"I thought you were dieting for the wedding?"

"Please, you know that's just something people feel compelled to say before they get married. Anyway, breakfast was hours ago. I'm starving."

"Why are you here? Shouldn't you be at work?"

"Half day, remember? Mason's picking me up from here." Daisy rolled her eyes at Daff's blank stare before elaborating, "I told you last night, Mason and I are heading to Knysna today for a cake tasting. And we're choosing our invitations." She gave an excited little squeal, and Daff couldn't help but grin at her sister's enthusiasm. Daisy was enjoying the planning process so much more than Lia had. Every part of it for Daisy was fun and exciting, while for Lia it had been a chore and she'd quickly regressed into a moody, bitchy bridezilla. Now, of course, they all knew that Lia had been stressed because deep down inside, she had known she was making a mistake. Daisy—as she had once told Daff with joyful tears in her eyes—had never felt more positive about anything in her life.

"Wouldn't eating now spoil the whole cake-tasting experience?" Daff asked.

"It'll probably improve it. If I'm hungry, any old thing will taste awesome to me and I wouldn't be making an informed decision. So you can totally share this with me." Daisy looked uncertain for a moment before adding, "Unless your mystery man will be joining you for lunch?"

"There's no mystery man," Daff denied, blushing furiously, and Daisy's loud, obnoxious snort of laughter told her that her sister wasn't buying that denial at all.

"Is he a local guy?"

"There's no guy."

"So where did this come from?"

"Maybe I made it myself."

"Please, you're a terrible cook. There's no way you made this."

"I ordered takeout from MJ's."

"This has never been, and will never be, on MJ's menu. So spin another tale."

Before Daff could respond, her phone, which was resting on the counter between them, rang, and Daisy's eyes widened when she saw the image and name that popped up on the screen.

Daff grabbed up the phone guiltily and jabbed the screen before lifting it to her ear and turning her back on Daisy. How could the man have such awesome sexual timing and such terrible timing everywhere else?

"Hey," she greeted furtively, and then her eyes slid shut involuntarily when his rough, no-nonsense voice echoed the greeting.

"How's lunch?" he asked.

"Haven't had a chance to sample it yet," she said in a near whisper, painfully aware of Daisy's flapping ears.

"Make sure you eat it."

"I will," she promised him, an involuntary smile coming to her lips. With anybody else she would have taken exception to the bossiness, but on Spencer it was kind of endearing, maybe because she knew his gruffness stemmed from a genuine place of concern. And she just didn't have the heart or will to be indignant.

"How was your meeting?" she asked.

"Still going. I took a quick break to call you." He'd interrupted work for her? For *her*? That made her feel way too special.

"That's—that's . . . I honestly don't know what that is." He chuckled at the candid statement.

"It is what it is. See you later?"

"Definitely," she promised him huskily. He disconnected the call, and Daff turned to face her avidly staring youngest sister nervously.

"Sooooo." Daisy drew the word out irritatingly, her elbows resting on the counter and her chin cradled in the palms of her hands. "Who's the Dick and does he really look like a cartoon penis in a top hat?"

Daff was grateful that she had so impulsively changed Spencer's name and pic on her phone.

"He's no one you need to concern yourself with."

"Come on, Daff. A little hint. Where did you meet him?"

"It's just a passing thing, Deedee. I don't see the need to discuss the matter with you. If it were serious, it would be different. But it's not. It's just . . . sex." She blushed a little, wondering why she felt like a fraud and a liar. And a traitor. She and Spencer had been clear on the matter. No-strings sex and no need to discuss this thing with family—especially not with nosy siblings.

"Fine, keep your secrets," Daisy said with a put-out little huff, and Daff exhaled in frustration.

"Come on, Deedee, it's still very new. I don't feel comfortable talking about it. Especially when I know it's not going anywhere."

"You'll let me know if anything changes? If it becomes serious?"

"It won't."

"I don't know about that; you didn't see your face when I first walked in here. You looked smitten." Such a dated word. Quintessentially Daisy. It struck Daff that both her sisters were a lot more suited to Spencer than she was. Sweet and innocent and exactly the type of woman a decent, old-fashioned guy like Spencer needed in his life. Daff wasn't sweet and she wasn't innocent. She was much too cynical. Still, she wasn't looking to settle down with the guy, so it didn't matter if they weren't compatible in any way other than sexually.

"I'm not smitten. He has a great body, a big dick, and can work wonders with his tongue," she said, being deliberately crude, knowing her sister—who had been a freaking *virgin* before Mason—would be silenced by that. "That's all I need from him."

To her credit, Daisy, who did look a bit queasy after Daff's frank statement, didn't back down.

"He sends you lunch and writes you love notes—there has to be more to him than just a nice body and a . . . and a big p-penis."

"Don't forget the talented tongue," Daff goaded, and Daisy glared at her. Daff waved the note in front of her face before continuing, "And this isn't a love note. He's telling me exactly where and how he wants to nail me next. Want to have a read? It's *very* educational."

"Sometimes it seems like you've never really left adolescence behind," Daisy said tartly. "You behave like the same boy-crazy hormonal teenager you were in high school. What's wrong with settling down?"

"Ugh, this again! Lia was the same. Why is it that the moment you find someone you're ready to settle down with, you expect everybody else to follow suit? We don't all want the same things in life, Daisy."

"So what *do* you want?"

"I don't bloody know. But why should I? Why can't I just figure shit out as I go along?"

"Maybe because you're thirty-two and directionless?"

"Well, we can't all be perfect little Daisy McGregor with the degree and the career and the amazing man, can we? Some of us are born fuckups."

"You're not a fuckup." Daisy rarely used profanity, and after getting over her surprise at the words, Daff was touched by her sister's immediate and vehement defense. "You're not. None of us think that. And maybe when *you* stop believing you are, you'll be able to move forward with your life."

"And how do you propose I move forward?" Daff had meant the words to be sharp and sarcastic, but instead they sounded almost . . . yearning.

"Quit this job, for one," Daisy said softly. "You hate it. You've never said as much, but I know you do. You're bored, and your active and intelligent mind is wasted here."

Daff said nothing, not admitting or denying Daisy's words, but surprised that her sister knew how much she hated the job. She had never divulged that information to anyone. Other than Spencer.

"I have to finish my lunch," she said quietly, not acknowledging Daisy's words. "If you still want half of this, I'll stick it in a lunch box for you."

"That's okay. Mason will be here soon, and we can get lunch en route. But, before I forget, the other reason I popped in was to tell you that Mason and I are hosting a dinner for our wedding attendants—well, most of you. Sam Brand can't make it, for obvious reasons. Just a fun evening so that everybody can get to know one another."

"We already know one another."

"Well, none of you have met Chris yet," Daisy said, referring to Mason's chef friend.

"When?"

"Saturday night. I hope you can make it."

"It should be fine."

"Feel free to invite your well-hung sex toy."

"*Daisy!*" she gasped, shocked, and Daisy grinned unrepentantly. Lately her sweet youngest sister had developed the tendency to astonish her. And that was quite a feat. Daisy's phone bleeped, and her smile softened when she looked at the screen.

"Mason's here." Mason's sleek, sexy BMW i8 drove up just as she said the words, and she waved at him through the plate-glass windows. "See you on Saturday?"

"Yeah."

Daisy had her hand on the door when Daff sighed and called her name. Her sister paused and looked back. "Enjoy the day, Deedee. I'm sorry about earlier."

Daisy let go of the door and came back to enfold her in a tight hug.

"Don't be silly. I shouldn't have pushed the way I did."

Daff ruffled Daisy's crazy curls and gave her a nudge toward the door.

"Your carriage awaits, and your handsome prince is looking impatient to get you to himself." They both watched Mason, who had vacated the car and was waiting next to the passenger door. He was shuffling from foot to foot in an attempt to stay warm in the frigid weather.

"We'll chat later," Daisy promised her before hurrying out to greet Mason. Daff watched as a goofy smile lit up Mason's good-looking face and he wrapped his arms around Daisy's cuddly figure, burying his nose in her neck for a brief instant before planting a hot kiss on Daisy's lips.

Daff blushed at the steamy exchange—Daisy was her baby sister, after all—and was about to yell at them to get a room before they started making babies right on her doorstep when Mason lifted his head and smiled at Daisy. The naked adoration on the man's face was evident to all, and Daff sighed softly. If she were a different person, she'd be envious. And she told herself that the only reason her chest felt so tight at the sight of the couple's devotion to each other was because of the happiness she felt for her sister. Nothing else.

His staff was gone for the day, and Spencer was just finishing up a few last-minute e-mails before heading home when his phone beeped. He tensed before looking at it, sure that it would be Daff bailing on tonight. He breathed a small sigh of relief when he saw his brother's name on the screen. Swiping his thumb across the screen to unlock the phone, his brow immediately furrowed when he saw the message.

Daff has a man. Know about it? Maybe an eighth for the stag?

Shit.

He thought about it for a second before replying.

How the fuck would I know about it? I'm not her bestie. She
doesn't braid my hair and tell me all her secrets.

He watched as Mason typed and typed and typed and then finally
rang. His brother didn't have the patience to send long texts.

"Yes?" Spencer snapped.

"Come on, Spence," Mason said without any of the usual niceties.
"You've been spending time with her lately. Hasn't she dropped any
hints?"

"We discussed the wedding and the party plans."

"Aren't you even curious about it?" Mason sounded surprised. "I
figured you would be, since you've got the hots for her."

"Not anymore." Spencer contemplated the elephant stain on his
ceiling, hoping lightning wouldn't strike him down where he sat.

"Apparently she has him listed as the Dick on her phone. And she
actually has a picture of a cartoon penis in a top hat as his profile pic."

Spencer swallowed back a surprised laugh, wondering what fit of
pique had led her to do that.

"No shit?" He could barely keep the laughter out of his voice.

"And he sends her lunch."

"How do you know all of this? Has she mentioned this guy to
Daisy?" Maybe paving the way to reveal their relationship to her family?
Spencer felt an elated bubble of hope in his chest at the thought. That
would be pretty terrific.

"Daisy was there when lunch was delivered."

"Oh. And what did she tell Daisy about the guy?" Spencer asked,
refusing to let go of that hope.

"Said she just needed him for his dick."

The bubble burst into a million sad little pieces, and Spencer glared
at his ceiling. He shouldn't have asked.

"Then why do you think she'd even want him at the party?"

"I just figured it would pad the numbers. And according to Daisy, Daff does seem a bit starry-eyed over the guy, even if she denies it."

"Yeah?" The bubble reformed, and Spencer sat up straighter in his chair.

"I told Daisy she was probably reading too much into it, but she wants her sisters to be happy and she worries about Daff."

"It's probably better not to interfere—you know how Daff can be. And honestly, we're starting to sound like gossipy old women, so I'd rather not speculate any further," he said firmly, and Mason chuckled.

"True. I think spending so much time with Daisy and her sisters has had an adverse effect on me. I'm way too involved with the gossip and the other chick stuff."

"You need a guy's night out."

"Tomorrow night?" Mason asked hopefully, and Spencer briefly thought about Daff, wondered if she'd miss him if they didn't spend a night together, and then grimaced. She wouldn't care. He knew that. They didn't have that kind of relationship.

Yet.

"Tomorrow night sounds fine. Tell your fiancée not to expect you back till the early hours of Saturday morning."

"Awesome."

Spencer was heading for his 4x4 when he saw her again, the young girl from the other night. She appeared to be loitering by his car, and when she saw him she immediately hastened away in the opposite direction. Spencer swore and increased his speed in an attempt to catch up with her. She was wearing the same huge jeans with a different shirt and a jacket that looked too thin to keep her warm in this weather.

"Hold up," he called as he darted after her. She was moving so fast that she was practically jogging now. "Charlie. Hey. *Stop.*" He had a longer stride and caught up with her in just a few steps, taking hold of her thin elbow in the process.

"I didn't steal anything," the kid growled in frustration as she tried to yank her elbow from his grip.

"I didn't think you did," Spencer appeased, letting go of her and backing off a couple of steps to give her more space. She looked torn between running and staying, and he could see her trying to assess the situation and figure out if he was a threat. He backed up another step, keeping his hands in sight all the time. She relaxed marginally.

"I just wanted to talk."

"About?" she asked warily.

"Wanted to know if we'll see you on Monday?" Her smooth brow furrowed, and she shrugged.

"Dunno." Now that he knew she was a girl, he could see why she disguised herself. She was quite pretty and, because of her circumstances, obviously felt the need to downplay that.

"Where are you staying? In the township?"

"No."

"With your family."

"That's none of your business."

"What about school? Are you attending Riversend High?" With everything that had happened with Daff this week, Spencer had forgotten to ask Principal Kane about her. He felt guilty about that oversight.

She shrugged again in response to his question. Typical teenager.

"Okay, well, I work at the sports store. If you ever need anything, please let me know."

"Why?" she asked suspiciously. "What's in it for you?"

"I've been where you are. I just want to help."

"I don't need your help," she snapped. Way too much prickly pride for one so young.

"Okay," he said, holding his hands up in a placating manner. "That's cool. I still hope to see you on Monday. We're doing that self-defense class."

"I'll check my schedule," she said sarcastically, and Spencer bit back a grin.

"You do that," he said seriously, trying to keep his amusement hidden.

"Can I go now?" she asked with a belligerent tilt of her chin.

"You're free to do whatever you want."

"See ya around," she said casually, turning away with a dismissive wave. Spencer watched her walk away, again feeling a swell of concern for her. He didn't think she had a permanent place to stay, and it worried him. She was young, vulnerable, and small enough for a strong breeze to blow over. Not ideal. He hoped like hell she would show up on Monday—something about her brought out all his protective instincts, and he wanted to be sure that she was safe.

He turned back to his car and saw that he was standing in front of Daff's store. She had closed up for the day already, and he wondered if she was headed straight to his or if she was on her way home for a change of clothes. He hoped it was the latter. It was silly for her to go home to change every morning before work. But he knew that bringing an overnight bag would feel a little too much like a relationship to Daff. So he doubted the stubborn woman would bring so much as a toothbrush.

He didn't know why he expected her for dinner, but she was a no-show. He ate a silent, solitary meal and glared at the empty chair across from his at the dinner table. Of course she wouldn't come—that wasn't the way this worked. He had a quick shower, changing into a pair of those pajamas she seemed to find so irresistible, and did some accounts. He was still trying to figure out an economically viable way to fix the plumbing at the community center. He could pay for the entire thing, of course, but this should be a community effort. He wanted people to get off their privileged asses and chip in. So far it looked like nobody else—aside from Mason, Oom Herbert, and Principal Kane—really gave a damn about these kids, and Spencer wanted to find a way to change that. He wanted his program to become something the entire town could be proud of. Maybe if they had a dedicated youth center. A safe haven where both the well-off kids and the at-risk kids could hang out and socialize. If Spencer and Mason had had a wider circle of friends, perhaps their grim home lives would have felt slightly more tolerable.

An idea started to bloom, and he began to jot down notes. He'd have to get Mason to sign off on it, but he was sure his brother wouldn't mind. He was about to pick up his phone to call Mason when the soft knock on his front door sent all other considerations fleeing.

Daff.

He went rock hard in an instant.

Just like Pavlov's fucking dog, he thought with a wry glance down at his straining crotch. He took a moment to will the erection away—his cock mocked him for even trying—before opening the door. She stood there, a cheeky grin on her face, her head tilted to the side and her hands planted on her hips.

"Hey there, big guy. What are you up to?"

"Nothing much." He stepped aside to let her in. She sashayed past him, leaving him to follow in her deliciously scented wake. She always smelled amazing. He couldn't tell if it was body wash, perfume, or just her shampoo. Again he wondered if it was vanilla or honeysuckle, and he was about to ask her when she sent him a cheeky peek over her shoulder.

"It's hot in here. Won't you take my coat?"

"Of course." He reached out to help her. She shrugged out of her coat, revealing first one bare shoulder, then the other, then the slim, naked column of her back, her pert, perfectly peach-shaped ass, and finally those gorgeous, shapely legs. His mouth immediately went bone-dry as he drank in the sight of her nudity. Then she turned around, and he nearly passed out when even more blood drained from his brain straight down to his now throbbing cock.

"Christ almighty," he breathed—prayed?—not quite sure where to look. At her beautiful face, adorned with a slightly nervous smile? Or maybe those pretty, perfectly shaped little pink-and-cream breasts? What about that delightfully dipped-in waist or that flat tummy? No, maybe his eyes should feast on the immaculately manicured V at the junction of her thighs. Yeah, that's where his eyes wanted to be; that's where his hands, mouth, tongue, and cock wanted to be as well. He groaned softly.

"Fuck me," he muttered, and her smile widened.

"That's the idea."

"You're fucking gorgeous."

"And you're a little overdressed."

Jesus. So much for his vow not to let her dictate the pace of this relationship. He'd had no intention of making love to her tonight, but how the hell was he supposed to resist this?

"Come on, Spencer, show me some skin," she pouted, tugging at his pajama collar, slipping her fingers between the gaps in the front to get at the skin beneath. He fought for control as he unfastened the top button and stepped back to tug it over his head and off. She gave a delighted little purr that turned into an undignified squawk when he unceremoniously pulled his top over her head and yanked her arms into the armholes before dragging it down over her hips and thighs.

He heaved a sigh of relief when she was somewhat covered and leaned in to give her shocked mouth a hot, brief kiss. She folded her arms over her chest and met his eyes defiantly. He was alarmed to see a touch of hurt beneath the bluster.

"Why'd you do that?"

"For my sanity," he said, smoothing a thumb over one of her cheeks. "You eat?"

"I'm not here to eat. Look, Spencer, this teenage petting business is not what I signed up for. I mean, it was cute at first, but it's beginning to get old. It's time we get down to business, don't you think?"

"That's a shame, really. Since I didn't get to pet you when we were teenagers, and I was just making up for lost time and lost opportunities."

He could see her fighting back a smile at those words, but she tamped down her amusement.

"Well, I think you've more than made up for lost time. So why not just get down to the nitty-gritty?"

"Hmm." His thumb moved from her cheek to the sensitive spot just below her earlobe. She shuddered, forgetting what else she'd been about to say, and leaned into his touch. He stroked his thumb to the hollow of her throat and lingered there while he dipped his head for another thirsty kiss. She opened her mouth and welcomed his tongue with an appreciative moan. Her arms wrapped around his neck and she strained up onto her toes, trying to get as close to him as she could, trying to dictate the pace again . . . He drew back, ignoring her frustrated sob.

"How was your day, darling?" he asked, and she glared at him.

"Are you kidding me with this?"

"With what?"

"This! Whatever the hell *this* is! What are you doing? This is not how it's supposed to go."

"How what's supposed to go?" he asked patiently.

"You're maddening," she seethed. "Our no-strings sex thing."

"I'm not too familiar with the rules of such a thing. I'm just playing it by ear."

"It's not that complicated! We have sex. That's it. You're being deliberately—*humph.*" He shut her up with another kiss. A long, deep, intense kiss.

Before she quite knew what was happening, they were on the sofa. She was flat on her back and he was nestled between her thighs, his hard cock grinding up against her mound.

"You feel so hot and hard, Spencer. I want to feel you naked against me. Please." Daff had never begged a man for sex. Had never really wanted to. She'd been happy to let her previous partners control the pace, the mood, the setting . . . the genre. That probably wasn't the right word, but that's what came to mind: the type of sex. Rough, gentle, oral (for men only, of course, selfish bastards), missionary . . . rough. Mostly rough. Scary rough. Spencer didn't seem like the type of guy who would take it to that place, but neither had her last partner. So Daff wanted to be the one to do the picking and choosing this time. She wanted to dictate the pace. But Spencer wasn't playing ball. He had his own set of rules, and it was confusing and frightening.

Did he want what the others had wanted? What they had assumed she would want and had then taken without real consent? If she offered it to him, that would still be a way of maintaining control, wouldn't it? She was mulling it over, only half-aware of him unbuttoning her top and tracing kisses down her chest. It was only when his hot, hungry mouth latched on to her breast that she was brought back to the very pleasurable present.

She gasped and buried her fingers in his hair, loving the more forceful tugs on her nipple. In their previous encounters, he had teased and tormented with nibbles and barely there little suctioning kisses. This was more like it. Deciding to go for it, to be brave and take matters into her own hands, she grabbed one of his large, busy hands and dragged it up over her breast and then her chest.

He stopped playing with her breasts and lifted his head to watch her. She smiled, brought his hand up, and sucked the tip of each finger into her mouth, loving the way his beautiful eyes darkened with each bit of suctioning. Then she did it, the bit she dreaded the most. The bit that always seemed to turn guys all the way on. She brought that big, strong hand to her throat and left it there. He frowned slightly, wrapping his palm over her slender throat but not doing more than that.

"It's okay," she promised him. Sounding braver and steadier than she felt. "You can squeeze."

She hated this part, hated how suffocating it was, how terrifying it felt to have her air cut off. Hated how much they seemed to love the discomfort it caused her. Spencer did nothing, his palm hot against her skin. He was staring intently down at her.

"Do it," she urged, hating the tension, dreading the inevitability.

"Do you really want me to?" he finally asked, sounding almost bored. His thumb was idly stroking her wildly pulsing carotid artery, and she swallowed. His question baffled her, and she had no idea what the right answer was.

After a moment's thought, she nodded, and his eyes narrowed before he smiled. The parting of his lips was slow and beautiful. He lowered his head and touched those lips to hers. The kiss was soft and delicate, his tongue coming out to trace the seam of her mouth. But when she parted her lips to allow him access, he retreated, lifting his head to look at her again. His hand was still at her throat, but there was no pressure yet, just that soft up-and-down sweep of his thumb. This was so much worse than usual. To follow up this tenderness with pain and humiliation would be unbearable.

"Just do it," she urged tightly, and he looked at her for a moment longer before his lips tilted at the corner and he shook his head.

"I don't think so."

What?

He stroked his hand away from her throat down the front of her body, sweeping between the shallow valley of her breasts before bringing it to the cleft of her pussy.

"There are so many other, more satisfying, things I could be doing with this hand." His voice was a rumble, and she groaned when his index finger found the swollen bundle of nerves at her center and proceeded to strum it delicately. She writhed in pleasure, completely overwhelmed.

"That's it, darling," he crooned. "Isn't this much better?"

He went back to her nipples, and the brief awkwardness of the moment was swept away in a tide of overwhelming lust. She arched her back, pushing her chest closer to his mouth, while she lifted her hips to encourage that softly stroking finger. Wanting him to put more effort into it. He lifted his head to grin at her, and then he was on the move again and Daff smiled as she watched his head travel down.

"Oh yes," she sighed when his lips closed over her clit, replacing his finger. Yes, this was definitely her new favorite thing. "Feel free to just set up camp down there," she invited him, and he chuckled. That huff of breath felt amazing on the straining, swollen knot that was the very center of her universe right now, and she shivered deliciously. Without lifting his busy mouth, he reached for one of her hands and pushed it toward her chest.

"Play with your nipples," he growled before going back to work.

Oh, with pleasure. She did as she was told, stroking, thumbing, and tugging at her hard nipples with both hands. He used his thumbs to part her pouting flesh, giving him unimpeded access to every sensitive bit of real estate down there, and he took full advantage, using his tongue to lave its way up the groove on one side of her clit and down the other. It traveled even farther down until she—*shockingly*—felt him probing for entry.

"Ohhhh my *God!*" she heard herself mewling. How long was his tongue? And how endlessly talented. It speared in and out of her clutching channel while his thumb took up the slack at her swollen clitoris. She felt so naïve in thinking—after the other night—that she now knew everything there was to know about cunnilingus, because she clearly knew absolutely nothing.

This was . . . it was . . . *transcendent.*

"Don't stop. Don't stop. Never stop," she chanted, moving her hips in time with every thrust of his tongue. Her hands fell away from her breasts to yank a couple of fistfuls of his hair; she knew it had to be painful, but she was barely aware of how rough she was being. Focused only on what he was doing with his mouth. Her thighs clamped over his ears, but that barely seemed to faze him, as he never lost pace. She was close. Very, *very* close. She felt herself melting all over his tongue as he took her higher and higher and higher.

Falling was inevitable. But she didn't care . . . she needed to fall. She wanted to fall. It was her destiny to fall. *Hard.*

His tongue plunged into her one last time before he dragged it all the way out and latched onto her clit and suckled her. It was the push she needed, and she went tumbling. End over end. Falling from such a great height was dizzying and disorienting and truly amazing. And totally terrifying.

She was crying again. It was getting embarrassing, this crying after non-sex. What was going to happen when they actually did the deed? Was she going to drown the man in her tears? He didn't seem to mind. He was holding her again, somehow wedging her between the back of the sofa and his massive bulk. Good thing he had man-size furniture, or the thing would never have accommodated them both. It was an inane thought, but it kept her from facing what a wreck this man was making of her.

"Better?" he asked a few long moments later, after her tears had finally dried up. She nodded and buried her face in his hard chest. She wriggled closer and felt his hard penis throbbing against her stomach. So big and hot, it was hard to ignore.

"That can't be very comfortable," she observed, and he shrugged.

"I'm a big boy, I can handle it."

"Yes, you are," she agreed pertly, stroking her hand over that impressive length so there'd be no misunderstanding her meaning. "But *I'd* rather be the one to handle it for you."

He groaned when she slipped her hand under his waistband and wrapped her fingers around that hard, thick length.

"You don't have to." He didn't sound very convincing, and she chuckled.

"I know, and that's why I want to." She felt his body ripple at the words and knew that she had scored a direct hit with that one.

"Not right now." His voice sounded beyond strained, and she rolled her eyes.

"I don't know why you're denying yourself. I'm right here. Ready, willing, and able to give you the best damned head you've ever had in your life."

Spencer couldn't think straight while she had her hand wrapped around him like this. But something felt . . . *off*, somehow. Like, what the fuck was up with that weird moment earlier? Why would she invite him to fucking strangle her? She had looked terrified and resigned at the same time, so *she* wasn't into it. So why the hell would she assume that Spencer was into erotic asphyxiation, for fuck's sake? It was bizarre. He would love a few minutes in a dark alley with whoever the hell had fucked her up so badly.

Spencer definitely enjoyed Daff more when she was wild with desire and couldn't control her responses to him. The second she regained her senses, everything she said or did felt practiced. Like she was going through some kind of sexual playbook. He liked that she was experienced, and he definitely enjoyed confidence in a woman. But this didn't feel confident, it felt rehearsed, and while his cock was more than ready to go, his heart and mind were throwing up huge red flags. He wanted

Daff, the *real* Daff, not whoever this woman with the plastered-on smile was. If he consented to this, it would feel like he was using her, and he wanted her to enjoy everything they did together. He didn't want her to feel uncomfortable or degraded.

"I have a different idea," he said, his voice hoarse with strain. "Why don't we take a shower and watch a movie?"

She gaped at him, her mouth literally falling open as she gawked at him in utter disbelief.

"I don't understand," she said, her brow furrowing. "Don't you want me?"

Oh hell.

"You know the answer to that," he said gently, pointedly thrusting in her grip and then cursing out loud as the sensation nearly undid him.

"Then why?"

He sighed and sat up, grateful when her fingers loosened around his penis. She withdrew her hand completely and sat up as well, folding her hands in her lap and staring up at him beneath that tumble of gorgeous brown hair. She looked confused and hurt and verging on pissed off. And he couldn't blame her for any of those things.

"Because," he answered her baffled question, "I don't think you actually enjoy giving the 'best damned head.' And I know that if I ask you straight up if you like it, you're going to give me another bullshit evasive answer."

"I don't have to enjoy it," she snapped. "As long as you do. Isn't that the point of a blow job?"

"Darling, do you think I didn't relish every fucking second of what I did to you earlier? The taste of you, the way you melted in my mouth, your sounds, your hands in my hair . . . biggest turn-on of my life. I could have feasted all night. Can you honestly say you would have enjoyed reciprocating as much?"

"How should I know? You didn't give me the opportunity."

Fair point.

"Daff, if you go down on me, I don't want it to be because you think you have to. I don't want you to ever feel forced to do anything. Everything we do here is meant to be for our mutual pleasure."

"And you're saying a blow job wouldn't have given you pleasure?"

"That's not what I mean, and you know it. And while we're on the subject, what the fuck was that other shit about?"

She flushed and evaded his eyes. "I thought we could try something interesting and different."

"Fuck that, you were hating every second of it. You did it because you thought you *had* to, didn't you? Because you thought I'd like it. You thought I'd enjoy cutting off your air and making you fight for breath. News flash, darling, I can make you gasp without deliberately restricting your fucking oxygen supply. And the thought of hurting you in any way makes me want to vomit. What fucking asshole made you believe that men want to hurt you?"

That seemed to hit the mark, and her lips trembled in her pale face. Her eyes skidded around the room, never once meeting his.

"I don't think we should do this anymore."

"Why? Because I'm hitting a nerve?"

"This experiment is over, Spencer. This is more stress than it's worth. It was supposed to be a little bit of fun for both of us, and you turned it into more than it is. I should have known better than to get involved with you." She got up and glared at him. "Why couldn't you just lie back and enjoy what I was offering, like a normal guy? Why did you have to make it weird?"

"I'm not the one who made it weird! Who gave you all these hang-ups?"

"I'm not the one with the hang-ups. What kind of red-blooded male won't take what I've been offering?"

"This kind." He jerked a thumb to his chest and glared at her, allowing her the height advantage because he didn't want her to feel intimidated when she already looked like she was close to her breaking point. "You were never completely on board, Daff. Admit it. And to be honest, neither was I. I don't want a no-strings sex thing. I want strings, lots of strings. I want a chance to get to know you, to spend time with you, to be a couple."

Spencer wasn't one for talking much, but sometimes shit needed saying and this was one of those moments. He could be an eloquent fucker when the mood struck, and right now, it was important to let her know exactly what he wanted.

"I don't want that. Not all women want that. If that's what you're looking for, then I'm not the woman for you. I don't do the normal couple thing, Spencer. I told you. It doesn't suit me."

He ran a tired hand through his hair and watched her helplessly. There was really no way forward from this point. He wanted more than he could have, more than she could or would give. So it was time to cut his losses and salvage the situation as best he could.

"We're going to have to figure out where we go from here, Daff. There's the wedding to consider."

She crossed her arms over her chest, hiking the pajama top dangerously high.

"We could just go back to the way things were before all of this madness."

"No. We should be friends." He couldn't believe he was sitting here saying this, while his cock was still at half-mast and he was willing that top to go just a couple of inches higher so that he could enjoy the sight of her nudity one last time. Friendship with this woman was literally the last thing he wanted, but if it was all he could have, then he would take it.

She looked hesitant.

"You can't just demand friendship."

"Why not? We get along. Have shit in common. We can be friends."

"I can't think straight. Can we talk about this tomorrow? I'm knackered and have to get home."

"Stay here." She stared at him like he'd gone off his head, which was fair, since it wasn't the most practical suggestion in light of the situation.

"No."

"It's late."

"Yes, so I should really get going." He acknowledged her words with a nod and a sigh. She walked to the front door, picking up her coat—which lay forgotten on the floor—along the way. She shrugged into it before he could assist her and patted her pockets in search of her keys.

"Do you have your phone?"

"Yes."

"Good. I don't like the thought of you driving alone at this time of night."

"I live five minutes away. Stop being such an old woman. I'll text you when I get home."

"Once you're safely indoors with your door closed and bolted behind you," he stipulated.

"Sure. Whatever." He couldn't resist it—he tugged the trapped hair at her collar free and she glared at him.

"Well, you never seem to get around to it," he explained, hiking a shoulder.

"Maybe I like it there. Maybe it's a neck warmer."

So touchy.

"Sorry, darling. It won't happen again."

"Yeah, that can't happen again, either."

"What?" he asked, baffled.

"The *darling* thing. Don't call me that."

"You said you like it," he reminded.

"It's not appropriate. What if you slip up and call me that in front of the others?"

This whole friend thing—if she even consented to it—was going to be challenging.

"We'll talk again soon," she promised him, then opened the door and left before he could say anything more.

Spencer sighed and resigned himself to a night with just his palm and a bottle of scotch for company. Same shit, different day, really.

Tomorrow would sort itself out.

CHAPTER NINE

Daff didn't know how she felt. Part of her was relieved that it was over, another was humiliated that he had called her out on all her bullshit, and another still was saddened that it had ended before it began. They hadn't really done much more than some heavy petting, but the orgasms he had given her were streets ahead of anything she'd ever experienced before. Truculent, taciturn, socially inept Spencer Carlisle knew his stuff in the bedroom. Who knew?

Well . . . Daff now knew. And she truly wished she didn't. How the hell was she supposed to act casual with him when they were around family and friends? And worse, he knew *other* things about her. He'd been way too on the mark with some of the stuff he'd said. She hadn't been fully sold on the idea of no-strings sex with him. She didn't like going down on a guy—at least, she hadn't with her two previous lovers. She felt like a cold fish in bed because their games had turned her off and that had felt like her failure. Apparently BDSM wasn't her thing, but they'd expected it to be. *Both* of them. Why?

Did she give off some kind of kinky vibe? Her very first sexual partner had tied her up, gagged her, and spanked her the first time they'd had sex. Not quite the initiation she'd expected. It had been frightening and intimidating, and he hadn't even asked her if she was okay with it.

Just assumed she would be. And then he'd been all kinds of smug about his performance afterward.

Thinking the fault was with her, Daff had said nothing, merely pretended to enjoy it. She'd gotten really good at faking orgasms. Jake's bag of tricks had expanded to include nipple clamps and blindfolds, as well as other handy restraints and harnesses that had made her feel claustrophobic and nauseous every time they had sex. The relationship had lasted for three years and had only ended when he got bored with her.

She shook her head. This trip down nightmare lane wasn't exactly fun, and she preferred never to think about Jake Kincaid ever again. Shar Bridges, a former high school friend, had introduced Daff to Jake.

Shar had introduced Lia to her douchebag ex-fiancé, Clayton Edmonton III, as well, and had promised that he was the perfect guy for Lia. Of course, with Shar being a total bitch and hindsight being twenty-twenty, none of them should ever have trusted her with their love lives. Shar had terrible taste in men and a mean streak a mile wide. And she had been a total rhymes-with-punt to Daisy for years. Why the hell the McGregor sisters hadn't booted that bitch and her entourage of mean girls years ago, Daff would never know.

Daff somehow managed to get home without paying real attention to her surroundings; luckily the one main road in town was empty this time of night. She let herself into the house and sent Spencer a quick message that simply stated: home.

Spencer was right—she had way too many hang-ups, and it had been a stupid idea to get involved with him in the first place. She couldn't stand sex, which was why her offer to Spencer had baffled her. A spur-of-the-moment impulse that had come from seemingly nowhere. And now look at her—the very first time she'd ever picked up the reins, the horse had thrown her and bolted. Naturally.

But the truly messed-up thing was that despite the abject failure, she had learned something new about herself. After the powerful orgasms she'd experienced with Spencer, she now doubted that she'd ever climaxed with a man before. She had never felt anything nearly as intense.

She now understood why Daisy looked like the cat that got the cream whenever she was around Mason. To think she'd *pitied* Daisy after learning her sister had been a virgin at twenty-seven. Now Daff envied her somewhat. Daisy had scored the jackpot with her first (and only) lover, while Daff would have been better off without hers.

She checked her phone to see if Spencer had responded to her text. The message had been read, but he hadn't responded. Not even with a dumb emoji. Her heart sank, and she realized that she was going to miss him. Maybe keeping him as a friend was worth considering.

She wasn't sure. It wasn't a decision she was ready to make, not when everything below her waist was still clenching after his unselfish pleasuring earlier.

She scrubbed a hand over her face and tiredly made her way to the bathroom for a shower. She fell into bed after that but couldn't get her roiling thoughts under control. So many bad decisions had led to this moment in her life, and she was buried beneath years of regret. So much regret.

She tossed and turned, going over every mistake, every stupid decision, every wrong turn, but she still couldn't pinpoint exactly where everything had gone so very wrong.

She knew she had to change something, had to better herself and her life. Find clarity and a way to rid herself of these pervasive feelings of inadequacy and hollowness. She wished that she could just wake up tomorrow and find herself living the perfect life. But she wasn't entirely sure what constituted a perfect life, and she had no idea what would make her happy. It was a grim and disturbing awareness.

"Hi, there." Lia waltzed into the boutique just before twelve the following afternoon, and Daff glared into her middle sister's cheerfully smiling face.

"Daisy sent you, didn't she?" Lia's smile wavered slightly before she righted it and blasted Daff with an even brighter one.

"I don't know what you're talking about. I thought I'd join you for lunch." She lifted her little strawberry-shaped lunch box and glass bottle of orange juice as proof. Daisy had chosen the worst possible spy; Lia didn't have a duplicitous bone in her body. But since Lia had given up her job as a minder at the local day care center last year, she had a flexible schedule until she found something new. So Lia was really Daisy's only choice in whatever recon mission she'd cooked up to figure out who Daff's mystery man was.

"Lia."

"Okay, fine. She told me to find out whatever I could about the"—she blushed and cleared her throat delicately—"the Dick. Why would you call him that? Why not Mr. McSexy or Mr. Big or something? Why refer to his anatomy?"

"Firstly, those references are so dated I'm embarrassed—and cringing on the inside—for you, and secondly, it wasn't so much in reference to his anatomy as to his personality." Not that she thought of him in that way anymore.

"Why would you date a guy you think is a . . . a . . . you know?"

"We're not dating." Daff shrugged. "And really, you're wasting your time. He won't bring or send lunch today. It's over between us." She forced down the pang of regret at the words.

"Oh. I'm sorry."

"Don't be. It was nothing." Daff averted her eyes, not wanting her sister to see the lie in them.

"Well, I'm here now. I might as well stay for lunch. What are you having?"

"I brought some fruit and a packet of chips." She was really going to miss Spencer's lunches.

"Ugh, that's not a proper lunch. You can share my—" The bell above the door interrupted her words, and they both looked up to see young Alton from SCSS walk in, carefully carrying a large-ish brown paper bag.

"Afternoon, miss. The boss asked me to deliver this to you." Shocked that Spencer would still do this, despite everything that had happened last night, Daff accepted the bag. "Careful, miss, there's soup in one of the containers."

"Okay. Thanks, Alton."

"My pleasure, miss." He grinned at her and retreated with a jaunty wave.

Daff carefully placed the bag on the counter and tore the note from the folded top. Ignoring Lia's shocked expression, she turned her back and read the short note through a haze of tears.

I'm sorry. I hope we can still be friends.

S

PS: And even if we can't be, don't expect me to stop sending your lunch.

Oh God. Why was he apologizing? The man had been nothing but amazing since this all began. He was right, she was always apologizing to him, but only because he deserved those apologies.

She blinked away the tears determinedly and cleared her throat before facing Lia again. Her sister still wore the same gobsmacked expression on her face, and Daff rolled her eyes.

"Okay, so it's Spencer. Whatever. It's over. Moving along swiftly, if you tell Daisy, I'm going to have to cut a bitch! And that bitch be *you*."

"I'm not going to be the one to tell Daisy, are you crazy? She'll freak out."

"She wouldn't," Daff scoffed before thinking about it for a moment. "*Would* she?"

"Daffy—"

"Don't call me that."

"Daffy," Lia continued stubbornly as Daff scowled, "you know she'll worry about the wedding and family dynamics and gatherings. She'd worry that it'd be awkward and that you or Spencer would always be making excuses not to be in each other's company. Baby Delphinium's christening . . . oh, here's Auntie Daff, but Uncle Spencer couldn't make it. Baby Dianella's first birthday, Uncle Spencer is the life of the party while Auntie Daff sits in a corner and sulks before leaving early. Daisy's thirtieth birthday bash, Daff comes for the first half of the party and Spencer for the second." Daff gasped indignantly.

"*Lies!* I'm the party closer, not Spence. He'd be home in his jammies"— his beautiful, beautiful jammies—"before nine. And also, Jesus, woman . . . you've just about plotted out Daisy and Mason's entire life together in under a minute. That's a little creepy. You need a proper hobby. And Spencer and I are adults, we'll make it work."

"Daff, last week you called the man bland and insipid and compared him to a mushroom." *Why* could no one let the mushroom thing go? "And that's just one sample from years of sniping and bitching at Spencer. You've never made it work."

"Well, now we have to, because of Daisy and Mason."

"Anyway, my point is, there's no way I'm telling her about this. It'll be a shoot-the-messenger type of scenario. I'd rather not be around when she finds out."

"She won't find out. I told you, it's over." Lia tilted her head curiously before pointedly looking at the paper bag on the counter between them.

"This is just Spencer being Spencer. He's concerned that I don't eat properly—"

"He's right," Lia inserted wryly.

"—and so, since we've decided to be friends, he's taken it upon himself to ensure I get at least one decent meal a day."

"That's so sweet," Lia gushed, and Daff sighed.

It really was.

"It's weird and I told him to stop. But he can be stubborn."

"Really? I never imagined that. He always seems so easygoing."

It was a little sad how few people *really* knew Spencer.

"So what exactly was going between you two and for how long? Was it already ongoing when you said those things last week? Was that like a cover-up to deflect attention from your relationship?"

If only. Daff regretted a lot of things in her life, but saying those things about Spencer within earshot of the man—no matter how unintentional—ranked up there among her top ten biggest fuckups.

"It began soon after I apologized to him. He started the lunch thing on Monday, we started the sex thing on Tuesday, and it ended last night. And here we are. TGIF, right?" She removed the carton of soup from the bag, along with thick slices of what looked like home-baked bread, a salad, and a bottle of juice.

"Three nights? That's it? What happened?"

"Nothing. It was an ill-advised endeavor from the start."

"So you . . . you *slept* with him?"

"Oh, I slept with him, all right," Daff recalled with a soft smile. "But I didn't have sex with him, if that's what you're wondering."

"I don't understand," Lia admitted, looking completely baffled.

"We did other stuff. Fooled around. Touched each other's naughty bits until it felt good." Lia went bright red, and Daff rolled her eyes. "Stop being such a prude. I wasn't half as crude as I could have been."

"Oh, believe me, I know. And I thank you for that. It's just that image is now seared into my brain forever."

"You *asked*," Daff said, and Lia winced.

"I know. So why did it end so quickly? And why didn't you, y'know, *do it*?"

"It was a mistake. A bad idea from the get-go. Spencer's a nice guy. A good guy. He deserves more than a fuckup like me."

"*Daff,*" Lia protested softly. "That's nonsense. Spencer—*any* guy—would be lucky to have you."

"No, they wouldn't. I'm so messed up, Lia," Daff admitted miserably, all semblance of wisecracking gone. "I'm trying to fix what's broken, but I can't be involved with anyone while I do that. It wouldn't be fair."

"Why? What do you think is wrong?"

Daff swiped at an errant tear, feeling foolish and childish but grateful for her sister's gentle, nonjudgmental regard and tone of voice. She also liked that Lia didn't argue with her about something actually being wrong. "Everything," she said softly. "This job, for one thing. I hate it."

"I know."

"It feels like everybody knew it before I did," Daff joked on a sob, and Lia reached over to squeeze her hand.

"We love you, we can tell when you're unhappy. And you haven't been truly happy in a long time. I think that's why Daisy wanted to know who you were seeing. She said you looked *happy* when you were reading his note yesterday."

Daff shrugged and ran the tip of her index finger around and around the rim of the plastic container holding the untouched soup.

"But I have news." Daff sniffed, forcing cheer into her voice and ignoring Lia's words. "In my first step toward a better life and a better me, I tendered my resignation this morning."

Lia inhaled sharply, and a huge smile instantly lit up her face.

"Oh my *word,*" she gushed. "That's wonderful news, Daff."

"I just have to work my two months' notice and this place is history."

"I'm so happy for you, Sissy," she said, coming around the counter to give Daff a hug. Her sisters had always called her Sissy when they were children. A nickname to acknowledge her big sister status. They rarely called her that now that they were adults, and the fact that Lia chose to use it in this moment brought a huge, emotional lump to Daff's throat. "What did Alison say?"

Daff giggled wetly as she recalled her boss's words.

"She said 'it's about damned time,' and she also said she always knew I'd come to my senses eventually and she'd lose the best manager she's ever had."

"Darned straight you are."

"Probably because she paid me peanuts and I was easy on her bank balance . . . *Ow!*" The last as Lia slapped her upside her head.

"Stop being so down on yourself. Yes, this place is quiet and boring during winter, but you said that it has always been her best-performing boutique in summer, and I believe that's largely because of you."

"Thanks." She grinned.

"So now what?"

"God, I don't know."

"At least I won't be the only one who'll have to listen to Daddy's lectures about the values of being a good, hard worker. Of staying the course. Steering ships from rocks. Navigating rough waters . . . I don't know, there seem to be a lot of seafaring references, I never understand half of it. Pro tip: just nod and keep saying, 'Yes, Daddy.' Never interrupt him with a 'but Daddy' or anything resembling an excuse. Just pretend to listen. He likes that."

"Sound advice." Daff laughed, feeling a lot lighter for having confided in her sister.

"So you and Spencer are friends now? Never thought I'd see the day," Lia mused as she opened her sickeningly cute lunch box to reveal the healthy-looking, bento-styled meal. Daff would never have the patience, but Lia lived for crap like that. One day, when she had kids, they'd probably find animal-shaped sandwiches and other cutesy surprises in their lunch boxes every day. Daff wasn't likely to ever have children, which was a good thing, because they'd probably open their lunch boxes to find nothing but lunch money. Or possibly two-minute noodles, depending on how motherly Daff was feeling.

"I mean, we're not bosom buddies or anything. We're just making an effort not to be shitty to each other. Although, to be fair, he was never really shitty to me. I suppose I'll be the one making all the effort, because Spencer's a good guy."

"I never thought I'd see the day . . . why were you always so mean to him?"

"It started in high school. I allowed Shar and her Sharminions to dictate my behavior. It was embarrassing that a kid like Spencer, with his worn clothing, his broken shoes, and his clumsiness—remember how clumsy he was during that gawky adolescent phase before he got all athletic and buff?—anyway, it was embarrassing that he had a crush on me. I was terrified that if I was nice to him, they'd think I liked him back or something." Daff was ashamed of her behavior now that she recalled it. She had made fun of him, of his clothes, his hair, the slight stammer he always seemed to have around her. And then—somewhere between fourteen and sixteen—Spencer had outgrown the nervous stutter and the clumsiness and had cultivated an aloof, bad-boy persona that Daff had secretly found intriguing. He'd still attempted to flirt with her, and when she was fourteen, he'd started writing furtive poems and letters that she'd mockingly shared with all her girlfriends.

The poems had stopped after his seventeenth birthday. The flirting, too. He'd been busy with the rugby, working hard, and then, a year later, he'd left for college. He was a bit of a sensation after his triumphant return to Riversend five years later, capitalizing on his short-lived but relatively successful rugby career by opening the most successful business in town and surroundings. But he hadn't socialized much, just dated here and there. So it had been a surprise to hear that he was dating Tanya Krige.

And then, one night, a year ago—shortly after his breakup with Tanya—he'd tried to flirt with her again. And because Shar and the rest had been around, Daff had toyed with him and then rebuffed him again. Old habits.

But she'd been interested and flattered. Then, later, she'd been *furious* and indignant when she discovered that he had asked his brother to distract—and "pretend" to like—Daisy while Spencer attempted to flirt with Daff.

She'd borne an irrational grudge against him since then, even after Daisy and Mason had fallen in love, though Daisy bore Spencer no ill will whatsoever. Daff had taken it very personally.

"Anyway, I'm not proud of the way I treated him in school. Their circumstances were difficult beyond our imagining." Daff shook her head in self-disgust. "I was a bitch and a bully."

"We allowed Shar and Zinzi"—Shar's best friend—"to influence our lives for way too long. You weren't the only one guilty of that, Daff."

"Daisy never bought into their bullshit, and she was relentlessly bullied by them because of it. And you were never a total bitch, Lia. You never lost sight of who you were. In this last year, since we stopped hanging out with them, I've come to see that everything I thought I'd achieved was just . . . I don't know . . . an illusion. I was so focused on shallow shit like being with the right guy, wearing the right clothes, saying the right things . . . that I don't know who I am without all that crap."

"I know who you are," Lia said, delicately nibbling away at a strawberry. "You're my sissy. You've always had my and Daisy's backs. You're fiercely protective and loyal. You're freaking smart, never mind what the aunties say. You're ambitious, but you've never found a focus for that ambition. Once you do know what you want, you're going to be unstoppable."

"There are . . . *other* things, too," Daff admitted uncomfortably, remembering the moment she'd invited Spencer to squeeze her neck. "But I can't discuss them with you. Yet. Maybe never. I don't know. It's something I have to work out for myself, but I think Shar may have had a hand in that, too."

"Gosh, she's like a supervillain. I mean, if not for her I'd never have met Clayton, either," Lia said, wrinkling her nose, thankfully not pressing Daff on the secrets she wasn't ready to divulge.

"Well, at least we don't have to deal with her any longer," Daff said. "We just have to figure out how to cope with the fallout of having her noxious presence in our lives for so long. And really, we can't blame her for everything. We have to own up to our own mistakes. We may have allowed her to manipulate us, but every decision we made was our own."

"True." Lia was quiet for a moment while contemplating her half-eaten strawberry. "So are you going to eat that tasty-looking soup, or are you just going to sit here moping all day?"

"Shut up." Daff grinned and finally popped the lid off the container.

"Knock, knock." Spencer looked up from his income and expenditure spreadsheet, close to the end of the day, to meet Daff's smiling eyes. She stood framed in the doorway of his tiny office, looking fantastic in a pair of faded skinny jeans, combined with a ruffle-fronted blouse, a slouchy cardigan, and scuffed brown cowboy boots. Her pretty hair was up in a ponytail. Her grin widened.

"Ah, the Clark Kent glasses. Nice."

"Hey?" he greeted cautiously. Not sure exactly where they stood at the moment. One thing was for sure—while it was frustrating as hell, it was never boring around Daff.

"I wanted to personally thank you for lunch and to tell you . . . one last time, so don't you dare roll your eyes, I'm sorry. *You* had nothing to apologize for. I was—" She looked off into the distance for a moment and shook her head with a smile. "Crazy. I mean, completely *nuts* this last week. And you bore the brunt of that. And—I'm going to say it again, brace yourself—I'm really, really sorry."

She looked . . . different. Lighter somehow, like the weight of the world had been lifted from her shoulders. It made Spencer happy just to see her like this. He wasn't sure what had changed, but it seemed to be a step in the right direction, and it suited her.

"May I sit?" she asked, indicating the rickety chair opposite his desk.

"Of course. Be careful, it's a little wobbly." She sat down cautiously and then met his eyes again. Sincerity shining from hers.

"You were right, I was never fully on board with our arrangement. And I wasn't comfortable with the idea of having sex with you. And that's through no fault of yours," she hastened to say. "It was all me. I do like you and I am attracted to you and the stuff we did . . . when I was in the moment, it was all *phenomenal*. Better than anything I'd ever experienced before. I wanted you to know that. But at the same time, after thinking about it, I'm really grateful that you didn't take it further. Clearly, I have a few issues to work out. But I do hope that we can be friends, Spencer."

"I'd like that," he said quietly.

Her eyes went suspiciously bright before she blinked a few times and cleared her throat.

"So guess what?"

"What?"

"I handed in my notice today."

"That's bloody fantastic. I'm happy for you, Daff."

"Everybody's been congratulating me on being unemployed." She chuckled. "It's bizarre."

"It's a fresh start," he corrected. "So what's next?"

"No clue. I have to figure out what I enjoy doing."

"There must have been aspects of working at the boutique that you liked and maybe could focus on."

"I'll think about it. Right now I'm just enjoying the feeling of having a whole world of possibility open to me. I feel optimistic and excited and ready to take on anything." No wonder she looked so damned radiant.

"I'll miss having you just down the road." He tried not to wince as he wondered if that was an entirely friendly thing to say. He was going to be second-guessing his every word from here on out.

"I'll still be here for another two months, so you'll have plenty of time to share lunch with me."

"And you wouldn't mind that?" he asked uncertainly, and she shook her head.

"No, but I think we should take turns bringing lunch. My turn next week."

"Like proper food? No salads. As a side it's fine, but don't give it to me as a meal."

"I know. Don't worry, I won't starve you."

"You're sure about this?" Somehow he had never pegged her as someone who enjoyed cooking, but maybe he was mistaken.

"Yep. Absolutely."

"You done for the day?"

"Uh-huh, just thought I'd pop in on my way home." She got up and smiled at him. "Thanks for listening, Spencer. I really want this to be a clean slate for us."

"It will be," he assured, getting up as well. He debated whether he should hug her or not but decided against it. It was too soon to touch her after everything that had happened between them. First he needed to retrain his body not to react whenever he touched her. Until he had his responses under control, they should probably stick to formal handshakes.

"Great." She hovered awkwardly for a moment, obviously debating whether to hug him as well before seeming to come to the same conclusion. "I'll see you soon."

"Tomorrow night, if I'm not mistaken," he reminded her.

"Oh yeah, the dinner. With everything that's happened, I'd almost forgotten. Anyway, see you then."

"Hmm." She grinned at the noncommittal sound—reading God knew what into it this time—and turned away. He tried his damnedest not to let his eyes drop—they were *friends* now, after all—but for fuck's sake, he was a red-blooded man and her ass looked spectacular in those damned jeans. He waited until she disappeared down the winding staircase before groaning and adjusting himself. This was *not* going to be easy.

We're having a girls' night! You've GOT to come over!!!

Daisy's text a couple of hours later was almost instantly followed by another, this one filled with crazy emojis—dancing chick, fireworks, beers, martini glasses, champagne bottle, more beers, wineglasses. Okay, Daisy seemed to be implying that there would be drinking involved. Daff rolled her eyes.

Maybe I've got plans, she replied. She didn't, of course. Her evenings had once again opened right up since she'd ended her no-sex sex thing with Spencer.

Ooh, with the Dick? Well, at least Lia hadn't blabbed. Daff hadn't been certain, since Lia really was an appalling liar. Luckily her fear of Daisy's reaction had been a great motivator to keep quiet.

I'll see you later, Daff responded, not bothering to reply to Daisy's question.

Crying face emoji.

You never tell me anything.

Nothing to tell. It's over.

Another sad, sad little face.

Fine! Bring tequila. Daff snorted in amusement—look at baby sister trying to be a badass. One shot of tequila and they'd probably have to scrape her off the floor.

I'll be there in an hour, she promised.

Daff let herself into Daisy and Mason's cabin and was greeted by a cacophony of female laughter and Peaches's high-pitched yapping. She made her way into the living room, where her sisters and a few friends—Tilda Stanford, Nina Clark, and Billie Greenspan—were all sprawled on the shaggy throw rug in front of the fire and guzzling down red wine like it was water. Tilda, Nina, and Billie were a few of the high school friends the McGregor sisters had won in the custody battle after their acrimonious split from Sharlotte Bridges and Zinzi Khulani. It hadn't been worth staying in contact with the rest. They were always on about materialistic crap. Daff had once bought into that nonsense, as had Lia, to a certain extent, all to fit in with a shallow group of women. Thankfully they were past that now.

"Ladies, I come bearing tequila and sours!" Daff announced as she entered the room, and the women all squealed.

Daff went to the kitchen, already familiar with the layout of the cabin, and grabbed the shot glasses, lemon, and salt before rejoining the rest and sinking to the floor with them. Peaches and Cooper immediately came over to give her a few slobbery welcome kisses before Cooper retreated back to his bed and Peaches crawled into Lia's lap.

"So what are we all talking about?" Daff asked as she poured the tequila shots and handed out the salt and lemon wedges.

"Tilda was saying Mason and I should have a blended name, like Kimye or Brangelina. Something like Daison." It reminded Daff of Spencer's attempt to blend his name with Daff's, and she smiled fondly.

"I said Maisy," Tilda corrected, and Daisy waved her wineglass at the other dismissively, spilling red wine all over the lovely cream rug. Lia grabbed the glass from Daisy before she could do more damage.

"Daison, Maisy . . . they're both awesome. I don't think Mason'll go for it, though, he'll say something boring like 'We'll just call ourselves the Carlisles, angel,'" she said in a gruff imitation of his voice. Which was sweet as hell and probably exactly what Mason would say. "But I don't mind being just the Carlisles. Or maybe the McGregor-Carlisles. We're still thinking about it."

"Would Mason double-barrel his name?" Lia asked, taking a tiny sip of wine. She was a cautious drinker.

"He says we'll have the same name no matter what, so that everybody can know I'm his and he's mine." Daisy said the words matter-of-factly, not even noticing the swoony sighs coming from the women around her. Even Daff barely prevented herself from sighing at the words, and she didn't have a romantic bone in her body. She shook herself and lifted her shot glass.

"To the future Mrs. Carlisle . . . or McGregor-Carlisle or Carlisle-McGregor. I wish you a life filled with nothing but love, Daisy Doodle."

"You had to spoil it, didn't you," Daisy complained, referring to the nickname, but still looked misty-eyed at the toast. Everybody—even Lia—licked their salt, downed their shot, gasped, and sucked on their lemons before upending the glasses on Mason's expensive, handcrafted coffee table.

"Where's Mason, anyway?" Daff asked.

"Suh-suhpensher took him out. Boysh night! S-sh-sho? Sho I figured we should have a la-la . . . *girlie* night!" The shot had definitely pushed Daisy over the limit, and she started giggling uncontrollably. "Sho? Izz not right. Sho . . . ?"

"God. How many drinks did she have before I got here?"

"A crapload of red wine," Tilda said. "And then that shot. I think the shot's knocked her on her ass."

Daisy was flat on her back and still giggling. Lia and Daff helped her sit up and propped her against the sofa. Her curly head lolled, and she still continued to giggle quietly to herself.

"Daisy, you're being a terrible host," Daff said sternly, trying to hide her amusement. They didn't often see their studious, earnest little sister let her hair down like this, and it was entertaining as hell. Daisy mumbled something in response and then chuckled again.

Ladies' night was a roaring success, even if their hostess was an incoherent mess and passed out on the floor. Mason returned home a little after one, looking a bit wasted as well, but by that time only Daff and Lia were still there. The other women had been picked up by Tilda's boyfriend about half an hour before. The dogs greeted Mason exuberantly and he took the time to give each one a couple of scratches before looking up and surveying the room. His brow furrowed when he saw Daisy passed out on the carpet.

"Oh good," Daff said drily. "Now *you* can take care of this."

Mason's eyes remained on his inelegantly snoring fiancée sprawled on the floor, and his expression softened.

"What happened?" he asked, his voice dropping to a whisper as he went down on one knee beside her supine body. He brushed her tangled hair out of her face and palmed one side of her face tenderly.

"She's wasted," Daff said as she dragged on her coat, while Lia did the same.

"What did you all get up to tonight?"

"Don't ask *me*." Daff snorted. "She was pretty much a lost cause by the time I got here. One shot of tequila and she went from hero to zero in about thirty seconds. I barely had time to speak with her. Lia and the rest got her completely hammered."

"Please, I didn't expect it to be a night of drinking. She lured me over here with promises of cocoa and rom coms."

Mason didn't appear to be listening to them anymore.

"Daisy? Angel, come on, let's get you to bed." She groaned and swatted his tenderly stroking hand away from her face, and he grinned at Daff and Lia. "She does hate having her sleep interrupted, doesn't she?"

"Since we were children," Lia confirmed.

"Always with the 'Five more minutes, Mommy,'" Daff said with a nostalgic smile.

Mason slid his arms beneath Daisy's limp body and picked her up, going from kneeling to standing with barely a wheeze. Daff couldn't lie to herself—that was pretty impressive. The guy's core strength was nothing to sniff at.

He made a few adjustments so that Daisy was more comfortably situated in his arms and then gave both Daff and Lia a pointed look.

"You'd better not be thinking about driving home. Nobody leaves until I get back downstairs. We'll organize an Uber."

"Lia's fine to drive, she can take me home," Daff said.

"I don't know if—"

"*Nobody* leaves," he reiterated sternly, interrupting Lia, and Daff cast her eyes heavenward, seeking patience from a higher source.

"Yes, sir," she snapped with what she thought was a credible salute, and Mason snorted.

"Get Daisy to teach you a proper salute sometime," he advised before heading toward the staircase and carrying Daisy up to their loft.

Daff wondered how Spencer was after his night out on the town. Was he drunk? She didn't think she'd ever seen Spencer drunk. Did he lose that quiet reserve when he got sauced? Or did he just get quieter? She was so tempted to take a walk over to his house just to appease her curiosity, but even in her slightly inebriated state, with her inhibitions down and her judgment somewhat impaired, she knew that was a terrible idea.

She sat down on the arm of the sofa, resigned to the fact that she and Lia would have to Uber home and dragged out her phone.

Are you drunk?

It took a few minutes for the reply to come through.

If ciurse

She lifted a hand to her mouth and stifled a laugh.
How novel.

Completely wasted? she prompted.

Ducking slaufhterd!$$!

"Who're you texting?" Lia asked, and Daff jumped.
"Jesus, what the hell are you? Some kind of ninja?" Lia had managed to come up behind her and was totally reading her texts over her shoulder.
"That says the Dick! So you're texting him, right?"
"Duh!"
"So what are you guys talking about? Friend stuff?"
"Oh my God! Go away . . . you're being such an annoying little sister right now."
"Well, I'm curious, you said you were going to be only friends from now on."
"I know what I said, and I'm sending my *friend* a text!"
"At one in the morning? Do you send your other friends texts at one in the morning?" Lia asked, folding her arms over her chest, looking smug because she seemed to think she'd made her point.
"I never have reason to send them texts at one in the morning."

"But you have reason to send *him* one, do you?"

"None of your business. Go sit over there and leave me alone, you obnoxious brat."

"Ooh, defensive," Lia said, sitting down on the chair closest to the sofa.

"Aargh!" Daff pointedly put her phone away and glared at Lia, but her younger sister just smiled back serenely.

"I'm just teasing, Sissy. You should keep texting him. You look *happy* when you're communicating with him. You had this ridiculous grin on your face."

Daff was about to respond when the sound of feminine giggling floated down from the loft. Mason's muted voice muttered something they couldn't hear, but Daisy's drunk, slurry voice carried down to them clear as a bell.

"Just let me pet it a little! *Please,* Mason."

Daff and Lia exchanged horrified looks. Mason spoke again, his voice low and urgent and unintelligible to them.

"Just a touch," Daisy purred. "It wants to play. *See?*" They heard Mason's low groan and Daff face-palmed—she would rather slice off her ears than hear this. Lia had her eyes closed and her lips were moving. Daff leaned a little closer. Was she praying?

"This can't be happening!" That's what Lia was saying. Just mumbling it over and over again.

"Let's just leave," Daff urged. "I can't sit here and . . ."

They heard Mason's heavy tread on the staircase and froze. He paused on the last step, looking a bit flushed and unable to meet their eyes. He hastened to stand behind one of the conveniently waist-high easy chairs.

"She gets a little . . . uh . . . affectionate after a few drinks," he muttered awkwardly. "I'll just send that Uber request and uh . . . yeah."

"You've turned my sister into a total horn muffin," Daff suddenly said, unable to resist.

"Daff!" Lia gasped, but Daff kept her eyes on Mason, who flushed even more. It was fun making the big, bad special-ops guy blush.

"She was a good girl before she met you, mister!" Daff continued, and Mason suddenly grinned.

"And now she's a sexy woman. Hashtag no regrets." He used air quotes as he said the last three words. It was kind of cute how he thought those two things would work together, and Daff choked back a laugh at the pithy response.

"I'm glad she's marrying you," Daff said. She had never completely forgiven Mason for his part in Spencer's stupid wingman plan, and it had loomed between them since then. But she couldn't deny that he made Daisy happy, and that had softened Daff's attitude toward him. But she now recognized that she genuinely liked the guy. She hoped that her sincerity was apparent in her voice. Judging by the way he smiled, it was.

"Thanks. That means a lot." Daff returned his smile. Happy that she and Mason could, once and for all, set aside the past and start anew.

A positive note on which to end an already awesome day.

CHAPTER TEN

Daff watched Spencer approach her shop the following afternoon and wondered if he was bringing lunch. It seemed pointless, since it was Saturday and they would both be closing shop in half an hour. They could go to MJ's or something instead. Like they had just a week ago. She shook her head, unable to believe how much things had changed, not just with Spencer but in her life over the last seven days.

"Hi, there," she greeted with a small smile when he finally stepped into the shop. He wasn't carrying any bags, so he definitely wasn't bringing lunch. He looked a little green around the gills, and she laughed. "A bit hungover today, are we?"

"Hmm." He sat down on his favorite chair and folded his arms on the counter, resting his head on them for a brief moment.

"I have some aspirin if you think that will help," she offered, hoping she sounded sympathetic. She definitely didn't *feel* sympathetic—she really just wanted to laugh. The man looked pathetic.

"Had some already," he grunted, lifting his head with effort to look at her.

"How did you manage to get through the day like this?"

"Claude took care of everything," he said succinctly. "I hid in my office all morning."

"For the love of his thighs, give that man a raise. He sounds like a saint."

"Oh, it's in the cards. Raise and promotion."

"Doesn't he already hold the highest position you can give at your store?"

"I've got some stuff in the pipeline. Will tell you when I can think straight."

"You done for the day?" Keeping her curiosity at bay. *What stuff?*

"Fuck yeah. I was just dead weight anyway."

"Lunch?"

"Hmm. Later. Will you go somewhere with me first?"

"Where?"

"Just a place I want to show you. I want your opinion. Please?"

"Yes, of course. I'm closing in twenty-five minutes." He snorted and looked around the empty shop pointedly.

"Close early. What're they gonna do? Fire you?"

"I've never closed early," she huffed. "Not once since I've been the manager here, and I'm not about to ruin my perfect record now."

"Fine. Wake me up when you're ready to go."

"God, you're such a baby. *I* drank last night, too, you know? You don't see me whining about it."

"Ten-minute nap. It's all I need . . ." His voice trailed off and the last word was followed by a light snore. She gaped at him, unable to believe that he'd fallen asleep just like that. She'd pay money to have that talent.

She shook her head and went back to her seat next to the till, digging out her romance novel—which she'd made very little progress on since Monday—and tried to concentrate on her reading. It was a lost cause. All she did was contemplate the top of his head and marvel at how shiny and silky that mane looked. Her eyes trailed down to the side of his face, the only part visible to her. The way his narrow, neatly trimmed sideburns met the line of stubble that darkened the lower half of his face. All uniformly short except for the ever-so-slightly darker patch beneath the center of his bottom lip, where his razor hadn't done as meticulous a job. Her eyes lingered on his mouth. He had the most beautifully shaped lips she'd ever seen on a man. Gorgeous, sulky curve on the bottom lip and the deep, shadowed groove of his pronounced philtrum with its accompanying thin Cupid's bow upper lip. Her eyes moved up from his mouth over the sharp, straight blade of his nose, that dimpled, lean left cheek—the only one visible to her—to his closed eye. His thick lashes were so long they cast shadows over the blunt curve of his cheekbone.

For a man who looked half-savage most of the time, he had surprisingly refined features. His heavy brows and deep-set eyes were what gave him that intense, untamed look, and when his hair was longer it definitely added to the image.

His eye cracked open, and he pinned her with a penetrating look. His gorgeous green eye looked somewhat bloodshot.

"I can feel you staring at me," he accused.

"Just wondering if you shaved this morning. This stubble is out of control." His eye slid shut again.

"Hmm." For a moment she thought that was all she would get, but he continued, "My five o'clock shadow tends to make an appearance at about nine thirty every morning. I should probably just embrace the beard."

"No, *don't*," she said so quickly she nearly sprained her tongue, and his eyelid lifted with seemingly great difficulty.

"Why not?"

"You'll look completely primitive with a beard, Spencer," she began derogatively, before stopping herself and adding honestly, "and you have a great jawline. Why hide it?"

"You think so?"

"Definitely."

"Stop interrupting my snooze."

"You only have fifteen minutes left."

"I'll make it a power nap."

"So where are we going?" she asked twenty minutes later. They were in his truck. He looked surprisingly refreshed after the short nap he'd taken at the boutique. Daff was still confounded by his ability to fall asleep seemingly on command. Who did that?

"I'll tell you when we get there," he said, and she huffed impatiently. Three minutes later they turned in to the woods just outside Riversend, and shortly after that, Spencer slid the truck to a stop outside a dilapidated old house. It was in the middle of a fairly large clearing in the woods, but the clearing was overgrown with weeds and long grass. The picket fence was rotted and falling apart, resembling crooked, broken, and yellowed teeth. The front yard was scattered with random debris: tractor tires, a rusty old mattress frame, a stack of rusted hubcaps piled in a heap. She could see glints of broken glass strewn all over. There was an old, rotten, and moldy sofa in the middle of the path leading up to the rickety porch.

Spencer stood at the crooked iron gate and simply stared at the house for a long moment before removing his sunglasses and meeting her questioning eyes.

"It's in worse shape than I imagined," he said, his voice wobbly and his eyes haunted.

"This is where you grew up, isn't it?" she asked softly, and he swallowed a couple of times before nodding.

"I haven't been back here in years. Not since I left for college." Not for sixteen years, then. He stepped through the gate and stopped. His reluctance to proceed was palpable.

"I left him here to fend for himself," he said, his voice virtually breaking.

"Who?"

"Mason. I left him alone in this fucking pit." He sounded disgusted with himself, and Daff very carefully—as if handling a wild animal—took his hand in hers.

"It couldn't have been this bad sixteen years ago, Spencer."

"It was a cesspool. Most of the broken glass in this yard came from Dad's rum bottles or Mom's crack pipes. Malcolm, Anita"—his parents—"and their friends did so enjoy their creature comforts. Malcolm and his cronies would sit on that sofa all day, just drinking and shooting the breeze. All things considered, they were okay parents. Didn't ever hit us or allow their friends to get handsy with us. Malcolm stuck around long enough after our mother died to give us a fighting chance at life. Left the day I turned eighteen. Happy fucking birthday to me, right?"

He ran his free hand roughly over his face and shuddered. Daff's hand clenched around his, and she just ached for the boy he'd been. The kid who suddenly found himself sole guardian to his underage brother, who worked several jobs just to get by. The boy *she*—Daff—had treated like dirt just because his scrupulously clean clothes had been threadbare, his shoes had been scuffed, with worn-down soles, and his hair had never been touched by a barber's scissors. While this was his home life, *she'd* made his school life hell of a different kind, and he'd never once had a bad word to say about her.

Her eyes flooded with tears, and she strove not to let him see them, knowing it would demolish his pride. He would misinterpret them as pity when all she felt was regret and shame.

"I'm sorry, this isn't why I brought you here," he said, his hand tightening around hers. "I wanted to see if the place was salvageable or if we'd be better off razing it to the ground."

"Why?" she asked hoarsely.

"I'm considering donating the land and everything on it to the town, on the condition that it's used to build a youth center. The main aim of the center should be to provide a safe haven for at-risk kids to come and play sports, learn skills, new hobbies. I was imagining a library, a gym, a sports field, tennis court, maybe a swimming pool and a cafeteria . . ."

"It's ambitious," she ventured cautiously.

"Unrealistic?"

"No, I just wonder where the funding would come from. Not just to build the place but to maintain it afterward."

"I spoke with Mase last night—before the drinking started—since he co-owns the house. Both he and I are willing to donate enough to kick-start the project. But we agree that the community should chip in as well, as this is to the town's benefit."

"That's where you're going to run into obstacles—a lot of the towns-people would be happy to help, but there are always a few who will be vocal about using the town's money to build something so expensive for kids from the poorer areas."

"Assholes, you mean?"

"Yes, but some of those assholes are pretty powerful," she reminded him, and he grimaced, acknowledging her point.

"This benefits everybody—if we make these kids feel valuable, give them something to do, keep them off the streets, there'll be less petty crime. And petty crime can lead to much worse."

"Did you ever . . ." Her voice trailed off; it wasn't her business.

"Yes," he said in answer to her incomplete question, and her throat went dry at the thought. Whatever he'd done was for survival, but she shuddered at the thought of what would have happened if he'd been caught. "After our mother died, our dad stuck around and sometimes threw money our way for food. Other times he used it for alcohol. At first we hung out behind MJ's a lot. Like hungry dogs. Occasionally, Janice Cooper . . . remember her? Played the piano a lot and then mar-ried that dentist and moved to Durban? Anyway, she used to sneak a few bread rolls and leftovers out to us. But she was terrified of getting caught and losing her job. I didn't want to put her in that position, she was nice. So I started shoplifting. I tried to keep Mase from figuring out where the food was coming from—I knew he'd follow my lead and I didn't want him to get caught. But of course he worked it out and took it upon himself to 'help' me. We only took food, nothing else. We knew people already thought we were troublemakers, and if we were caught stealing—" He shook his head, no need to elaborate. "So, yeah, I know what I'm talking about. I know what desperation can drive a kid to and how lethal boredom can be as well."

"So how do you start something like this?"

"Well, we'll have a look through this dump to see if anything's worth saving. Then I'm going to have to figure out how much it will cost to renovate this place versus just razing it completely and building from scratch. Once we know exactly how much everything will cost, we'll have to figure out where the money will come from."

"And you brought me because—"

"Because I value your opinion, and because—" He sighed before slanting her a quick look. "Mason bailed on me. Apparently Daisy's completely useless today after you guys got her drunk last night, and that means Mason has to sort out the cooking for the dinner party tonight . . . and I didn't want to come alone."

Daff felt warm and gooey inside—okay, so she was his second choice, but she understood why Mason was his first choice. They had history with this place and maybe a few ghosts that needed to be laid to rest. But Spencer thought enough of her to bring her in his brother's stead. And he *valued* her opinion. Nobody had ever said anything like that to her before.

"So let's have a look at this place," she said, and, still holding her hand, he tugged her toward the raised porch. He stopped at the steps and winced.

"I'm not sure how safe this is," he muttered, assessing the broken slats in the steps.

"Just be careful," she said and gingerly stepped onto the first step. It only barely held her weight. Spencer decided to skip the stairs completely and climbed straight onto the porch. The boards groaned beneath his weight, but held.

The front windows were all shattered, and the walls—which had once been white—were covered with mold and years' worth of graffiti. The front door was nonexistent.

She watched him square his shoulders and take a deep, bracing breath before moving over the threshold into the gloomy interior.

Spencer was only dimly aware of Daff's hand tightening as his childhood came flooding back. There, that was where he had once found his mother passed out in a puddle of her own vomit with a needle sticking out of her arm. All of six years old, he'd been terrified that she was dead. Over in the corner was where—when one of his parents remembered to feed them—he and Mason had eaten. Here's where the TV had stood. Mason and Spencer had sat for hours just staring at the screen, flipping between only three channels and fantasizing about the glamorous lives those rich soap opera people led. Pretending to be them and learning from them. Of course, one day they'd come home to find the TV gone, sold for "Mommy's medicine."

It seemed like a lifetime ago, and yet he could still remember everything so vividly. The fear, the hunger, the sadness, and the uncertainty. It had been no way to grow up, and he wanted this place to become a symbol of hope rather than of poverty, desperation, and fear.

He clung to Daff's hand, his only lifeline in this turbulent tsunami of memories, and continued to walk through the nightmare that was his childhood.

Daff trailed behind Spencer; she wasn't sure he was aware that he was quietly narrating as he went along. Just little snippets of information, like finding his mother passed out with a needle in her arm when he was six. *God*. It was horrible to imagine him growing up like that, to imagine any child growing up like that, and she was beginning to understand his need to offer help and guidance to as many at-risk kids as he could.

It was a pretty big house, all on one floor, and when they reached the last room, he stopped before going inside and looked at her.

"Mason and I shared this room. Malcolm said we didn't have to share, but I liked to keep Mase close to me. He was a scrawny kid, and while our parents kept their shadier friends away from us, I still didn't trust them not to hurt my brother. So we shared a room until the day I left."

"It must have been hard leaving him here when you went to college."

"He was only sixteen. I was going to stay. Or try to figure out a way to take him with me. But he was stubborn. Insisted he'd be fine, said that me getting a degree would eventually improve both our lives. I would have lost the scholarship if I got caught sneaking him into student housing with me. It would never have worked.

"By then he was already working at MJ's and had a few other jobs, so he'd have money for food and stuff. I sent extra money every month. It helped that the house was ours. And we both knew that nobody cared enough to check how Mason was getting along after I left. He just kept telling the teachers, when they bothered to ask, that Malcolm was back."

"But why not ask for help?"

"They would have shoved him into foster care. We were taken into care for a time after my mom's overdose when I was six, and it wasn't ideal. The older kids were bullies; the adults were bigger bullies. He was two years away from being a legal adult. We figured we could make it work. I hated it, worried about him every single day, and then, when he was eighteen, the little asshole went and joined the fucking army. In another country."

"Making you worry even more," she said astutely, and he glowered at the memory.

"Hmm."

They stepped into the room and gaped. It was reasonably clean, had cardboard shoved into the window to keep the wind out. A mattress had been dragged into the least drafty corner and was neatly covered in a flowered comforter. There were a few cans of tinned food, along with a can opener and a spoon, neatly stacked on a box at the foot of the mattress, a stack of romance paperbacks carefully arranged, in alphabetical order, on the floor at the head. A flashlight was placed on top of them.

"Somebody's living here," Daff whispered, and, grimly taking in every detail of the room, Spencer nodded.

"Hmm. I think I know who it is."

"You do?"

"This kid, I think she's new in town. I've seen her around a couple of times. Dresses like a boy to disguise the fact that she's female. I was worried that she was in some kind of trouble." He shook his head sadly as his eyes continued to sweep from one item to the next. "I was hoping it wouldn't be this bad."

"Should we wait for her?"

"She won't come near the house with the truck parked outside. I'll have to find another way to approach her. I hate the thought of her in this old place. It should have been condemned years ago, and who knows what other itinerants come through here. Girl or boy, they won't care—she's young, small, and pretty much defenseless despite her prickly attitude."

"Will you call the police? Having her in custody is better than to risk leaving her here another night, isn't it?"

"She won't be here another night."

"What do you mean?" she asked, confused by his statement. "You're coming back here?"

"After the dinner party, yeah," he confirmed. "I'll park farther away and walk up to the house."

"Won't that scare her?"

"We have the cops pick her up and she's lost to us. They'll stick her in the system. Maybe Oom Herbert or Father O'Grady can help me find her a temporary home until we can figure something out."

"You can't do this for every lost child, Spencer. You have to use the system and make it work for you."

"And I will, it's just this one . . . it feels different."

She considered his strong profile and felt the most overwhelming surge of admiration mixed in with tenderness for the man. He really was quite *remarkable*. More people should aspire to be like Spencer Carlisle. He had a genuine concern for others that—considering his background—was extraordinary. He could so easily have gone in another direction, could have made different choices, could have allowed his circumstances to engulf him and suck him into the same vicious circle as his parents. But he hadn't—instead he'd learned empathy, had aimed higher, had taught old-fashioned values to his brother and had pushed them both to want more and *be* more.

Daff was starting to feel things for Spencer Carlisle she'd never felt for any man before, and she wasn't entirely sure what those feelings meant. Or how to cope with them.

He led her back to the truck, and she remained silent and introspective until they were back on the road to town.

"So what's the verdict on the house?" she asked.

"I don't think it can be saved," he said. "Do you?"

"No, you're definitely going to have to demolish and rebuild it." She paused before sighing deeply. "I'm pretty sure you're going to meet some resistance from a few members on the town council over this, Spencer."

"I know. Mason and I will work out a solid business model for the project before presenting it, have all our ducks in a row, so to speak."

"You could raise money through charity drives and fund-raisers," she suggested. "My mother and I are always having dinners and functions to raise money for the animal shelters. It's small-scale, but we can find a way to do something similar for the youth center. Mom and Dad are in the country club—Dad hates it and rarely goes, but I could ask my mother if she could convince some of her friends to talk to their husbands. There are some very influential people at that club."

"You'd do that?"

"No child should go through what you and Mason did growing up," Daff said softly, her voice hitching on the words. "And no child should be so alone in the world that they're forced to sleep on the floor of a condemned building. What you're trying to do for these kids is amazing. I'm sorry I didn't know exactly *how* amazing before today."

He'd already parked his truck behind her car outside the boutique and was watching her gravely while she spoke.

"I don't want you to pity me," he growled.

"Oh, I don't pity you, Spencer. I *admire* you." He looked completely baffled by her words, and she smiled. This guy definitely wasn't used to compliments.

"Uh . . . lunch?" he asked, changing the subject quickly, because he was clearly embarrassed by her words.

"It's getting late; I think I'll just grab something at home while I get ready for tonight."

"Eat something decent," he reminded her.

"Will do." On sheer impulse, she breached the gap between them and dropped a quick, completely chaste kiss on his beautiful mouth.

"What was that for?" he asked after she moved away, his voice husky.

"I just wanted to thank you for today. It means a lot that you value my input."

"You're the smartest woman I know, Daff," he said, and she laughed dismissively.

"Come on, you've met my baby sister, haven't you? You know, the vet?"

"Daisy's book-smart. You're intuitive, witty, and street-smart. Exactly what I needed today." Daff had had so many men compliment her on her looks, commenting on how cute she was, how pretty her eyes or how lovely her hair. None had ever shown any interest in her mind. Her opinion was neither sought after nor welcome. Spencer's words meant the world to her, and she wasn't sure if she wanted to cry or simply wrap herself around him and take comfort and shelter in his arms for days. In the end she did neither, but the warmth blossoming in her chest felt life altering.

"You don't look too bad for someone who was at death's door this morning," Spencer observed when Daisy let him into the cabin later that evening. She looked cute in a short, flirty dress and with her brown curls allowed to riot around her head. She wrinkled her freckled nose at him before showing off the famous McGregor sister grin. She pushed her heavy, dark-framed glasses up the short bridge of her pert nose and inspected him carefully.

"You don't look half bad yourself. Mason told me you were pretty wasted as well last night. I don't imagine you had an easy time of it this morning."

"Hmm," he agreed, trying not to shudder as he remembered how perfectly awful he'd felt that morning.

"Not an experience I'd be keen to repeat any time soon," he said as she led him into the dining and living area.

"Believe me, I can relate." She laughed, then waved a hand at the assembled group of people who were milling around and chatting. "Well, as you can see, everybody else is here already. This is Chris."

"Yes, of course, nice to finally meet you," Spencer said, taking the man's hand in a firm handshake. Even Spencer could appreciate the guy's charisma and good looks. He was tall and lean, with a muscular physique and angular, dramatic features. Spencer could see how he would have been a sensation in the modeling world, where he'd been quite a big deal. Spencer was more interested in the guy's cooking abilities. Apparently he was a brilliant chef, and Spencer had been meaning to visit his restaurant.

"*Oui*, I am happy to meet you, too. Mason speaks of you often," Chris said. Congolese, he spoke with a thick French accent, which caused every woman in the room to sigh. Spencer could practically feel the breeze on his back from all the sighs and barely refrained from rolling his eyes. He looked at Daff, who was standing with Tilda; both of them were staring at Chris, practically with their tongues hanging out and then whispering to each other like giddy schoolgirls.

Seeing Daff moon over the guy made Spencer feel a little less charitable toward him, but Chris continued to talk and was so damned likable that it was hard to harbor ill feelings toward the man. After all, the guy couldn't help it if he was a chick magnet.

Daff practically swooned when Chris smiled at her, and Spencer gave her another piercing look while reminding himself that he had no right to feel jealous. They were just friends. She could gush over whomever the hell she wanted to. Still, it was hard to convince himself of that when she'd come on his tongue only two nights ago.

"Hey, how'd it go this afternoon?" Mason asked, handing him a beer. Spencer took it without thinking—having no intention of drinking tonight—and tore his eyes from Daff with difficulty to focus on his brother. It brought his other immediate concern to the forefront.

"We have a problem."

"That bad, huh?"

"What? Yeah, the house is a write-off, but that's not the problem. That kid . . . the girl from the other night? She's squatting there."

"Shit." Mason rubbed a hand over the nape of his neck and scowled into his beer. "You sure?"

"Pretty sure. Somebody's living there, definitely female if the romance novels lying around are any indication. And it's so neat and orderly, I don't know why, but she immediately sprang to mind."

"You call the cops?"

"I want to give her a chance, Mason. You know what will happen if the cops show up. She'll either make a run for it and wind up God knows where, doing God knows what. Or she'll get caught and lost in the system." Mason was too young to remember when they were taken into care, but Spencer did, and while he knew foster care worked for a lot of kids, he and Mason hadn't been so lucky. He'd spent nights clinging to his brother, terrified that the other kids would hurt them again. Or that an adult would punish them for being too loud, or too slow, or too fucking present. It had only been for a few months, but it was the first time in his life that he'd appreciated his parents and the fact that life could be a whole lot worse.

"Where do you intend to put her? Finding a place for her at this time of night will be almost impossible."

"I'll call Oom Herbert or Father O'Grady about finding shelter for her tonight, and then we can figure out something more permanent in the morning."

"I don't know, Spence, it seems crazy."

"She deserves a chance, Mase."

"Maybe the best chance we can give her is to let the system take care of her."

"I'm not calling the police," Spencer insisted. He refused to budge on this issue—the girl needed someone in her corner.

"Have it your way, but you're not traipsing out there alone tonight. You know nothing about the girl, she could be part of some gang. There could be others with her."

"She's alone."

"You're irrational. I'm coming with you."

"Hey, guys, sorry to interrupt this intense conversation." Daisy looked at Mason questioningly, and he shook his head abruptly.

"Later," he said curtly in response to her look, and she raised her eyebrows, pursing her lips, clearly displeased with Mason for the terse response.

"Anyway, as I was saying, sorry to disturb, but dinner will be served in just a minute, so if you don't mind taking a seat, Spencer," she said with a gracious smile, which disappeared when she looked at Mason. "Your brother and I will bring out the food."

She flounced away, and Mason face-palmed.

"You shouldn't have snapped at the little woman, there, brother," Spencer said gleefully. Not in the least bit sympathetic, especially since he was a bit frustrated with his brother as well for not seeing his point of view on the situation with the girl.

He joined the rest at the long dining room table, making sure he grabbed the seat next to Daff before Chris could, which was stupid, since she had taken a center seat and the other man could easily have sat down on her left. Instead, Chris slanted Spencer a knowing smile and moved to the other side of the table, graciously seating himself between Tilda and Lia and directly opposite Daff, which was still not ideal.

Mason and Daisy returned from the kitchen, serving dishes in hand; they both looked relaxed and Daisy was smiling, so Spencer assumed that Mason had done some smooth talking in the kitchen.

"We had something fancier planned," Mason explained and then directed an affectionate smile at his fiancée. "But Daisy wasn't feeling too great today, so you can't enjoy her awesome cooking and will have to be content with my meager offerings instead."

"Stop," Daisy begged, flustered, her cheeks flushed. "I was going to bore you all with a roast lamb. Mason's beef goulash is so much better."

"Your roasts are fuc . . . uh, *freaking* amazing, angel," Mason complimented sincerely. Spencer knew he meant it—his brother couldn't stop rhapsodizing about Daisy's cooking and baking. Especially her baking. And Spencer had to admit, her breads were pretty good. Daisy looked like she was about to respond, but she was interrupted.

"Oh for *God's* sake! Feed your guests instead of your egos, people," Daff snarked, and Spencer bit back a chuckle. She was entirely irreverent and had no absolutely no patience with the mushy stuff.

Daisy shot her sister a look but said nothing in response to Daff's outburst and merely placed a steaming dish of fragrant goulash in the center of the table, along with a basket of fresh, delicious-smelling bread. Mason added a green salad and a bowl of jasmine rice to the fare and uncorked a couple of bottles of pinot noir. He went around the table filling glasses as required, and after he and Daisy were seated at each end of the table, they smiled at each other like lovesick teens.

Spencer was reaching for the bowl of salad when Mason spoke, and he sat back with a sigh as he recognized that it was a *speech* of some sort.

Fuck.

"We'd like to thank you all for joining us at our very first dinner party as an engaged couple," Mason said, his words sounding rehearsed. He tugged at the collar of his shirt and cleared his throat. "I'm no fucking—sorry—no good at this kind of stuff. But Daisy says we should let you all know how much you mean to us. But I think you all know, right? Else we wouldn't fucking—*fuck*, sorry—uh, we wouldn't have you in our wedding party, right? Anyway, just. Thanks." He looked pained and glanced at Daisy, seeking her approval, and she grinned, throwing him a cheeky thumbs-up and a wink. Relieved that the *touching* speech had been short-lived, Spencer reached for the salad again. But, of course, Daisy started speaking and he sat back again, feeling like an idiot. He felt a kick against his shin and glowered at Daff, who sneaked a quick eye roll his way. He fought back a laugh.

"I'd also like to thank you all. I want this to be fun for everyone, and I hope that you all know that even if—when—I go a little crazy over the next few months, I absolutely adore each and every one of you.

Just knowing you'll all be a part of our big day means so much to both of us. We love you guys."

Well, that was . . . kind of sweet, actually, and Spencer felt a swell of affection for the lovely woman who had stolen his brother's heart. Chris lifted his glass.

"To Daisy and Mason. Your love for each other is truly wonderful to witness, and I'm sure I speak for all of us when I say that we wish you the happiest of marriages."

Of course, perfect Chris would say the perfect thing. Spencer tried not to be exasperated by that. Nobody expected Spencer to make a spur-of-the-moment toast—it would be an abject failure. He already broke into cold sweats when he thought about the best man speech he'd have to make. So he lifted his glass and added his "hear, hear" to the chorus and touched glasses with everybody at the table.

Finally, they were able to eat.

"Don't know about you, but I was genuinely worried that that would go on for hours," Daff muttered into his ear after they'd both piled their plates, and Spencer chuckled.

The sound seemed to draw stares from around the table, and Spencer scowled back at them all uncomfortably.

What the fuck?

Gradually everybody went back to their chatter and he turned to Daff questioningly.

"They're not used to hearing you laugh so freely, that's all," she informed him, and he felt his brow lower even farther.

"Does everybody think I'm some kind of monster?" he asked under his breath. She shook her head.

"Of course not, don't be ridiculous. They just think you're serious, that's all."

"That's not good. Serious people are assholes."

"Not true. They're just . . . serious."

"*You* thought I was an asshole," he reminded, and she huffed querulously.

"That's because *I* was the real asshole. Trust me, nobody thinks you're an asshole."

"So you *don't* think I'm an asshole?" he prompted, and she graced him with an affectionate smile.

"Shut up and eat your goulash."

"You eat. What did you have for lunch today, anyway? Have some more rice, you barely have a thimbleful on your plate." He reached for the rice and attempted to pile another spoonful onto her plate. She blocked his hand.

"Jesus, and you have the nerve to call *me* rude? You can't just put more food on my—"

"Oh dear God," Daisy chimed in dramatically. "Spencer's the Dick, isn't he? You're the Dick?"

"Daisy, what the fuck?" Mason's voice was laden with comical incredulity, and Daff and Spencer froze in midsquabble. They met each other's eyes sheepishly, acknowledging that the jig was up.

"I've been called that on occasion," Spencer admitted.

"You *know*?" Daff asked out of the corner of her mouth, and he smiled at her.

"That you have me down as the Dick on your phone? Word gets around. And seriously, a penis in a top hat? Can I see it?"

"Shut up," she sulked, folding her arms over her chest and turning her focus on her truly horrified-looking sister. "In case you haven't noticed, we're in shit here."

Spencer frowned, not sure how to deal with the situation other than to brazen it out—but that wasn't something that was in his nature.

"Daff, how *could* you?" Daisy asked at the same time as Mason glared at Spencer.

"Seriously, bro?"

"What's going on?" Tilda asked nervously while Chris sat back with a grin on his face, watching the drama unfold. Lia leaned over to whisper urgently in Tilda's ear, clearly filling her in on the situation, if Tilda's widening eyes and shocked gasps were anything to go by.

"Daffodil, a word, please," Daisy said pointedly and then got up to stalk in the direction of the kitchen. Daff hesitated and then sighed in resignation.

"Wish me luck," she said to the table at large and followed Daisy.

Spencer watched her retreat before turning to meet his brother's furious regard.

Mason just nodded in the direction of the front door.

"Really? Outside? It's fucking freezing, man."

"The house is small."

"Your fault, you could have built a bigger one, planned for a family."

"Spence!" Mason hissed warningly, clearly not interested in his delay tactics, and Spencer put aside his napkin and headed toward the front door with Mason in tow.

"This is so much more exciting than we were expecting, *non?*" he heard Chris say as he left. "Well . . . no use letting this beautiful food go to waste, ladies. Let's eat."

CHAPTER ELEVEN

"Before you say anything, it's over," Spencer explained once they were out on the porch.

"No shit?" Mason seemed remarkably unperturbed, compared to how furious he'd looked in the house. Spencer guessed that most of his brother's "outrage" had been affected for Daisy. "You okay with that?"

"Well, it wasn't anything, really. We didn't . . ."

"No details, if you please. I just need to know two things."

"Yeah?"

"Are you okay?"

"It wasn't what it should have been. What it could have been. She wasn't ready. I don't know if she'll ever be ready for that kind of relationship, not with me. So we've decided to be friends."

"That ties into the second thing . . . I need to know that this business between you guys won't become a problem, Spence. You're my brother, I love you, and I'd hate for you to get hurt, but you and Daff need to make sure your shit doesn't spill over at family events. We have a whole family to think about now, Spence. It's not just you and me against the world anymore. We have sisters and parents to consider as well."

Spencer stretched his lips into what he hoped was a semblance of a smile and tried to hide the pang of hurt he felt at his brother's words.

What the younger man didn't seem to grasp was that *he*—Mason—now had a whole family to consider. Not Spencer. Spencer's family still consisted of only Mason. And while to Spencer it was still him and his little brother against the world, Mason had gone and acquired other loved ones. And he was happy for his brother, it was everything he wanted for Mason, but Spencer felt lonelier than he'd ever felt in his life.

"Daff and I are fine. Has there been any tension between us tonight?"

Mason considered his words before shaking his head. "You two were more relaxed in each other's company than I've ever seen you."

"Well, aside from the sex stuff—"

"God." Mason pinched the bridge of his nose.

"Aside from the sex stuff," Spencer continued, as if Mason's disgusted outburst hadn't occurred, "there was a lot of talking, and we've resolved some issues. She's actually quite . . . special."

That made Mason pause, and he squinted at Spencer in the dim light spilling from the front windows.

"Spence . . . don't fall for her," Mason warned him, and Spencer forced another smile.

"Don't worry, Mason, I won't fuck up the family dynamics."

"I just don't want you to get your heart broken, man," his brother said uncomfortably, and Spencer shifted, the touchy-feely stuff also not sitting too well for him, even while his brother's concern warmed him. Especially after feeling sidelined by Mason's new family just moments before.

"We're friends. That's all."

"We're just friends," Daff said as soon as she got to the kitchen, where Daisy stood waiting.

"You said you just wanted him for his—" Daisy clapped a hand dramatically over her mouth as Daff's exact words came back to her.

"*Oh my God!* I'll never be able to look at him again! Not without hearing those words over and over again in my brain."

"What words?" Daff asked, baffled by her sister's weird reaction.

"About his . . . *you know?*" Understanding dawned, and Daff couldn't hold back a laugh at Daisy's truly appalled expression.

"I could lie and say he has a small dick," she teased, and Daisy clapped her hands over her ears.

"Don't talk about his penis *ever* again! Ew, ew, *ew!* *Why* did you have to sleep with him? Why couldn't you leave him alone? He's about to be my brother-in-law."

"You told me to get along with him, and you know that's the only way I get along with guys." The look on Daisy's face brought her up short—her sister looked genuinely furious.

"*Stop* it! This isn't a joke, Daff. Not everything's a joke and not everything's always about you and *your* wants and *your* needs." Daisy swiped at a couple of errant tears, and Daff was immediately contrite. She reverted to wisecracking when she was stressed, nervous, or on the back foot, and it definitely wasn't the right approach this time.

"Deedee," she said in a soft, pleading voice. Her sister deserved honesty. "I'm sorry. I'm so . . . *confused* where Spencer's concerned. But I promise you, this won't mess up your big day or our family gatherings, and I don't want it to mess up tonight any further, either. Spencer and I aren't . . . *intimate* anymore. We never were. Not really. We did some stuff. But not the main stuff. Anyway, none of that's important. What's important is that I like Spencer, I want to try to get along with him. He's a nice guy and I'm sorry it's taken me so long to figure that out."

"But you were fighting at dinner," Daisy reminded her, dabbing beneath her eyes with a napkin.

"*That?* That wasn't fighting, it was playing."

"It was?"

"You're so used to seeing us—*me*, really—fight, so that's all you saw. Look closer next time."

Daisy peered closely at Daff, which wasn't quite what she had meant.

"You look different," Daisy marveled. "Happier."

"Well, I quit my job, I have an awesome new friend, and my sister's getting married to a great guy. What's not to be happy about?"

"And it's *that* easy? Being friends after nearly being lovers?"

"We're trying to make it work."

Daisy graced her with a tremulous smile.

"It's not just about the wedding, Daff. I don't want either of you to get hurt. I hope you know that."

"I know that." Daff gave her sister a quick, tight hug. "Now how about we go eat that goulash? I'm starving and—*don't* tell Spencer—I skipped lunch."

The rest of the evening was actually quite pleasant. While Daisy and Mason watched Daff and Spencer closely, they continued to enjoy each other's company. In fact, the scrutiny made them feel unified. Daff enjoyed that, she had never been great at team sports, but that's what she and Spencer felt like tonight—a team.

Spencer kept checking his watch and she knew he was concerned about the girl, but after the evening had already been disrupted, he stoically stuck it out, not wanting to ruin it any further by leaving early. So they formed three teams of two and played a raucous game of 30 Seconds. The teams were Tilda and Lia, Daff and Spencer, and Mason and Daisy. Chris, claiming that his poor English made him a terrible game partner, sat out to be the timekeeper. It was a crazy-fast board game that had one partner trying to explain a list of five objects or people without saying any of the words on said card. There were lots of raised voices, rule disputes, and disgust at partners for not guessing correctly. It was hilarious, and Daisy and Mason won by the narrowest of margins—mostly because they knew each other's verbal shortcuts and body language so well already.

After the game ended, Daff could see that Spencer was keen to get going, so she sidled up to him and dropped a hand on his arm and tugged him to one side.

"I'm going with you," she said under her breath, keeping their conversation private.

"No." His voice brooked no argument.

"I don't think you should go alone."

"I'm not. Mason is coming."

"I'm still going with you, and if you don't take me, I'll just follow you in my car anyway."

"Daff," he began, his eyes and voice exasperated. "I don't want you there. It's no place for you."

"That girl is going to be *terrified* to have two huge men sneaking up on her in the middle of the night," she pointed out. "I want to ensure you don't scare the poor thing half to death."

She made sense and she knew he knew it. She could see it in the way he hesitated.

"Fine, but you're going to have to stay way back."

"That completely defeats the purpose," she argued. "I should be with you when you go into her room. Why should I hang back? *Unless* . . . are you expecting trouble? Are you placing yourself in danger, Spencer?"

"No, of course not!" And yet he evaded her eyes.

"Spencer!" The word came out as a warning, and he glowered at her.

"We can't be sure she's alone, okay? So just give us a chance to check out the situation and then I'll call you in."

"If you get yourself hurt, I'm going to be pissed at you! And I'll unfriend you before I even friend you."

"What the fuck does that even mean?"

"Like on Facebook? It's funny because we haven't friended—" He continued to look at her blankly, and she gaped at him. "Spencer, you *are* on Facebook, right?"

"Would I be weird if I'm not?"

"Oh God. Let's just get going . . ." He helped her into her coat—of course—and said a few hurried goodbyes to the rest of the group.

"I'll drive," Mason said once they were outside and led them to his Jeep. They all piled in, and Daff wrinkled her nose at the smell of wet dog. Mason often took Cooper for a run on the beach, and the interior of his Jeep had acquired the permanent odor of wet pooch.

The drive was conducted in grim silence, and a few minutes later Mason drew the car to a stop on the dirt road. It was far enough from the house for the headlights to not have been spotted.

Both men exited, and Spencer sent Daff a warning look.

"Don't you dare move from here. I'll send you a text if it's clear."

"Fair warning, if you don't contact me within five minutes, I'm calling the police and then I'm coming to find you."

"Don't you dare leave this car if you don't hear from us. And keep the doors locked. Use the horn if you see anyone or anything strange."

"Hmm."

"What the fuck is that supposed to mean?" he asked, irritated, and she smiled sweetly, happy to turn the tables on him for once.

"Figure it out."

His glower deepened and she met it full on, making sure her glare matched his. It was a good one, and she hoped he appreciated it, despite the dark.

"Be careful," Daff urged when he turned away. "And keep my sister's fiancé safe while you're at it."

He threw her an inscrutable look over his shoulder before he walked away. Mason paused at her open window.

213

"Mason—" He threw her a quick grin, as if knowing what she wanted to say, even if Daff herself didn't have a clue.

"Don't worry. I'll watch out for him. I have a black belt, you know?"

"In what?" she asked dumbly, and his grin widened.

"Everything."

Daff watched the two men walk away. They left the safety of the Jeep's headlights in seconds, and soon all she could see of them were the dim lights of their phones before those disappeared completely, too.

Her stomach began to turn as she imagined all kinds of disturbing scenarios. What if there *was* a gang of men waiting? What if they were armed? What if they hurt Spencer? Or Mason? Daisy would be devastated.

She fiddled with her phone, willing Spencer's message to come through. In order to take her mind off the situation, she tried to think about the girl and what they were going to do about her.

Trying to figure out potential solutions, she decided to contact someone who always knew exactly the right thing to do.

The house was dark and quiet. Mason did a quick scan of the perimeter and then stealthily went from window to window before making his way back to Spencer.

"Looks clear. Just the girl. I can't be entirely sure because of the cardboard in that window, but it doesn't look like anyone's in the room with her. I don't know how she hasn't frozen to death by now."

"She's lucky; it hasn't been too cold this winter. Do you mind fetching Daff? I don't want her to walk up here alone. I'll wait."

"You sure you want to do this?" Mason asked quietly.

"It's the right thing, Mason. I feel really strongly about this."

"I'll get Daff."

"Thanks."

Mason left and Spencer sent Daff a quick text to let her know that his brother was coming for her. After sending it he shoved his hands into his pockets and glared at the ramshackle building that used to be his home. In the dark it didn't look too bad—almost welcoming when you couldn't see the broken glass and piles of scrap lying about. This place that had been both safe haven and hell from one moment to the next. He shook his head and tried to keep the memories at bay.

It wasn't long before he heard soft footfalls on the gravel path leading up to the house, and he turned and watched the dim lights come closer and closer.

Daff came up to stand right beside him and quite shockingly slipped her small hand into his and squeezed comfortingly.

"My parents have agreed to take her for the night," she said by way of greeting, and he felt his brow lower.

"I don't want to inconvenience them."

"Don't be silly—they want to help, and you're family."

Was he?

"You mean Mason is family?" he clarified.

"Don't be a dumb-ass, Spencer," she dismissed. "They're doing this for you, not Mason."

"But . . ."

"So where is she?" Daff interrupted him, and Spencer—still confounded by her words—pointed toward the house.

"Let's go, then."

"Uh, be careful on this path," he warned her, gathering his senses.

"Yep. Got it."

When they were outside the room, Daff signaled for the men to stay back and stepped confidently over the threshold, making enough noise to alert the girl that she was coming. Charlie was probably always on alert, sleeping in a place like this, and her flashlight came on immediately.

"Who's there? I have pepper spray," she warned them, her voice high and thin with fear. *Pepper spray*, for God's sake. Like that would keep anybody who meant to do her harm away.

"It's okay," Daff said soothingly, and Spencer saw her lift her hands in a placating manner. "My name is Daffodil McGregor. I'm not here to do you any harm. But you can't sleep here, Charlie. It's dangerous."

"How do you know my name?" the girl asked suspiciously. "I didn't tell you my name."

"My friend Spencer is here, too. He wants to help you."

"He should mind his own business." Charlie raised her voice, clearly meaning for Spencer to hear her words, too.

"He cares about your well-being."

"I'm not a charity case. I have a right to be here."

"This is private property," Daff said gently.

"I have a right to be here!"

"No, you don't, Charlie," Spencer said, stepping into the small ring of light provided by the girl's and Daff's flashlights. "We want to take you somewhere safe. And warm. You can have a bath and something to eat and not worry about anybody hurting you."

She was sitting up on the thin mattress, her eyes huge and terri-fied. She looked small and helpless, and Spencer's protective instincts immediately came to the fore.

"I don't want to go to a shelter."

"It's not a shelter," Daff told her, moving forward slowly so as not to spook her even more. "I promise you. It's my parents' place, they're looking forward to meeting you."

"I don't need your charity."

"It doesn't have to be charity," Daff said. "You can pay them back eventually."

Charlie's big eyes shifted to Spencer, and he could see fury mixed in with her terror.

"I only came here to tell you Malcolm is dead," she spat out. "I was going to leave after that."

Spencer felt the blood drain from his face, and he sensed Mason moving forward to stand beside him.

"*What* did she just say?"

"How do you know that name?" Spencer demanded, glancing around the room wildly, wondering if they'd left any family documents behind. How else would this girl know their father's name?

"He had liver cancer. He died three months ago." She folded her arms belligerently and lifted her chin to glare at them.

"*Fuck,*" Mason whispered from beside Spencer. He took a step forward, peering closely at the girl. "Fuck me."

"How do you know Malcolm?" Spencer asked again, and Mason grabbed hold of his elbow painfully.

"Look at her," he whispered. "The eyes, the cheekbones, that fucking glare."

Spencer looked and staggered, his mouth dropping open.

"How old are you?" he asked hoarsely, and that stubborn jaw tilted even higher while her expression remained mutinous.

"He wanted me to find you and tell you what happened. And I have, so I'll be leaving in the morning."

"Over my dead body." Spencer bristled.

"You can't tell me what to do," she fumed.

"I fucking can and I fucking will," Spencer dictated. "I'm the head of this family, and as the youngest member, you *will* do what I say!"

He sensed Mason gaping at him and Daff turned to stare as well, her head swiveling from Spencer to Charlie and back again. He heard her swear shakily as she finally took in the resemblance.

The girl—his *sister*—leapt to her feet, looking ready to flee, but she had nowhere to go, not with Mason and Spencer blocking the door.

"Take it down a notch, lord and master," Mason said drily before moving toward the girl. She watched him approach, her eyes wary, her thin body tense. She looked like a cornered animal. "Hey, Charlie . . . so Malcolm was your dad, yeah?"

A hesitant nod.

"And where's your mother?"

"S-she died of an overdose four years ago. When I was ten." So Malcolm's taste in women hadn't changed. He did have a thing for addicts.

"And Malcolm took care of you since then?" Mason asked.

"When he remembered I was there." She shrugged and Mason snorted.

"That sounds like dear old Dad, all right," Spencer said scathingly.

"We'd really like it if you stuck around a bit, Charlie," Mason continued. "I've always wanted a sister."

"How'd you know—" She looked startled that they'd seen through her thin disguise, and Spencer barely kept himself from rolling his eyes.

"The girl thing?" Mason asked, a smile on his lips. "I knew immediately. It took big bro over there a minute to figure it out. If we could see it, others can, too. It's not safe for you out there, Charlie. Let us help you. Please."

The girl hesitated, obviously confused, but Spencer could also see the yearning in her eyes, the desire to be warm and safe . . . to *belong*. He knew that feeling. Had experienced it often in his youth, and if the bastard weren't already dead, he could have killed Malcolm for making all the same mistakes with this fragile child. For letting her to grow up in an unsafe environment, for allowing her to know fear and hunger, and then for fucking abandoning her.

At least the bastard had done one thing right—he'd sent her to Spencer and Mason. But he should have sent her sooner. The thought of this girl, their *sister*, for Christ's sake, growing up the way he and Mason had was just horrifying. And even though this situation had completely thrown him, Spencer was going to make damned sure that she never knew such deprivations again.

He wasn't aware of Daff coming up to stand beside him until her arm crept around his waist. He was grateful for her tacit support, because he was still reeling. He was desperate to make this child stay and not sure how to keep her from bolting the moment they let her out of sight. Mason's approach was clearly working more than Spencer's instinctively autocratic one had. So he let his brother do the talking and tried his best to keep his expression neutral, not wanting to terrify her.

"What do you say, Charlie? Will you come with us? Give us a chance to be your big brothers?"

"I don't need any big brothers. I don't need anyone. I can take care of myself," Charlie stated belligerently, folding her arms over her flat chest. "But . . . I'll go with you for tonight only."

"Thank you," Mason said and looked at Spencer, who—surprise, surprise—found himself incapable of saying anything at all. He nodded curtly and turned away. Daff gave him a brief squeeze and left his side to approach Charlie.

"I'll help you pack. You love reading, huh? I'm sure you'll want to pack these," she said brightly, gesturing toward the paperbacks. "My sister Lia has quite a stash of romance novels as well. I'm sure she'll be happy to swap with you. Or lend you some. My other sister, Daisy, has also been trying to find a home for some of her books. So if you're interested—"

"Books are heavy. I keep my favorites, but I can't collect more. They're difficult to carry."

She was very well-spoken and evidently well educated. Spencer wondered when she had dropped out of school, because clearly she was no longer going, since she was fucking squatting in a derelict building. They'd have to look into guardianship and start thinking about putting her back in school. He knew he was getting ahead of himself, but he felt . . . purposeful. Important. *Needed.* Even if she would never admit to needing him.

He'd come out here tonight, looking to help a stranger, and had found family. And she for damned sure was going to get his help whether she wanted it or not.

The drive back was silent as Mason drove straight to the McGregor farm, even though Spencer was having second thoughts about leaving Charlie there. What if she bolted during the night? He wanted to turn and talk to her, engage her in conversation, encourage her to speak about herself and ask questions about Mason and him, but his tongue felt thick and the words wouldn't come. It was weird. Spencer never had problems speaking to the kids in the youth program. He'd been proud of his ability to draw them out and befriend them. Now, when it mattered most, he couldn't find a single word to say.

Thank God for Daff, who kept up a running commentary in the back seat beside the girl. Telling tales of growing up on the farm, of her sisters, the ill, injured, or stray animals their father and Daisy had frequently adopted. More stories about her mother's cooking, about the ridiculous fights she'd sometimes had with her sisters. Her childhood sounded idyllic. Spencer would have killed for a family life like that, and one quick check over his shoulder told him that Charlie had longed for the same.

He shifted his attention to Mason and, in the dim light, he could see the fond smile on his brother's lips. Mason had obviously heard some of these stories before and didn't find them as alienating as Spencer—and possibly Charlie—did. Maybe because he already felt a sense of belonging where the McGregors were concerned. It was a bizarre sensation to feel instant kinship with the girl, while at the same time feeling farther away from his brother than ever before.

The McGregor farm was fully lit when they drove up, and Dr. and Mrs. McGregor, along with Lia and Daisy—who had heard the news via a quick call from Mason—all spilled out onto the porch. They wore warm, welcoming smiles, and, as Spencer watched, his newly discovered sister was instantly engulfed in love and warmth. The girl looked tiny, lost, and overwhelmed as she stood in the center of the small cluster of people. Her thin arms clutched protectively around her ratty backpack. Mason was among the crowd, and Spencer felt a stark sense of loss and envy as both Mason and Charlie were claimed by the McGregors.

"The warm and fuzzies can get a little overwhelming, right?" Daff's voice sounded from beside him, and, startled, his eyes dropped to hers. He hadn't realized that she wasn't among her family, and he instantly felt less isolated.

"Why aren't you over there fawning?"

"The poor kid's intimidated and overwhelmed, and my family can be a bit much sometimes. Figured it best to sit it out on the sidelines with you."

With him.

"So . . . how much of a mind fuck is this for you?" she asked bluntly, and he shook his head.

"I can't wrap my head around it yet. All I know is that she needs us and I'll for damned sure make certain that we're there for her."

"And you're sure she's . . . you know? Related to you?"

"She has more than a passing resemblance to both Mason and me," he pointed out.

"That's true. That scowl is unmistakable. But are you going to get DNA tests or anything?"

"A birth certificate will do me," he said easily. "If Malcolm's name's on it, she's ours."

"Fair enough." She was quiet for a moment before continuing. "But it seems irresponsible to just take someone in off the street."

"I don't think she's been on the streets for too long, she doesn't seem hardened enough. Which is all the more reason for us to take her in. She wouldn't last much longer out there. She's been lucky so far." The thought of everything that could have happened to her on the streets sent a cold shudder down his spine.

"I just don't want anyone to take advantage of you and Mason," Daff explained. "You guys are wealthy and people know that. And they find ways to exploit generosity and kindness."

"If that's her plan, she'll soon find it's a crappy one, since it means having to go to school and then college and then working her ass off to pay part of her own tuition, because she needs to understand the value of hard work."

She giggled, and he looked at her, surprised by the sound.

"You sound like a dad."

He replayed the words in his head. The thought kind of pleased him. Maybe there was hope for him yet.

"Do I? I have no clue what a real dad sounds like," he said with a perplexed shrug. The movement brought attention to the fact that her hand was in his again. It was starting to feel like it belonged there, and he tried to veer his thoughts off that dangerous path. He couldn't think of Daff in those terms.

Friends didn't hold hands, and if they kept touching like this, he'd lose sight of the true nature of his and Daff's confusing relationship. He subtly moved his hand out of her hold and folded his arms over his chest while he continued to watch the touching tableau of developing kinship in front of him.

She didn't say anything, just pushed her hands in her coat pockets.

"Come on in, everybody," Mrs. McGregor invited them. "I have no idea why we're all on the porch, it's freezing out here. Let's get in out of the cold." She dropped an arm around Charlie's shoulders, not acknowledging the girl's tension. "Would you like some hot chocolate, sweetheart?"

"I've got to get going," Spencer muttered as the larger group splintered and headed into the house.

"Well, you can't. Your ride's just gone inside for some of my mom's awesome hot chocolate. Guess you're stuck with us for a little while longer."

This time Daff tucked a hand into the crook of his elbow and tugged him toward the house. He allowed her to pull him into the large, warm kitchen, where everyone had congregated. Mrs. McGregor was in her element, bustling around, making sure everyone had a cup of something. She beamed when she caught sight of Spencer.

"Hello, Spencer, would you like a cup of hot chocolate as well? Tea? Or something stronger?"

"The chocolate's fine, ma'am," he murmured and then remembered his manners. "Please. Thank you."

"Please, call me Millicent," she invited him, and he was appalled by that idea. It seemed disrespectful to just call her by her first name. He cleared his throat and threw her an awkward smile and a short nod.

His eyes drifted to the girl sitting at the kitchen table; she had her head down and looked completely overwhelmed. The mug of chocolate sat untouched on the table in front of her.

"She should go to bed." The words sounded harsh and way too loud, dropping into one of those odd silences that sometimes fell over a group of people. The girl's beautiful green eyes—so striking against her light-brown skin—lifted and met his. They were seething with anger and resentment. She probably thought he was trying to tell her what to do again. But he knew how terrifying this all had to be for her and thought she might need a little space and some privacy to process everything that was happening.

Everybody else was staring at him, too, and he flushed, uncomfortable with the unwanted attention.

"Of course, this is all new and a little scary, I'm sure," Mrs. McGregor said and then smiled at Charlie. "Why don't I show you to your room? If you don't mind, I'd like to give your clothes a wash, but you can wear some of Daff's and Lia's stuff in the meantime. I'm sure you'd love a hot shower or bath, wouldn't you? Just to get the cold out of your bones."

She led the girl out, chatting amiably all the way. Charlie looked over her shoulder as they left, her eyes seeking and finding Spencer's. Even though she seemed to resent him, he was familiar, and sometimes the devil you knew was a lot less intimidating than the one you didn't. A huge part of him wanted to drag her to his home and take care of her there. But he wasn't equipped to care for a young girl. Not yet. He would make sure there was a room ready for her in no time. She was his family, and it was only right he be the one to take care of her.

When Mrs. McGregor and Charlie were out of earshot, everybody left in the kitchen seemed to exhale collectively.

Mason ran his hands through his hair and looked at Spencer with a helpless shake of his head.

"Now what?"

"We have to get her papers, start looking into legal guardianship."

"You sure that's the right course of action?"

"I don't see what other options we have."

"She may have other family, on her mother's side."

"Yeah. No. I'm not down with that. Where were they when her mother died? They left her with Malcolm for four years. Even if they are out there, they're not getting her. Now that we know she exists, are you really cool with someone else taking care of her?"

"Of course not, but it's a lot to put on you, Spence. Daisy and I are leaving in a few short months, and you'd be left shouldering the bulk of the responsibility on your own."

"We could always take her with us," Daisy suggested softly. Her arm was hooked through Mason's and he seemed to be hanging on to her for support.

"*No.*" Spencer was aware that he'd barked the word, but he couldn't help himself. "She'll stay with me. I have the space. And you guys will be newlyweds—you need your privacy."

"You can make these decisions later," Dr. McGregor intervened quietly. "Charlie is safe for now, and Millicent and I will be happy to take care of her until you've figured out your next step."

"With all due respect, sir, I can take care of my own family."

"I know that, son, and you've done an admirable job over the years. But you're a part of *our* family now, and it always helps to share the burden."

Why did they all refer to him as "family"? It made him uncomfortable. He'd done nothing to earn his way into this family. Mason was marrying into it, Spencer wasn't. And while everything in him yearned to belong, it just seemed too easy and completely undeserved.

"Just until we get the legalities sorted out," he grudgingly relented, ignoring the whole "family" thing.

"I think our immediate concern is preventing her from bolting. The kid looks skittish," Mason said, and Spencer sighed. How had things suddenly become so complicated? Just a week ago, his biggest concern had been his store expansion. Seven days later, he was entangled in the most confusing relationship he'd ever been in, with the world's most complicated woman. His brother was leaving again, and he had a stag party to plan, a best man's speech to write, and a frickin' baby sister who'd popped up out of nowhere.

Millicent McGregor came back downstairs, the smile gone from her face, replaced by a troubled frown.

"That poor child is way too thin and so guarded. Gaining her trust is going to take some doing. Such a pretty little thing, even if she does try to hide it under that gruff exterior. I suppose it comes from pretending to be a boy. I'm so happy she found her way home to you boys," she said, reaching over to squeeze Spencer's hand. "She has no idea how lucky she is to have you two."

Did she really think that? The sincerity shining from her eyes certainly seemed to confirm that she believed what she was saying, and everybody else in the kitchen was nodding in agreement.

"Anyway, I've put her in Daff's old room for now. And I gave her some of you girls' clothes. I hope you don't mind?" she asked but didn't seem too concerned over the reply. "She's just having a shower now."

"Do you think she'll run away?" Lia asked quietly.

"She's too tired for that tonight. And if she means to sneak out first thing in the morning, she'll have a tough time of it, what with your father's tendency to rise with the birds. I think she'll stay put for now."

"It's been an exhausting and eventful evening; I think we'll head home. Get some rest," Mason said, casting his eyes around the room for affirmation. Daisy and Daff nodded, but Spencer hesitated, reluctant to let the girl out of his radius.

"She'll be fine, Spence," Mason murmured, and Spencer nodded. As long as she didn't think they'd abandoned her.

"Can you tell her we'll be back in the morning? To talk?" he asked Mrs. McGregor gruffly, and she smiled reassuringly.

"Of course I will."

"Rough week, huh?" Daff muttered in the car, en route to Mason and Daisy's place.

"Hmm." *Rough* was understating it.

"I want you to know I'm here for you if you need someone to talk to. I have younger sisters, too, and they can be a total pain." She raised her voice so that Daisy could hear the last bit, and the younger woman—whose curly head was resting on Mason's shoulder—casually stuck up a middle finger in response.

"See what I'm dealing with? No respect." Spencer peered at her smiling face, clearly visible only when they passed a streetlamp. She was smiling, looking so fucking approachable and beautiful.

He wished . . . he wanted . . .

He shook himself. What he wished or wanted didn't signify. Still, he couldn't stop himself from reaching out and cupping her cheek in the palm of his hand.

"Thank you. For tonight. For coming. It meant a lot." They passed another light, and he could see the small smile on her lips. She lifted her hand to cover his, stroking her palm over the backs of his fingers.

"I'm happy I went." He turned his hand until her fingers were caught in his grip and brought them to his mouth to kiss the backs of her knuckles.

"This week may have been a bit rough and slightly bizarre and ever so surreal. But I have no regrets," he told her, and her fingers squeezed around his hand.

"I'm happy to hear that," she said, and, in what appeared to be a completely impulsive move, gave him a quick peck on his cheek.

Daisy turned her head to look at them, her curiosity evident despite the car's dim interior.

"Are you guys sure you're *just* friends?" she asked softly. Her voice was speculative. Daff's fingers tightened around his once more before she replied.

"Never been more certain of anything in my life," she said sincerely, and Spencer swallowed past the lump of emotion in his throat and smiled.

CHAPTER TWELVE

"Why are you being so secretive? Why can't you just tell me what your plans are for this place?" Daff asked, crunching into a crisp green apple while she spoke and peering at Spencer closely. He'd been making vague references to potential changes and expansions to SCSS for weeks now, and it was driving her crazy.

He was peeling an orange and gave her one of those inscrutable looks that always drove her a little crazy over the top of his glasses. He just looked so freaking hot and stern. He couldn't seem to maintain the stern expression this time and grinned, looking almost boyish in his excitement.

"I think I can talk about it without jinxing it now. Since the plans were approved this morning," he said, his smile widening. "I'm adding a gym and juice bar up here. Top-of-the-line equipment, world-class instructors, and we'll be offering everything from personal fitness training to Pilates to yoga to kickboxing. I want SCSS to be a one-stop shop for all your fitness needs. Buy the gear downstairs; use it upstairs."

"Oh my *God*, Spencer, that's freaking amazing!" Daff enthused, and his chest expanded at her praise. He looked prouder than a new father.

"Better still, I'm opening a second branch in George early next year. Claude will run it for me."

Daff squealed, genuinely excited for him. She knew how much the store meant to him. After weeks of shared lunches, she still learned something new about him every day, but his pride in this store was something that had always been evident.

She leaned back in the rickety desk chair that she had claimed as her own and stared at the ceiling.

"You know that once you start renovating up here, you're going to lose Nelly, right?" she asked, referring to the elephant-shaped stain above his desk. She had named it Nelly the very first time she'd brought him lunch here.

"Nah, I'll ask them to save that ceiling board for me and frame it or something. I need something to look at when I'm concentrating."

They talked about the expansion plans a bit more, while at the same time spitballing ideas for Daff's future career.

"Maybe you could be a yoga instructor," Spencer speculated. "You're constantly wearing yoga pants in your free time anyway."

He'd noticed that, had he? Since they'd put an end to their no-sex sex thing, he'd been really good about not flirting or treating her in any overtly sexual way, but she'd caught him staring at her ass a few times. Mostly when she wore yoga pants, come to think of it. It made her feel better about the hankering she felt for him every time she got within five feet of the man.

"I'm sure it would be a great career opportunity for me if I didn't suck at yoga," she dismissed, and his eyes widened.

"For someone who's not very good at it, you own a shitload of yoga pants."

"Yeah? I also own a ton of jumpsuits, but that doesn't mean I want to be a fighter pilot." He choked at her words and then laughed.

"I'm picturing a fighter pilot in some of those jumpsuits women wear these days," he elaborated, and she giggled. "In all seriousness, when Claude leaves this branch, I'll be looking for a new manager," he said pointedly.

"Keep looking, mister," she said, taking another bite from her apple. "Because I'm leaving the whole managing gig behind permanently."

She just wished she knew what to do instead. The two months had practically flown by and she had just a week of work left. She was already training a new woman to take her place, but Daff still had no clue what she wanted to do.

"So has Charlie loosened up about moving?" Daff asked, changing the subject, and Spencer winced. It was a bit of a sore subject. Charlie was still living with the McGregors and, after a rocky start—she'd attempted to run away twice—seemed to be settling in nicely. Mason and Spencer had contacted an attorney, and because Charlie had no other living relatives, there was no disputing their claim to dual guardianship. They'd had social workers in for interviews, undergone rigorous evaluations, and had both been deemed fit guardians for the girl. It was a lengthy process, but the ball was rolling.

The only hitch was Charlie. She refused to accept that she required any form of care and barely gave Spencer the time of day. She was getting along well with Mason now, thanks to Daisy, and had even spent a weekend with them, sleeping on the new sofa bed Mason had acquired especially for her.

Daff knew that the girl's rejection troubled Spencer. It was clear that he desperately wanted to find a way to communicate with her, but every word he said to her sounded like a command, and Charlie didn't respond well to orders. It was painful to watch. Daff had attended a couple of his youth outreach sessions, and it wasn't like the man didn't know how to speak to teens. He just sucked at talking to Charlie.

And Daff was beginning to understand that when someone meant more to him, his attempts at communication became even clumsier. It made her view all those past aborted attempts at flirtation in a whole new light.

"I asked her if she wanted to choose the decor for her room. She told me she didn't care, since she wouldn't be staying there anyway." His dark brows furrowed at the recollection.

"Did you ask her? Or *tell* her?"

"I don't follow."

"Spencer, when you speak with Charlie, you have this tendency to"—how to put this tactfully?—"bark orders at her. She doesn't seem to respond well to that."

"She doesn't seem to respond well to *me*," he said somewhat morosely. "She hates me. Leaves the room every time I enter it. But of course, she and Mason get on like a house on fire."

And he felt excluded.

Her stupid heart just about broke at that revelation. And she wasn't sentimental. Except, where Spencer was concerned, she found she had a sentimental and emotional streak a mile wide.

"You just have to be patient, Spencer," she said. "She doesn't hate you, she just doesn't know you very well yet. And you *have* to use a different approach when speaking with her. Suggest instead of command. Request, don't order."

"She's a kid. What good are suggestions and requests when she has no idea what's good for her?"

"She's a teenage girl. A confused one. She went from being an only child to a youngest sister, with just about everyone telling her what she can or can't do. She undoubtedly feels powerless. You and she are more similar than you know. And I'm not just talking about those matching glares . . . think about it. From the bits and pieces she's revealed over the last few weeks, it's safe to assume that she ran the house, took care of her dying parent, and kept things from falling apart. That was *your* job growing up. Of course you're going to butt heads now. You're both used to steering the ship . . . oh my *God*, I sound like my father." She raised a horrified hand to her mouth. Her father—unhappy that she would be unemployed soon—had been giving her his seafaring-themed pep talks/lectures, pretty much like Lia had predicted he would. Apparently Daff had absorbed more of his words than she knew.

Still, Spencer looked thoughtful. Something she'd said clearly resonated with him.

"Think about what approach would work on you and go with that," she suggested.

He rested his elbow on the desk and his chin on his thumb and absently stroked his index finger over his lower lip. Back and forth, back and forth . . . Daff was mesmerized by the movement and longed to run her own finger and then definitely her tongue over the firm softness of that lip as well. He was staring up at Nelly while he considered her words. He started plucking at the lip with thumb and index finger, and Daff bit back a groan.

The more time she spent with him, the more she wanted him. She couldn't recall ever really desiring a man this much, and she couldn't be sure if it was because he was now off-limits or because every moment spent with him was quite *wonderful*, really.

He was so easy to be with. She never had to put up a pretense with him. In his own gruff way, he always had something kind to say. Just last week when she had sprouted a zit, he had grinned and told her she looked cute, even though Daff had known she looked downright hideous. She didn't feel the need to dress up; he always had a gleam of appreciation in his eyes no matter what she wore. It was nice. *He* was nice.

Watching him with the teens he tried to help was also eye-opening. The patience and care he exhibited. She recalled how willing he'd been to put his entire life on hold to help Charlie, even before he knew what she was to him. The man would give the clothes off his back to help a child in need, and Daff often felt a little intimidated by his sheer *goodness*. She wasn't good. She wasn't kind. And even though she wanted him, she knew that what they had now was best. Spencer needed someone like him. Someone who was kind and decent.

"What time's the meeting tonight?" she asked in an attempt to break free of her melancholy thoughts. He was still dead set on building the youth center and would be meeting with the town committee that night to pitch the proposal he and Mason had been working on for weeks.

"Seven." His eyes dropped back to hers and he stopped worrying at his lip.

"How do you think it'll go?"

"I know Oom Herbert, Principal Kane, and your dad are on board. I think Father O'Grady would be keen on the idea, too, but I'm not too sure about Alderman Motlaung and Mrs. Salie." Mrs. Salie was the librarian.

"I don't think Mrs. Salie is a concern. But you may have your work cut out with the alderman. There's been talk about him being a mayoral candidate next year, and a lot of his party's campaign sponsors probably won't support the youth center."

"Hmm." He went back to worrying his lip, and Daff stifled a moan.

"Anyway," she said, starting to pack up the remnants of their lunch, "I should get back to work."

"Hmm." He was staring at Nelly again and only shifted his attention back to her after Daff got up to leave. "Daff?"

She stilled and watched him cautiously.

"Yes?"

"Do you think Charlie would like a day out? Maybe to explore and shop and stuff?"

"I think she'd like that."

"Would you . . ." He paused as he considered his words carefully. "Could you join us? She probably won't go if it's just me."

"When are you thinking of doing this?"

"Sunday?" Just two days away. The thought of spending an entire day with him definitely appealed.

"Suits me," she said, striving for casual, and he looked relieved. As if she weren't at the point where she would move heaven and earth for this man.

"Appreciate it."

"I'll see you soon," she promised him and turned to leave again.

"Daff?"

"Yes?"

"I'm glad we're friends." The words were soft and heartfelt and yet left Daff feeling hollow and disheartened. Because it didn't matter if what they had now was best—she definitely no longer wanted to be this man's friend. She wasn't sure *what* she wanted, but it was definitely more than what they currently had.

"Me too," she said, her voice muted and her smile an effort.

She left without another word.

Spencer watched Daff leave and heaved a frustrated sigh before running both hands through his hair. The woman was driving him crazy. Her warm smiles, so scarce in the past—and never aimed at him—were ever present these days. Sometimes it physically hurt not to reach out and touch her. He still wasn't able to convince his body that they were just friends, and the amount of self-relief and/or cold showers he'd been forced to submit to over the last six weeks was becoming ridiculous. He had to consider the possibility of lessening his exposure to her.

Maybe depriving himself of her company, going cold turkey, as it were, would be the eventual solution to his dilemma. But it was something he could only consider doing after the wedding. Luckily, that was just a month away now. After that he'd be sure to keep his distance. It would be easier once she was no longer working down the road and the lunches stopped.

And he definitely wouldn't be seeing much of the McGregors after Mason and Daisy left. Which was why he had to get Charlie comfortably situated at his place before that happened. If she didn't wind up going to Grahamstown with Daisy and Mason after all—something that was starting to look like a distinct possibility.

Asking Daff to join him and Charlie on Sunday probably hadn't been the wisest move, either. But if he asked Mason and Daisy to come, Charlie would give all her attention to Mason. He'd noticed her doing that more and more lately. Mason and Daisy had suggested a small family dinner, just the four of them, a couple of weeks ago, and the girl hadn't said a single word to Spencer the entire evening. And yet, she and Mason seemed to have hit it off immediately.

Spencer felt left out.

Every night he went home yearning for Daff, missing his brother, and longing to spend time with his new sister. Occasionally he went out to Ralphie's, often inviting Mason, who always joined him but rarely stayed out longer than a couple of hours. The younger man was too distracted with wedding and moving plans. So Spencer was usually left to finish his drinks alone. Someone would occasionally stop by for a word, but for the most part everyone left him alone. He felt like a fucking island, being buffeted by heavy winds, rain, and waves from all sides and at risk of disappearing completely beneath the raging waters.

On the bright side, his plans for expansion were steaming ahead, and the youth center looked like it would become a reality soon. At least that was something in the huge ocean of nothing his life had become.

He shook his head firmly. God, he was turning into a morose fucker. It was time to get his life back under control. And he would start with Carlotta "Charlie" Carlisle. A fourteen-year-old little wiseass who had seen way too much shit in her life wasn't about to get the better of him.

Daff was at Daisy's later that evening, helping her sisters and mother with seating arrangements for the wedding, when Mason came striding in. Charlie was idly fidgeting with the little magnetized cards, looking bored out of her mind. They all—with the exception of Charlie—sat up expectantly and watched Mason's face closely. His expression gave nothing away and he dropped a kiss on Daisy's neck on his way to the refrigerator for a beer.

"Well?" Daff prompted when he twisted the cap off, leaned against the kitchen counter, and took a thirsty drink, still without saying a word.

"The project got the green light," he said with a grin, and the women squealed in excitement. Daff's eyes went to the front door, looking for Spencer. He would be thrilled and shouldn't be left to celebrate this momentous occasion alone.

"Where's Spencer?" she asked. "He must be ecstatic."

"Whatever *that* looks like," Charlie droned, and Daff shot the girl an irritated look, even though it was probably exactly what Daff herself would have said just a few months ago.

"*Watch* it, Carlotta Carlisle," she warned, and the girl glared at her. Daff had sussed out pretty early on that Charlie absolutely hated her given name—*join the club, sister*—and had filed that useful bit of knowledge away until she could use it.

"He stayed behind to go over a few additional details with the committee."

"What was the overall reaction?" their mother asked.

"Pretty good. A few naysayers as we expected, but when Captain Van Breda wholeheartedly backed the project, saying he was all for something that was likely to keep problem teens off the streets, most of the town got behind it, too."

"That's fantastic," Lia exclaimed. Daisy couldn't stop grinning, and Daff felt quite uncharacteristically giddy with happiness. She knew how much this meant to Spencer and had desperately wanted it for him. She'd wanted to attend the town meeting and voice her encouragement but had promised Daisy ages ago that she would help with the seating arrangements. They'd considered changing their plans, but Spencer wouldn't hear of them postponing anything and their father had promised to be very vocal in his support of the project.

"So how's this going?" Mason asked, coming up to focus on the seating chart on a mini whiteboard. "Need my help?"

"Not this time," Daisy said with an easy smile. Mason had proven invaluable when they'd been struggling over the same task for Lia's wedding. Because of her asshole ex-fiancé's extended family and her need to please everyone, Lia had invited some problematic guests, and it had been a nightmare trying to find the right tables for them. Mason had sorted it out with admirable efficiency.

Fortunately, Daisy's guest list was smaller and her guests less complicated. Everybody started discussing the wedding again, and Daff bit back a frustrated groan. She wanted to hear more about the youth center and to ask what Spencer's reaction had been. It was annoying that everybody else seemed to have moved on from something so momentous.

She got out her phone and checked her messages. Nothing from Spencer. Why hadn't he texted to tell her his news? Surely he'd want to share it with her?

Congratulations! So happy for you!!! She sent the message hastily and waited. But the message remained unread. Disappointed, she watched the screen a moment longer before shoving the phone into her pocket. And then dragging it back out a second later to check it again. Still nothing. She checked the alert volume and put it back into her pocket.

The next half hour dragged by, and even though Daff constantly checked her messages, Spencer didn't contact her. She knew he was probably busy with those "additional details," but it was killing her not to talk to him about this. After six weeks of hearing about all the hopes he had for that place, for it to finally come to fruition . . . Daff wanted to share in that joy with him. It almost physically hurt her not to be there with him right now.

"Daffy," Daisy exclaimed, and Charlie sniggered when Daff glared at her sister. "What's going on with you? You're squirming like you have ants in your pants."

"Well, you'd know what that looks like, wouldn't you?" Daff scowled. Daisy and Lia burst into laughter.

"Yeah, sorry not sorry!" Daisy hooted, and Mason frowned.

"What's this now?"

"We once put actual ants in her pants." Lia chortled at the recollection.

"Oh, I remember that." Now their mother was laughing, too.

"God, sometimes you guys really suck," Daff muttered when Mason and even Charlie joined in on the laughter. "Some of those little bastards nearly crawled up my cooch."

"*Daffodil!* Language!" their mother admonished, clapping her hands over Charlie's ears. The teen squirmed, still laughing, as she tried to free her head from Millicent McGregor's hold.

"You put soap on our toothbrushes," Daisy reminded her gleefully. "You had it coming."

"Ugh. Keep laughing, I'm heading home . . . to chuck your caterpillars in the dustbin."

"You wouldn't!" Daisy gasped.

"*That's* where the caterpillars disappeared to?" Mason asked, his eyes still alight with laughter.

"I so would! Come and find them in the trash tomorrow," she taunted with a wave as she grabbed up her purse and hastened to the front door.

"*Daff!*"

"Night, all!" Daff called cheerfully as she slammed out of the house to a chorus of Daisy's frantic calls and everybody else's laughter. Once she was outside in the cool night air, she leaned back against the front door and turned her attention on Spencer's dark home just yards away. She could sit on his porch and wait for him, but it was a chilly spring night and there was no telling when he'd be back. Especially since he wasn't answering his texts.

She considered calling him, but knew that if he hadn't even seen her text, then his phone was probably off.

I'm so sorry I wasn't there to celebrate with you tonight. I know how much this means to you. I wish I could have been there. She contemplated her message for a long time before adding a sad face, followed by a heart and a kiss. Before she could think about it too long, she sent the message and trudged to her car.

She was getting ready to climb into bed nearly an hour later when her doorbell rang. Startled, she froze for a second, wondering who on earth it could be at nearly twelve at night.

Her phone buzzed and she picked it up from the nightstand and grinned when she saw the message: Open the door, Daffodil.

She hastened to the front door and, after a quick peek through the window to confirm who it was, threw back the bolts and yanked the door open. He strode inside without a word and shut the door purposefully behind him.

"You know I hate it when you call me Daffo—" Her words were cut off when his strong arms wrapped around her waist and yanked her to his chest. He sighed and buried his face in her hair. She smiled contentedly and snuggled there, rubbing her face against his well-defined pecs, while her own arms wound around his back and held on tight.

This.

This, right here, was perfection.

"You did it," she whispered, and he shook in her arms, mute testimony to how much that center meant to him and how afraid he'd been that it would be rejected. His grip around her waist loosened, and his hands reached up to cup her face and tilt her head back.

"Daff . . . *darling*." He hadn't used the endearment in weeks, and Daff shuddered in response to it. He watched her for a moment and then, without any hesitation at all, lowered his head to claim her lips in the hungriest, hottest kiss she'd ever experienced. There was no subtlety as his tongue swooped into her mouth and simply claimed her, and for once, Daff was happy to be claimed. Her hands trailed to his shoulders and up around his neck as she gave and received in equal measure.

He moved, hooking an arm around her waist and carrying her with him until she felt the wall at her back. He lifted his head and caged her with his body while she quivered in his hold. His forearms rested on the wall on either side of her head.

"I can't be your friend," he whispered, his lips finding the sensitive spot beneath her ear and nuzzling. "I don't want to be your friend. I want more."

She nodded in response to his words, unable to find her voice, her body warmed by the intense waves of heat coming off him. In this moment, she wanted more, too. No reservations, no insecurities, and no worrying about who was in control of what. They could both be captains of this freaking ship and ride out this storm together.

"God, Daff, I *burn* for you." He lifted his mouth and swept it up her throat and seared his way to her hungry mouth. He cupped her face again, palms on her cheeks. He used his thumbs to tilt her head back. His tongue found her mouth, and it felt like she was welcoming him home. Her hands stroked over the hard planes of his torso and up over his chest, where her fingers found the taut masculine beads of his nipples, evident even through the thick fabric of his shirt. She smiled when he jerked beneath her touch—it thrilled her when he reacted to her like that. Made her feel powerful.

With Spencer, she felt sexy and confident because she had no doubt that he wanted her, just the way she was. With all her flaws and quirks and craziness, he still wanted *her*.

"Again," he demanded, and Daff's hands moved back up to his chest, kneading and exploring hungrily along the way.

"Daff, darling," he grated, lifting his lips just enough to say the words. "You know what I want, don't you?"

"Yes."

"Say it," he commanded, and she smiled again.

"To take a shower and watch a movie?" she teased, and he half laughed, half groaned, clearly recognizing the ludicrous suggestion as his own.

"Never mind. I'll just show you." He kissed her again. A little more roughly this time, his tongue unapologetically forging its way into her mouth. She sighed happily when it demanded a response from hers. She buried her hands in his soft, springy hair and pushed herself against him while he murmured something inaudible against her lips. He swung her into his arms, the gesture outrageously romantic, and, without lifting his mouth from hers, strode blindly toward the bathroom.

"Do you know where you're going?" she asked with a breathless giggle, and he paused outside her open bedroom door.

"I do now," he growled, and she thrilled at the intense masculinity in his voice. Forceful men didn't usually do it for her, but on Spencer it was mind-blowingly sexy. Because she knew he'd never do anything to hurt her. He strode into the room and then paused to shove the door shut with his booted foot.

His mouth was on hers again, and Daff was dimly aware of a dizzying sensation that could be attributed to either his fantastic, all-consuming kiss or the fact that he'd swung her around to deposit her on the bed. He settled himself between her spread-eagled thighs and unabashedly ground his hard length up against her aching core.

The move had her nearly arching off the bed in reaction, but he settled her down with a gentler kiss before lifting his mouth and staring down into her flushed, dazed face with his wondering, heated gaze.

"You're so fucking gorgeous," he said thickly. He reached for her tank top and shoved it up over her small, naked breasts. Daff lifted her chest toward him, proudly displaying herself to him, inviting him to taste and touch, but he simply knelt between her thighs and stared at her with such burning intensity that she uncharacteristically found herself blushing.

"Hmm." This time it really *was* just a sound. One of yearning and appreciation. The sound a starving man would make at the dinner table.

He reached out and thumbed both nipples gently and she nearly came off the bed in response to that.

"Love how sensitive these are," he muttered, his thumbs circling the aching centers now, tormenting her by not touching her the way she needed to be touched.

"Spencer, please," she begged, and he reluctantly lifted his burning regard from her breasts to her eyes.

"Still trying to meet that sex deadline, are you? There's no rush, darling," he teased gently. He dropped another hot kiss on her lips, and she wrapped her arms around him and dug her fingers into his strong back. He was still wearing too many clothes. Why was he *always* wearing too many clothes?

She forgot about the disparity seconds later when he lifted his head and trailed his mouth over her sensitive skin, all the way down to her chest. Once he reached the slope of one aching, taut breast, he planted soft, gentle kisses around the crest of her nipple and Daff shuddered when she felt his hot breath against her sensitive flesh.

"Oh God, Spencer. Oh please. *Please*," she begged unashamedly, and he put her out of her misery by drawing the tight, aching bud into his hot mouth, suckling so hard that the pleasure was almost pain. He lifted his head and planted a sweet, apologetic kiss on the aching nipple before moving over and gracing her other breast with the same treatment.

He straightened, still kneeling between her spread thighs, looking as fiercely beautiful as a demigod. She didn't know how it had happened, but she noticed that the fly of his jeans was unsnapped, revealing that hard, gorgeous column of flesh straining between his thighs. She reached for it, and he gently pushed her hand away.

"Not now, darling," he denied her, and she cried out in frustration.

"I want to touch you."

"I know. I want you to. But that thing has a hair trigger right now. One touch from you and it's going off."

She huffed impatiently and he smiled at her, the strain evident on his face. He gently pushed her hair out of her face and kissed her again.

"Beautiful Daff, you mean the world to me," he said, and the words caused a lump to form in her throat. Did she? How could she? She wasn't sweet like Lia, or clever and witty like Daisy, she didn't have a kind heart like Spencer. She was just Daff. Mouthy, sarcastic, and confused.

"Stop thinking about it," he instructed firmly. "And stay right here in this moment with me."

"Spencer," she whispered helplessly.

"Right here, with me," he maintained. "Daff. Look at me. I'll make it worth your while."

She lifted her eyes to his, and he grinned.

"Keep looking," he coaxed and then rewarded her by unfastening the top button of his shirt and dragging it over his head. He tossed the shirt aside and she nearly sighed at the familiar sight of his gorgeous chest. She reached up to touch all that smooth, firm flesh and was delighted when his muscles bunched and jumped beneath her fluttering touch.

"Oh God, Spencer. You're magnificent," she said in awe, and his grin widened. She lifted her head and started trailing her lips over his warm, smooth, and slightly salty skin. Her mouth found his taut nipples and began to voraciously lick and suck the sensitive flesh.

"You're just so—" The rest of whatever he was saying was muffled against her neck, which he kissed and sucked before he found his way back to the lure of her mouth.

He dragged his head up to peer down to her pouting breasts in unabashed hunger. They were both topless now, Daff in her panties and Spencer in his jeans. He reached down reverently to cup her breasts with both hands, testing their weight in his palms, his thumbs finding and teasing her nipples again. He stalled there, spending so much time on her nipples, Daff found herself uncomfortably overstimulated, dizzy and disoriented. He had to stop—he was literally driving her insane with pleasure.

"*Spencer,*" she pleaded. "I can't stand it anymore. Please."

"Hmm." His mouth clamped over a nipple, the suction bordering on painful, and his hand burrowed beneath her panties, where his thumb stroked her clit while his middle and index fingers buried themselves inside her tight, wet sheath. She shuddered and screamed as she came almost immediately. He continued suckling on her nipple while his free hand stroked the other, prolonging and intensifying her powerful orgasm. She screwed her eyes tightly shut and fought for breath. Her complete focus was on the pleasure he was giving her.

When she finally stopped clenching around his fingers, she melted onto the bed in a boneless, exhausted, sweaty heap of satisfaction. She was still trembling from her release and feeling more than a little shattered by the sheer magnitude of her orgasm. Spencer dragged her panties off, tearing them a little and leaving the ruined and soaked garment tangled around one of her ankles.

"Okay, darling?" he asked gently, and Daff barely found the energy to shake her head.

"No. Damn you. I'm not." It took everything in her not to cry like a baby again. What was it about the orgasms this man gave her that made her dissolve into an emotional heap every single freaking time? He kissed her again, and she was vaguely aware of him tugging something from the back pocket of his jeans. He got off the bed to very carefully drag off the offending denim garment. Good thing, too. Those damned jeans had overstayed their welcome.

God, he had superlative thighs. Heavy, well defined, and gorgeously muscled. A sportsman's thighs. Her mouth went dry as she watched him climb back onto the bed. Brandishing that massive erection like a club, he clambered between her thighs, and she gawked at that huge thing so comfortably resting on top of her naked mound. It throbbed in time with his heartbeat, and the red, plum-size glans shone with moisture. She unthinkingly reached down to pet it.

"Uh-uh," he rasped, intercepting her hand. "Hair trigger, remember?"

Daff stared mutely up into his beautiful, savage face.

She couldn't believe they were finally going to do this. It felt so right. There was no overthinking it, and she was happy in this moment to trust Spencer not to abuse the power she was ceding to him.

She watched him open the little foil package and drag the latex up over his hardness. Afterward he sawed that sheathed column up and down against her cleft and she groaned, more than ready to go again.

"Spencer," she whispered, thrusting up against him, wanting so much more. She felt open and exposed, but she didn't care if he could see right into her soul. Not anymore.

"Darling Daff," he growled, intensifying the sawing against her clit. He never quite allowed her to come down from her previous climax, and it was driving her crazy because while she felt sated, she didn't feel finished. Finally, he reached between them and took hold of his shaft, placing himself at her entrance. Very slowly and very gently he eased himself inside. Daff whimpered at his impossible size, bigger than anything she'd ever felt before. She craved more and moved impatiently against him, even while his largeness felt uncomfortable. He refused to rush, doing this in Spencer time. And Spencer time crept along at a snail's pace.

"You're so tiny, tell me if it hurts." Everybody was tiny next to him, but Daff appreciated his concern and, considering the size of him, was grateful now for the slow pace he had set. She sobbed slightly at the stretching fullness. He really was uncomfortably big. Sensing her uneasiness, he reached down and found her clit with his thumb. All thoughts of discomfort fled as her body blindly followed instinct and moved restlessly beneath his. He hissed in reaction when she thrust her hips against him.

"No, darling, don't move. I don't think I can—" She ignored him and pushed up even farther, grinding herself against his hand as she sheathed him almost completely. Spencer groaned, sounding almost pained, and swore shakily when she slid down, guiding the rhythm for now, before pushing back up to gain another inch.

Sweat beaded his brow and his eyes shut in concentration as he remained completely still, allowing her to set the pace. Daff widened her thighs even more and planted her feet flat on the mattress as she slowly slid down his hard length again. He moved his knees under her butt, giving her more control, while her shoulders remained flat on the bed. Her bum was on his lap and angled just enough to give her complete and unrestricted access to his penis. Using only her feet for leverage, she slid slowly up and down his shaft. His hands moved to her straining breasts, strumming her nipples, while his eyes slid back and forth between her face and the sight of his hardness sliding in and out of her softness.

"Spencer," she whispered, one hand reaching up toward his face, and he lowered himself just enough for her to hook her palm around his neck and drag herself up until she was straddling his lap and her breasts were flattened against his chest.

"You feel so good," she sobbed, loving this so much. Her other arm flung around his neck, and he buried his face in her neck. She felt him huffing for breath against her skin while his arms wrapped around her waist.

She wasn't sure who was directing the pace anymore, and she didn't really care. It was all give and take in this moment, and she felt his breath quickening against her.

"I can't much longer, Daff," he groaned. "Going to fucking come."

"Good," she huffed as she continued to rock against him. He felt wonderful inside her. Filled her completely. He belonged right there for all eternity. The thought scared her, but she shoved it aside as she focused on her building orgasm.

"Spencer," she entreated, not sure why she was pleading with him when he was doing *everything* right. He yanked her closer with one strong arm while bracing his other hand on the mattress behind her. He maneuvered her until she was flat on her back and he was propped above her, and this time there was no mistaking who was in charge as he slammed into her. His face hovered above hers, his eyes entangled with hers. He was dripping with sweat, his biceps and shoulders bulging as he held his weight off her.

She grunted with each thrust, the sound guttural and in no way, shape, or form ladylike. There was nothing ladylike about her at all in this moment, and she didn't care. This was primal, it was fierce, it was *perfect*.

Her legs drew up and wrapped around his taut, thrusting butt, and she felt everything inside her draw tight. His green eyes shone into hers, bright with emotion and gleaming with moisture.

"Come for me, Daff," he whispered. His voice—the quietest thing in the room—was barely audible against the wet, slapping sounds of their lovemaking. And because he asked, she did. With a single high-pitched cry, she came. Hard. Endlessly and agonizingly. It was the most amazing thing that had ever happened to her, and she was glad, *fiercely* glad, that she was sharing it with Spencer.

She was still at the pinnacle when she felt him tense, groan, and then shudder in her arms, and they both floated down to earth together. He wrapped himself protectively around her, as if to shelter her from the world, and in his own quiet way made her feel safe and protected and cherished.

CHAPTER THIRTEEN

She didn't cry. She thought perhaps she was too wrung out to cry. She *felt* like crying, but she felt like laughing, too. She felt like running a mile or sleeping for days. She felt restless and contented. Wrong and right. Her emotions were jumbled up inside her, and it was both terrifying . . . and exhilarating.

All she knew for sure was that she felt safe in Spencer's strong arms. Welcome and at home. It was a powerful and addictive feeling, and while she knew it should probably scare her, she didn't really have the energy to worry about it now.

Spencer was quiet. He hadn't said a word since their breathing had evened ages ago. She would have thought he was asleep if not for the gently stroking hand on her naked back. She was wrapped in his arms, her head on his bicep and her face against his chest. One of her hands rested on his waist, and the other was curled up against his chest. She never wanted to move.

"You okay?" he asked after another few minutes had passed.

"Yes."

"I'm not sorry this happened, Daff," he said, sounding almost defensive, and she smiled against his chest.

"Neither am I." Sex had never been like this for her before. So emotional and intense. It had never felt this natural and beautiful, either. No toys or ropes, no whips and chains. Just them . . .

Spencer and Daffodil, giving and taking in equal measure. Daff had never really known it could be like that, and yet, that's how she'd always known it *should* be.

"And I want to do it again," he asserted, sounding stubborn, and her smile widened. She lifted her head so that he could see it.

"Good," she said. His brow lowered in confusion, and she stretched up to kiss him lightly before lowering her head back onto his bicep.

"And I don't want a no-strings thing this time." Daff sighed and pushed herself up to face him, sitting cross-legged with her hands folded in her lap. He sat up, too, dragging a sheet over his hips and hiding that beautiful, burgeoning erection from her.

"You're bound and determined to talk about this now, aren't you?" she asked, pushing her messy hair out of her face.

"Hmm." She grinned at the huffy sound.

"You're going to have to give me more than that, big guy. You're the one who wants to talk."

"Just like to know where things stand, is all," he groused.

"Why should we put a label on it? Why can't it just *be*? You're always overthinking things."

"I just want people to know—" He stopped abruptly, as if thinking the better of what he'd been about to say.

"Uh-uh, I'm curious now," she said. "You'd better finish that sentence."

"I just want people to know that you're with me, that's all."

"I told you, I don't do that whole ownership thing anymore."

"Yeah." He looked moody and unsettled and confused. And boy, could she relate. "I just don't know how to do *this*."

"What?"

"Casual. Like it means nothing, when it fucking means everything."

"I don't know how to be what you want, Spencer," she whispered. Unsettled by his words. By how much they echoed the way she felt about their encounter.

"That's okay, darling," he whispered back, cupping the side of her face. "You already *are* exactly what I want."

There was no way to respond to that. None. For a man of few words, he often found just the right ones to say at just the right time.

She shook her head and smiled at him.

"I really don't know what to do with you, Carlisle." She sighed sadly, and he smiled.

"Right now? I have a few ideas." He pointedly looked down at the tent that had formed in his lap and she giggled lightheartedly, only vaguely aware that she was seeing him through a haze of tears again.

"Yeah? Do enlighten me."

The night passed in a beautiful blur of orgasms and laughter. Once he'd stopped asking difficult questions and expecting impossible things, they'd gone back to the easy relationship that had developed between them over the last few weeks. It was surprisingly uncomplicated, even with sex thrown into the mix.

"You have the sexiest legs," she said during one of their breaks. They were sitting naked on her bed and eating the awful leftover pasta she'd cooked for dinner two nights ago.

"Hmm? I could say the same about yours."

"These scrawny chicken legs have nothing on yours." Her eyes drifted to the surgical scar on his left knee, and she pulled a face. "Do you ever miss it?"

"Miss what?" he asked absently, his eyes riveted on a dab of pasta sauce that had dropped to her naked breast.

"Playing." He dragged his hungry scrutiny from the sauce to stare at her blankly, and she laughed in disbelief before elaborating even further, "*Rugby*. Do you ever miss playing it?"

He grinned sheepishly before shrugging.

"Honestly? And this stays between us. I fucking hated it. Hated every single thing about it. I never liked the sport, but it was my ticket out of here. I was relieved when I tore my ACL. I could have done the rehab, gone back, played again. But it was the excuse I was looking for to get out. I'd already gotten what I wanted out of the sport. It was time for me to move on with my life."

She laughed incredulously at that revelation.

"I prefer cricket," he continued conspiratorially, and she laughed even harder. She didn't even know why she found it so funny, but it just made her admire him more. He'd done whatever the hell it took to better himself—what was not to admire? The man was amazing.

"Now, if you don't mind," he said seriously, "I hate to see good food go to waste."

He bent over and finally claimed the errant drop of sauce that had trickled its way down to her nipple. It was a long time before either of them spoke again.

It was nearly dawn when she told him her most shameful secret. She didn't know why she did it—it just came out, and she found herself grateful for the dark while she spoke.

"I don't think I ever really *liked* sex before," she blurted out into the night. The darkness helped, as did Spencer's quiet breathing and patient silence. The up-and-down movement of his hand on her arm never faltered.

"My first lover—not first boyfriend, I've had a lot of boyfriends. I haven't slept with most of them." She cleared her throat after that awkward confession. "Anyway, my first lover—Jake—he was charming and nice. He seemed perfect. He was an out-of-towner, one of Shar's friends. Great background, wealthy family, the works. Everything a stupid twenty-year-old girl aspires to. He was a good kisser." She could feel Spencer starting to tense beneath her, obviously not keen on hearing about Jake's kissing prowess. She patted his chest comfortingly, mutely begging for patience, and she could feel him force himself to relax.

"When I thought I was ready, I let him know that I was willing to, you know . . . ?"

"Hmm." It was all the encouragement she needed, and she gulped before continuing.

"He took me to this place he was renting in Knysna. It all started pretty innocently, the kissing and petting and stuff. I was relaxing, enjoying it, but when I was naked he . . . he picked up his brush and spanked me." Spencer tensed again, and she patted him once more. Feeling the need to comfort him, because nobody had ever comforted her. Nobody had ever even known about this until now. It was a lot harder to talk about than she'd expected, but she'd started this and she *would* tell him the rest of it.

"I don't know why. He made it seem normal and said something about all girls loving a good spanking." Spencer's hand had stopped stroking her arm and just lay there. Not moving at all. "I felt . . . well, I don't know how I felt. I was confused. I didn't like it. It had taken me out of the moment, so to speak. He went back to kissing me and playing with my breasts, but he pinched my nipples too hard. It hurt. He kept asking me if I liked the stuff he was doing, and I suppose saying I did made him escalate it a notch every time. But I liked the kissing and the stroking. Not the other stuff. He would kiss me and lick me and say, 'You like this, don't you?' and just when I said yes, he'd pinch me, or slap my butt, or do something painful. It was so confusing."

Spencer's breathing was no longer even and quiet; it was starting to sound ragged and labored, and she wasn't sure if she should continue.

"What happened?" he asked after she'd lapsed into a silence that lasted a beat too long.

"He flipped me onto my stomach, kissed me some more, touched me, played with me, made me feel good. Then he said, 'This is okay, right?' I remember feeling more relaxed, finally enjoying it and saying that it was fine . . . but he had a b-ball gag just slightly in my line of vision. I didn't notice it. But when I said it was fine, he said he knew I'd be game and put it in my mouth. He tied my hands to the headboard and spanked me again, with something else. I don't think it was the brush." She took a deep, bracing breath. Reliving it made her feel so dumb. Why hadn't she known how manipulative he was being? Why hadn't she seen it until years after it had all ended?

"And then he d-did his thing," she said hoarsely. She hated telling Spencer—good and kind and gentle Spencer—these things. She didn't want him to know her as this awful, stupid *person* who had allowed these things to happen. Didn't want him to recognize her as a fraud who acted tough but submitted to such degradations. But at the same time, she needed him to know every ugly detail about her. Needed him to understand what he was getting into if he insisted on being with her. So she forced herself to continue.

"I didn't like it. It was my first time and I *hated* it. It hurt, it was humiliating and awful, but he acted like it was completely normal. Afterward, he untied me. Snuggled up and said I was amazing, but maybe I could move a bit more next time, squirm a little, get all the way into it. Girls loved it once they got used to it."

She shook her head and plucked at the bedspread, staring blindly into the darkness.

"I never got used to it. Three years in that so-called relationship and I never, ever got used to it. And he didn't care. I was the submissive he was looking for, a naïve, stupid virgin who thought there was something wrong with her for not enjoying the mortification of being tied up and spanked and blindfolded and gagged . . ."

"And asphyxiated?" His voice sounded harsh in the darkness, like he'd chewed on nails as a snack.

"That came toward the end of our three years. It was *terrifying*. His grip got tighter and tighter each time. And it lasted longer and longer." Spencer started stroking her arm again, in an attempt to soothe her.

"After that, I had a series of boyfriends, but every time we got intimate, they started behaving strangely, trying to tie me up and stuff . . ." She shook her head, still completely baffled by that. "It scared me. I didn't want to be with another man like that, so I always ended it before it went further. I thought maybe I gave off some kind of vibe. I don't know, like something about me just screamed *submissive*. It's weird, because I don't *feel* like a submissive. I was a stupid, naïve girl with Jake. I didn't know better. But I feel like I have a sign pinned to my back or something. Anyway, a few years ago, around the time you started getting serious about Tanya, I started seeing Carter, another out-of-towner."

"Hmm. I remember," Spencer grated. "Seemed like a total asshole to me."

"He was. I thought, he's an out-of-towner, maybe it'd be different. Our first time together was normal, nothing earth-shattering, just nice, vanilla sex, so I relaxed. But things got freaky after that. More choking, if you can believe it—" She shook her head in disbelief before continuing. "The last time, he didn't stop until I passed out."

Spencer swore viciously and she started, understanding that maybe she shouldn't have laid that zinger on him so casually, but he stroked her arm reassuringly and she relaxed again. "Anyway, that's when I gave him his marching papers and decided that relationships weren't for me. Besides the bizarre sex crap that always seems to happen to me, I don't like myself when I'm in a relationship with someone. I really wanted to start liking myself."

It took everything in Spencer not to jump out of bed, get dressed, and go hunting for the motherfuckers who had hurt Daff. How could she speak about it as if it were normal? She might have thought she'd given consent, but that Jake fucker had definitely manipulated her into giving it. If Spencer could get his hands on any one of them right now, he would show them what it felt like to be fucking strangled until you passed out.

And why the fuck did they all go that way, anyway? Something was up with that. Daff had her hang-ups—probably because of the fucked-up shit she'd had to deal with in the past—but all Spencer wanted to do was cherish her. Not hurt her or humiliate her. He couldn't imagine anyone wanting to do anything different. It didn't add up.

"Are you sure these guys didn't talk to one another? Maybe some of them spread rumors about what you supposedly liked?" he speculated, and she shrugged.

"I thought that, too, but it didn't explain Carter. And I mean, stuff like that gets out, right? I figure if it was the guys talking to one another, there would have been rumors. You would have heard it if there was a rumor like that out there, don't you think?"

"Don't know. I don't really mingle too much."

"If you'd heard a rumor like that about me, would you have . . ." Her voice trailed off, but he knew what she was asking.

"I don't need your subjugation to get my rocks off, darling," he said quietly.

Daff was quiet for a moment as she thought about the woman she'd been, the people she'd spent time with, and wondered if their former friend Shar Bridges had known about the bondage stuff. She had introduced Daff to Jake. It was the first time the possibility occurred to Daff, and it made her want to find Shar and violently rearrange her smug, perfect face.

"What are you thinking about?" he prompted gently, and Daff shook her head. She had once, foolishly, considered Shar a friend, but the shallow woman had only ever been interested in what would benefit *Shar*. What did she have to gain from sabotaging Daff's relationships?

Daff wasn't sure, but her gut—while historically shitty at reading Shar—told her that the woman was somehow involved.

"I'm not sure, but I think Shar might have had a hand in telling those lies about me," she said, feeling sick inside. "Why would she do that?"

"Jealousy, maybe?"

"Why would she be jealous?"

"Well, you're prettier, smarter, more likable than she is, for starters," Spencer said with a shrug, and Daff smiled at that sweet response.

"I just felt so idiotic," she said with a deep sigh. "Maybe I was just being a total prude, you know? I know I'm supposed to be this modern woman and it's okay to enjoy a bit of kinky sex now and then. But I didn't. I didn't enjoy it. I just felt demeaned, and maybe I made myself feel that way, but . . ."

"Daff, you're overthinking it," he said soothingly. "You don't like BDSM and there's nothing wrong with that. Your partners should have asked if you were okay with it instead of assuming that you would be."

"Jake asked."

"*Jake* asked jack shit! The way he presented these questions to you was ambiguous, to say the least. You thought you were agreeing to other things, and he fucking knew it. He tricked you and then made sure to gag you before he did all the things he knew you *would* have protested to."

"I must seem so weak and foolish to you now," she whispered, and he heard the absolute misery and shame in her voice.

"Oh no, my darling." He lowered his voice to match hers. "*Nothing* you've told me tonight changes how I think of you."

"But I—"

"No. Daff—" He moved his hand to her face and stroked her damp cheek. It *killed* him that these memories had made her cry, and he wanted to murder someone because of those tears. But he kept the savage fury he felt leashed, wanting her to feel only tenderness in his touch. "You did nothing wrong. He took advantage of your innocence and confusion. It was an assault."

"No, I consented to everything."

"Darling, you didn't know what you were consenting to."

"But I didn't say no."

"You *couldn't* say no. He shoved a gag in your mouth."

"Afterward, when I knew . . . I still allowed it. I allowed everything else. For three years. What's wrong with me?"

"Did you love him?" He tried to keep the tension he felt out of his body, dreading her answer. Not knowing what he would do if she admitted to loving an asshole like that, when she wouldn't even give Spencer a shot at a real relationship with her.

Daff considered his question for a moment. Why *had* she stayed with Jake for so long?

"I thought maybe I did. But I think I kind of hated him. I just . . . I think I was afraid of being a failure and maybe afraid of being alone. I was so young, and I thought being in a relationship was everything. I didn't have a degree, I didn't have what I thought of as a proper job, I was afraid—" She stopped speaking abruptly, the nascent thought almost revolutionary. "All my life I was told I was cute but not very bright, and I should find a man to take care of me. Aside from his sexual proclivities, Jake was every girl's dream, and I thought he was what I needed."

"Your *fucking* aunts," Spencer muttered, sounding pissed off. "Why would they sabotage your self-worth like that? I thought family's supposed to lift you up and make you feel special."

"I think they thought they were complimenting me. Daff's the cute one, Lia's the pretty one, and Daisy's the clever one," she intoned before snorting in dark amusement. "More like Daff's the neurotic one, Lia's the needy one, and Daisy's the insecure one."

"I swear to God, if they start carrying on about this crap at the wedding, I'll—" He paused and she felt him shrug. "I don't know. Steal their dentures and force them to eat popcorn and apples or something."

She surprised herself by giggling.

"Badass!" she teased.

"You know it." She lifted her hand to cup his jaw, and he leaned into her touch.

"Spencer, I think this whole year for me has been about proving that I *can* take care of myself. That I can live alone, I can quit my job, I don't need a man, and . . . I don't know, I can find what really makes me happy."

"I get it," he whispered, covering her hand with his own. He turned his head and kissed her palm tenderly.

"So this thing between us . . . I can't. The timing . . ." Her voice trailed off.

"I know." His voice was a gentle rumble and filled with nothing but understanding. Her tears overflowed, and she tried not to let on that she was crying. But somehow, despite the darkness, he knew.

"Don't, Daff. Don't cry. I'm here for you. In whatever capacity you need me."

"I just don't want to label this."

"But *this* exists?" She could hear the question in his voice and nodded.

"It does. But no boundaries, Spence. No parameters. No labels."

"I see."

"*Do* you?" she sobbed. "Because I don't even know if I do."

"Ssh." He kissed her palm again. "I won't be yet another thing for you to worry about, darling. No labels. Just *this*."

He turned until he was on his back and she was straddling him, his hard shaft pulsing beneath her wet nakedness.

"Condom?" she asked, her voice wobbling with excitement. Even after everything they'd done that night, she still couldn't get enough of him. Of *this*. And she had *never* been on top before. She was practically quivering in anticipation.

"I left a few on the nightstand," he grunted, arching up against her. She hissed in pleasure at the contact and fumbled around in the predawn grayness until she found what she was looking for. She had him sheathed and poised for entry in moments, and when she finally sank down and accepted him into her body, they both sighed blissfully.

Nothing had ever felt more perfect.

Neither of them got any sleep after that, and about an hour and a half later, after sharing a quick and naughty shower, they left Daff's place—Spencer to dash home for a quick change of clothes before work, and Daff heading straight for the boutique.

Despite her exhaustion, Daff couldn't stop smiling for most of the morning. Definitely out of character for her, and she was happy that Steph, the manager in training, didn't come in on Saturdays. She even found herself humming a couple of times, and when her phone rang at eleven and the cartoon penis flashed onto the screen, her heart did a weird little loop-the-loop in her chest.

"Hey," she hummed.

"Do you still have me listed as the Dick in your contacts?" he asked without any preliminaries, and her smile widened.

"Yep. But I'm thinking of changing it to Mr. BAD." No response, and she knew that Spencer, being Spencer, probably didn't get it. So she elaborated, "Y'know? Big-Ass Dick?" He was quiet for a beat, and then he chuckled.

"Yeah?" He sounded half-embarrassed, half-flattered.

"Only the truth."

"Well, then—" He gave another huffing little laugh, and Daff would bet decent money that he was probably blushing. He cleared his throat before changing the subject. "Just checking in to see if you're okay."

"I'm fine. Feeling a bit achy. You?"

"Same. I miss you." She rolled her eyes while grinning so broadly it felt like her cheeks would split.

"Shut up. You saw me like three hours ago."

"Too fucking long ago. Want to have lunch at MJ's?"

"Nope."

"Oh." He sounded disappointed.

"I want to order takeout from MJ's, head to your place or mine, and not surface again till tomorrow."

"That sounds doable."

"Meet you there after one?"

"Yeah. Don't know how I'm going to last that long without you." *Damn it.* Why did the man have to be so freaking adorable?

"Later, Mr. BAD," she singsonged and disconnected the call with a swipe of her thumb. After that she leaned on the counter and daydreamed about him and all the things they had done last night and would do later. The man was frighteningly addictive, but Daff had decided not to worry about that. To just enjoy this for however long it lasted. Just another leg—extremely vital—on her journey of self-discovery.

That evening, after a day of nothing but *fantastic* sex mixed in with periods of long conversation about everything and absolutely nothing, Daff and Spencer sat cuddled on her sofa, blindly staring at the bright images on the television screen. Daff's head was on Spencer's bare chest. He had very thoughtfully brought a pair of pajamas for his sleepover, of which Daff was wearing the top and Spencer the bottoms. Her legs curled over his lap, and she was more interested in his relaxed breathing and strong, reassuring heartbeat than she was in the movie on TV. She didn't even know what it was—something with UFOs and way too much talking. She kind of resented the stupid movie, because right now Spencer seemed more interested in *it* than he was in Daff.

Jealous of a movie. What in the actual fuck was up with that?

It wasn't like the man hadn't showered his undivided attention on her all day. She had been his entire focus for hours, but Daff felt like a junkie. She discovered that she absolutely craved his every look, touch, and smile. She hoarded them and found herself recalling everything he'd said and done with absolute clarity. It wasn't even about the sex— well, not *entirely* about the sex; he made her feel absolutely precious. She found his gentle and thorough lovemaking so much more appealing than anything else she'd experienced before. His reverent touches, appreciative compliments, and long, lingering kisses made her feel like a shy young girl around her first crush, yet she hadn't felt awkward or unsure around him once today.

She snuggled closer, and his arm, which was resting casually across her shoulders, tugged her even nearer. She lifted her face and buried her nose in the nook where his neck met the strong curve of his broad shoulder. He smelled clean and faintly like lavender after using her soap in the shower. Combined with his unique masculine musk, it was almost irresistible. She planted a soft kiss in the spot, and he tilted his head until his cheek rested on top of her hair.

Her hand, which had been resting on his flat stomach, crept up over that spectacularly ridged abdomen, enjoying the feel of every hard, smooth inch as she explored her way up to the gorgeous pec that her cheek was resting on. She watched as his nipple drew tight and smiled in complete feminine satisfaction. She didn't touch it but brought her hand to rest in the shallow valley between his impressive pecs. She walked her middle and index fingers down between his six pack, along the happy trail of silky black hair there. She ignored his ragged inhalation of breath, too focused on watching the way his muscles twitched as her fingers stepped lightly over them. They reached the indentation of his navel, and she paused as she contemplated her next move. Spencer's heart was racing beneath her ear, and his breathing came in gasps.

She circled her index finger around the sensitive oval of his belly button before her fingers continued on their little trek down the now slightly wider trail of silky hair. When her fingers reached the elastic barrier of his pajama bottoms, they paused again, and she became aware of the fact that Spencer had gone completely still. Even his breathing had stopped.

She took the higher road, literally. Instead of burrowing beneath the waistband, her hand glided over the top and found his straining length beneath the fabric. She slid her palm over his hard, thick shaft and cupped him possessively. His breath exploded from his chest on a long groan, and it was all Daff could do to stop herself from groaning in sympathy. She wanted him again. She couldn't get enough of him. She climbed on top of him, straddling his lap, and allowed herself one quick grind up against him before she lifted her warm wetness all the way off him.

His hands went to her hips as he tried to drag her back down, but she smiled into his strained face before putting her own hands over his and pulling them away.

"Nope. I'm driving this bus, mister. Just keep your hands to yourself."

"You're killing me, Daff," he said hoarsely.

"You'll survive." She lowered her head and latched her mouth onto his neck and sucked, knowing that the pressure was too strong and uncaring of the mark she'd leave there. He loved it, throwing his head back to allow her more access. His arms were stretched out over the back of the sofa, and for now he followed her rules and kept his hands well away from her.

Daff kissed her way down over his chest, lavishing attention on his nipples, and his hips bucked, sneakily stealing another quick grind against her naked core. She hissed at the scalding sensation and bit back a cry of pleasure.

"Keep that penis under lockdown, Spencer. It's not allowed to join the fun and games yet," she instructed sternly, and he practically sobbed in response to that. Her mouth went back to his nipples before following the same trail down his torso that her fingers had just moments ago. She crawled off the sofa until she was kneeling between his spread legs, her hands braced on each hard, thickly muscled thigh, spreading them farther apart to allow her better access.

Her lips reached the same barrier her fingers had, and she lifted her face to contemplate the pajama bottoms thoughtfully. Her hands crept up to the waistband, and her fingers folded over the elastic and tugged. When they didn't budge, she looked up into his strained face.

"Lift your tight little butt, big guy, I've got work to do here."

"Daff?"

"Don't make me ask again," she warned him, feeling a little giddy with the extent of her arousal. She kind of liked bossing him around like this. She was drenched with need, and every time he wordlessly obeyed one of her commands, her lady bits clenched painfully. He closed his eyes and did as she demanded, lifting his hips just enough for her to tug his pajamas down over his lean hips. They snagged over the rigid pole of his penis, and she gently lifted the elasticized waistband up and over his pulsing staff.

She groaned hungrily when he was exposed to her and licked her lips at the beautiful sight just inches from her face.

Spencer wasn't sure what her endgame was, and he watched her intently as she examined his aching cock without making a move to touch it. He was happy to let her play and discover, knowing that after years of feeling helpless during sex, she needed the opportunity to explore the true extent of her power over him.

Her small hand wrapped around his penis and peeled it away from his stomach, and he hissed in response to the sensation of her tight fist closing around him. He looked at her silky hair, unsure of what to expect, and then sighed in relief when he felt her hand begin to stroke him, slowly and sensuously. His breath was shuddering unevenly in and out of his lungs and, unable to resist, he reached down with both hands to caress her hair gently. Just this touch—surely she wouldn't begrudge him this touch.

"Feels good, darling," he encouraged hoarsely. "Feels so . . . Oh my *God*!" The top of his head just about blew off when he felt the first tentative stroke of her tongue on him. She licked him delicately, like she would an ice cream cone, along the top, down the sides, then back up to the top. His hips jerked abruptly and uncontrollably before he tried his best to minimize his movements, not wanting to scare her off. His resolve lasted only as long as it took for her to add a little suction, and that was when he cried out, his eyes welling with tears of bliss and frustration. His hands curled into fists in her hair. His instinct was to thrust, but he knew he couldn't. *She* needed to control the movement. But dear God, it was killing him. Until finally, *miraculously*, she found a rhythm.

"Oh . . . *Jesus*!" She increased her suction, took more of him, moving her lips up and down the hard shaft so damned sweetly that he nearly wept at the incredible sensations. But—"Daff, you've got to stop . . . Stop, darling, I can't hold off for much longer."

To his eternal regret, she lifted her mouth to look at him.

"Why?" she pouted. For the first time, he noticed that her other hand was between her thighs as she took her own pleasure while giving it to him. It made him so fucking happy that she was taking enjoyment from this act, which had seemed so distasteful to her before, that for a moment he lost his train of thought.

"Uh. Because, I'm going to come," he finally remembered to reply, and as if on cue his cock throbbed in her hand, which was encircled around the base.

Daff frowned, confused by his words. Of course he was going to come—that was the point. She wanted him to come. It was such a turn-on having him in her mouth, feeling his helpless responses to her every touch and kiss.

Who knew?

"I want to taste you," she said resolutely, her voice sounding embarrassingly sexy even to her, and before he could respond, she went back to her task and this time didn't let up until he cried out hoarsely, the sound filled with a crazy mix of anguish and ecstasy, and came so copiously she could barely keep up.

She loved how, during his orgasm, which looked and felt mind-blowing, his grip on her head never tightened. He never took over the rhythm or shoved himself all the way to the back of her throat. He allowed her to decide how much she was willing to take and she adored that about him. Her regard shifted to his face; his eyes were screwed shut, his head thrown back, and the cords in his neck were strained. He looked beautiful, primal and fierce, and seeing him like that sent her over the edge. She lifted her mouth from his waning hardness and cried out as she came violently and powerfully. She went limp and was dimly aware of him dragging her trembling body up until she was cradled in his lap, his softening penis fitting snugly against her bottom.

He planted little kisses all over her face and claimed her mouth for a hot, deep, very thorough kiss. Another surprise. In her—admittedly crappy—experience, guys didn't like to kiss her after she'd gone down on them.

"Thank you," he whispered, sounding completely drained.

"No, thank *you*. That was such a turn-on."

"Hmm?"

"Yes."

"Why did you—" He didn't complete the question, but she knew what he wanted to ask.

"Well, for starters, this movie blows. It's boring as hell. So I found something more entertaining to do." She heard the deep rumble of his chuckle beneath her ear and smiled. "I *loved* it. Now stop overanalyzing crap again. And you'd better get used to the bj's, dude. Because the menu has changed and you're now on it."

He laughed outright at that.

"Cheesy, McGregor."

"Give a girl a break, Carlisle. You've tired me out. My brain is on autopilot. And don't change the channel—this movie is the perfect sleep aid."

They went to bed early and, exhausted from their day of excessive sexual indulgences, they did nothing but sleep—naked and wrapped up in each other's arms—all night long.

The following morning, Spencer cracked open an eye and groaned at the bright sunlight flooding the small bedroom. He flung an arm out, looking for Daff, wanting to introduce her to his morning wood, but she was nowhere to be found. He frowned and sat up. The room was empty.

Panicking for a moment, concerned that she was once again sporting a pair of cold feet, he flung the bedcovers aside and jumped out of bed, intent on finding her and kissing her doubts away. He was headed toward the bedroom door when it creaked open and Daff carefully shouldered her way in, clutching a breakfast tray in her hands. She looked startled to find him standing just on the other side of the door.

"Oh, you're up," she said, sounding a little disappointed. "I fixed us some breakfast." His eyes swept down to the tray in bemusement. Two cups of coffee, scrambled eggs, bacon, and toast. And a fresh flower in a slender vase. He peered at the flower closely.

"Is this a daffodil?" She went bright red at the question.

"It's the only flower I could find out in the garden. Daisy planted a crapload of daffodils when she first moved in. I'm pretty sure she did it to annoy me or something. She knows I hate them. Anyway, they're the only ones in full bloom this time of year."

"Why do you hate them? I love Daffodil . . . s."

Daff rolled her eyes at Spencer's lame little quip, but he barely cracked a smile and she blinked uncertainly.

"Let me help you with that tray," he offered, and the awkward moment slipped by. "This all looks awesome, thank you." They retreated to the bed and sat cross-legged facing each other. Daff aimed an exasperated look at his lap.

"You couldn't put on your pajamas?" she asked, tossing a pillow into his lap to cover up his eager erection. She was wearing his top as usual, and it was modestly tucked over her lap, concealing her from his hungry scrutiny.

"Couldn't find them." He shrugged. "Besides, putting them on just to take them off again seems like a waste of time and energy."

"Uh-uh, Spencer, no time for any rumpy-pumpy this morning, boy-o. We're taking Charlie out, remember?"

"*Fuck*. I forgot." He'd made arrangements to pick her up at ten this morning, and while Charlie hadn't seemed too enthused, Daff's mother had ignored the girl's surly reaction and had cheerfully agreed that Charlie would be ready and waiting for them.

"I figured. But you can't cancel."

"I know. I wouldn't." Of course he wouldn't. He took his commitments seriously, and he would *never* disappoint the girl. Even if she probably wasn't really keen on the idea of spending the day with them.

"What's the time?" he asked while hastily gulping down his coffee.

"Eight thirty, no rush. Enjoy your breakfast." He ignored her words and continued to gobble down his breakfast, occasionally buttering a piece of toast and hand-feeding it to her when she ate too little and too slowly for his liking. Daff rolled her eyes but accepted the offerings.

"I said there was no rush, Spencer," she said when he'd polished off the meal in record time.

"Hmm." He wiped an arm across his mouth, moved the tray aside, and then focused a predatory look on her. "Rush through breakfast, take my time through dessert."

"Oh."

In the end they wound up rushing anyway. After a lengthy and satisfying morning session, they broke all speed records to get showered and changed before dashing over to the McGregor farm in Spencer's truck.

They had just parked in front of the farm when Daff glanced over at Spencer and gave a horrified shriek. He jolted and shot her an alarmed look.

"What the fuck?"

"Oh my *God*! Your neck."

"What? Is it a spider?" He sounded so panicked that for a moment she forgot her own horror and stared at him in fascination.

No way.

"Are you afraid of spiders? Is big, bad Spencer Carlisle terrified of a teensy, weensy wittle spider-wider?"

"Is it a *spider*, Daff?" he asked urgently, starting to dust at his clothes and his hair. He looked completely freaked out. She clapped a hand over her mouth, trying her best not to laugh, and he glared at her before hopping out of the truck and doing the spider dance, all flapping arms and flailing legs.

Daff was hosing herself with laughter. She practically fell out of the truck and rounded the front of it to watch him flail around. It was too much. This massive specimen of man afraid of a tiny bug. It was absolutely adorable.

"Did I get it?" he asked after he stopped flapping around, both his hair and eyes completely wild.

"Th-there wasn't one." She forced the words out between the gales of helpless laughter. "N-no spider, Spenc . . ."

"What the *fuck*, Daff? Why did you say there was?"

"I—I didn't . . . it's the . . . you have . . ." She was bent over, hands braced on her knees as she tried to compose herself. This was serious. He couldn't talk to her mother looking like that. But she just couldn't stop laughing. "Hi-hi-hickey. Neck!"

She lifted a hand to point, and he clapped his palm over his neck, somehow looking even more horrified than he had just moments ago. It set Daff off again, and they were both unaware of the group of people on the porch now watching them in bemusement.

"So what's going on, guys?" It was Mason. Why the hell was Mason here? Daff looked up to see her entire family on the porch, watching her and Spencer. Her mother had a small smile on her face while everybody else just looked befuddled.

"Uh . . ." Daff pointed at Spencer. "Spencer's afraid of spiders."

"Yeah. He's a regular wimp with creepy-crawlies, made *me* get rid of them when we were growing up. When we got older, I used to charge him for the service. Take note, kid." This last as an aside to Charlie, who had her best rebellious teen face on.

Spencer, still clutching a hand to his neck, was staring back at everybody silently. He looked confused, trapped, and so unutterably defenseless that it just about broke Daff's heart.

She straightened and walked over to where he stood, always completely separate from everybody else, and stepped into his little bubble of isolation, taking his free hand into hers.

"Wrong side of your neck, big guy," she informed him beneath her breath, and his eyes dropped to hers. He looked so achingly vulnerable, and she smiled up at him.

"Just *this*," she said. "Spencer and Daff."

She clutched his big hand between both of hers, and he lowered his hand from his neck as he lifted his head to face her entire family and his.

CHAPTER FOURTEEN

"Why are you guys here so early?" Daff asked Mason as she approached the wide-eyed group. Spencer hesitated for a brief moment but followed before she had to tug him along behind her.

"Daisy and I were dropping Charlie off. She stayed over at ours last night."

Of course she did. And she'd probably had an awesome time, and now, with that fresh in her mind, she'd have to spend a day in Spencer's mediocre company. He felt like an ass for resenting his brother a little for that. And for resenting Charlie for so easily creeping into Mason's affections. He was jealous of the sibling relationship he saw blooming right in front of his eyes and pained by the one that he seemed to be losing with Mason, as well as the one that he couldn't get off the ground with Charlie.

Daff's hand tightened around his, and he was once again grateful for her support. It still blew his mind that she'd taken his hand so damned easily, right in front of her family and everybody. Like she was claiming him, like she was proud for the family to know about them. He knew he shouldn't read too much into it. It wasn't permanent. Her feelings for him were nowhere near as intense as his were for her, but still this gesture felt . . . significant. And for the first time, he felt like he was wanted and belonged.

"Come on, kid. Time's a-wasting, and we have shitloads to do today."

"*Daff.*"

"Sorry, Mum," she said cheerfully. "*Craploads.* We have craploads to do."

Charlie reluctantly peeled herself away from the group. She already looked like she belonged with them, and Spencer felt that pang of envy again. It wasn't an admirable trait, and he felt like a shallow asshole. He should be happy that she was fitting in.

Charlie skulked past him and Daff and clambered into the truck.

"See you guys later," Daff chirped. Spencer lifted a hand in farewell, and Daff only released his hand when it was time for her to get back in the truck.

The first five minutes of the drive was silent, and Daff reached over to put on some music while Spencer stretched his mind for something to say to Charlie. He felt like an idiot around this child. He could never seem to find the right words. Maybe because it meant so much to him.

"Eww!" Charlie exclaimed after a few minutes, finally breaking the increasingly awkward silence. "You have a *love bite.*"

Shit! Spencer sighed in exasperation. Of course that would be the first thing she remarked on.

"Who did that? Did *you* do that?" she demanded of Daff.

"Of course I did," Daff shocked him by admitting. She turned in her seat to grin at Charlie. "It's an awesome one, isn't it? I'm quite proud of it."

"Oh *eeeewww.*" The girl's disgust was actually quite comical, and for the first time she struck Spencer as a normal teen. It relaxed him somewhat. "Stop talking about it."

"*You* brought it up," Daff said with a shrug. "So what did you do at Daisy and Mason's last night?"

"Watched movies and stuff. It was okay."

"Yeah? I love my sister, but she talks about the wedding a *lot*." Spencer checked the rearview mirror to gauge the girl's reaction, and she bit her lip uncertainly. Obviously not wanting to betray Daisy. "Right?"

"Daisy's nice," Charlie finally said, and Daff nodded.

"I know. So nice. *Too* nice. God, she was such a Goody Two-shoes growing up. Lia was worse. But Daisy was *clever*, too. Always with her nose in a book, which is awesome and all, but it made Lia and me look bad. And Daisy never knew about makeup and stuff." Spencer slanted Daff a curious look, wondering where she was going with this.

"Do you know about makeup . . . and stuff?" Charlie asked after a beat.

"Of course I do," Daff said nonchalantly. "I could give you some makeup tips if you like."

"She's a little *young*, Daff," Spencer said, and she threw him a look of exaggerated, openmouthed shock.

"A woman is *never* too young to learn about makeup, Spencer," she admonished, wagging a finger in his face, and Spencer bit back his response when Charlie giggled at her words. The sound was so sweet, carefree, and innocent that it took the wind clear out of his sails.

"Sorry, ladies. I stand corrected," he said meekly. When he sneaked another peek at Charlie, he was rewarded by the look of astonishment on her face. Daff reached over and squeezed his thigh in approval.

"Anyway, how can you handle all the lovey-dovey stuff over at Daisy and Mason's?"

"They kiss a lot," Charlie admitted, sounding faintly disgusted. "Nobody needs to see that from old people."

"Tell me about it." Daff groaned. "Fair warning though, kid. It won't be as often, or as gross, but you'll see me kiss your big brother a bit today, too."

"Ugh, *no*. What's wrong with all of you?" she squeaked, and Spencer hid a grin. He was so damned thrilled that she hadn't protested his title of "big brother." Daff had slipped it into the conversation so insouciantly that Charlie had just accepted it, instead focusing on the grosser revelations in the sentence. His hand dropped to where hers still rested on his thigh and he squeezed her fingers gratefully.

"It feels good to kiss," Daff said. "You'll find out soon enough."

"No, she won't," Spencer snapped, and Daff rolled her eyes. "No kissing, Charlie. Not until you're thirty-five."

"Jeez. Big brothers. Your poor boyfriends are going to have a hard time getting past Spencer and Mason."

"Daff, stop corrupting my sister—" The word slipped out without thought and caught all of them unaware. Daff's lips curled into a smile and Charlie, quite shockingly, said nothing in protest to his claim. He met her eyes in the rearview mirror, where she was eyeing him speculatively, as if she couldn't make up her mind about something.

"I like Cooper and Peaches," Charlie said, unexpectedly changing the subject, her eyes narrowing as they held his.

"Is that right?" Spencer asked, and she nodded, her eyes challenging. He grinned and she blinked, looking completely thrown by his reaction. "You know Mason and Daisy are taking the dogs to Grahamstown with them, right?"

"I know."

"Guess I'll have to get you a dog of your own," he said nonchalantly and released her eyes to focus his attention back on the road.

She said nothing in response to that, but Spencer felt lighter and happier than he had during any previous interaction with Charlie. His hand clung to Daff's for the rest of the fifty-minute drive to Mossel Bay.

The morning was pretty pleasant. Spencer let Daff and Charlie chatter on. The teen was recalcitrant at first, selfishly hogging her words, and he really couldn't blame her. Not when he often did the same thing, especially around strangers. They leisurely explored the small coastal town for about forty minutes before Daff dragged Charlie off for some shopping—*no boys allowed*—and left Spencer to wander around on his own for a while.

He stopped in front of a small, upmarket jewelry store and scanned the window display for the longest time before venturing in for a closer look at the wares. Maybe a small gift for Daff? He wasn't even sure if she was into jewelry. Although she always seemed to be wearing necklaces and stuff, he wasn't certain how she would receive a gift such as this, but he couldn't resist. He imagined her in sapphires—they would look amazing on her skin and bring out the blue notes in her gray eyes. Or maybe rubies, to match her gorgeous, velvety soft lips. She wouldn't go for diamonds, not his colorful Daff.

He inspected the bracelets and necklaces, the earrings and the charms, and in the end, not sure how it happened, walked out with a ring. A rose-gold ring with a pear-cut peach sapphire. It had a warm vibrancy to it that reminded him of Daff.

And there was no fooling himself—it was an engagement ring. An engagement ring for a woman who wanted no strings and who would probably run screaming for the hills if he so much as hinted at marriage.

Spencer was fucked and he knew it.

Spencer seemed tense during lunch. He could barely meet her eyes, and Daff wondered if Mason or Daisy had contacted him while she and Charlie had gone to do their "lady shopping." It wouldn't surprise her, since she'd received a **WTF** text from Daisy about half an hour earlier. Daff hadn't responded, fed up with having to explain herself to them. They would have to trust that she and Spencer were adult enough not to drag the family into a divisive brawl after this thing between them ended.

Spencer watched Charlie dig into her burger, his eyes protective, a small—almost proud—smile on his face.

"Why are you staring at me like that?" the girl snapped irritably, more observant than Daff had assumed. Spencer looked startled to have been caught staring but recovered quickly.

"Tell me about your home life with Malcolm. After your mother died," he invited her, and Charlie's brow lowered, looking so much like Spencer in that moment that Daff's affinity for the girl grew even stronger.

"Maybe I don't wanna," Charlie grumbled sulkily, and Spencer nodded.

"You don't have to. I was just curious."

"Why don't you tell me about *your* life with Malcolm," she retorted, challenge lighting her eyes. "After your mother died."

The corner of Spencer's mouth lifted, and he stole one of Charlie's fries and popped it into his mouth. He washed down the potato with a swig of soda.

"You have your own fries," Charlie pointed out.

"Sorry, force of habit. I usually grab a few of Mason's. It pisses him off."

"Why do you do it?"

"Because I can," Spencer admitted, and Charlie watched him thoughtfully, again with that speculative spark in her eyes. "So after my mother died, Malcolm stuck around till my eighteenth birthday. He left when I turned eighteen, he probably figured I was old enough to take care of Mason by then."

"That was a douchebag move," Charlie said, sounding way more adult than her years.

"I think we can safely agree that he was a negligent asshole," Spencer said with a bitter smile, and Charlie nodded.

"But he tried," she whispered.

"He did. Sometimes he'd surprise us with takeout, sometimes he'd give me money to get some food for the house, and other times—"

"He'd buy alcohol and forget you existed for days on end?"

"Pretty much, yeah."

He took a sip from his soda and still avoided eye contact with Daff. What the hell was up with that? It bothered her more than she would have expected.

"How long was he sick?" Spencer asked.

"A few months. It was very fast."

"Who helped you? After he died?"

"Neighbors. A social worker. They were going to put me into care, but I left before they could. Malcolm had some money hidden inside his mattress. He told me about it a couple of weeks before he died. It wasn't a lot, but it got me this far. He told me to find you and Mason after he was gone. He was always talking about you guys."

"He *was*?" Daff could tell that the information stunned Spencer.

"He had old newspaper clippings about your rugby stuff and a magazine with some gross almost-naked pictures of Mason in it." Mason had been an underwear model for a very brief moment in time. Spencer looked completely astounded and couldn't seem to find an adequate response to her revelations. He seemed unable to process the words and just sat there blinking at Charlie for a few moments.

"I guess Malcolm was okay. Some of his friends were a bit creepy, but if anyone looked at me the wrong way or said something . . . *bad* to me, he'd never allow them back. I was scared that one day he wouldn't notice and—" Her voice trailed off, and Daff's heart clenched for the young girl. She looked small and lost sitting there in one of Daff's cast-off dresses. Her short hair growing out into a cute cap of dark, silky waves.

"You were very brave living through that, Charlie," Spencer said. "You should *never* have been made to fear for your safety. I know you're used to taking care of yourself. I know you don't need my help. But it would mean a lot to me if you would accept it. I have to make up for all those years I wasn't there to keep you safe."

"I mean—" Charlie's eyes left Spencer's, and she glared at her plate. "It's not like you knew."

Daff, who had been holding her breath after Spencer's heartfelt little entreaty, released it on a wobbly sigh. Charlie's eyes lifted shyly back to Spencer's, and Daff could have cheered for both of them.

"I'm bossy and I don't talk much and will probably tell you no a lot, but I'd really like it if you'd consider living at my house," Spencer said in an awkward rush, the tips of his ears going pink.

The girl lifted one of her fries and twirled it between two fingers as she contemplated Spencer's pitch.

"I suppose it wouldn't be too bad. Especially not with my new dog to keep me company."

"As long as you understand that it's time for you to start being a kid. I didn't get to be a kid. I want that for you, Charlie. But that means following my rules, okay?"

"What rules?" Charlie asked suspiciously.

"I'll try to keep them fair. But off the top of my head, stuff like curfews, cleaning up after yourself—and your dog—and studying hard."

"Sometimes I get angry and don't want to talk," Charlie said, sounding for all the world like she was revealing what she considered to be her worst character flaw.

"Yeah? Me too. Maybe we can synchronize it so that we're angry together and not speak for hours?"

Charlie giggled, and the look of vulnerable gratification on Spencer's face made Daff reach for his hand under the table. She was shocked and disappointed and more than a little hurt when he moved his hand before she could take hold of it.

"Maybe it won't totally suck to live with you," Charlie said after a long pause, and the tension left Spencer's shoulders. He finally met Daff's eyes, and she was heartened by the intensity she saw in them. He groped for the hand he had just rejected and clung to it tightly.

"Great," he rasped and then cleared his throat before continuing. "You can redecorate the room any way you like, and maybe you can move in after the wedding?" That would give her nearly a month to get used to the idea.

"Sounds okay," Charlie said, keeping it casual. "When can we get my dog?"

"We can pick one out from the shelter after you move in."

"If I didn't want to move in, would I still get a dog?" she suddenly asked cynically, and Spencer smiled at her.

"I said you could, and I'm a man of my word." His voice was solemn and utterly believable. His answer seemed to satisfy Charlie.

The rest of the day was lovely. Spencer's strange behavior over lunch had disappeared like a rogue cloud on a sunny day, and Daff attributed it to the high-stakes conversation with Charlie. He was back to normal now, happy to hold Daff's hand, comfortable with eye contact and even the occasional bit of PDA from Daff, despite Charlie's gagging faces every time they kissed.

After dropping Charlie off at the farm, they made a quick stop at Daff's to pick up a change of clothes and less than an hour later found themselves snuggling, in their pajama halves, in front of the TV and watching a cooking show. Both were wiped out after the past twenty-four hours and stared blankly at the screen. Not talking much, just sharing a bowl of popcorn and vegging out.

"Mason sent me a text. Asked me what the fuck we were up to." Spencer broke the comfortable silence close to forty-five minutes later, and Daff, who had been on the verge of dozing off, jerked to attention. Wiping some drool from her mouth and hoping she hadn't gotten any on his chest.

"Oh? What'd you say?" she asked, her voice slurred.

"Told him we had no idea but once we figured it out it would be none of his fucking business anyway." Daff snorted and pushed her hair out of her face to stare at him. Sadly, she couldn't see much past the stubbled ledge of his firm jaw.

"And what did he say to that?"

"Just said 'okay' and left it at that."

"I wish it were that simple with Daisy."

He graced her with another of his gorgeous smiles. "I told him to pass the sentiment along to her, and he said 'sure.' I think you'll be fine."

Daff giggled and scooted up to kiss him lightly.

"My hero."

"And don't you forget it."

Sam Brand readjusted his hold on the duffel bag strap and lifted his hand to knock on Mason Carlisle's front door. Judging by number of cars parked outside and the sound of voices and laughter coming from the interior, they were having some kind of gathering. Not ideal. His intention had been to surprise Mason and his bride-to-be, not ruin a dinner party. He shook off the uncertainty. His cab had left and there was really nothing to do but knock. He was here—no going back now.

The knocking set off a frenzy of barking and he sighed. Yeah . . . this was going to ruin whatever party the couple were hosting. The door swung open, and the unmistakable figure of Mason Carlisle stood silhouetted in the doorway. The guy said nothing for a moment, then huffed in surprise.

"Fuck me! Brand? What the hell are you doing here, man? We weren't expecting to see you till the stag party."

"That's just a couple of days away, mate. I finished up some business early and figured, I'm in the neighborhood, might as well pop in. I don't mean to intrude on your party, though."

His buddy engulfed him in a quick, manly hug and then stepped back.

"Define 'neighborhood,'" Mason invited.

"I was in Mozambique," Sam informed him drily. "Just a hop, skip, and a jump away from here."

"One thousand three hundred kilometers, give or take, is nothing, really." Mason shrugged. "Come on in, man. We're just having Daisy's sisters and Spencer over for dinner. Nothing fancy, just a family gathering. The ladies are working on some last-minute wedding stuff, and Spencer and I were starting to feel a little outnumbered. I can't wait for you to meet my Daisy."

"Are her sisters hot? Single?"

"Hands off, bro. No flirting and no fucking."

"You know how to ruin a good time, mate," Sam grumbled as he followed Mason's broad back into the house. He absently petted each dog, a big yellow Lab and a small, poofy ball of some kind. Mason led him into a dining room, and four pairs of eyes gawked at him curiously. He instantly reconned the room, noticing about a dozen different things before his eyes halted and went back to *her*.

Well, hello, Miss Priss. Despite the two other interesting-looking women present, this beautiful buttoned-down little thing immediately snagged and held his attention. She looked like a church organist, a librarian, or a strict teacher. Everything about her was neat and prim and proper. Not a hair out of place, and Sam immediately wanted to ruffle her perfect plumage. Everybody else was blatantly staring at him, but *she* dropped her eyes and totally rebuffed him.

Well, then . . . challenge accepted.

Why was he staring at her? Lia refused to meet the stranger's eyes. He was so overt about it, too. It was embarrassing. She sneaked another peek, and thankfully his attention was diverted by Mason, who was proudly introducing Daisy to him.

Compared to Mason and Spencer, this man wasn't the best-looking guy in the room by far. He wasn't the tallest or the biggest, either. He looked to be about five foot eleven and had a spare build that complemented the faded jeans and black Henley he was wearing. Short, spiky dirty-blond hair and a rugged face that looked like it had been out in the sun and wind too long. He had piercing ice-blue eyes with expansive laugh lines radiating from the outer corners. She wasn't sure if they were indeed caused by laughter or from squinting into the bright glare of the sun for long hours at a time. Add that to the deeply tanned hue of his skin and you had a man who was made for the outdoors. He had a *presence* about him that instantly made the room feel claustrophobic.

Lia watched him hug Daisy, lifting her off her feet until she squealed. He put her down and turned to the rest of the table again to acknowledge them with a grin.

"Spencer, Lia, Daff, this is my friend Sam Brand," Mason told the room at large, and Lia's eyes drifted shut for a moment.

Of *course* he was Sam Brand. Her partner for the wedding. He was supposed to meet them in Plettenberg Bay the day after tomorrow for the mother of all bachelor-slash-ette parties, as Daff had dubbed it. What was he doing here? They had just started dinner, and Daisy quickly arranged a setting for him directly opposite Lia. He accepted the seat with a charming smile, his cheeks creasing attractively.

Something about him got Lia's back up and put her on immediate alert. So when he focused those intense eyes on her, she pretended not to notice his interest, focusing her attention on her napkin instead.

"So I didn't quite catch your name," he said. His voice had an appealing raspy undertone to it. It sounded like he'd damaged his vocal cords at some point in the past and had been left with this husky rasp.

She pretended not to hear him, instead picking up her fork and resuming her meal. Not that she could taste anything—it was like all her senses were being hijacked by the man across the table, and she definitely did not appreciate that at all.

Daff watched her sister, wondering what the hell was up with her. Lia, who always had a smile and kind word for everybody, was positively frosty to the new addition at the table. Daff was seated beside Sam and opposite Spencer, who looked distracted. He was distracted a lot lately. They spent most nights together and he was affectionate in bed, a considerate and gentle lover. But since she'd finished working at the boutique a few weeks ago, their lunches had stopped, and she missed the connection they used to share *outside* bed.

She turned her attention back to Lia and Sam Brand. The man hadn't prompted Lia for her name again and instead turned to Mason, who was at the head of the table directly to Sam's left. Daff tried to catch Lia's eyes, but her sister was suddenly very interested in her plate, eating with more focus than the meal required.

Sam Brand was an interesting, lively addition to their evening, and soon everybody was laughing at the comical account of his journey from Maputo to Riversend over the last twenty-four hours. Seemed like it had involved just about every mode of transportation imaginable. They were all hooting about a story involving a woman and a chicken in a public taxi when Lia abruptly excused herself. Nobody else seemed to think anything of it, but Daff watched as Sam Brand's predatory eyes tracked her sister's movements.

Daff leaned toward him, a bright smile plastered to her face—by now the conversation had flowed in a different direction and nobody was paying attention to them.

"Back off, Brand," she growled. "She's not interested and you're making her uncomfortable."

He turned to her with a laconic grin on his face, and Daff decided in that instant that she probably wasn't going to like this suave asshole.

"I'll wait for *her* to tell me that herself," he murmured in that crisp British accent of his and then leaned in, a conspiratorial smile on his face. "So . . . *what's* her name?"

"Ugh . . ." She turned away from him and met Spencer's brooding gaze. He was a serious man, but lately he looked downright gloomy every time he looked at her. She wanted her Spencer back. The man who shared his rare smiles and incomprehensible sense of humor with her. The man who couldn't seem to get enough of her company. Lately it seemed like he went out of his way to avoid her when they weren't making love.

Lia returned a few moments later, looking less strained. She smiled gratefully when Spencer, in typical fashion, stood and held her chair out.

"So why were you in Maputo, Sam?" Mason asked.

"Looking to expand the business," Sam explained, and Mason nodded. The two men had co-owned a personal protection company until Mason had sold his half to Sam for a vast amount of money.

"Yeah, just like we always talked about. There's decent business down here, but I want to set up the African base in the Cape and use it mostly for recruiting and training new officers."

"Makes sense." Mason nodded. "Does this mean we'll have more opportunities to see you?"

The guy's eyes went back to Lia's downcast head, and Daff did *not* like his smile.

"Oh, I think that's a definite possibility."

"I didn't like that guy at all," Daff bitched to Spencer a couple of hours later after they'd returned to his place. She was applying lotion to her legs; she loved the way Spencer's eyes usually followed every sweep of her hands. But tonight he barely spared them a look. Maybe they were becoming familiar with each other's routine and it was old hat to him now. She tried not to think about possibly boring him and instead continued her little anti-Brand campaign. "He's too smooth and too arrogant and he's *way* too interested in Lia."

"Hmm?" There was surprise in the sound, and Daff cast him an exasperated look. He was standing in the doorway of the en-suite bathroom, watching her while he brushed his teeth vigorously, one powerful shoulder propped against the door frame.

"Don't tell me you didn't notice?"

"Things on my mind," he said around his toothbrush.

"You seem to have a lot on your mind lately."

"Hmm," he agreed before turning away and heading into the bathroom. She heard him spit, rinse, and clean the basin and his toothbrush before he sauntered back into the room. He crawled onto the bed and straight between her recently moisturized legs. "*This* on my mind."

He kissed her, and she melted with a blissful sigh and happily accepted his all-consuming, minty-fresh kiss. Of course the kiss led to other incredible wonders, and afterward Daff stretched blissfully as she considered the fact that every time with Spencer was absolutely amazing. He didn't have a bag full of tricks to keep things spicy, but he didn't need them. The man was extremely goal oriented and focused, and when he was in bed with her, he treated her like she was the center of his universe. At first it had been unnerving, being the sole recipient of all that attention. But now she craved it, and she felt like she would wither away if he were to deprive her of it.

It was early, she could tell from the hazy light in the room, and she heard the shower running. He was getting ready for work. Because of the expansion plans, he had been spending longer hours at his office. The renovations would start next week and the shop would be closed for two weeks in December, which was his most profitable time of year. He wasn't thrilled about it.

Daff lay curled up beneath the covers, feeling lazy and disinclined to move. Her mind fluttered from one topic to the next while she hovered in that happy place between complete wakefulness and sleep. Charlie's room was just about done, and she would be moving in next week, so Daff and Spencer would probably have to spend more time at Daff's place. He probably wouldn't stay over anymore, because he wouldn't feel comfortable leaving the girl alone overnight. That was just the way he was made. Charlie was his responsibility and he'd promised to take care of her, and staying out all night wouldn't be fulfilling that promise.

Daff was going to miss him. She'd miss this, the intimacy they'd built between them. The comfortable ease of his quiet companionship. Even with him being so withdrawn recently, she still preferred his company over most others'.

The shower switched off, and she listened to the familiar sounds of him drying off and then brushing his teeth—he did this weird humming thing whenever he brushed. In anyone else it would have annoyed her, but she found it endearing in Spencer.

She pushed herself up when he finally emerged from the steamy bathroom and smiled at him.

"Morning," she greeted, and his lips quirked.

"Hey. Go back to sleep, darling," he said, his voice pitched low. "It's barely six."

She sank back down under the covers and watched him get dressed. Every movement he made was quick and efficient. When he was fully dressed, he ran his fingers through his damp hair, not bothering with a brush, and strode over to the bed. He sat down on the side closest to her and dropped a kiss on her lips.

"I have back-to-back meetings today, so my phone will be off," he said.

"See you tonight?"

"Maybe. Depends on how late the meetings run. I'll still have some paperwork to do after that."

"Okay."

"I'll text you if I have the time."

"Okay." She wanted to insist he *make* the time to text her, but that wasn't her place. She couldn't make demands on his time, just as she didn't expect him to make demands on hers. That wasn't how *this* worked.

"Have a good day," he urged, dropping another kiss on her mouth before exiting the room abruptly. She heard the front door open and shut moments later. It was unusual for him to not even have coffee before heading out, so he was definitely pushed for time today.

Daff contemplated her own day. She really had absolutely nothing planned. Three weeks of unemployment, and she was already bored out of her skull. Who knew she'd miss going to that damned boutique every day? Maybe she hadn't hated it as much as she'd thought. She shook her head, disgusted with herself for being so damned wishy-washy, and got up.

She tugged on her pajama top and contemplated her bare feet on the cold hardwood floor for a moment before padding over to Spencer's gorgeous oak bureau and yanking open drawers until she found his socks. She smiled fondly at the neat arrangement and dug around for an old pair of rugby socks. Her hands hit an unusual object and she tugged it out before thinking the better of it. She was about to shove it back when she recognized it as a small velvet jewelry box. She stared at it for a long, blank moment, stunned to realize that Spencer had been this serious about Tanya.

Maybe she was wrong; maybe it wasn't an engagement ring. But what else would be in a box this size? Earrings? Possibly. She scrutinized the closed box for a long moment, torn between her conscience and the need to know. Had he lied about the depth of his feelings for Tanya?

Slowly, against her better judgment, everything in her screaming to just *put it down*, she cracked open the lid. She inhaled sharply at the first sight of the beautiful ring nestled in the small, dark-velvet interior of the box.

Warm rose gold, with a pear-shaped pink stone framed by tiny diamonds, it was absolutely stunning. She couldn't imagine flashy Tanya ever liking a discreet, beautifully elegant ring like this. She lifted it from the box with trembling fingers and noticed etchings on the inside of the narrow band.

Don't look, Daff! Just don't! her conscience shrieked, but she was already going to burn in hell for this, so she might as well go all in. She held it up and peered closely at the small, elegant script engraved inside the band.

Daff, my only love. S

"No," she whispered, her throat going dry. Her hands started shaking so much she dropped the ring. It landed on the floor and rolled a short distance before losing momentum and teetering to a stop.

"Oh Spencer. Why did you do this?" The words were barely audible, and she continued to gape at the ring in horror. Like it was a snake poised to strike at any moment.

"Daff?" Spencer's low and uncertain voice came from behind her, and she whirled around to see him standing in the bedroom doorway, his travel coffee mug clasped in one hand.

She looked trapped. Her eyes wide in her ashen face, her breath coming in shallow gasps. One hand clasped around the empty ring box.

Fuck.

"I—I was looking for s-socks," she stuttered, and he nodded, putting his mug on the bureau and striding toward her. She flinched slightly, and he tried not to take it personally. He reached for her hand

and removed the box from her slack hold. His eyes scanned the floor until he saw the ring lying about a meter away.

"Why do you have that?" she asked, her voice getting stronger and filled with anger and accusation. Spencer ignored her and bent to pick up the ring and gently place it back into the box. "You shouldn't have that. I don't want this."

"I know," he said placidly, trying not to show how much her words hurt him.

"So *why* do you have it?" she practically screeched. He lifted his face to the ceiling, fighting for control, trying to keep it together. "Why would you ignore my wishes like that? When you know this isn't what I want."

Always about *her.*

Finally, reaching the end of his tether, Spencer met her angry and confused eyes.

"Because I fucking *love* you, Daff!" He fought for control, but the words still flew out of his mouth at a louder volume than he intended. He brought it down to an angry whisper. "Because I want to marry you and spend the rest of my sorry life with you. Because *this*"—he waved the box angrily in her face—"this is what *I* want! It's what I need."

Finally running out of steam, he blinked rapidly, forcing the blurriness from his eyes.

"But I know it's not what *you* want," he continued, his voice softening and his heart breaking. "And that's why it's been lying at the bottom of my fucking sock drawer for weeks."

"Spencer—"

"It's okay. I'm not proposing, Daff," he reassured quietly. "But I can't do this anymore."

"Wh-what do you mean?" Her eyes were bright with tears, and it *killed* him to see them. He had never meant to make her cry.

"I've known, since I bought this ring, that I can't do this. I love you, Daff. With everything in me. But you don't want that love, and it's breaking my heart—" His voice cracked on the last word and he cleared his throat, trying to maintain his composure and do this right. "It's breaking my heart to be in this nonrelationship with you. I've tried to be what you want, do this your way . . . but that's not the kind of man I am. I'm an all or nothing guy, Daff. I want the world to know that we belong to each other. I want to be able to show you how I feel, *tell* you how I feel. I want us to . . ." He shook his head and simply said, "I want *us*."

"Spencer."

"You're wonderful," he told her. "You're beautiful, kind, sweet, amazing, smart, funny. You're everything. Don't forget that, Daff. Never let anyone make you feel like you're less. Because you're not. You're *everything*."

"Spencer, please, don't." She was sobbing now, doubled over, her arms folded protectively over her stomach.

"After the wedding—"

"No, Spencer," she begged, but he had to remain resolute.

"After the wedding, I think it would be better if we saw each other only when absolutely necessary. For family events."

She keened softly at his words, and Spencer found himself unable to resist dragging her into his arms and comforting her, despite what it cost him to touch her. He felt the dampness seep down his cheeks, and he choked back his own sobs.

"I love you so damned much," he told her before kissing her one last time. He stepped back, looked into her beautiful, tear-drenched face for a long moment.

And let her go.

CHAPTER FIFTEEN

Daff and Spencer still spoke over the next day and a half—they *had* to—stilted conversations about party plans, travel arrangements, and accommodation. Last-minute snags and fixes.

Daff felt far removed from everyone and everything. She made the right noises, smiled when she had to, and even cracked a few jokes. And never once looked like her heart was dying in her chest. But it was, she could feel it. It hurt at first, sharp and intense and overwhelming, but soon a welcome numbness set in and she was able to function with relative normalcy.

She had no other choice; her sister was getting married and she had promised that her thing with Spencer wouldn't affect the wedding or their family dynamic. It had been an easy promise to make, because never in her wildest imaginings had she understood how very much the reality of being excluded from Spencer's life would hurt.

Two days later, they set off for Plettenberg Bay. Daff and Spencer had rented a couple of minibuses, deciding that it was the most convenient transportation option. Daff was in one van with the women, and Spencer in the other with the men.

"So here's the deal, ladies," she called to the group as they set off. "My baby sister's getting married next week—" She paused and allowed a few moments of rowdy catcalling and howls from the peanut gallery.

"We're having a full-on hen at a separate venue from the guys, but we're meeting up with the sausage party later at a nightclub for some dancing and partying deep into the night. Transportation back to the hotel has been arranged, and there are rooms reserved for all your drunken asses. So there's no need to worry about anything. Just make sure you have an awesome time. And remember to take a shot when somebody says 'wedding,' 'bride,' 'bridesmaid,' 'groom,' 'hung like a horse,' 'crazy married sex,' or 'Mason loves Daisy.' Oops, that's seven shots to start you off!"

More crazy cheers, and Daff passed shot glasses around but warned them, "Don't give any to Daisy, not until later! We want her to be conscious for most of the evening!"

"Hey!" Daisy protested good-naturedly but happily passed on the first shots of the evening.

Daff sent a tacky veil and silk sash that read "Mason's Bride" to the back of the bus, and a couple of the ladies decked Daisy out in her hen finery. She also handed out other specially commissioned party favors—hats, glasses, and T-shirts, all pink and sparkly, with "Daisy's Hens" printed somewhere on them.

She smiled while everybody giggled and oohed and ahhed over the selection, but her eyes drifted to the minibus behind theirs. She hadn't seen Spencer that day, but she knew he was back there. She wondered how he was doing. He wasn't great at public speaking, and she knew hosting something like this was going to be hard for him. She was tempted to text him to find out how it was going. But she knew better.

She wanted to curl up into a ball and cry every time she thought about his words to her that last time. He loved her and she'd broken his heart, and it killed her to know that. He didn't deserve to have his heart broken—he deserved to be loved back, completely and without reservation. But Daff didn't know how to do that. All she knew was that not having him around, never having him around again, hurt more than anything she'd ever experienced before. She didn't want to lose him, but she didn't know how to give him what he wanted.

Everybody was starting to get into the swing of things and, job done for now, Daff sat down and faced forward, taking out her phone and blindly staring at the bright screen. Hoping everybody would think she was making last-minute arrangements. Someone sat down next to her, and she plastered a bright smile on her face and looked up to see Lia. Her sister was staring at her with grave eyes, so Daff widened her smile, even though her cheeks were aching.

"Hey, Lia, everything okay?"

"You tell me," Lia said under her breath, her words barely audible above the rowdy group in the back.

"Everything is going according to plan and—"

"*Daff,*" her sister interrupted sharply, and Daff's smile wavered. "Tell me what's going on. You look so sad."

"I *do?*"

"Sissy, you're crying," Lia said quietly and handed her a tissue. Daff lifted a hand to her cheek, horrified to find it wet.

"I'm going to ruin the party," she lamented, and Lia shook her head.

"Nobody noticed, just keep your eyes front and pretend that we're talking."

"We *are* talking," Daff pointed out, discreetly swiping at her face.

"What happened?"

"This isn't the time or place."

"Is it Spencer? Did you guys have a fight?"

"He bought a ring," Daff said, more tears slipping down her cheek.

"But that's wonderful, Daff."

"Of course you would think that, it's your ultimate goal in life," Daff said bitterly, then immediately felt like a bitch when Lia looked like she'd been slapped.

"Hey, at least I *have* goals," Lia pointed out scathingly, recovering quickly. And it was almost enough to make Daff smile.

Way to go, Lia!

"So . . . you're *not* happy about the ring?" Lia clarified, and Daff shook her head.

"*Why* would he do that? When I specifically told him that I wasn't into traditional relationships and that I was happy with what we had."

"Because he loves you and wants more?"

"So he says. But if he loves me, why can't he accept me as I am? Wouldn't he be happy to just be in my life?"

"And if you love *him*, why can't you accept that he wants what he's never had? He wants someone to love, someone to make a family with. I think he wants to belong, because he never has before."

Daff stared at Lia, the words echoing in her mind. She felt like someone had ripped a veil from her eyes and she was only now seeing things clearly.

Of course he wanted a family. She just had to look at his house to see that. Of *course* he wanted to belong. No matter how awkward he seemed around her family or how he kept himself apart from them, he always looked at them with something close to yearning in his eyes. It was entirely possible that he wasn't deliberately keeping himself separate, he just didn't know how to fit in. Or *where* he fit in.

"I'm very fond of him, but I don't love him," she finally protested weakly as the rest of Lia's words sank in. Her sister rolled her eyes exaggeratedly.

"Please. You look at the guy like he hung the sun," Lia dismissed.

"That's just lust," Daff said, sounding completely unconvincing even to herself.

"I've never seen you look happier or more content than you are around Spencer. You adore him."

Yes, she did. There really was no point in denying that fact.

"I'm not cut out for marriage, Lia."

"Why not?"

Daff thought about it and shook her head in bewilderment. "Reasons." And yet she couldn't think of a single reason right at that moment.

"Do you think he'll treat you badly?" She didn't even bother answering that stupid question. Spencer was quite incapable of harming even a fly.

"Do you think he won't support your decisions?"

Daff thought about his gentle, nonjudgmental encouragement when she'd quit her job and shook her head helplessly.

"Okay. Let me ask you this . . . do you want to be with other men?"

The thought was so repulsive that Daff was quite unable to hide her reaction from Lia.

"Is he boring? A bad conversationalist? I mean, I know he's quiet, but you guys always seem to have *something* to talk about."

"He's not boring," Daff defended with a glare. "Look, I just don't like labels, Lia. Why do we have to give what we have a name?"

"Okay, so you'd be fine with nobody knowing the true nature of your relationship and chicks always hitting on him because you didn't put a ring on that?"

"That's such archaic thinking," Daff protested, while at the same time feeling nauseated at the thought of Spencer with some other woman. A woman who wouldn't understand him. Who wouldn't appreciate his occasional lapses into silence. And who definitely wouldn't know that there were about fifty possible interpretations for one mild "hmm."

"How long would you expect this tenuous sexual thing without labels to last? A few months? A couple of years? How do you introduce him to people? As your friend with benefits? Your casual lover?"

"I don't know, okay? I just don't think marriage is the right fit for me!"

"Why not?"

"Because I—" *Don't deserve it!*

I don't deserve . . . him.

Daff stopped herself before she completed the sentence. Horrified to hear the silent words screaming loudly in her mind. Why would she think that? Why would she feel so inadequate?

She thought about Spencer's words to her: *Never let anyone make you feel like you're less. Because you're not. You're* everything.

And Daff finally recognized that *she* was her own worst enemy. She was the one who thought she was less. Who thought she didn't deserve good things and happiness. She had allowed complete assholes to grind her self-worth to dust, and once they were out of her life, she'd taken over the job herself. And Spencer, unfailingly kind and loving Spencer, who had made her feel cherished and important, had been the one she'd inadvertently been punishing for everyone else's sins.

She gulped down a sob, and Lia put an arm around her shoulder and squeezed her close.

"You're okay, Sissy. You'll be fine."

Daff nodded and plastered another smile on her face, trying to keep the cheerful façade in place for Daisy's sake. But she wasn't sure if she'd ever be fine again.

The hen party was a smashing success, and by the time they hooked up with the guys, everybody was well and truly sauced. Daisy was just loud and drunk enough to be hilarious. She launched herself at Mason when she saw him, for all the world like someone who hadn't seen her man in months. Mason wasn't much better; he wouldn't stop snogging her.

The guys were all wearing "Mason's Stag Bros" T-shirts, and Mason himself was topless. Someone had crudely painted "Daisy's Man" on his back and "This belongs to Daisy" on his truly magnificent chest, with an arrow pointing down to his crotch. He had lipstick kisses all over his neck and shoulders, which would have been dodgy if not for the fact that all the guys had lipstick smeared over their mouths and halfway down their chins.

Clearly they'd been up to some crazy shit. Daff knew that Mason had invited their dad along, but she was kind of relieved that the older man had politely declined the invitation. He'd said he'd be fine staying home to play a few rousing games of Scrabble with Charlie and their mother. She didn't think the party would have been quite as crazy if their father had been present.

Her eyes scanned the crowd until she spotted Spencer's huge shoulders on the other end of the dance floor. He had a drink in each hand and was about to make his way back to the party when a couple of nearly naked *skanks* rubbed themselves up against him. One of them ran her hand up his chest, and Daff felt her brows slam together. When the other woman curled her hand around his bicep, she clenched her teeth and heard herself growling.

One of the little slags put her hand on his cheek, and he tilted his head enough for her to go up onto her toes and say something directly into his ear.

"Uh-uh," Daff snapped, and before she knew it she was halfway across the dance floor, pushing her way through throngs of writhing people. She wasn't sure what her endgame was—her only objective was to get their hands *off* Spencer!

"Spencer," she barked when she reached the threesome, raising her voice so that he could hear her above the music. He was smiling at them. Why was he smiling at them? His head jerked up when he heard her voice, and his eyebrows rose clear to his hairline when he saw her folded arms and her scowl.

"What's up, Daff?" he asked warily.

"Thought you might need a hand carrying those drinks," she offered. And he lifted a powerful shoulder nonchalantly.

"I'm fine."

Daff's eyes tracked to the two women, one of whom still had a hand on Spencer's arm. Her eyes lingered on that hand as she entertained dark thoughts of ripping each scarlet acrylic nail off those slender fingers. That would teach her to lay hands on Daff's man.

Only he wasn't her man. Was he? Not according to her own rules, and especially not after Spencer had ended things between them. He was a free agent—he could flirt with whomever he wanted, date anybody, sleep with every woman under the sun. Daff had no claim on him. She had revoked that right.

She ran a hand over her throbbing forehead. The tension and stress of the last few days, combined with the music and alcohol, had given her the worst headache.

"You okay?" Spencer shouted, shrugging off the woman's hand to move closer to Daff. He completely ignored the other women, his attention wholly focused on Daff, and she choked back a sob as she recognized the look in his eyes as concern . . . for her.

His reaction was utterly instinctive, the behavior of a man who wanted to protect someone he cared about. This was the man Spencer was, the man he couldn't help being, and Daff loved him for it.

She loved him!

She took a moment to process that thought. She examined the emotion from every angle and felt . . . relieved. Not panicked or terrified, but relieved. Because *of course* she loved him. How had she not seen that sooner? And how could she have tried to curb the very thing about Spencer that made him special? She had attempted to stifle his protective instinct by minimizing their relationship. By lying to herself and him and referring to what they had as a *thing*. In refusing to give it a name or any importance, she had basically communicated to him that he didn't have the right to care about her, to worry about her, or to *love* her.

And Spencer wasn't wired like that.

And seeing him with these women, Daff finally began to understand that perhaps *she* wasn't wired like that, either. She *wanted* everybody to know that he was off-limits and belonged exclusively to her. Suddenly Daff found herself wanting those strings. She wanted this man so thoroughly bound to her that he would never get away again.

She gaped at him in slack-jawed bewilderment—the epiphany, so long in coming, sent her reeling—and it took a moment to register the alarm on his face or hear his words.

"—going to be sick?" he yelled, the music all but drowning the words.

"Uh, I-I'm fine," she said, and he gave her another long, searching look.

"Great," he said dismissively. "I've got to get these drinks back. See you later."

And with that, he walked away. Without so much as a backward glance. Leaving Daff to feel completely abandoned. Despite knowing that this sense of loss she felt was entirely her own doing.

"So you're Dahlia." Lia trembled at the sound of the dark, silky voice murmuring directly into her ear. She immediately knew who the voice belonged to, of course—the man hadn't taken his eyes off her since the stag party had collectively strutted into the nightclub an hour ago. She'd been expecting some kind of contact from him, and sure enough, here he was, standing so close she could smell his delicious aftershave and feel his breath stir her hair.

She shut her eyes, drew in a deep, fortitudinous breath, and turned to face him. Crumbs, he was much too close; if either of them inhaled too deeply, her chest would scrape against his. He was just four or so inches taller than her five foot seven, and—with her heels—their eyes were nearly level. He was smiling, and somehow that display of even white teeth did not make him seem approachable or friendly, but predatory.

It was disconcerting.

"Yes," she replied. Not really wanting to talk with him. Thankfully the pulsing music and strobe lights made it almost impossible to have a decent conversation. So she gave him a wholly fake smile before dipping her head to take a sip of her drink. She drank too fast and then grimaced when the frozen margarita gave her brain freeze.

"Stick your tongue to the roof of my mouth," Sam Brand shouted in her ear. Completely appalled by the lewd suggestion, she backed away and glared at him, one hand pressed to her chest. His smile transformed into a roguish grin and he, once again, breached the space between them to yell into her ear. "For the brain freeze. Stick your tongue to the roof of your mouth!"

She watched him in confusion, not sure if she'd imagined the "my" the first time or if he was messing with her. Brain freeze forgotten in her complete confusion, she waved him off.

"I'm fine," she said, raising her voice to be heard. Then, remembering her manners, "Thank you."

"It's loud in here! Want to go someplace quiet to . . . talk?" Well, she certainly hadn't imagined that suggestive pause and gave him her most quelling look. The one Daff often described as the "cock burn." It wasn't a term Lia would ever use, but the look was usually pretty effective.

It had no effect on Sam Brand. He continued to watch her expectantly. She sighed, recognizing that she would have to use her words on this one.

"No. I would not like to go anywhere with you—" Okay, that seemed a little rude, and being rude was completely out of character for Lia, so she added a polite disclaimer. "Right now."

"Yeah, I get it, your sister's hen party. I'm cool with that. Want to dance?"

"Uh. No."

"No problem, we can stand here and yell at each other."

"I see my, uh . . ." Lia scanned the area, but none of her friends were currently nearby. Daff was on the other side of the dance floor talking to Spencer—it didn't seem to be going well—and Daisy and Mason were barely visible in their dark corner. They seemed to be having a fine time feeling each other up. Everybody else was scattered all over the place.

"So what do you do?" the gorgeous man next to her bellowed into her ear.

"Mr. Brand, I don't think—"

"Sam."

"Right. I have to go to—uh . . ."

"Dahlia—" Ugh, Lia didn't much care for her name, but asking him to call her by the shortened version would be sending the wrong message, so she left it. "I think you're incredibly sexy. I never imagined the whole librarian thing ever appealing to me, but fuck me, babe, on you it's scorching hot. I just wanted to get to know you a little better."

"Why?" she asked bluntly, and he laughed.

"I like a woman who can get straight to the point," he said, and she started to fold her arms defensively, forgetting about the margarita and spilling some of the freezing liquid all over the front of her pretty new blouse. The thin material immediately soaked through, beading her nipples and bringing up every lacy little curl on her white B-cup bra in lurid detail beneath the black lights. The corner of his mouth lifted in very sincere appreciation. He plucked the margarita glass from her hand, and she immediately crossed her arms over her soaked and practically naked chest.

"You need to get out of those wet things," he informed her, a gleam in his eye, and she frowned.

"Well, I think that's my cue to call it a night," she said, relieved for an excuse to get away from him.

"You could just ditch the blouse and party in that pretty little thing you're wearing beneath it. It's quite modest by some other standards in here."

Lia went bright red at the thought of parading around in her bra and tucked her hands beneath her armpits in an attempt to cover herself even more.

"Good night," she said sternly and turned away.

"Whoa, sweetheart, you can't go out reeking of tequila and unescorted in that see-through shirt. There are a lot of arseholes out there."

And yet—despite his amiable grin—Lia felt like she was in the company of the biggest a-hole of them all.

"I'll be fine," she said, keeping her voice frigid, but his smile never faltered.

"I'll accompany you back to the hotel. Maybe we can have a nightcap."

"Mr. Brand, I really don't think that's necessary," she negated primly.

"Sam . . . and maybe I don't really have a nightcap in mind."

"I know what you have in mind."

"Yeah?" His face brightened. "Then we're on the same page."

"No. We're not."

"Come on, Dahlia, it's just a bit of fun and fucking."

She gasped and her eyes widened. No man had ever spoken to her so bluntly before, and it was . . . different. Not appealing, but not entirely repulsive, either. More like intriguing.

"You're interested, I can see you are," he said, latching on to her hesitation.

"You're unbelievably crude, Mr. Brand, and I don't believe we'll get along. So why don't we just part ways here? Before you say something to make me dislike you even more."

"Aw, come on, sweetheart, you clearly need to loosen up a bit. I can help you with that."

After the debacle of her failed wedding, everybody had been treating her with kid gloves. She had to admit it was really kind of refreshing to meet someone who didn't walk on eggshells around her. Someone who didn't treat her like some fragile little porcelain doll that would break at the first sign of rough handling.

She tilted her head and openly assessed him.

"My wedding was called off at the eleventh hour last year," she told him, watching closely for his reaction. He did nothing more than raise a cocky brow.

"Yeah? Good to know you're a free agent, sweetheart. Married women are off-limits. I don't do messy or complicated."

"There are plenty of other available women here," Lia pointed out.

"None of them are you," he yelled, raising his voice even more when an annoying electronic beat started thumping and the crowd cheered. People swarmed around them, but nobody touched them. It was as if Sam Brand created his own invisible force field and people automatically knew to go around it. He was standing so close to Lia that she was afforded the same protection that invisible shield offered him, and it felt like—despite the throngs of people around them—they were in their own private little oasis.

He was staring fixedly at her, his unnerving and unflinching scrutiny making her feel vulnerable and exposed, but she found herself quite unable to look away. Her eyes dropped to his beautiful mouth and then back up to his magnetic blue eyes.

"How's that nightcap looking, Dahlia?" he asked, that irrepressibly wicked grin flirting with the corners of his mouth.

"My name's Lia."

Two days later, just barely recovered from Friday night's colossal hangover, Daff sat curled up on her sofa, her hands wrapped around her coffee mug as she took in the collection of personal debris she had been sifting through over the course of the last few weeks in her ongoing quest toward self-improvement.

The jazz albums, Japanese cookbooks, art history books, sketchbook and oil paints, a drum kit, a guitar, a surfboard, a collection of noir film DVDs, most of them unwatched, binoculars from that time she'd taken up bird-watching, her dad's old golf clubs—she'd have to return them—and so many other gadgets and doodads that she had collected over the years. Obtained, not out of any genuine interest in learning a new hobby or craft, but to impress her current man of the moment.

The pile on the floor was embarrassingly large and served as mute testament to what had gone wrong with all those relationships. None of those guys had shown the slightest interest in getting to know her and, worse, Daff hadn't showed any of them her true self, either. She hadn't trusted them enough to reveal her weaknesses and insecurities. Her pathological need to impress them by adopting *their* interests and hobbies had doomed each and every relationship from the start. It had started with Jake, of course, and despite the way that had turned out, she had continued on the same self-destructive path for years.

She took a sip of her coffee and thought about what she and Spencer had shared. She had gone out of her way to give it no labels. Had done her best to ensure that it meant nothing . . .

And yet it had been her healthiest relationship with a man *ever*. They had talked, laughed, made love, and talked some more. He'd been genuinely interested in her likes and she in his. Spencer Carlisle was a man any woman would be lucky to have, and he'd wanted *her*. Not because of some bullshit, fake mutual interest she had cultivated, but because he had seen the real, cranky bitch Daff, with her many, many insecurities, and yet somehow still loved her. He did not want to change her, or improve her, or educate her, he just wanted them to belong to each other.

Why was that so hard for her to accept?

She set aside the mug and got up to pad to her bedroom. She went straight to her closet and retrieved the shoebox she had stowed on the top shelf. She took it back to the living room and sat down on the nearest armchair, holding the box in her lap. She took a deep breath, removed the lid, and smiled fondly at the slips of yellowing notepaper. There were more than she remembered. She lifted the top one and unfolded it. Spencer's handwriting, bold and masculine even when he was a teenager, was scrawled across the lined paper.

Daff, your eyes

Are like stars in the skies

And for all your smiles

I would walk a thousand miles

She raised a hand to her mouth and stifled a half laugh and half sob. His poetry was kind of atrocious, but it must have taken phenomenal courage for the shy, reticent boy Spencer had been to write and then present this to the more popular Daff. She refolded the page along the well-worn crease and picked up another.

She unfolded and recognized it with a sad pang. The last note he'd ever sent her. She'd never shown it to anyone. Even though she'd cruelly taunted him by sharing his sweet little love rhymes with Shar Bridges and her ilk, this letter had felt too personal, and she'd experienced an instinctive need to protect his privacy along with his dignity.

Daff,

I know my letters and poems have embarrassed you, and I'm so sorry I put you through that. I wanted you to know that I like you and I didn't know how else to show you. I love coming to school every day and seeing your beautiful smile. I wish you would have shared one with me . . . just once. It would have meant the world to me.

I won't bother you again.

Yours,

Spencer

Daff wiped a tear from her cheek as she reread the letter. He had been about seventeen at the time, and her fifteen-year-old self—the selfish, vain girl she had been—hadn't *truly* understood what she had meant to the quiet boy who rarely spoke with anyone other than his brother. Even after becoming something of a sensation on the rugby team in his senior year, he had still remained quiet and removed from his peers.

Daff read each slip of paper, bittersweet tears sliding down her cheeks as she thought of the boy he had been, of the man he was. She was a fool for letting him go. She knew it.

She regretted it.

But she wasn't sure she was brave enough to fix it.

"I don't know *why* I can't have a TV in my room, all the other kids at school do," Charlie whined, and Spencer hid a grin at the unfamiliar high pitch in her voice. She was starting to behave like a typical young girl, concerned about the way she looked, her hair, what the other kids at her school had. She had started attending the local high school just three weeks ago and seemed to be settling in nicely. She even had a couple of friends.

She would be moving in with Spencer next week, and her room was nearly complete. She'd surprised him by going pink and girly. Somehow he'd expected something darker, more Goth. But now that she didn't have to hide her femininity, she was embracing it. It was odd to see her in skirts and dresses. With her short hair and skinny frame, they didn't quite suit her, but she was starting to gain weight and looking healthier by the day. Spencer loved that she felt safe enough to behave and look like a girl again. And—while frustrating—he enjoyed her displays of temper and adolescent sulks, which meant that she felt secure enough in her position here not to tiptoe around on her absolute best behavior.

"You don't need a television when we have a perfectly good one in the living room," he said, addressing her latest grievance.

"Yeah, but I probably won't want to watch the same crap you watch."

"Hey, watch the language," he warned her, and she rolled her eyes.

"*Crap* is so not a swear word."

"Yeah, well, I say it is."

"Oh my God. Your rules are so arbitrary. Why do you have to be such an old man sometimes?" He merely raised a brow to that, and she huffed dramatically.

They were at Spencer's place having some lunch after an "epic" shopping trip, for some "absolute, must-have" last-minute finishing touches to Charlie's room. Spencer didn't see what was so essential about a pod chair, or a weird pink fur rug, or whoever the hell that sulky teen boy in the ridiculously expensive framed poster was, but he'd had a blast getting the items for her. And the tasks took his mind off Daff—and the huge gaping hole she had left in his life and his heart.

God, he missed her. He felt so lost and lonely without her. Being with her on her terms didn't seem so bad compared to the constant, dull ache he now carried with him. With Daff he'd felt a sense of belonging, and not having her in his life made him question whether the traditional bonds he sought were as important as he'd once believed they were.

"So are you and Daff not, like, together anymore?" Charlie's subdued question completely threw him, and he blinked at her dumbly.

"I—uh . . . well, we weren't really together," he explained awkwardly, and she took a sip from her soda before daintily picking up a french fry and biting it in half.

"You seemed like you were."

"It wasn't serious."

Charlie dragged the other half of her french fry through some mustard, drawing patterns on the plate, and shrugged.

"You guys looked at each other the way Daisy and Mason do, and *they're* getting married. And you look sad lately." The last bit was mumbled self-consciously, and her eyes dropped to her plate. She was clearly uncomfortable making such a personal observation about him, while Spencer was more than a little shaken up that his overwhelming grief had been so evident to this young girl who barely knew him.

"Yeah," he said gruffly. "I am. I miss her. A lot."

He blinked rapidly, horrified when his vision blurred.

"Uh, so how do you like your dress for the wedding?" He changed the subject and left the table abruptly, ostensibly to get a bottle of water from the refrigerator. He took a moment to compose himself while his back was to her.

"It's pretty. Daisy says it's exactly like the other bridesmaid dresses, only theirs are knee-length and mine is long. I've always wanted a long dress. And I've never been a bridesmaid before."

Shortly after Charlie had moved in with the McGregors, Daisy had insisted that her new sister be included in the bridal party. Charlie had initially played it cool, but it was clear to see that she was very excited about it. Spencer didn't know how complicated these things were, but evidently it had taken some doing getting a dress organized for Charlie on such short notice. But somehow, apparently against all odds, they had managed to pull it off. Spencer turned to face the smiling teen and felt his own mouth quirk in response to her sheer happiness. He really didn't care about the particulars—what mattered was the end result. And—if Charlie's bright and excited face was anything to go by—the result was pretty damned great.

He was so damned grateful for Charlie. So happy to have the opportunity to provide a stable home for her. He had no real idea how to raise a girl, but he knew where she came from and he would make damned sure that nothing in her life from here on out was anything like she had experienced in the past.

"I'm glad you're here, Charlie," he said, that gruffness creeping back into his voice, and this time Charlie was the one blinking rapidly.

"I guess I am, too," she finally admitted, then added with that usual air of teenage insouciance, "I mean, you're not *that* bad for a boring old fart. And you *are* letting me have a dog."

It was an ambush, plain and simple. Daff knew Shar Bridges would be at the only salon in Riversend for her bimonthly dye job and caught her as she exited the salon.

"Why the hell did you tell all of my boyfriends that I was into BDSM?" Daff launched at the other woman without preamble. Firing on all cylinders was the only way to get results with Shar, and Daff knew that stating her suspicion as fact would get the most honest reaction from the other woman.

"Daff. I hear you've been spending time with that mouth breather Spencer Carlisle. Slumming, are we?"

Daff inhaled deeply. Oh man, the bitch was courting a slap, and it would be Daff's greatest pleasure to lay one on her.

Don't lose focus, Daff! Keep it together.

"Answer the question, Shar."

"Why should I?" Shar asked laconically, showing her disinterest in Daff and anything she might have to say by keeping her focus on her phone and lazily scrolling through her texts and e-mails.

"Oh, I don't know . . ." Daff mused. "Maybe because of Ryan Casey? Or Dirk Pieterse? And let's not forget Bryan Pienaar."

Shar's head shot up, and she went paler with each name Daff itemized.

"You *wouldn't!*" Shar gasped, and Daff's lips quirked.

"I so would. And those are just the names off the top of my head. If I *really* put my mind to it, I'm sure I could come up with many more. Now you tell me what I want to know, or your husband and I are going to have a very interesting conversation." Shar was married to an extremely wealthy man, old enough to be her father. She loved the lifestyle that went hand in hand with being his wife but cheated on him quite indiscriminately. The older man cheated on her, too, but they both enjoyed pretending nothing was amiss with their marriage.

"I remember you once telling us that Frank's an old-fashioned man . . . cheating's all well and good as long as you're discreet about it, right? He won't like learning that half of the town knows that you're sleeping around on him."

"You and your fucking sisters," Shar hissed suddenly. "With your perfect parents and your perfect lives and your perfect bond. You were always so perfectly fucking insufferable."

"Why did you tell those lies about me?" Daff pressed, ignoring the bitter diatribe.

"It wasn't a lie, though, was it? You stayed with Jake for three years, and he was heavily into that shit."

"Wait, you didn't tell Jake I was into bondage?"

"No. You saw Jake and decided you wanted him. And perfect Daffodil McGregor always got exactly what she wanted. Jake and I were . . . I *liked* him." Daff blinked in surprise.

"But you introduced us," she reminded her, a little blindsided by the revelation that Shar had liked Jake.

"Because he took one look at you and forgot all about me, didn't he? He demanded an introduction, and that was it. Daff got the guy. Of course, I knew about his little bondage games—I quite enjoyed them."

"You and Jake were sleeping together when I met him? Why didn't you say something?" Why was she only hearing this now?

"Right. Like I'd let you know that you managed to steal the guy I wanted. How smug that would have made you."

"You were my friend. I would have backed off," Daff said incredulously. How had Shar developed such a skewed view of Daff and her sisters? Her unfounded jealousy had made her irrationally competitive.

"Whatever." Shar shrugged, flipping her artificially blonde locks nonchalantly. "It's ancient history now. The fact is you stayed with Jake for three years, so you must have been into the BDSM stuff. After you broke up, I thought it would freak out a few of your potential boyfriends if they knew about your particular kinks, but they never seemed particularly fussed by it. So no harm, no foul."

Daff stared at the other woman for a long moment and then smiled. She was relieved to now know why men had behaved the way they had with her. And simultaneously surprised by how little it actually mattered to her now that she *did* know. She wasn't even angry with Shar. Just sad for her. She had allowed petty jealousy and vanity to ruin her perception of the women she had called her friends. She was a sad, pathetic, desperately vain woman who deserved pity more than hatred.

But right at this moment, Daff felt neither emotion toward her. She felt curiously apathetic and keen to get away from the woman and the messed-up past she represented.

"Jake Kincaid?" Daff said, leaning toward Shar confidentially as she spoke. "You could have had him. All you had to do was tell me you liked him. Because that's what friends do. But you wouldn't know that, would you? Because you've never been a true friend to anyone. Now, if you'll excuse me, I have to go slumming with my man. You know the one? Big, gorgeous, sexy Spencer Carlisle."

With that, Daff turned away from Shar and the past. More than ready to fight for the man and the future she deserved.

Monday seemed endless. The expansion that Spencer had been so excited about just last month now couldn't ignite a flicker of interest in him, and he passed just about every nonessential task to Claude.

The day dragged on, and all he could do was stare at Nelly. Mason was out fishing with his buddy Sam and kept sending selfies of them posing with huge fish. Apparently the fishing at the river mouth—*Kleinbekkie*—was "epic as fuck" today. Spencer seriously considered ditching work to join them, but in the end he couldn't even summon up enough interest to play hooky.

After eight hours of doing absolutely nothing, he left the store right at the stroke of 5:00 p.m. and went straight home for an evening of much the same. He was contemplating dinner and his lack of appetite when he saw her. Just sitting on his porch swing and watching the car come up the drive.

She didn't move when he got out and watched him somberly as he climbed the three steps up to his large porch. There were three midsize cardboard boxes at her feet and he kept his attention on those, because it hurt less than looking at her.

"What are you doing here, Daff?" he asked her feet.

"These are for you," she said, getting up. The movement automatically drew his scrutiny to her face, and he locked eyes with her and found himself quite unable to look away. Was it his imagination, or was she as miserable as he was?

"What are they?"

"This"—she gestured to the boxes as a whole—"is not who I am."

What the fuck was that supposed to mean?

CHAPTER SIXTEEN

"What?" She had the grace to look embarrassed and shrugged self-consciously.

"It's a gesture," she admitted, her cheeks flushing. "Just, please . . . go with it, okay?"

Confused, Spencer peered at the boxes again. They weren't taped shut; the flaps were just folded over.

"I'm supposed to open them?"

"Yeah, of course, Spencer," she said, sounding a little exasperated. "Why else would I say they were for you?"

He lifted his hands, palms up, trying to placate her. She looked apprehensive and kept lifting her forefinger to her lips as if to chew before remembering that she had kicked that habit and lowering it again. The little display of nerves bolstered him a bit, and he warily sank to one knee in front of one of the boxes and opened it up.

He didn't know what he'd expected, but it definitely wasn't a stack of Miles Davis CDs.

"You like jazz?" he asked, confused.

"No," she said, her voice soft as she sank back down onto the swing. "I hate it. But Jeremy Boothe loved it. I dated him for about two months five years ago. And during that time I absolutely *loved* jazz.

Jeremy and I could talk about jazz for hours. He thought we had a real connection. We had so much in common."

Spencer lifted the small stack of CDs and turned them over, staring at them for a long time before putting them aside. He sat down on the porch step and reached into the box again and withdrew a pair of binoculars. He looked at them curiously for a moment before turning to face her. Her eyes were shining with tears, but she forced a little smile.

"Peter Weyland, three years ago, also two months. He was an out-of-towner, a keen bird-watcher, and I took him to all the best bird-spotting sites in the Garden Route. I knew them all, you see, because I absolutely *adored* bird-watching."

"I see," he said, dropping the binoculars, uncaring where they landed. His eyes remained riveted to hers, and one of the tears that had been threatening slid down her cheek and hung from her trembling chin for a long moment before dropping to her fidgeting fingers. She seemed unaware of it and just kept watching him steadily.

"There's more," she prompted him, and he nodded without looking at the box again.

"I know."

"It's important," she said, her voice quiet.

"It's not."

"I also have a guitar. I'm quite proficient at it. I learned to play when I was dating Aaron Marks. He was an aspiring musician."

"I remember him," Spencer said, keeping his voice carefully neutral even though his heart was breaking for this beautiful, intelligent woman who had felt the need to pretend—for fucking *years*—to be someone she was not. When she was amazing just the way she was.

"A-and I have a surfboard, cookbooks, all these really shitty black-and-white movies, a—"

"Daff," he said, inserting just enough volume in his voice to halt the stumbling tide of—what she clearly considered—guilty admission. "Stop. I just want to know which one of those fuckers loved eggs."

She made a wet, snorting giggling sound and covered her mouth and nose in horror. He dug into his sweatpants and dragged out a clean hankie and handed it to her. She accepted it gratefully and blew her nose before shaking her head ruefully.

"Nobody carries hankies anymore."

"I do." She nodded and twisted the handkerchief between her fingers.

"The eggs? That was Byron Blake, back in the sixth grade. He offered me an egg-mayo sandwich and I liked him, so I accepted it."

"That far back, huh?"

"Told you I was messed up. To be fair, none of them really *expected* me to lie about my interests. That was all me, in my sad attempts to be interesting to them. This past year was the first time I found myself without a boyfriend of some kind, and I found it kind of liberating to just do what I wanted to do."

He nodded, unable to take his eyes off her. The tip of her nose was pink, her cheeks were blotchy, and her eyes were red. She wasn't a pretty crier, but he couldn't remember her ever looking more beautiful.

She sniffed messily and reached for another box, a shoebox that had been tucked away out of sight beside her hip.

"Daff, I told you I don't need to see—"

"*This,*" she interrupted firmly, "is who I always longed to be."

He scrutinized the box for a couple of heartbeats before reaching for it. She seemed reluctant to relinquish it, and that raised his curiosity.

He opened the box and stared at the neatly folded slips of notepaper for a moment. They looked familiar. He lifted one and opened it and felt his face go bright red as he instantly recognized what it was.

"You *kept* them?" he asked hoarsely. Frankly, he was amazed his voice actually worked.

"Every single one of them."

He cringed and opened the note again.

"God, this is awful," he muttered.

"I love it. I loved all of them. I was such a bitch, Spencer. But I couldn't bring myself to part with a single one of them. They were so sweet."

"I was a horny, troubled teen."

"Don't you *dare* denigrate my love poems. I never understood why you kept giving them to me. I didn't deserve them, not the way I behaved, reading them out loud and making fun of you in front of the other girls. I was horrible. Even now I can't really explain why I did those things, except that I was really scared the other girls would think I liked you back and I'd never hear the end of it. Fitting in meant so much to me; I was so shallow. And every time I read one of your poems, I felt worse about myself, because I could never be the girl you seemed to see."

"It was a long time ago."

"I wanted to be this girl, Spencer. I really did."

"I put a lot on you, Daff. My home life was shitty. You were this perfect and beautiful girl and I built this fake romance up in my head. You would make my life different and wonderful and worthwhile. It was unfair. I did to you what all those other assholes did—I placed my expectations on you. I'm so fucking sorry."

"No, Spencer. You're nothing like the rest of them. So many of your notes asked questions and showed interest in *me*. Did I take sugar in my coffee? What was my favorite movie? What was my opinion on"—she laughed softly—"on Hanson?"

"I hated those little assholes," Spencer recalled, shaking his head. She giggled outright at that.

"Anyway, my point is, you were different. You cared. You wanted to know me. You didn't expect me to like what you liked. And while none of the other guys expected me to like what they liked, either, in the end, none of them actually cared enough to ask me about any of my other interests. They just accepted that I was this perfect, feminine reflection of them. I liked what they liked, and that was it."

She got up again and snatched her box of badly written poems back. She placed them carefully on the swing. He couldn't believe she'd kept them—it made his heart feel so fucking huge in his chest, he thought it was about to burst.

She straightened and lifted her chin to look at him. He remained seated and perfectly still, curious to see what was next.

Daff sucked in a deep, shuddering breath and dropped the coat she'd been wearing. It was too damned hot to wear a coat in late October, but she was making a gesture and it required a reveal.

His eyes drank her in . . . okay, maybe they didn't so much drink as kind of hop from place to place. He clearly hadn't been expecting saggy sweatpants, flip-flops, and a ratty old T-shirt.

"Spencer, I can't say I truly know who I am. Not just yet," she admitted softly. "I think I'm kind of a work in progress. I hate eggs, I hate jazz, I fucking *hate* bird-watching—it's boring as hell. I like slouching around in my oldest, comfiest clothing. Sometimes I don't wash my hair for days, and in winter I wear long skirts and yoga pants, like, *all* the time because I'm too lazy to shave my legs. I have no idea what the hell I want to do with the rest of my life, but I think maybe I kind of *liked* managing that stupid boutique, so maybe I'll go to business school and study marketing or something. I enjoyed coming up with creative ways of appealing to customers. Who knows? I'll go to college and work it out from there. I'm not perfect; I get zits and bloated and cranky as hell when I have PMS, and sometimes I don't shave my armpits. I—"

He got up so quickly, she didn't have time to react, and he had his arms wrapped around her and his mouth on hers in two seconds flat. Daff sighed and leaned in to his kiss, feeling like she'd just come home.

"You're so fucking beautiful, Daff. And when you turn into a hairy yeti in winter, I'll still think you're gorgeous. Maybe—but probably not—I'll pop your zits for you." He grimaced comically. "Yeah, probably not, but I'll yell my support from the other room if you feel the need to pop them yourself."

"Spencer," she whispered, snuggling her face into his neck. "My gesture. You're ruining it."

"Sorry. But not really sorry."

She sighed.

"That's supposed to be 'sorry not sorry.' I have much to teach you, grasshopper," she intoned gravely, and he grinned. "Anyway, I was *going* to say, I can't say I truly know who I am . . . but I do know that I *like* myself when I'm with you. And I think that's because I'm not trying to be this perfect woman around you."

"I don't want a perfect woman, Daff, I want *you*—" He paused and then grimaced. "That sounded so much better in my head."

"Spencer," she said, grabbing his head in her hands and holding it steady so that she could look into his eyes. "I've been so miserable without you. I love you and I don't really think I can live without you. So I want those strings."

"Daff, we don't have to rush into—"

"*Strings*, Spencer! They're important, because I would prefer not to have to peel more skanks off you in the future. I want them to know you're off-limits. That you're *mine* and I'm yours."

"Fine . . . but you're going to have to allow me time to work on my own grand gesture, because I want to marry you, Daff, but I'm not fucking proposing to you on a porch full of your ex-boyfriends."

She giggled.

"This shit is all headed for the charity shop tomorrow, you know that, right?" he warned her, and she nodded, finding herself quite unable to stop smiling. He caught her eyes and smiled back.

"I've been miserable without you, too, darling," he said, and she melted at the sound of the endearment. "I never want to be without you again. So please. You have to be sure this is what you really want, Daff."

"No take-backsies, Spencer. My life is too damned desolate without you."

"Daff, it's not just me, it's also—"

"Charlie. I know, Spence," she reassured, reaching up to cup the side of his face with her palm. She loved the feel of his stubble abrading her skin. "You guys are a package deal. As long as she's clear that there's going to be a lot of embarrassing kissing and stuff in her immediate vicinity."

He grinned.

"I'll make sure she understands that some things are just as inevitable as the tides."

"Why are we still talking?" Daff asked, going onto her toes to steal a kiss. "I want to ravish your gorgeous bod, Carlisle. Stop delaying the inevitable."

He growled and grabbed her ass and hauled her up against him. Confident in his strength, she hooked her arms around his neck and her legs around his waist while he supported her butt in his palms and ate her mouth.

"You're the best thing that's ever happened to me, Spencer," she breathed when they came up for air moments later. "And I've decided that I deserve you."

He grinned shyly, that sweet smile that had so ensnared her heart, and anointed her lips with the gentlest of kisses.

"That's my girl."

EPILOGUE

"So last week was fun," Sam Brand, who stood next to Lia for the bridal party picture, said into Lia's ear, and she shot him an appalled look. How could he be bringing that up *here* at her sister's wedding? Where anybody could hear him?

The ceremony had been beautiful, of course. Perfect and romantic, everything that Lia had hoped hers would be. Daisy and Mason's vows—which they had written themselves—hadn't left a dry eye in the crowd. Lia was happy for Daisy, but she couldn't help but feel a stab of envy as well. If Clayton had been a better man—the *right* man— Lia could have been the one exchanging vows with a man who treasured her and loved her above all else. Instead, this was her sister's wedding and Lia was saddled next to *this* man—who was interested in nothing but bedding her—for the duration. And he kept making excuses to touch her and *breathe* on her and brush against her and now he was speaking to her.

About something that he'd promised never to talk about again. The biggest—okay, maybe second biggest—mistake of Lia's life.

"We're not discussing this here," she whispered from the side of her mouth. "Or ever again."

"C'mon, Lia. I'm leaving tomorrow, and since Daisy and Mason are moving, it's not likely you'll ever see me again. I'm single, you're single—"

"So help me, if you say 'let's mingle'—"

"Let me make you tingle," he finished, ignoring her interruption. She gasped again, fighting back unwanted images of her stupid, drunken mistake the other night. It was completely uncharacteristic, and she was not going to repeat it. No matter how great he smelled right now, how enticing that roguish grin looked, or how mind-blowingly fantastic his body was beneath that tuxedo.

None of that mattered. Lia learned from her mistakes, and there were a lot of truly nice men here today. She glanced over at Sam Brand and caught him staring at her breasts and fought the urge to cover herself up with her hands. Lots of nice men here who were interested in more than just her boobies.

The photographer now wanted shots of just the bridal couple, and as the rest of them heaved relieved sighs and turned to walk away, Sam placed his palm in the small of her back, ostensibly to lead her through the departing group. She shuddered at the intimate warmth of his hand resting so close to her butt and tried to glare at him, but it was a bit demoralizing when you were trying to freeze a guy with a glare and he reacted by smiling.

"You're so cute when you try to look stern, princess. You should get a pair of those half-rim glasses just so that you can glare at me over them. God, this is becoming a fully realized fetish," he groaned in dawning self-recognition. "But I don't even care. It's hot. *You're* hot. Let's go somewhere and fuck."

"You're just so . . . *ugh*. The other night shouldn't have happened," she snapped, her voice low.

"The other night was awesome," Sam recalled with a nostalgic smile. "I lost track—how many times did you come? Four times? Five?

We could try for seven tonight. After all, I have to give you something to remember me by."

"Mr. Brand . . ." He sighed, the first sign of annoyance he'd shown her.

"Sam. Or Brand. Just drop the 'mister'—it's weird when you've had my cock in your—"

"Oh, *please* stop." She held up both hands and his mouth snapped shut. "I don't usually sleep with strangers. It's not who I am. I'm Dahlia McGregor. I teach Sunday school, volunteer at animal shelters, I want to be a kindergarten teacher, for crumb's sake. I don't *have* these kinds of conversations with men."

"I get it," he said, his voice placating. "You wanted to break out of your shell for a night. Be a bad girl. But here's the deal, princess. I'm not a stranger anymore. So it's okay for us to have one more night. And tomorrow I'm out of your life for good. And you can go back to being Miss Priss and teaching the homeless to play harpsichord or whatever the fuck it is you usually do in your boring suburban daily life. But why not take this one moment out of time and walk on the wild side? With me."

"You look so sexy in that tux, Carlisle," Daff said with a salacious grin as she took in Spencer's fine form in the traditional black-and-white tuxedo.

"Hmm?"

"You know you do." She winked, the gesture teasing a small lip tilt from him. He was pale, and his forehead gleamed with sweat. She grabbed the crook of his elbow to halt their progression into the marquee where the reception had been set up and went onto her toes to kiss him.

"You'll be fine," she whispered encouragingly.

"I've never spoken in front of a crowd of people before," he groaned, looking absolutely terrified. "I'm going to make a gigantic dick of myself and ruin my brother's wedding."

"Don't be ridiculous, you're going to rock this."

"Mason should have made Brand his best man. Or Chris. Both of them are smooth fuckers who could charm the scales off a snake. I can't even charm the collar off a puppy."

"Please, you can charm the panties off me. And despite many rumors to the contrary, that's *not* an easy feat." Another grin.

"I don't think I've told you how cute you look in that poofy skirt, darling," he said, and she was happy that he'd forgotten his anxiety long enough to tease her, but that was beyond the pale. She looked like a frickin' Disney princess. She didn't *do* Disney princess. And she didn't do lilac. But it was better than that hideous yellow her mother and sisters had threatened her with.

"I look silly."

"You look stunning," he pacified, stroking his hand down her arm. "Absolutely beautiful."

"Thank you, handsome," she said, somewhat mollified, and reached up to straighten his tie. "Now, why don't we get in there and get these speeches out of the way so that we can party and go home, where you can charm the panties off me?"

Just like that, his nervousness was back, and she lovingly traced her index finger over his tense jawline.

"Spencer, Mason chose you because you're his big brother. You're the best . . . no, the *only* man for the job. You've got this."

He inhaled deeply and loosely hooked his arms around her waist.

"I love you so much." She swallowed down the lump of emotion at those words. They were so simple, yet meant so much. She would never get used to hearing them from him.

She took his hand and led him into the tent.

When the moment arrived, Daff squeezed Spencer's thigh before he got up, and he gave her a nervous smile. Her steady gaze calmed him. He still couldn't quite believe that she returned his feelings. Just last week his life had been a total wreck, and today, with Daff by his side, he felt like the tallest, strongest, proudest man alive. She was his very heart and soul. And as he stood, his eyes touching on all the familiar faces around him, his heart nearly overflowed with love.

This was his *family*. Not just Mason and Charlie and Daff, but all of them. Daisy and Lia, their parents, their crazy old aunts . . . they had all accepted him into their intimate family circle long before today. He huffed a laugh at the revelation, and when he felt Daff's familiar hand creep into his, he looked into her beautiful eyes and grinned. She returned the smile widely.

Love you, she mouthed, and he nodded, his hand tightening around hers. He lifted her hand and bent his head to drop a kiss on her knuckles and proclaim to anyone who wasn't yet aware that she was his, he was hers. They belonged.

He looked at Daisy and Mason, who were sitting so close together they might as well be sharing a seat. They were staring back at him expectantly, and Spencer exhaled slowly.

This was his family, his friends. And the woman he loved.

Hmm, he thought, contentment settling in his veins. *I've got this.*

ABOUT THE AUTHOR

 Natasha Anders was born in Cape Town, South Africa. She spent nine years working as an assistant English teacher in Niigata, Japan, where she became a legendary karaoke diva. Now back in Cape Town, she lives with her opinionated budgie, Oliver; her temperamental Chihuahua, Maia; her moody budgie, Baxter; and the latest addition to the family, sweet little Hana the Chihuahua. Readers can connect with her through her Facebook page, on Twitter at @satyne1, or at www.natashaanders.com.